Tolkien the Medievalist

Tolkien the Medievalist explores how Tolkien's creative worlds were shaped by his own scholarship on medieval literature. In trying to create a "mythology for England" in the space of his fiction, Tolkien inevitably drew upon extant medieval languages and literatures.

This is the first recent collection to examine anew the question of Tolkien's medievalness. Interdisciplinary in approach, the essays explore Tolkien's position within the context of twentieth-century medieval scholarship and religious movements and his use of various works of medieval literature as a palimpsest for the development of his own ideas.

In the first section, essays focus on how Professor Tolkien invested his professional interests in his writing and how those works and the movements of his day may have affected his fiction. The second and third sections focus on specific episodes, characters, concepts, and images and how they correspond to medieval literary antecedents, in Old Norse, Old and Middle English, medieval Latin, and in medieval Catholicism. In the fourth section, essays explain how mythological retextualization in his fiction assumes a medieval form.

Essential reading for all scholars interested in J. R. R Tolkien, this work will also be of vital interest to those working in the fields of medieval history and literature, literary history, and literature in the early twentieth century.

Jane Chance, Professor of English, teaches medieval literature and J. R. R. Tolkien at Rice University, Houston, Texas. Among her seventeen books are *Tolkien's Art: A Mythology for England*, *The Lord of the Rings: The Mythology of Power*, and two guest-edited issues of *Studies in Medievalism*. She also edits two series, the Library of Medieval Women and the Greenwood Guides to Historic Events in the Medieval World.

Routledge Studies in Medieval Religion and Culture

Edited by George Ferzoco, University of Leicester and Carolyn Muessig, University of Bristol

This series aims to present developments and debates within the field of medieval religion and culture. It will provide a broad range of case studies and theoretical perspectives, covering a variety of topics, theories, and issues.

1 Gender and Holiness
Men, Women and Saints in Late Medieval Europe
Edited by Samantha J. E. Riches and Sarah Salih

2 The Invention of Saintliness
Edited by Anneke B. Mulder-Bakker

3 Tolkien the Medievalist
Edited by Jane Chance

Tolkien the Medievalist

Edited by Jane Chance

Routledge
Taylor & Francis Group
New York London

First published 2003
by Routledge
270 Madison Ave, New York NY 10016

Simultaneously published in the USA and Canada
by Routledge
2 Park Square, Milton Park, Abingdon, Oxon, OX14 4RN

Routledge is an imprint of the Taylor & Francis Group

Transferred to Digital Printing 2008

© 2003 Selection and editorial material, Jane Chance;
individual chapters, the contributors

Typeset in Baskerville by Taylor & Francis Books Ltd

All rights reserved. No part of this book may be reprinted or reproduced or utilized in any form or by any electronic, mechanical, or other means, now known or hereafter invented, including photocopying and recording, or in any information storage or retrieval system, without permission in writing from the publishers.

British Library Cataloguing in Publication Data
A catalogue record for this book is available from the British Library

Library of Congress Cataloging in Publication Data
Tolkien the medievalist/edited by Jane Chance
p.cm – (Routledge Studies in medieval religion and culture)
Includes bibliographic references and index.
1. Tolkien J. R. R. (John Ronald Reuel), 1892–1973 – Knowledge and learning. 2. Medievalism – England – History – 20th century. 3. Fantasy fiction, English – Medieval influences. 4. Literature, Medieval – Appreciation – England. 5. Middle earth (Imaginary place).
6. Medievalism in literature. 7. Middle ages in literature. 8. Mythology in literature. I. Chance, Jane, 1945 – II. Series.

ISBN10: 0–415–28944–0 (hbk)
ISBN10: 0–415–47348–9 (pbk)

ISBN13: 978–0–415–28944–3 (hbk)
ISBN13: 978–0–415–47348–4 (pbk)

Contents

Contributors

Douglas A. Anderson's first book was *The Annotated Hobbit* (Houghton Mifflin, 1988; revised edition 2002). He has also overseen the corrected texts of *The Hobbit* and *The Lord of the Rings*, published by Houghton Mifflin (US), and HarperCollins (UK), and is co-author (with Wayne G. Hammond) of *J. R. R. Tolkien: A Descriptive Bibliography* (Oak Knoll Press, 1993).

Jane Chance, Professor of English, Medieval Studies, and the Study of Women and Gender at Rice University, has published seventeen other books on Old and Middle English, medieval mythography, medieval women, and modern medievalism, including revised editions of *Tolkien's Art: A Mythology for England* (Macmillan, 1979; University Press of Kentucky, 2001) and *The Lord of the Rings: The Mythology of Power* (Twayne/Macmillan, 1992; University Press of Kentucky, 2001), and guest-editions of two issues of *Studies in Medievalism*, on *Medievalism in the Twentieth-Century* (1982; rpt., 1991) and the *Inklings* (1991).

Christine Chism, Assistant Professor in English at Rutgers University, New Brunswick, New Jersey, is interested in medieval romance, drama, and travel narratives. She has published articles on late medieval alliterative poetry, Chaucer, and the fifteenth-century Robin Hood ballads, and her book, *Alliterative Revivals*, was published by the University of Pennsylvania Press in 2001.

Leslie A. Donovan teaches interdisciplinary courses on medieval culture and on Tolkien in the University Honors Program at the University of New Mexico. Her background and current research emphasize Old English and Old Norse literature, and she has recently published a book titled *Women Saints' Lives in Old English Prose* (Boydell & Brewer, 2002).

Bradford Lee Eden is currently head of Bibliographic and Metadata Services at the University of Nevada, Las Vegas. He has a master's degree in library science from Indiana State University (1984) and a Ph.D. in medieval musicology from the University of Kansas (1991). He publishes extensively in librarianship, metadata, medieval music and liturgy, and Anglo-Saxon studies, and has a lifelong interest in dragons and a love of all things Tolkien.

Jonathan Evans is Associate Professor of English and Director of the Medieval Studies Program at the University of Georgia. He teaches courses in Old English language, *Beowulf*, and medieval literature; he has published articles and essays on Old English, Old Norse, C. S. Lewis, and J. R. R. Tolkien in reference works and scholarly journals, including the *Dictionary of Literary Biography*, the *Journal of Folklore Research, Style, Semiotica*, the *Journal of English Linguistics*, *NOWELE*, and the *Journal of English and Germanic Philology*. His essay "The Dragon-lore of Middle-earth" was published in *J. R. R. Tolkien and his Literary Resonances* (Greenwood Press, 2000).

Mary Faraci is Professor of English at Florida Atlantic University, where she serves as the Director of English Undergraduate Studies. She teaches courses in English linguistics, literature, and composition. Her publications include linguistic approaches to the works of Jane Austen, Saul Bellow, and Dante. An essay on the contributions of the lexicographer Herbert Dean Meritt to Old English studies has been accepted by *Language and Style*.

Verlyn Flieger is Professor of English at the University of Maryland at College Park, where she teaches courses in Tolkien, Arthurian myth and legend, and medieval epic and myth. She is the author of two books on J. R. R. Tolkien, *Splintered Light: Logos and Language in Tolkien's World* (Eerdmans Publishing, 1983), soon to be republished by Kent State Press, and *A Question of Time: J. R. R. Tolkien's Road to Faërie* (Kent State Press, 1977). She is co-editor with Carl Hostetter of *Tolkien's Legendarium: Essays on The History of Middle-earth* (Greenwood Press, 2000).

John William Houghton, Chaplain and Chair of the Department of Religious Studies at the Episcopal High School of Baton Rouge, studies Anglo-Saxon appropriation of late antique ideas and has published articles on Alcuin, Bede, and Dunstan as well as on Tolkien.

Andrew Lazo is a Ph.D. student in English at Rice University, Houston, Texas. His research interests focus on C. S. Lewis, regarding especially myth, medievalism, and theory. He has contributed to *Seven* and done archival research at the Marion E. Wade Center.

Michael W. Maher, S.J., is an Assistant Professor of History at St. Louis University. His area of research in Early Modern History emphasizes popular religion and the role of the Jesuits in promoting approved religious practice. He received his doctorate in history from the University of Minnesota, and advanced theological degrees from the Jesuit School of Theology at Berkeley.

Gergely Nagy is a Ph.D. student at the University of Szeged, Hungary, writing his doctoral dissertation on the possible integration of Tolkien's texts into a poststructuralist theoretical framework. His professional interests include medieval English literature, specifically Arthurian romance and Malory. Nagy has also published essays on Sir Thomas Malory and Geoffrey Chaucer.

Margaret A. Sinex is Assistant Professor in the Department of English and Journalism at Western Illinois University, where she teaches medieval British literature and historical linguistics. Her publications examine Anglo-Latin literature and in particular the twelfth-century author Walter Map.

Richard C. West holds graduate degrees in both medieval studies and library science. He is Assistant Director for Technical Services at the Kurt F. Wendt Library at the University of Wisconsin-Madison, and the author of *Tolkien Criticism: An Annotated Checklist* (Kent State University Press, 1970; 2nd ed., 1981) and several articles on fantasy literature.

Miranda Wilcox is a graduate student in the Medieval Institute at the University of Notre Dame, Indiana, studying Old English language and literature. She received her bachelor's degree in English from Brigham Young University, Provo, Utah.

Acknowledgments

Thanks to Paul Szarmach and Timothy Graham for allowing us to organize three sessions on Tolkien at the Thirty-Sixth Annual International Congress on Medieval Studies held at Western Michigan University, Kalamazoo, Michigan, in 2001, from which the nucleus of this volume of new readings sprang. In the audience for our sessions were a *New York Times* journalist, Stephen Kinzer, who interviewed panelists for an article about Harry Potter and *The Lord of the Rings*, and an editor of the Routledge series on Studies in Medieval Religion and Culture, George Ferzoco, Director of Italian Studies at the University of Leicester, who urged us to send the completed volume to him and his co-editor, Carolyn Muessig, for consideration. What a delight now after thirty years of patient waiting to see that the popular has become the canon – that the mythology of J. R. R. Tolkien, far from incurring the critics' opprobrium, as it did for so much of Tolkien's professional career, has in fact become the critics' subject.

For this volume, Terry Munisteri, our Rice University English departmental editorial assistant, has assisted by bringing the essays into line with the requisite house style. All of us are grateful to her for her many fine suggestions. Jamie Cook, the department secretary, over time has mailed, copied, and e-mailed various messages and attached files (and whole books and essays) back and forth across the Atlantic and the United States; she also aided in typing corrections to the text. Andrew Yerkes, a graduate student in English, also retyped portions of the text; we are grateful to the Dean of Humanities, Gale Stokes, for subsidizing this necessary work and the index. Last but not least, Andy Dimond, a Rice University Century Scholar who opted to assist with my research on Tolkien and mythology as his project for 2001–3, undertook to recheck citations and documentation in the book. I am indebted to Rice University's Vice President for Enrollment, Ann Wright, and Assistant Director of Admissions Jennifer Wilson for encouraging me to participate in this new program, and also very appreciative of Andy's help in bringing this project to completion.

Certain spellings of words preferred by Tolkien have been retained throughout – Dwarves, sub-creation, fairy-stories, Middle-earth, and so forth.

Permission to reprint a revised version of John W. Houghton's essay, which originally appeared as "Augustine and the *Ainulindalë*," in *Mythlore* 79 (1995): 4–8, has been granted by the editor, Dr. Theodore James Sherman. Permission to quote from J. R. R. Tolkien's *The Fellowship of the Ring*, *The Return of the King*, *Letters*, "Mythopoeia" (from *Tree and Leaf*), as well as *The Silmarillion*, has been granted by HarperCollins Publishers Ltd.

Permission has been granted for publication in the United States of extracts from the following works:

From *The Fellowship of the Ring* by J. R. R. Tolkien. Copyright © 1954, 1965, 1966 by J. R. R. Tolkien. 1954 edition copyright © renewed 1982 by Christopher R. Tolkien, Michael H. R. Tolkien, John F. R. Tolkien and Priscilla M. A. R. Tolkien. 1965/6 edition copyright © renewed 1993, 1994 by Christopher R. Tolkien, John F. R. Tolkien and Priscilla M. A. R. Tolkien. Reprinted by permission of Houghton Mifflin Company. All rights reserved.

From *The Letters of J. R. R. Tolkien*, edited by Humphrey Carpenter with the assistance of Christopher Tolkien. Copyright © 1981 by George Allen & Unwin (Publishers) Ltd. Reprinted by permission of Houghton Mifflin Company. All rights reserved.

From *The Return of the King* by J. R. R. Tolkien. Copyright © 1955, 1965, 1966 by J. R. R. Tolkien. 1955 edition copyright © renewed 1982 by Christopher R. Tolkien, Michael H. R. Tolkien, John F. R. Tolkien and Priscilla M. A. R. Tolkien. 1965/1966 edition copyright © renewed 1993, 1994 by Christopher R. Tolkien, John F. R. Tolkien and Priscilla M. A. R. Tolkien. Reprinted by permission of Houghton Mifflin Company. All rights reserved.

From *The Silmarillion*, Second Edition by J. R. R. Tolkien, edited by Christopher Tolkien. Copyright © 1977 by The J. R. R. Tolkien Copyright Trust and Christopher Reuel Tolkien. Copyright © 1981 by The J. R. R. Tolkien Copyright Trust. Copyright © 1999 by Christopher Reuel Tolkien. Reprinted by permission of Houghton Mifflin Company. All rights reserved.

From *Tree and Leaf*: including the poem "Mythopoeia" by J. R. R. Tolkien. Copyright © 1964 by George Allen & Unwin Ltd. Copyright © renewed 1992 by John F. R. Tolkien, Christopher R. Tolkien, and Priscilla M. A. R. Tolkien. Copyright © by The J. R. R. Tolkien Copyright Trust. Reprinted by permission of Houghton Mifflin Company. All rights reserved.

Houston, Texas
February 2002

Abbreviations

"Beowulf"	"*Beowulf*: The Monsters and the Critics"
Biography	*Tolkien: A Biography* by Humphrey Carpenter
*BLT*1	*The Book of Lost Tales, Part 1*
*BLT*2	*The Book of Lost Tales, Part 2*
EPCW	*Essays Presented to Charles Williams*
FGH	*Farmer Giles of Ham*
FR	*The Fellowship of the Ring*
H	*The Hobbit*
"Homecoming"	"The Homecoming of Beorhtnoth Beorhthelm's Son"
"Leaf"	"Leaf by Niggle"
Letters	*The Letters of J. R. R. Tolkien*
LR	*The Lord of the Rings*
Monsters	*"The Monsters and the Critics" and Other Essays*
"OFS"	"On Fairy-Stories"
RK	*The Return of the King*
Shadow	*The Return of the Shadow*
Shaping	*The Shaping of Middle-earth*
Silm	*The Silmarillion*
"Smith"	"Smith of Wootton Major"
TL	*Tree and Leaf*
TR	*The Tolkien Reader*
Treason	*The Treason of Isengard*
TT	*The Two Towers*
UT	*Unfinished Tales*

1 Introduction

Jane Chance

J. R. R. Tolkien's *The Lord of the Rings* was recently named "Book of the Century" in a survey of 25,000 British readers. The trilogy has sold over a hundred million copies worldwide since its publication in 1954 and has been translated into twenty-five different languages (most recently, Chinese). Tapping into Tolkien's enormous popularity, producer Saul Zaentz (*The English Patient*) and director Peter Jackson (*The Frighteners*) launched a $400-million film adaptation of *The Lord of the Rings*; shooting began in 1999 on location in New Zealand. With the growing interest in the filming of Tolkien's epic – the first of three full-length features that appeared in Christmas of 2001, to be followed by the next two on consecutive Christmases – there has been a parallel rise in interest in his writings and books about his writings. Copies of the 1955 British first edition, first printing, of the trilogy (with dust-jackets) recently sold on eBay for over $19,000, for example.

What is it that makes this "fairy-tale" appeal to readers of all ages in so many different countries? Why has its reputation increased in the years since Tolkien's death? And what information does one need to appreciate the fantastical world that Tolkien created – with its own history, geography, and mythology – inhabited by peoples speaking fourteen different languages, all elaborately constructed by this medievalist scholar who taught at Oxford?

Although various critical studies of Tolkien appeared in the 1970s, in the past few years there has been only one new collection of essays about Tolkien's writing and literary sources, both fiction and nonfiction: *J. R. R. Tolkien and his Literary Resonances: Views of Middle-earth*, edited by George Clark and Daniel Timmons (2000). The recent hard-cover collection of scholarly essays by Tolkien scholars, *Tolkien's Legendarium: Essays on "The History of Middle-earth"* (2000), about the British medievalist's background mythology – the twelve volumes of *The History of Middle-earth* compiled by Christopher Tolkien from his father's unpublished drafts – has just been published by Verlyn Flieger and Carl F. Hostetter. The very important *J. R. R. Tolkien: A Descriptive Bibliography*, by Wayne G. Hammond and Douglas A. Anderson, appeared in hard cover in 1993 through Oak Knoll Books (significant because of the many reprintings and revisions published during Tolkien's lifetime and thereafter, and therefore valuable to book collectors). New editions and reprintings of *The Hobbit* and *The Lord of the Rings* have been produced by HarperCollins in Great Britain, the press to which Allen

& Unwin (Tolkien's original press) was sold: a millennial *The Lord of the Rings*, with CD-ROM, published in seven small volumes (with the seventh being the appendices), in 1999; and, in 2000, a one-volume, leather-bound *The Lord of the Rings*, following the success last year of a similar leather-bound *The Hobbit* (the first printing of the former sold out in two months this year and has just been reprinted).[1] Harold Bloom compiled a collection, *Modern Critical Interpretations: J. R. R. Tolkien's Lord of the Rings*, for Chelsea House in 2000, reprinting previously published and now canonical essays on Tolkien, a collection similar in intention (but superior in quality) to Katie de Koster's *Readings on J. R. R. Tolkien* (2000).

That this commercial and popular interest in Tolkien has been propelled by popular interest in the trailer on the film of *The Lord of the Rings* – the most downloaded internet film trailer in history – is obvious. In addition, Tolkien has come to be accepted by high academic culture in varying ways: through the journal *Seven*, dedicated to the writings of the Inklings (see Hood, 59–71); through the 1992 conference on Tolkien held at Oxford, whose proceedings have been published (see Reynolds and GoodKnight); and through the acceptance at the International Congress on Medieval Studies for 2001 at Western Michigan University in Kalamazoo of three sessions on Tolkien.[2]

One way to understand Tolkien's popularity that has emerged, slowly, over the forty-five years since the publication of *The Lord of the Rings* is to acknowledge the indebtedness of his creative work to the medieval languages and literatures he professed at Oxford and other universities over his lifetime. In the interval since his death, scholars have come to embrace the view that Tolkien was attempting to create what his biographer Humphrey Carpenter has termed a "mythology for England" in the space of his fiction by creating an imaginary world with its own languages, history, cultures, origin, and peoples.[3] Tolkien achieved this aim, scholars believe, by drawing not only on the extant languages and literatures in Old and Middle English, but also on those languages that influenced the cultural and historical development of Great Britain, namely, Finnish, Welsh, Old Norse, and Old High and Middle German – as a "tribute to England." Tolkien's desire to attempt this in *The Hobbit, The Lord of the Rings*, and *The Silmarillion* has been most fully expressed in Tolkien's letter to the publisher Milton Waldman, letter 131, written in response to the Collins editor's request to explain how *The Lord of the Rings* relates to *The Silmarillion.* The text of the long letter (over ten thousand words) was published in full when Humphrey Carpenter's edition of Tolkien's *Letters* appeared (1980–81), although it had also been published in excerpted form in Carpenter's *Biography* (1977) (Tolkien, *Letters*, 143–61). In this circa-1951 letter, Tolkien expresses his desire to

> make a body of more or less connected legend, ranging from the large and cosmogonic to the level of romantic fairy-story – the larger founded on the lesser in contact with the earth, the lesser drawing splendour from the vast backcloths – which I could dedicate simply: to England; to my country.
> (*Letters*, 144)

This "mythology for England" (his biographer's words) was necessary because of what Tolkien understood as

> the poverty of my own beloved country: it had no stories of its own (bound up with its tongue and soil), nor of the quality that I sought, and found (as an ingredient) in legends of other lands. There was Greek, and Celtic, and Romance, Germanic, Scandinavian, and Finnish (which greatly affected me); but nothing English, save impoverished chap-book stuff.
>
> (*Letters*, 144)

Where Tolkien turned to find the stuff and fabric of this "mythology for England" was clearly the medieval world he knew so well from his scholarly studies: he had labeled an early notebook on which he began the work now known as *The Silmarillion* "The Book of Lost Tales" (*Biography*, 90). Later, in his description of the criteria he sought to match in his creation of this lost world as described in the letter to Waldman – those of "tone" and "quality" – he invoked British and Celtic "beauty":

> It should possess the tone and quality that I desired, somewhat cool and clear, be redolent of our "air" (the clime and quality of the North West, meaning Britain and the hither parts of Europe; not Italy or the Aegean, still less the East), and, while possessing (if I could achieve it) the fair elusive beauty that some call Celtic (though it is rarely found in genuine ancient Celtic things), it should be "high," purged of the gross, and fit for the more adult mind of a land long steeped in poetry.
>
> (*Letters*, 144)

By "Celtic" Tolkien meant what made up that body of faërie mythology common to Great Britain and its outposts and suggests at first glance those Elves so dear to Tolkien.

Over the past twenty-five years, Tolkien scholars have argued in various ways about the meaning and scope of Carpenter's phrase "mythology for England" – that is, whether it refers to the specifically Old and Middle English works of literature Tolkien himself discussed in his nonfiction prose, to his work as a tribute to his nation (with all that means in the 1930s and 1940s), or to his desire to write a "true English epic" (meaning Anglo-Saxon epic) – and about its origins in what was apparently Carpenter's conflation of Tolkien letter 131 (to Waldman) and letter 180, to someone named "Mr. Thompson," but not actually a phrase written by Tolkien.[4]

Despite the recurrence of this phrase in such previous studies, the implications of Tolkien's medievalness has only been touched on. Three previous books from the late 1970s and early 1980s have focused on Tolkien as a professor of Anglo-Saxon and a teacher of Old and Middle English Language and Literature. First, Mary Salu and Robert Farrell's *J. R. R. Tolkien, Scholar and Storyteller: Essays in Memoriam* (1979) in three sections examines Tolkien's life, the study of Old and Middle English (that is, essays on medieval English subjects by his former students, colleagues, and friends), and Tolkien's use of the romance, philology, and the New Testament. Second, *Tolkien's Art: A "Mythology for England"* (1979; 2001) by Jane Chance (Nitzsche) sketches Tolkien's interest in medieval literature in his minor works, *The Hobbit*, and *The Lord of the Rings*. Third and last, Thomas A. Shippey's *The Road to Middle-earth* (1982; 1992) examines Tolkien's use of individual medieval words and his philology as a means of accessing his medievalized literature.

No other collection or single monograph has examined anew the question of Tolkien's medievalness, his capturing of that medieval form or theme or symbol for his own mythologized fiction.[5] On the other hand, since Tolkien's death a collection of his letters has appeared (1980), and his long-languishing *The Silmarillion* has been completed and published by his son Christopher Tolkien (1977). In addition, other works Tolkien did not succeed in completing during his lifetime – earlier drafts or alternate recensions, including *Unfinished Tales* (1979; 1980) and the twelve-volume *History of Middle-earth* (1983–95; 1984–96) – have subsequently appeared in print, thanks to Christopher. Two additional children's stories have also been recovered – *Mr. Bliss* (1982) and *Roverandom* (1998) – as well as several editions and translations of Old and Middle English poems, completed by Tolkien's own former students (Tolkien, *The Old English Exodus* [1981]; *Finn and Hengest* [1982; 1983]; and *"The Monsters and the Critics" and Other Essays* [1983; 1984]).

With this fuller knowledge about Tolkien's life and thinking about his own work, of which we now have everything of value, it is time to reconsider the question of Tolkien's medievalness and to offer new and more informed ways of reading Tolkien. Within this fuller context of posthumous works by and about Tolkien's mythology, *Tolkien the Medievalist* will demonstrate in varied fashion how Tolkien from the beginning responded to his modern contexts by retelling his medieval sources and adapting his medieval scholarship to his own voice. Tolkien was, over time, influenced by his own personal medievalism, his profession as a medievalist, his relationships with other medievalists, and his own mythologizing in constructing his major fiction. Interdisciplinary in approach, the essays in the collection will explore Tolkien's position within the context of twentieth-century medieval scholarship and religious movements such as the Oxford movement in Britain, and his use of various works of medieval literature as a palimpsest for the development of his own ideas. In the first section, chapters focus on how Professor Tolkien, as a philologist, fairy-story writer, editor of Old and Middle English poems, citizen and Roman Catholic, and friend of C. S. Lewis (a fellow Inkling), invested his professional interests in his writing, and how those works and the movements of his day may have affected his fiction. In the second section, chapters focus on specific episodes and how they correspond to medieval literary antecedents, in Old Norse, Old and Middle English, medieval Latin, and medieval Catholicism. In the third section, the chapters discuss how his mythological retextualization in his fiction assumes a most medievalized form.

The concluding section involves computer technology as a form of "recontextualization" to indicate some ways in which Tolkien's intentions as a mythmaker can be more fully understood.

In the first part, on the modern contexts of Tolkien's medievalism and scholarship, Douglas A. Anderson – in "'An industrious little devil': E. V. Gordon as friend and collaborator with Tolkien" – examines Tolkien's collaboration with Eric Valentine Gordon (1896–1938) on their edition of *Sir Gawain and the Green Knight* (1925). The two philologists also worked together on several other editions, including *The Pearl*, *The Wanderer*, and *The Seafarer*, but with the early death of Gordon these projects were left uncompleted or were finished posthumously by Gordon's widow. Gordon's precise scholarship and graceful style, as manifested in his solo work – namely, *An Introduction to Old Norse* (1927) and an edition of *The Battle of Maldon* (1937) – and his friendship with Tolkien both motivated and influenced Tolkien's own scholarship and creativity, especially in Tolkien's "sequel" to "The Battle of Maldon," "The Homecoming of Beorhtnoth Beorhthelm's Son" (1953).

In chapter 3, Verlyn Flieger, in "'There would always be a fairy-tale': J. R. R. Tolkien and the folklore controversy," investigates Tolkien's key essay "On Fairy-Stories" in the context of folklore studies and its various schools in the late nineteenth and early twentieth centuries, all of which contended for hegemony within this new and just-formed discipline. Tolkien's terminology in his essay – "nature myth," "disease of language," and "Comparative Philology" – resonates with the identifying hallmarks of early folklorists such as Müller, Dasent, Lang, and others. His citation of their work in philology, anthropology, and mythology is set against his own personalized disagreement with their theories, one connected to his emerging, still developing creative mythology. In large part, his reaction to the folklore controversies can be used to read his own fiction as an illustration in practice of his theory in "On Fairy-Stories."

In chapter 4, "A kind of mid-wife: J. R. R. Tolkien and C. S. Lewis – sharing influence," Andrew Lazo examines the interinfluence of Tolkien and his friend and fellow medievalist C. S. Lewis by focusing on an unpublished letter by Lewis about Tolkien and his influence on him and by isolating one night (11 May 1926) when they had a row about the differences between religion and mythology and their appropriateness in their fiction. Tolkien's subsequent writing of the poem "Mythopoeia" served to mark the turning point in their literary relationship and friendship. Although the two British scholars shared interests, professions, and a field, and spent much of their lives talking about books (their own and others') and enjoying social experiences, their real bond lay in their writing and reading of each other's work and the influence each had on the creative function.

In chapter 5, "'I wish to speak': Tolkien's voice in his *Beowulf* essay," Mary Faraci argues that – despite the fame of Tolkien's 1937 essay, "*Beowulf*: The Monsters and the Critics," for its pivotal role in directing Anglo-Saxon studies to the study of the literary text itself and away from its historical and anthropological contexts – it remains relatively unknown as a work of linguistic artistry, particularly speech-act theory. In his rescue of *Beowulf* the poem from *Beowulf*iana – that is, scholarly study that ignores the poem's artistry – Tolkien uses several voices to construct his argument. His second nature in his dramatization is that of storyteller: by using the ancient Greek distinction between the active voice and the middle voice, Tolkien removes himself, the "I" in the essay, from the critics blind to its artistry. The "I" functions in the ancient middle voice inflection to perform the difficult task of perceiving the poem's art previously hidden from *Beowulf*'s "experts." That is, Tolkien's "I," as the subject in relation to the criticism process, acts as effected "inside the process" of the action of the verb (this volume, p. 58). In contrast, the critics occupy the role of the ancient active-voice inflection: the subject acts as agent outside the process of the action of the verb. The result is the dramatic projection of the "I" as questor of permission to release the monsters from their mistaken representation in *Beowulf*iana by these critics, who then assume the position (relative to the hero Beowulf) of the adversarial dragon.

Chapter 6, by Christine Chism, "Middle-earth, the Middle Ages, and the Aryan nation: myth and history in World War II," places Tolkien as professional medievalist within the historical context of the period before and during World War II, when Tolkien wrote the *The Lord of the Rings*. During this period the "Germanic" medieval sources that Tolkien loved – medieval languages, legends, and sagas in Icelandic, Germanic, Gothic, and Anglo-Saxon – were (mis)appropriated by the German Aryan movement, which created a conflict in his writing. In "ruining, perverting, misapplying, and making forever accursed" (this volume, p. 63) these legends, Aryanism made it impossible for Tolkien to ignore the ethical dilemma of his own imaginative inspiration from such legends and their effect on his sense of morality, religion, and nationalism. Because Tolkien casts the sub-creator in "On Fairy-Stories" (1939) as an analogue to God when he endows humanity with his own image, when humanity's sub-creating replaces devotion to God with an obsession to the imagination, does humanity then take the place of Lucifer? Chism argues that Tolkien rehearses this question in the actual extended writing of *The Lord of the Rings*, itself "a tale of renunciation," specifically, Frodo's renunciation of the Ring when he returns it to its origin, which takes on the additional symbolism of Tolkien's own renunciation of the act of writing this epic, the last extended narrative he completed. Thus are justified those structural narrative (and generic) flaws in *The Lord of the Rings* – structural delays, deferrals of ending, doublings and reduplications of narrative artistry – so criticized by Christine Brooke-Rose. "Middle-earth unfolds, grows more intricate, more peopled, more culturally diverse, more deep as we wander through it, but it blooms forth only in the shadow of its own immanent destruction," Chism notes.

> The Ring – that weirdly empty, weirdly powerful object around which the narrative assembles itself – interrogates the imaginative capacity for world-creation itself. ... The loss of the Ring consigns Middle-earth to the joys and depredations of history – and this consignment to history is costly. It is no accident that the loss of the Ring maims Frodo forever and disenchants

> Middle-earth. ... And, finally, I argue, it is no accident that the writing of this renunciatory narrative occupies dark night after dark night, during a time when Germany was mobilizing and recasting heroic '"Germanic' ideals" to articulate and impose its own terrifying new world.
>
> (This volume, p. 64)

In the next part – on the medieval texts and contexts Tolkien appropriated as models in his mythological fiction – Verlyn Flieger begins chapter 7, "Tolkien's Wild Men: from medieval to modern," by considering the archetypal outsider, the figure of the Wild Man drawn from the Babylonian epic of Gilgamesh, the biblical Nebuchadnezzar, European folklore, Chrétien de Troyes's twelfth-century romance *Yvain*, the *wodwos* in *Sir Gawain and the Green Knight*, Sir Thomas Malory's Lancelot, and elsewhere in medieval literature to understand how Tolkien reshapes this topos in his own fiction. Among the many manifestations of the outlaw Wild Man is Beorn in *The Hobbit*, Ghân-Buri-Ghân in *The Return of the King*, Strider (Aragorn in rough disguise), Túrin Turambar in "The Tale of the Children of Húrin," and even Gollum, Tolkien's most brilliant creation. Also participating in the typology of the Wild Man, at least in his struggles with madness, is Frodo Baggins himself.

In chapter 8, "The valkyrie reflex in J. R. R. Tolkien's *The Lord of the Rings*: Galadriel, Shelob, Éowyn, and Arwen," Leslie A. Donovan works with Old Norse and Old English types for Tolkien's women in the trilogy. Often criticized for his paucity of female characters and presumably, therefore, his latent misogyny, Tolkien has also been defended for appropriately reweaving medieval epic materials that do not emphasize women in their thematic or structural conventions. However, Donovan contends that the few women in Tolkien's epic derive their especial importance from the "valkyrie reflex" found in Germanic heroic literature and Scandinavian myth and heroic legend. Deriving from these valkyrie traditions, Old English women characters function as heroic, cultural, and moral models for the women in Tolkien's texts. Thus, Tolkien pairs Galadriel and Shelob, Arwen and Éowyn, and Rosie Cotton and Lobelia Sackville-Baggins to transcend the conventional medieval moral polarities between generosity and selfishness, hope and despair, and loyalty and treachery.

Chapter 9, by Miranda Wilcox, "Exilic imagining in *The Seafarer* and *The Lord of the Rings*," traces the Old English elegiac theme of exile articulated in those works. Wilcox argues that Frodo, the primary exiled character, is coupled with the voluntary exiles of the Elves; in addition, despite the mortality of the Seafarer and the immortality of the Elves, similarities in theme, imagery, symbolism, and characterization exist between the Old English poem *The Seafarer* and Elvish poems in the *The Lord of the Rings*. Both the Seafarer, the speaker in the elegy, and the Elves, especially Legolas, reveal a longing for the sea; it functions as a source of imagery and background in both accounts. Both the Seafarer and the Elves regret the departure from their comfortable present life to an unknown future life and death, and to the afterlife in the case of the Seafarer. In *The Seafarer* the glorious arrival of spring signals the time of man's departure from this world and, simultaneously, his ambivalence toward this change; so also Frodo must depart Lothlórien on his quest, and the Elves, fated to diminish, must leave Middle-earth. The sea, then, represents a "transcendent bridge" between the mortal and the immortal. Because the sailors in both narratives are not depicted as arriving at their final ports, both remain fixed eternally in the text between the misery of mortality and the hope of future joy. This moment of simultaneity records a glimpse of the experience of exile in both medieval and Tolkienian worlds.

In chapter 10, "'Oathbreakers, why have ye come?': Tolkien's 'Passing of the Grey Company' and the twelfth-century *Exercitus mortuorum*," Margaret A. Sinex demonstrates Tolkien's indebtedness to medieval Latin sources in the construction of a group and their political history in *The Lord of the Rings*. Aragorn's command of the "Sleepless Dead" in Tolkien's *The Return of the King* can be contextualized within several twelfth-century Latin narratives, some of which stress the threatening military might of Hellequin's hunt, and others, the penitential purpose of the troop of wandering dead. These prescholastic treatments of the *Exercitus mortuorum* have particular relevance to Tolkien's episode in several key ways. In Tolkien, we see a creative version of the crucial relationship of exchange between the dead and the living, in which the living perform suffrages (prayers, masses) for the spiritual peace of the wandering penitents. The relationship of exchange is present, as is the spiritual purpose, but the direction of the service is reversed (as the dead serve the living). In Aragorn's demand for military aid, we also find the binding nature of vassalic ties that transcends death and obligates the living to fulfill the requests of the dead so often stressed in the twelfth century. (The transcendent tie is present, but again, the dead serve the living.)

Further, as Jean-Claude Schmitt and others have noted, certain twelfth-century texts used the theme of the furious army to criticize the second estate for misdirecting its war-making potential, thereby dooming its members to their agonized, penitential roaming. Readers of Tolkien learn that the King of the Mountains once misused his own military might by withholding it during Isildur's war against Sauron. And finally, the *Exercitus mortuorum* participated in twelfth-century political ideology in another way as well. For often, the service the dead perform for the living (frequently in the form of crucial information) helps to found a dynasty or ensure its survival and protect its possessions. While members of the "Shadow Host" render military service (rather than give information), their decisive aid ensures the survival of Isildur's line and the protection of all Aragorn's possessions (most notably Minas Tirith).

In the third part, we turn to the texts and contexts of medieval patristics, theology, and iconography, and a sampling of the ways in which Tolkien incorporated cosmogony and religion from patristic and scholastic commentaries and the artistic representation of theological issues from the Middle Ages and Renaissance. In chapter 11, "Augustine in the cottage of lost play: the *Ainulindalë* as asterisk cosmogony," John William Houghton examines the relationship between Tolkien's *Ainulindalë* in *The Silmarillion* and Augustine's commentary on Genesis. In "asterisk" Houghton borrows a term used by T. A.

Shippey to mean the understanding of a world-view conveyed by the philologists' use of a prefixed asterisk to denote lost words (or languages) they have reconstructed. In this sense Tolkien's *Ainulindalë* – the first tale of *The Silmarillion* – represents neither of the models of cosmogony inherited by the early Middle Ages – the hexameron with its six days of creation found in Genesis, the Old English *Hexameron,* and the *Timaeus* of Plato – but instead, a third account of creation, an asterisk cosmogony in the Elvish creation myth told by Eriol, an Angle who lived before the historical Angles migrated to Britain, and Ælwine, an Anglo-Saxon seafarer. Houghton's point is that this fictional myth of creation actually fits easily into a Christian-Neoplatonist synthesis of the two major models of cosmogony as demonstrated by Augustine's commentary on Genesis.

Bradford Lee Eden, in chapter 12, "The 'music of the spheres': relationships between Tolkien's *The Silmarillion* and medieval cosmological and religious theory," explores the medieval concept of the "music of the spheres" as it relates to Tolkien's work on Middle-earth, specifically, with the creation scenes given in *The Silmarillion,* as well as with continuing lines of relationships that appear throughout this work, *The Hobbit,* and *The Lord of the Rings.* Tolkien's use and reuse of ancient and medieval mythology from a number of traditions is well known, but his use of medieval cosmological and mathematical concepts surrounding music and its relationship to creation, life, and the unfolding drama throughout the history of Middle-earth has not been explored in depth. This chapter provides introductory background and insight on just how thorough Tolkien was in his use of the "quadrivium" concept in the creation of Middle-earth in relation to the Boethian and Neoplatonist traditions in particular.

Jonathan Evans, in chapter 13, "The anthropology of Arda: creation, theology, and the race of Men," analyzes the early history of Men and posits a theory of "Man" that isolates this category as an idea of the human in Middle-earth divorced from whatever assumptions we may have about humankind as a species common to earth. In Evans's consideration, "Man" represents a separate race and not "the 'default' category of sentient beings." Drawing on philology, theology, and literature – Tolkien's and Milton's, most specifically – Evans dramatizes by contrast the special relationship between the creator and the created in Tolkien's theological anthropology, and by analogy, the relationship between Tolkien as author and the nature and role of the species of Man in his mythological fiction. Man's fall becomes one of several in Middle-earth rather than the focal point, as it is in traditional Christianity.

Chapter 14, "'A land without stain': medieval images of Mary and their use in the characterization of Galadriel" by Michael W. Maher, S. J., explores the attributions given to the character of Galadriel, particularly those that are similar to the representations and attributes of the Virgin Mary. Although Marian imagery and piety embrace nearly two thousand years, this work limits itself to a small part of the imagery particular to the Middle Ages and its subsequent resurgence in the Gothic revival and the Oxford movement of the mid-nineteenth century.

For modern Christians, the received vocabulary of Marian piety has been reduced to images approved by the post-Tridentine church filtered through such devotions as Lourdes and Fatima and then reconfigured by the norms of devotion established by the Second Vatican Council. During the Middle Ages, a far greater body of literature existed that fueled popular images and stories concerning the Blessed Virgin, not all of which found its way into the orthodox canon of the post-Tridentine church or the experience of contemporary devotion. Such works and images include prayers to the Virgin, litanies, seasonal antiphons, and artistic representation and texts by theologians such as Bonaventure and Thomas, as well as popular texts such as the *Golden Legend*.

Maher does not argue that Galadriel is an allegorical figure pointing to the Blessed Virgin. Tolkien himself states his dislike for allegory in his introduction to his trilogy. Rather, Maher demonstrates how knowledge of medieval imagery of Mary and what that imagery represents creates a better understanding of the character of Galadriel and Tolkien's relationship with the other characters in his trilogy.

In the last part – on Tolkien's *Silmarillion* mythology and medieval retextualization and theory, primarily in *The Silmarillion* – Gergely Nagy, in "The great chain of reading: (inter-)textual relations and the technique of mythopoesis in the Túrin story," examines the peculiar interconnectedness of several Tolkien texts, using the story of Túrin as a guideline. The allusions to this story in *The Lord of the Rings* give rise to both readerly and critical considerations: to understand the allusions, the reader needs another text to serve as a context. From the critical point of view, the question concerns the status of the allusions (genuine allusions to an existing (con)text/"pseudo"-allusions, cited to supply depth and perspective).

The context is provided in *The Silmarillion*; but the *Silmarillion* story becoming a primary text in its own right, the same critical question of genuine versus "effectual" depth remains standing with the text's claim of the existence of sources. These "sources" are to be found in other treatments of the story (in *Unfinished Tales*, *The Book of Lost Tales*, etc.); however, all claim to be founded on others, to be retextualizations of other texts. These retextualizations in various genres also represent the stages of the story's development. The perspective and depth (which our critical question examines) seem to be produced by the very linkage of texts, as each establishes itself as a context or a retextualization of another one.

Interpreted in terms of Tolkien's textual world, these interconnected texts represent the development of the tradition of the Túrin story *within* the secondary world; in a critical interpretation, however, they show the artistic creation of that development in literary texts. Within his secondary world, Tolkien "simulates" the evolution of mythical/legendary material and the emergence of several retextualizations, in various genres, resulting from it. This understanding of myth as continual retextualization shows that all texts in the Tolkien corpus and the interrelations between them are essentially important to the critical appreciation of his artistic methods to achieve the complex effect of the depth of mythology and mythological text.

Finally, Richard C. West, in chapter 16, "Real-world myth in a secondary world: mythological aspects in the story of Beren and Lúthien," focuses on Tolkien's use of the gods and heroes of world mythology, legend, and folklore in relation to the story of Beren and Lúthien. A tale especially important to Tolkien – the names of the two lovers are etched on the shared tombstone of Tolkien and his wife – exists in several recensions, none of which can be singled out as his preferred version. Among the various myths and legends recalled by the tale are the *Volsunga Saga*, the Calydonian Boar Hunt, Robin Hood, Rapunzel, Orpheus, and Ishtar. Within these tales appear common themes: the disapproving father, the rival lover, the quest, the bride-price, the magical animal ally, the tragic victory of death over love, and the triumph of love over death. Despite the apparent patchwork-quilt nature of the tale as it appears in Christopher Tolkien's publication of *The Silmarillion*, it is deeply moving and carefully crafted.

What this volume can do, ultimately, is to suggest new ways in which Tolkien's medievalness and his medievalism informed and shaped his fantasy, through the collaborations he enjoyed professionally and the academic debates in which he participated at a particular moment in contemporary history, through the actual literary and mythological contexts he spent most of his life understanding, and through the modes and genres he revitalized – retextualized – in the fantastic histories of Middle-earth he created.

Notes

1 See the Millennium edition for the seven-volume format (London: HarperCollins, 1999). For the single-volume format, see *The Lord of the Rings* in the original "India paper" deluxe edition, with slipcase, published by Allen & Unwin (London, 1968); and again, but without a slipcase and printed on regular paper, in 1991 (London: HarperCollins); and with a slipcase and in limited numbers, in quarter-leather (London: HarperCollins, 1997).

2 About half of the chapters in this volume were first delivered as papers in shortened form at this annual international conference. The three sessions were also organized by Jane Chance. We are grateful to Medieval Institute director Paul Szarmach at Western Michigan University for allowing us to assemble in dialogue about Tolkien.

3 See *Biography*, 89. Carpenter sees a hint of this desire as early as in his undergraduate years in comments he wrote about the Finnish epic, the *Kalevala*.

4 See especially, for a treatment of the specifically Old and Middle English works of literature Tolkien himself discussed in his nonfiction prose, Chance, *Tolkien's Art*; for Tolkien's work as a tribute to his nation, see Lobdell (*England and Always*); and for his desire for a "true English epic" (meaning Anglo-Saxon) as manifested in five figures of his mythology, Eärmendil, Ermon and Elmir, Ælfwine, and Ingwë, see Carl F. Hostetter and Arden Smith, "A Mythology for England," in Reynolds and GoodKnight, 281–90. For the origin of Carpenter's phrase "mythology for England" from a conflation of letter 131 and letter 180, see Anders Stenström's discussion of "mythology" in "A Mythology? For England?" in Reynolds and GoodKnight, 310–14.

5 See the annotated bibliography of items up to 1990 in Chance and Day, 375–88. See also the more recent essays by Bruce Mitchell, Tom Shippey, Andy Orchard,

Jonathan Evans, George Clark, and others: Mitchell's "J. R. R. Tolkien and Old English Studies: An Appreciation," in Reynolds and GoodKnight, 206–11; Shippey's "Tolkien and the *Gawain*-Poet," in Reynolds and GoodKnight, 213–20; Orchard's "Tolkien, the Monsters, and the Critics: Back to *Beowulf*," in Battarbee, 73–84; Evans's "The Dragon-lore of Middle-earth: Tolkien and Old English and Old Norse Traditions," in Clark and Timmons, 21–38; and Clark's "J. R. R. Tolkien and the True Hero," in Clark and Timmons, 39–52.

Part I

J. R. R. Tolkien as a medieval scholar

Modern contexts

2 "An industrious little devil"

E. V. Gordon as friend and collaborator with Tolkien

Douglas A. Anderson

In early 1922, E. V. Gordon was hired as a lecturer at the English department of Leeds University. J. R. R. Tolkien had been at Leeds since the autumn of 1920 as Reader in English Language (from July 1924, as Professor of English Language), and not long after Gordon's arrival, Tolkien recorded in his diary that "Eric Valentine Gordon has come and got firmly established and is my devoted friend and pal" (*Biography*, 104). They soon began to work together on what would be their only collaboration to reach print, a major edition of the Middle English poem *Sir Gawain and the Green Knight.* Tolkien found Gordon to be "an industrious little devil" (105), and, as Tolkien's biographer Humphrey Carpenter has observed, Tolkien had to work fast to keep up with Gordon.

In the summer of 1925, Tolkien was elected to the Rawlinson and Bosworth Professorship of Anglo-Saxon at Oxford, and though he taught at both Leeds and Oxford for the autumn term, by early 1926 he had left Leeds and moved on to Oxford. The simple fact of geographical distance made collaborating with Gordon less easy, though the two men did work extensively on several projects. Gordon's early and unexpected death in 1938 robbed Tolkien of a close friend and collaborator. Humphrey Carpenter has suggested that Gordon was in fact Tolkien's "ideal professional collaborator" (*Biography*, 140) – that is, someone who could not only work with Tolkien but also make him surrender material to the printer. Gordon's friendship with Tolkien lasted for the better part of two decades, and a study of that friendship and of Gordon's own life and achievements is overdue. Here, in a short space, I can give only a general outline and delve into a few of the specifics.

Eric Valentine Gordon was born on Valentine's Day, 14 February 1896, in Salmon Arm, British Columbia. He was educated at Victoria College and at McGill University College, both in Victoria, British Columbia. He was elected one of the eight Rhodes scholars from Canada in 1915 and went to University College, Oxford, where he was tutored by Kenneth Sisam, who would soon become one of the central figures at Oxford University Press, and Percy Simpson, who is now remembered mainly for his Oxford edition of Ben Jonson's works.

In 1916, Gordon joined the Canadian Field Artillery in order to serve in World War I, but he was discharged as medically unfit. He spent the remainder of the war working for the Ministries of National Service and of Food. He returned to University College in 1919, where in the following year he was tutored by J. R. R. Tolkien. In 1919–20, C. S. Lewis was also at University College, and Gordon and Lewis certainly knew each other at the time. Through Tolkien, in the late 1920s and early 1930s, they came to know each other well. Gordon got his B.A., a second, in 1920.[1] He remained in Oxford and began working on a B.Litt., which he left uncompleted when he accepted the position at Leeds.

Two Oxford figures were important to both Gordon and Tolkien: C. T. Onions, the great lexicographer of the *Oxford English Dictionary*, and Kenneth Sisam, the scholar and publisher.

In 1919, Onions, in his role as an adviser to the Oxford University Press, offered Tolkien the chance to do a short book, "The English Language before the Conquest." Tolkien was then working on the *Oxford English Dictionary*, and probably he found that he didn't have the time for such a project. He did accept a second opportunity, this being to compile *A Middle-English Vocabulary* to accompany an anthology, *Fourteenth Century Verse and Prose*, already being compiled by Sisam. Years later (in 1932) Onions would found the journal *Medium Ævum*, which he edited for many years. Its many distinguished contributors would include Gordon, Tolkien, C. S. Lewis, and several other members of the Inklings, the circle of Lewis's and Tolkien's friends that began meeting in the 1930s to read aloud to each other their own compositions.

Kenneth Sisam's relationship to both Gordon and Tolkien was complex. Like Gordon, Tolkien had also been tutored by Sisam, and years later Tolkien would say that he counted himself fortunate to have attended Sisam's Old English lectures as an undergraduate. But when Tolkien was late in delivering the manuscript of his glossary, Sisam's anthology was published without it in October 1921. This was the first of several disappointments between the two men.

Onions and Sisam seem to occupy, in Tolkien's life at least, almost antithetical positions. On Onions's death in 1965 at the age of 91, Tolkien referred to him in a letter as "my dear old protector, backer and friend" (*Letters*, 353). Sisam, however, was Tolkien's rival in 1925 for the Anglo-Saxon Chair, and in the election process itself both candidates had tied in votes for the position. The vice-chancellor of the university cast the deciding vote for Tolkien. Openings for Oxford chairs were not frequent, and this proved to be Sisam's only chance at such a position. There was possibly some resentment. Some other colleagues felt similarly, like Eugène Vinaver, who wrote on Sisam's death in 1971 that "everyone knows what a terrible mistake Oxford made when they by-passed him for the Chair of Anglo-Saxon" (Sutcliffe, 270).

Peter Sutcliffe's informal history of the Oxford University Press gives an interesting picture of Sisam:

> To some of [his] contemporaries, … Sisam seemed a hard man …. He was certainly unyielding, often stubborn, and on the rare occasions when he was

> persuaded to change his mind there was a rumbling and creaking of machinery unaccustomed to shifts of gear.
>
> (Sutcliffe, 270)

Sisam had strong opinions about press policies, preferring books with a minimal amount of editorial apparatus. Both Gordon and Tolkien, on the other hand, wanted space for large glossaries and more notes. They desired to compile major editions rather than junior university textbooks. In the end, Gordon found ways to work with Sisam. Tolkien did not. After *Sir Gawain* appeared in April 1925, Gordon published two further books with Oxford University Press – *An Introduction to Old Norse* (1927) and *Scandinavian Archaeology* (1937) – whereas from 1925 through the end of Sisam's tenure in 1948, Tolkien published almost nothing more with Oxford.[2]

Both Tolkien and Gordon enjoyed Leeds immensely. They worked hard to build up the English department and found pleasure in the work. They formed a Viking Club for undergraduates, which met to drink beer, read the sagas, and sing drinking songs in Anglo-Saxon and Old Norse. A number of these songs were distributed as stenciled sheets. One of their most promising students was A. H. Smith, who, soon after earning his Ph.D. at Leeds in 1926, became known as a distinguished scholar of place-names and, from 1930, a professor at University College, London.

While at Leeds, Gordon's papers began to appear in print. When Tolkien became seriously ill with pneumonia in 1923, Gordon was allowed to take over Tolkien's responsibility for the review chapter on philology for *The Year's Work in English Studies 1922*, thereby earning the right to contribute the chapters on Old English and Middle English in the annual in subsequent years. Both Gordon and Tolkien published poems and translations in local Leeds magazines and anthologies.

Gordon and Smith collaborated on an extensive article, "The River Names of Yorkshire." Gordon wrote solo articles on the Scandinavian influence in Yorkshire dialects, and in the years afterwards he would cover other topics, such as place-names and their origins, the historical dating of certain events in poems, and the backgrounds to various Icelandic sagas.

Gordon visited Iceland twice, and his interest in the Icelandic language led him to try the experiment of inviting Icelandic students to study English at Leeds, while they at the same time provided opportunities for their fellow students to learn Icelandic. The response led to the founding of an Icelandic honors course.

Gordon and Tolkien were also active locally with the Yorkshire Dialect Society. Gordon, in particular, assisted with their Dialect Gramophone Recording Scheme, an attempt to preserve a record of local dialects. Gordon also lectured to the society on 30 November 1930. His paper, "The Vikings in Yorkshire," was very popular and provoked a lively discussion.[3]

Gordon's first book had been his and Tolkien's edition of *Sir Gawain*, which was published in April 1925. Tolkien had been primarily responsible for the text and glossary, while Gordon contributed the greater part of the notes. Soon after its publication they began work on an edition of *Pearl*, which went through several nearly finished versions but remained unpublished for more than a decade after Gordon's death. A few offshoots of this work on *Pearl* did reach print. In 1932–33, Gordon and C. T. Onions collaborated on a series of two articles in *Medium Ævum* on textual points and the interpretation of *Pearl*.

Tolkien left his Leeds post at the end of 1925, and in January 1926 Gordon was named as his successor to the Professorship of English Language. In 1927 Oxford University Press published Gordon's hefty anthology, *An Introduction to Old Norse*. It contains a long introduction, a grammar, and a moderate glossary (Tolkien is thanked for reading proofs of the grammar, and for making valuable suggestions and corrections), along with a wide-ranging selection of extracts from the *Elder Edda* and a large number of the sagas.

In 1929, Gordon arranged, for the Leeds University Library, the acquisition of the private library of the late author and historian of Copenhagen, Bogi Thorarensen Melsteð (1860–1929). This purchase of some seven thousand volumes formed the basis of the Leeds University Icelandic collection, which to this day remains one of the best Icelandic collections outside of Iceland and Scandinavia. In 1930, for his services to Icelandic studies, Gordon was awarded the Knighthood of the Royal Icelandic Order of the Falcon by Christian X, the King of Iceland and Denmark. Soon afterwards he was elected Honorary Fellow of the Icelandic Society of Letters.

On 30 July 1930, Eric Valentine Gordon married one of his students, Ida Lilian Pickles, a local girl from West Yorkshire (she was born in 1907 in Wakefield, just south of Leeds). The marriage took place at a parish church in nearby Liversedge. Ida Pickles had come to Leeds University around the time of Tolkien's departure and earned a B.A. (with honors) in 1928. She continued at Leeds and earned a Ph.D. in 1930 for her thesis, "A Topographical Study of the Sagas of the Vestfirðir." The couple would have four children, three daughters and one son.[4]

In February 1931, Gordon was appointed Smith Professor of English Language and Germanic Philology at the University of Manchester. He took up the post in September of that year and held it until his death. The Arthurian scholar Eugène Vinaver followed Gordon to Manchester in 1933; a few years later he and Gordon would collaborate on a comparison of the text of the alliterative *Morte Arthure* and the Winchester manuscript of Malory, the latter of which was discovered in 1934.

Like many other academics of the time, Gordon supplemented his income as an examiner in English literature for many universities. Around 1933, after a *viva voce* examination at Oxford where Gordon, Tolkien, and C. S. Lewis were examiners, Lewis poked fun at his two philologist friends in a short verse in alliterative meter: "Two at table in their talk borrowed / Gargantua's mouth. Gordon and Tolkien / Had will to repeat well-nigh the whole / That they of Verner's law... / Heard by hearsay. / Never at board I heard / Viler vivas" (Carpenter, *Inklings*, 55). (Of these lines Tolkien retorted that during these sessions Lewis's voice was the most often heard.) Gordon also served as external examiner for the University of New Zealand for the last seven years of his life.

In 1932, the London publisher Methuen began a small series of books that would comprise Methuen's Old English Library. The series had two general editors, A. H. Smith and Frederick Norman, both of University College, London. These books were intended to be small, student editions, and Gordon and Tolkien were signed up to collaborate on two. Tolkien would be the senior partner on *The Wanderer*, while Gordon would be the senior on *The Seafarer*. As early as 1933, these two editions were announced for publication, but Tolkien and Gordon soon found that they had problems over length. Eventually they decided to do both poems in a single volume, probably in order to allow themselves a slightly larger glossary. These editions were essentially complete by the mid-1930s, but Gordon passed away while the manuscripts awaited reduction and final revision. Only Gordon's work on *The Seafarer* would ever appear in print, under his wife Ida's name, an edition that was eventually published in 1960.[5]

On 25 November 1936, Tolkien delivered his landmark lecture, "*Beowulf*: The Monsters and the Critics," to the British Academy in London, and Gordon arranged for Tolkien to repeat the lecture for the Medieval Society at Manchester a few weeks later on 9 December. (Tolkien's train was late, and Gordon temporarily entertained the audience with an account of the Norse settlements in Greenland.)

In 1937, Gordon published two books. The first, published in March, was his translation of Haakon Shetelig's and Hjalmar Falk's *Scandinavian Archaeology*, in its time an impressive pulling-together of archeological findings with linguistic data (assembled from literature) on many aspects of the Old Norse way of life, including dwellings, weapons, boats, dress, diet, and religion. Gordon's next book, the last to be published in his lifetime, was his edition of *The Battle of Maldon*. It was the fifth book in Methuen's Old English Library, and it appeared in June 1937. Tolkien is acknowledged for reading the proofs and making many corrections and contributions. Gordon goes on to say that "Professor Tolkien, with characteristic generosity, gave me the solution to many of the textual and philological problems discussed in these pages" (*Battle of Maldon*, vi).

Also in 1937, Tolkien and Gordon were each contacted by BBC Radio to broadcast in their poetry series. Gordon was asked to discuss Old Norse poetry, and Tolkien, Anglo-Saxon. Gordon broadcast on the Icelandic Eddas on 30 December 1937. Tolkien's contribution, titled "Anglo-Saxon Verse," followed as the next in the series on 14 January 1938.

In July 1938, Gordon suffered an attack of gallstones. An operation was quickly undertaken to remove his gallbladder. The operation itself went well, but then things went very wrong, and Gordon died on 29 July 1938 at the age of 42. A postmortem disclosed that two suprarenal glands had ceased to function, an undiagnosable, preexisting condition that would have been untreatable once discovered, and which would have inevitably resulted in a slow and painful death. Gordon's body was cremated on 2 August 1938.

A correspondent of *The Times* (London) wrote on 4 August 1938 to supplement the short obituary of Gordon that had run three days earlier, calling him

> an untiring worker, quick of eye and penetrating of mind … . For him philology was no dry-as-dust matter of word-forms, but a humanity, the study of life and thought. He was thus an inspiring as well as a solid teacher.
>
> (*The Times*, 4 August 1938, 12)

Gordon's widow was left to raise four children on her own. Her professional philological qualifications fortunately enabled her to take over some of her late husband's teaching duties. She remained a lecturer at the University of Manchester from 1938 to 1960 and a senior lecturer from 1960 to 1968. She visited Iceland twice to study saga literature, and in 1970 she was a visiting professor at the University of Victoria, in British Columbia. This latter position has an interesting connection with her husband, for the University of Victoria, founded in 1963, is the successor to Victoria College, where E. V. Gordon had studied in the early teens.

After Gordon's death, Tolkien took over the edition of *Pearl*, which, with Tolkien's approval, Gordon had nearly completed on his own, though in late 1937 Gordon had asked Tolkien to come back as a collaborator on the project. Tolkien planned to finish it as a duty to his dead friend and former student, but he proved unable to do so, and after more than a decade it was passed back to Ida Gordon, who began the final revision of it in 1950. Tolkien continued to assist, but Mrs. Gordon found it necessary to reduce the size of the edition.[6] *Pearl* was finally published in June 1953. It appeared solely under E. V. Gordon's name, though it probably should have been credited as a collaboration with his wife, Ida Gordon, such was her extensive contribution to the final work.

E. V. Gordon's *An Introduction to Old Norse* was revised by A. R. Taylor in 1957, but the only major change in contents was to remove the fragment Gordon had used of *Hrafnkel's Saga* and include the full saga instead. Ida Gordon assisted in the process of updating the book. In 1967, the Tolkien and Gordon edition of *Sir Gawain* was revised by Tolkien's former student (and his successor to the Merton Professorship of English language and Literature at Oxford, which Tolkien held from 1945 to 1959) Norman Davis.

Ida Gordon published only a small amount professionally. By 1960, when she had finished her husband's edition of *The Seafarer*, she published it under her own name, feeling that there had been a revolution in the understanding of the poem since her husband had worked on it, and that a new approach had been necessary.[7] Her other work includes a couple of articles on *Gisli's Saga* (offshoots from her doctoral thesis), a study entitled "Oral Tradition and the

Sagas of Poets," an essay on the themes in *The Wanderer* and *The Seafarer*, and an essay called "The Narrative Function of Irony in Chaucer's *Troilus and Criseyde*."

Ida Gordon's short book *The Double Sorrow of Troilus: A Study of Ambiguities in "Troilus and Criseyde"* was published by Oxford University Press in 1970. Her most recent publication is a small pamphlet, a translation of *The Dream of the Rood*, published in 1993 by the Groam House Museum in Rosemarkie, Scotland. Now retired and in her nineties, Ida Gordon lives in Scotland.

By a rough count of their primary professional publications during their respective lifetimes, Gordon and Tolkien published nearly the same amount. The main difference is that Gordon published his work over a span of about fifteen years, while Tolkien's output is spread out over nearly forty, an estimate that does not count the years of his retirement. Tolkien published three books (plus two posthumous ones), roughly nineteen articles, and only two book reviews,[8] while Gordon published four books (plus a posthumous one), sixteen articles, and fourteen book reviews (covering twenty-one books), some of which are long enough to be considered as articles.

There is no doubt that Tolkien would have been extremely interested in all of Gordon's professional work, which ranges through the fields of place-name studies, Old English, Middle English, and Old Norse and into a few miscellaneous areas. In a short space, I am here able to cover only a small number of points with Tolkienian relevance.

First, there are a few examples of a direct influence of Gordon's work on Tolkien. The ink drawing of an Old Norse hall, presumably by Gordon himself, which appears in his *An Introduction to Old Norse*, seems to have provided the model for Tolkien's own illustration of Beorn's Hall published in *The Hobbit* (Hammond and Scull, 122–23).

And in his essay "Tolkien and 'The Homecoming of Beorhtnoth,'" Tom Shippey has written at length about Tolkien's verse-play, which is a kind of sequel to *The Battle of Maldon*. Tolkien's poem was first published in 1953 as a contribution to *Essays and Studies*, where, as a literary creation, it fits somewhat uneasily. Tolkien had certainly written it before 1945, and Shippey points out that some of Tolkien's commentary, published along with the poem, seems to have been composed in direct response to Gordon's statements in his 1937 edition of *The Battle of Maldon*. However, the inspiration for Tolkien's poem seems to predate Gordon's edition by some years. Christopher Tolkien has published a fragment of an earlier conception of his father's verse-play (then in rhyming dialogue), which he dates to the early 1930s, and he references a still earlier text (*Treason*, 106–7). Thus, while the verse-play itself might have existed before Gordon's edition, the additional commentary, added by Tolkien to the poem (probably in order to justify its inclusion in a collection of literary criticism), may be the only part directly influenced by Gordon's work.

Tom Shippey has also written of the influence of Bothvarr Bjarki from *Hrolf Kraki's Saga* on the character of Beorn in *The Hobbit* (*Road to Middle-earth*, 73), so it is highly interesting to tie this influence directly into Gordon's work. At Leeds, one of his and Tolkien's students, Stella Marie Mills, had translated it as *The Saga of Hrolf Kraki* under Gordon's guidance. It became her only book when Blackwell's published the translation in 1933. The volume is dedicated to Gordon, Tolkien, and Onions, and for publication Gordon contributed an introduction. Mills got her B.A. at Leeds in 1924, and Tolkien helped her secure employment in Oxford after his return. For a time she worked with Onions on the *Oxford English Dictionary* before she joined the staff of St. Joseph's Catholic Primary School in Oxford. For the rest of her long life she was a close friend of the Tolkien family.

Gordon's introduction to *The Saga of Hrolf Kraki* is very interesting, as is the translation itself, about which Gordon wrote:

> The translation is a faithful one in the truest sense of the term; it is close to the original in spirit, and yet is not over-literal … . Here at last we have a translator who is willing to treat realistic writing as realistic, and has no desire to impose colour upon it, as William Morris and his many imitators have done. Morris added this heavy colouring of his own with such literary mastery that it is not surprising that most translators since him have followed him as closely as they could: but it is not faithful to the original.
>
> (Gordon, "Introduction," *The Saga of Hrolf Kraki*, xi)

Gordon also wrote a lengthy and highly praiseworthy review of S. T. R. O. d'Ardenne's doctoral thesis, published as *An Edition of "Þe Liflade ant te Passiun of Seinte Iuliene"* (1936). The thesis was done under Tolkien's supervision and arguably contains more of Tolkien's own thoughts on early Middle English than anything Tolkien himself published. D'Ardenne admitted privately that the book should have appeared under their joint byline, but by being published under her name only it enabled her to become elected as a university professor.[9] Gordon, who certainly recognized Tolkien's generous input but was careful not to disclose it, wrote that "there is probably no other edition of a Middle English text with so many new contributions and discoveries in it" (Review of *Þe Liflade*, 137).

In his reviews and articles, Gordon's enthusiasm for literature, especially for the sagas, is infectious, and his criticism frequently just. He considered *Hrafnkel's Saga* to be "a jewel of narrative art, even among Icelandic sagas, and especially renowned for its excellent structure" ("On *Hrafnkel's Saga*," 1). But in writing on *Kormák's Saga*, Gordon notes, "though the author of *Kormáks saga* failed to make the best of the superb material which he had at hand, he has at least the credit of preserving for us some of the finest skaldic verses that have survived from the Viking age" ("Traditions," 64). And Gordon's style could be at times very witty and engaging. In reviewing an edition of the most considerable medical work known in Old Icelandic, Gordon observed that

> the manuscript was evidently written by men (two principal scribes) who had difficulty in reading their original, perhaps because of ignorance of the

> subject. They left a number of blank spaces where they were unable to decipher the word in the original, and the corruptions are numerous. If it is really true that misprints in medical encyclopædias of to-day have been the death of men who thought it unnecessary to consult a doctor, there are enough errors in this manuscript to be as fatal as a plague.
>
> (Gordon, Review of *Old Icelandic Medical Miscellany*, 76)

Of his miscellaneous writings, Gordon's own prose translations from the *Elder Edda* are memorable. It is a pity, though, that he translated only three selections – *Thrymskviða*, *Volundarkviða*, and *Atlakviða*. Gordon also published a few interesting poems, a ballad of Tristram and Isoult adapted from a Scandinavian version, a translation in skaldic meter of a short verse composed by Skuli, earl of the Orkneys, in the twelfth century, and an English rendering of a short work by Ibsen.

Some of Tolkien's and Gordon's poetic work appeared side by side under strange circumstances in a small volume entitled *Songs for the Philologists*. In 1936, their former pupil A. H. Smith set his students at University College, London, the task of printing on their Elizabethan printing press a small edition of the stenciled Leeds songs (using an uncorrected version, as Tolkien later noted, and altering a number of the verses that had specific references to Leeds). A small number of copies were printed up as a book before Smith realized that he had never asked Tolkien or Gordon for their permission, so the copies remained undistributed. Tolkien first learned of the book in 1940, when one of Smith's colleagues wrote him to ask for retroactive permission, by which time most of the printed copies had been destroyed by a fire in the building. Many of the poems in *Songs for the Philologists* were Tolkien's, but those by Gordon include three versions of "When I'm dead don't bury me at all, just pickle my bones in alcohol" – in Old English, in Gothic, and in a Scottish dialect – and another poem, "Su Klukka Heljar," an Icelandic version of "The Bells of Hell." Gordon probably never knew of the volume's existence, and *Songs for the Philologists* is the greatest rarity among Tolkien's publications (Hammond and Anderson, 293–94).

Of Tolkien's nonacademic work, we know that Gordon did read, sometime in the mid-1930s, Tolkien's unfinished poem in alliterative verse, "The Fall of Arthur." And Gordon certainly knew of Tolkien's aspirations as a poet, for a number of Tolkien's poems – some jeu d'esprit, others more serious – were published in magazines and small anthologies while both men were at Leeds.

Gordon also knew *The Hobbit*, for Tolkien sent him one of his author's copies on publication in September 1937. But it seems unlikely that Gordon would have known of his friend's invented mythology as it existed prior to Gordon's death in 1938, most of which has now been published in the first five volumes of Christopher Tolkien's series, *The History of Middle-earth*. Tolkien seems to have kept these writings pretty close to himself, certainly in the years before the publication of *The Hobbit*.

Whether Gordon would have enjoyed *The Lord of the Rings* is really a different matter. As a question of taste, perhaps he, like C. S. Lewis, would have delighted in it, or, like some medieval scholars, he might have felt that Tolkien's time would have been better spent in finishing up any number of his outstanding scholarly projects. Gordon's wife certainly belongs in the latter group, for she wrote in a 20 April 1982 letter to the Tolkien scholar John D. Rateliff,

> I ought to tell you that I have very little interest in the Tolkien of *The Lord of the Rings*. In my opinion that side of him robbed us of a very fine medieval scholar who might have done so much more work of lasting value like the *Gawain* & *Pearl* editions.

E. V. Gordon's scholarship is without question rewarding in its own right, but those interested in the scholarship and literary background of J. R. R. Tolkien will also find Gordon's work to be illuminating and relevant for study. One conclusion derived from such close study is inescapable: Humphrey Carpenter's characterization of Gordon as an ideal collaborator for Tolkien must be discarded. Gordon had as little influence as anyone in persuading Tolkien to finish the projects he was working on. Otherwise, the bibliographies of both men would have several additional entries.[10]

Notes

I am grateful to the following people for assistance on this paper: Dr. Robin Darwall-Smith, Archivist, University College, Oxford, for information on the college records of E. V. Gordon; Susan E. Seright, Curator, Groam House Museum, Rosemarkie, Scotland, for sharing information from Ida L. Gordon; John Garth, for literary detective work; Wayne G. Hammond and Christina Scull, for help on several points; and John D. Rateliff, for a transcription of his letter from Ida L. Gordon.

1 Gordon's Oxford M.A., which did not require any additional study or course work, was awarded in 1926.

2 During Sisam's tenure, a few of Tolkien's essays and an introduction by Tolkien to another man's work did appear in books published by Oxford University Press, but Sisam does not seem to have been involved in any of these projects, which may have been overseen by different people or by a different division of the press.

3 This paper was not published. Another unpublished paper, "The Earliest Runes," was presented by Gordon to the Viking Society for Northern Research on 19 January 1926.

4 The Gordons' eldest child, Bridget Mackenzie, followed her parents academically and was a lecturer in Old Norse at Glasgow University.

5 In 1969 the Methuen Old English Library published an edition of *The Wanderer* by T. P. Dunning and A. J. Bliss, both of whom, coincidentally, were Tolkien's former students and contributors to his festschrift, *English and Medieval Studies Presented to J. R. R. Tolkien on the Occasion of His Seventieth Birthday* (1962), ed. Norman Davis and C. L. Wrenn.

6 In her preface, Mrs. Gordon states: "I wish to make it clear that there has been considerable rewriting, and that if, in the process errors or obscurities have crept in, the blame must be the reviser's. Some sacrifice of the original material there has been, especially in the Introduction" (*Pearl*, iii). Mrs. Gordon continues with warm thanks to Tolkien, whom she says added valuable notes and corrections, and responded generously to queries.

7 In the preface, Ida Gordon writes:

> When my husband, Professor E. V. Gordon, died in 1938 he left an uncompleted draft of an edition of *The Wanderer* and *The Seafarer*, on which he had been working in collaboration with Professor J. R. R. Tolkien. And my first intention, with Professor Tolkien's approval, was to bring into final form that edition. But by the time I was free to begin the work there had been a revolution in the study of these poems.
>
> (I. Gordon, *Seafarer*, vii)

She goes on to relate that, in order to keep the size compatible with the plan of the series, she had chosen to do just one poem, *The Seafarer*, because of its more challenging theme. She again thanks Tolkien "for some notes given to me with his usual generosity" (*Seafarer*, vii).

8 The count of Tolkien's academic publications is based on that devised by Tom Shippey in his article "Tolkien's Academic Reputation Now," adding to it a few book reviews not cited therein.

9 See Hammond and Anderson, 278. Tolkien and S. T. R. O. d'Ardenne collaborated on a few later articles and planned a major edition of another Middle English work written in the same dialect, *Seinte Katerine*, but Tolkien never found the time, and d'Ardenne eventually finished the edition with E. J. Dobson. *Seinte Katerine* appeared in 1981.

10 Since this chapter was written I have learned of Professor Jean Barman's forthcoming book on E. V. Gordon's aunt and mother, *Sojourning Sisters: The Lives and Letters of Jessie and Annie McQueen* (Toronto: University of Toronto Press, 2002).

3 "There would always be a fairy-tale"

J. R. R. Tolkien and the folklore controversy

Verlyn Flieger

In March of 1939, with World War II about to begin, a middle-aged Professor of Anglo-Saxon at Oxford with a private hobby of inventing myth and languages took time out from both occupations to deliver the annual Andrew Lang Lecture at St. Andrews University in Scotland. Surprisingly, Tolkien's talk, twelfth in the series, was the first to deal with Lang's work in myth and folklore. He called his lecture, which he later expanded and published as an essay, "On Fairy-Stories."[1] In it, he recalled that his own taste for fairy-stories was "wakened … on the threshold of manhood, and quickened to full life by war" (*EPCW*, 64).

The war to which Tolkien referred was not the one about to start but its predecessor, soon to be known as World War I. Nevertheless, it is not difficult to track the connections that might have linked fairy-stories, the past war, and the one ready to start as he spoke at St. Andrews. World War I began in August of 1914. In September of that year John Ronald Tolkien, then a 22-year-old student at Oxford awaiting military call-up, wrote a fairy-tale poem titled "The Voyage of Eärendel," about a celestial mariner who sails west to seek peace for Middle-earth. It was the beginning of his invented mythology (*Biography*, 71; *BLT*2, 267, 277n).

Tolkien's so-called mythology for England has been much discussed among scholars of his work,[2] and his own words about his motive in undertaking such a project have usually been taken at face value:

> I was from early days grieved by the poverty of my own beloved country: it had no stories of its own (bound up with its tongue and soil), not of the quality that I sought and found (as an ingredient) in legends of other lands. There was Greek, and Celtic, and Romance, Germanic, Scandinavian, and Finnish (which greatly affected me); but nothing English, save impoverished chap-book stuff … . I had a mind to make a body of more or less connected legend … which I could dedicate simply to: to England; to my country … . I would draw some of the great tales in fullness, and leave many only placed in the scheme, and sketched. The cycles should be linked to a majestic whole, and yet leave scope for other minds and hands, wielding paint and music and drama.
>
> (*Letters*, 144–45)

The concept is clear, and the entirety of Tolkien's Silmarillion cosmology as published in *The History of Middle-earth* series fits the description like Cinderella's slipper. However, the historical and intellectual backgrounds from which that concept emerged have been too little considered.

The two coincident events mentioned earlier, the start of Tolkien's mythology and the start of World War I, were themselves coincident with a third, not a beginning this time, but an end. This was the close of what Richard Dorson calls the "golden century" of British folklore studies, 1813 to 1914 (*Peasant Customs*, 1:ix; hereinafter *PC*). More than mere chronology connects all three. While the start of war was not the inspiration for Tolkien's mythology, which had been taking shape in his mind for some time, the immediacy of the conflict and its threat to European national identities if Germany should prevail may well have acted as a spur. The outbreak of hostilities had the opposite effect on the golden century. The exigencies of war slammed the door on the first burst of international cooperation in this newly formed area of research.

An often republished essay, "On Fairy-Stories" is usually read in the context of Tolkien's own work as his creative manifesto, explicating the principles he was even then putting into practice in his own mythological fiction. As early as 1937, two years before his St. Andrews lecture, he had begun the sequel to *The Hobbit* requested by his publisher, George Allen & Unwin, which after long labor became *The Lord of the Rings*. Begun as "the new Hobbit," as Tolkien called it, this project began almost immediately to veer away from the children's story tone and content of the earlier book, gravitating toward the older and much darker material of the Silmarillion mythology originally intended "for England." It seems reasonable to suppose that his theoretical discussion of fairy-stories would be colored by his practice and the standards set out in the lecture by those he was even then engaged in developing through his own experience.

There is, however, a wider and more complex intellectual and historical background into which both the lecture and the fiction fit, for the principles set forth in his essay were not just the working template for his own story, but a direct reply to and argument against the then current major folklore theories. At the time Tolkien spoke at St. Andrews, the golden century – the first fine, careless rapture of folklore studies – was long over. Nonetheless, the questions that had concerned the folklorists – which according to Dorson were "[t]he origin and dispersion of the Aryans, the mythopoeic view of early man, the animistic philosophy of savages, the survivals of primitive belief among peasants" (*PC*, 1:x) – together with the Sherlockian search for answers and the close inspection of trees that left researchers unable to see the forest, were all still operable factors. By 1939 it was time to review and reevaluate the state of the question, and Tolkien, no folklorist but a mythmaker, felt (though he modestly denied it) equal to the task. Much of his argument in "On Fairy-Stories" was both a capsule history of and rebuttal to the theories of the folklore movement.

The issues over which the folklorists disagreed are precisely the topics Tolkien deals with in his lecture, and which he counters with his own more imaginative analysis of the nature and appropriate uses of fantasy. To enter the debate,

Tolkien selected three names representing the major and contending schools of theory that generated and carried on the controversy. From comparative philology he took Max Müller and his follower George Dasent, and from evolutionary anthropology he took Müller's chief opposition, Andrew Lang.

Tolkien faulted all of them and the theories they represented for "using the stories not as they were meant to be used, but as a quarry from which to dig evidence, or information about matters in which they are interested" (*EPCW*, 47). In his view, they were not reading stories at all; they were examining data, a process which to him was a gross misuse of the enchantment, what he called the quality of "faërie," that he found in fairy tales. His answer began with a discussion of what fairy-stories were not and was followed by his judgment of what they were and how they worked. The result was an on-the-spot forging of his own working theory, hammered out on the anvil of the folklore controversy.

From each contending school of thought he plucked a phrase or idea to address, which he then used as topic sentences in his lecture. From Müller he took "nature myth," "solar mythology," and the concept of mythology as "a disease of language," all of which were staples of Müller's groundbreaking first essay, "Comparative Mythology," published in 1856. From Lang he took the idea of human maturation as the model for cultural evolution. This had led Lang to the conclusion that the matter of fairy-stories was "primitive" and the consequent assumption that the stories themselves were only fit for children, concepts he spelled out in one of his most widely read books, *Custom and Myth.* From Dasent's introduction to his translation of Moe and Asbjörnsen's collection of *Norske Folke-eventyr*, rendered in English as *Popular Tales from the Norse*, Tolkien took an extended metaphor, the "soup" of story and the "bones of the ox" from which it is boiled.

Some background is necessary here. The origins of folklore research go back to the gentleman antiquaries of the sixteenth and seventeenth centuries: John Leland, William Camden, and John Aubrey. Their investigations into the antiquities of England were, to begin with, chiefly topographical and included Stonehenge, Avebury, and a variety of other monuments, mounds, long barrows, and standing stones. The first great literary flowering came in the eighteenth century with the ballad collections of Thomas Percy and Francis Child. Late in the eighteenth century, the German Johannes Gottfried von Herder argued persuasively for oral traditions rooted in the language of the unlettered "folk" as the repository of any country's cultural identity. It was an idea whose time had come, and by the early nineteenth century the hunt was on, no longer for actual ruins, but for narrative folk traditions as reservoirs of national spirit.

This was Dorson's "golden century," the era of the great collectors. The brothers Grimm in Germany, Moe and Asbjörnsen in Norway, Elias Lönnrot in Finland; in the British Isles John Francis Campbell of Islay in Scotland, Sir John Rhys in Wales, Thomas Croker and Jeremiah Curtin in Ireland, and Thomas Keightley – all turned to the "folk" to discover a mythic past. Their research was coincident with a resurgence of interest in cultural and national identity. Germany had not long been a united nation when the Grimms began looking for philological material to validate that unity. Likewise, the Celtic outposts in the British Isles, Ireland, Scotland, and Wales were reaching for and finding evidence of a cultural history independent of English hegemony. An especially notable success was that of Elias Lönnrot, whose collection of Finnish folk songs, arranged and published as *Kalevala*, had given his native Finland, for centuries the shuttlecock of Russia and Sweden, a national identity.

For all this nationalistic fervor, however, once the stories were collected and set down it became uncomfortably clear that they were made of pretty raw material: incest, rape, bestiality, child murder, cannibalism, and the like. Two of the Grimms' stories Tolkien mentions in his lecture – "The Frog-King" and "The Juniper Tree" – are ample illustration. "The Frog-King" is about a princess who promises to marry a frog if he will retrieve her ball from a well. When he does indeed fetch her the ball, she is faced with the disagreeable prospect of fulfilling her promise and marrying the frog. The fact that the frog magically and at the last minute turns into a handsome prince is irrelevant to the real frisson of the story, the monstrous notion of a young woman going to bed with a frog. This is made explicit in the narrative when the frog jumps on to her pillow as she prepares for the night and demands to share her bed.

"The Juniper Tree" hinges on cannibalism. The story tells of a wicked stepmother who murders, cuts up, stews, and serves her young stepson to the boy's father for dinner. The boy's stepsister (a more loving relative than her mother) saves the bones from the stew and buries them under a tree in the yard, from whence the boy is resurrected as a bird. This "gay and vengeful bird-spirit," as Tolkien describes it ("OFS," 128), brings about the death of the stepmother by dropping a millstone on her. As with "The Juniper Tree," the taboo is not violated, for the father, though ignorant of the content of the soup, inexplicably loses his appetite. Nevertheless, the concept is introduced.

The proper Victorians were properly horrified at such goings on, and then the search began for anything that could explain or justify the apparent barbarities (such as child murder, anthropophagy, and bestiality) and logical inconsistencies (such as just how a union between a girl and a frog could be consummated). In Britain the battle lines were drawn between the mythologists and the anthropologists, more specifically between Max Müller and Andrew Lang. Müller used comparative philology, relying heavily on Greek and Vedic sources, and found the origins he sought in evidence from Sanskrit, Homeric Greek, and the comparison of Indo-European (or as he termed them "Indo-Aryan") languages. The search for Aryan roots was full of pitfalls, and it did not take long for some collectors to fall into them and to look for what they wanted to find instead of finding whatever was there. Nazi Germany was the extreme and ugly culmination of the early Indo-Aryan theory.

Müller introduced his argument in an epochal essay "Comparative Mythology" (1856), later reprinted as volume 2 of his four-volume *Chips from a German Workshop* (1867–75). Here he proposed that myths as we have them arose through verbal misapprehension (Dorson, *PC*, 67), the late misunderstanding of early, primarily Sanskrit Vedic names for celestial phenomena. In what he called the "mythopoeic" age, the concepts arose of the Aryan gods. As the migrations of the Indo-Aryan people splintered them into separate groups, so their language and its related mythology splintered into various offshoots. In this process, the original true, "nature/solar" meanings were forgotten, surviving only in mythical words and phrases that were retained although their original referents were forgotten.

The stories and names that then developed to explain these phrases constituted Müller's notion of mythology as "a disease of language," that invalid understanding from which new stories – the myths as we know them – were created (Dorson, *British Folklorists*, 162; hereinafter *BF*). The natural phenomena originally referred to – sun, wind, dawn, night, sky, earth – were replaced by heroic personifications – Apollo, Zeus, Herakles. Müller's conclusion was that by tracing the words back to ancient forms it was possible to arrive at their original referents. He was constrained by his own catchphrases, for his interpretation of mythology as a disease implied a previous state of health, a state presumably expressed in the "original" language of solar mythology. Moreover, the assumption that there had been an "original," therefore "true" solar meaning that had been lost had the predictable but deplorable consequence of elevating the "Aryan" peoples and languages to primacy, and by implication denigrating the non-Aryan "others."

When you look for things, you are apt to find them, and pretty soon Müller was finding solar mythology everywhere and seeing solar heroes in every myth he examined. Any time a hero went into a cave or traveled from east to west or died in battle – that was the sun setting; a hero vanquishing a dragon was the rising sun conquering the night, and so on. Those who followed in Müller's wake elaborated his theory but stuck to his methods. Adalbert Kuhn, described by Dorson as "one of the foremost of the philological mythologists" and chief proponent of the "lightning school" (*BF*, 171), proposed a variation that substituted lightning for the sun and found electrical phenomena in Zeus and Indra and lightning-related fire in the story of Prometheus. Kuhn expanded Müller's theory to include a variety of weather phenomena – clouds, lightning-bolts, thunder – but did not substantially change its direction.

Müller's philological principle ruled uncontested for nearly a decade before it was, as Tolkien put it, "dethroned from the high place it once held in this court of inquiry" (*EPCW*, 50). The dethroner was Andrew Lang, who opposed Müller vigorously and vociferously for more than twenty years and finally toppled him. Lang's *Custom and Myth* attacked comparative mythology for its self-limitation to Aryan-speaking peoples and replaced philology with anthropology. To his credit, Lang avoided the Aryan/racial pitfall, but only to fall into the trap of social Darwinism, a pit of almost equal size and naïveté. His approach was grounded in the notion that humanity had evolved culturally from a "primitive" to a "civilized" state. He "demolished the hypothesis of disease-of-language and filled the vacuum with a continuous chain of savage survivals" (*BF*, 1997).

In Lang's view, the rawer aspects of the tales were the relicts not of some lost language of celestial mythology but of "primitive" – therefore "savage" – cultural practices. His evidence was assembled from studies of contemporary, so-called primitive peoples such as Native Americans, Australian Aborigines, Zulus, Hottentots, Melanesians, Polynesians, Samoyeds, and West Highlanders. Not the history of Indo-Aryan languages, said Lang, but the ritual and totemic customs of contemporary primitive societies can explain the seemingly irrational, at times horrific subject matter of myths and fairy-stories. "The origin of the irrational element in myth and tale is to be found in the qualities of the uncivilized imagination" (quoted in Dorson, *BF*, 297). His view of "the uncivilized imagination" as the earliest or childhood stage of human cultural development led directly to the concomitant assumption that in a postchildhood – that is to say, modern – world, fairy-tales would only, indeed could only, be enjoyed by children.

Although by the time he gave his lecture the golden century was long over, Tolkien was by no means the only one of his generation to respond (whether negatively or positively) to the intellectual climate of opinion arising out of the controversy. Others had read the folklorists and taken their words to heart. The first novel in C. S. Lewis's so-called space trilogy, *Out of the Silent Planet*, has his protagonist, a philologist, taking notes on the language of Malacandra (the planet Mars). In the next volume, *Perelandra* (i.e., Venus), this language turns out to be Old Solar, an original speech common to the entire solar system but now entirely lost on Earth.

It is not difficult to hear an echo of Indo-Aryan theory in the antiquity and originality of Lewis's lost tongue or of Müller's solar mythology in the name Lewis bestows on his fictive language. Lewis's good friend and his and Tolkien's fellow-Inkling Owen Barfield devoted much of his B.Litt. thesis, later expanded and published as *Poetic Diction*, to addressing Müller's theory. Tolkien, the one bona fide mythmaker in the group, was unique only in basing his answer on practice as well as theory.

Let us turn now to Tolkien's lecture, which left neither the philologists nor the anthropologists much room to maneuver. Addressing Müller and through him his followers, Tolkien dealt summarily with disease as either a cause or a result. He first rejected Müller's famous phrase and then reversed it: "Mythology," he maintained, "is not a disease at all … . It would be more near the truth to say that languages, especially modern European languages, are a disease of mythology" (*EPCW*, 50). But the idea that either was a "disease" of the other was countered by his proposal that language, myth, and human consciousness arose together, simultaneously and indivisibly.

This was to Tolkien so central and important an idea that he returned to it several times. "To ask what is the origin of stories, however qualified," he said, "is to ask what is the origin of language and the mind" (47). In his view, mythmaking is neither a late nor a degenerate function of language separated from its roots. A myth is not a cutting grafted onto a new stem but an organic and self-consistent whole, with its own inner consistency of reality. Having established the point, he nevertheless said it again: "The incarnate mind, the tongue, and the tale are in our world coeval" (50). Language, story, and human imagination are inborn faculties in the human organism. No one of them has a pathological relationship to any of the others.

That said, Tolkien next addressed the concept of "solar" or "nature" myth. In his view, Müller's notion – that gods were originally natural forces, that they eventually diminished to legends and finally dwindled to fairy-stories – would be

> the truth almost upside down … . The gods may derive their colour and beauty from the high splendours of nature, but it was Man who obtained these for them, abstracted them from sun and moon and cloud; their personality they get direct from him.
>
> (*EPCW*, 51–52)

His counterexample, a gage thrown down to Müller and his Greek and Sanskrit etymologies, is from a mythology that he vastly preferred, the Norse.

Using Müller's own weapon of philology and expanding the argument to include the "lightning school," Tolkien offered Thórr as a typical case of "Olympian nature myth," glossing Thórr's name as the Norse word for thunder and suggesting Thórr's hammer, Miöllnir, as lightning. He then went on to point out what to him is the important and obvious fact – that beyond these characteristics, Thórr has also a personality that is absent from thunder or lightning. The question of which came first, the phenomenon or the character, Tolkien suggested, is a meaningless one. Take Thórr as far back as you can and you will still find a story about a recognizably human personality, for, he declared, "there would always be a 'fairy-tale' as long as there was any Thórr. When the fairy-tale ceased, there would be just thunder, which no human ear had yet heard" (*EPCW*, 52).

Turning to George Dasent, Tolkien took Dasent's metaphor of "the soup," elaborated it, and then reapplied it. Dasent had said, "We must be satisfied with the soup that is set before us, and not desire to see the bones of the ox out of which it has been boiled." Tolkien agreed, but he went on to imply that Dasent had said the right thing for the wrong reason. He dismissed Dasent's "soup" as "a mishmash of bogus pre-history founded on the early surmises of Comparative Philology" and found little to value in his "bones," which he described as "the working and the proofs that led to these theories" (*EPCW*, 49).

I suggest that it was not mere coincidence that led Tolkien to make such a statement in 1939. Dasent's stance was blatantly and stridently racist, described by Richard Dorson as "praising the Aryans and denigrating non-Aryans in the crassest racist terms" (*PC*, 2:572). Dasent had seized on the "Aryan" component of the Indo-Aryan theory to make what may have been implicit in his folklore peers chillingly explicit in his own discussion. Where Müller had focused on language, Dasent focused on race. Such phrases as "the popular literature of the race," by which he meant the Norse or Germanic, and "tales which England once had in common with all the Aryan race" (quoted in *PC*, 2:598, 599) make his position clear.

There was nothing to stop Dasent from publishing his opinions, and while they seem clearly indefensible now, at the time he reflected the cultural chauvinism of many scholars of his generation. But, by the time of Tolkien's lecture, these were no longer simply the theories of folklorists but the explicit principles behind Nazi Germany and its war machine, just then gearing up for action. I don't think it is stretching too much to read in Tolkien's words an implicit condemnation of the exemplar and worst illustration of Dasent's Aryan emphasis. Tolkien countered by focusing on the story rather than on its ancestry (whether "Aryan" or not). He declared that by the "soup" he meant "the story as served up by its author or teller," which he found effective, and that by "desire to see the bones" he meant its sources or component material, which he did not (*EPCW*, 49).

Tolkien elaborated Dasent's extended metaphor of soup, ox, and bones, adding the pot or cauldron of story, and also the cook, the largely unknown storyteller, but only to illustrate the futility of inquiry into origins. Despite his own taste for philology, he felt that "desire for the bones was not the most desirable purpose" of reading, and that it worked to the detriment of the story itself. While conceding that fairy-stories are "very ancient indeed," and that they are found "wherever there is language" (49), he very quickly dealt with the major questions of independent evolution (which he called invention), diffusion (which he called borrowing in space, i.e., through migration), and inheritance (which he called borrowing in time). Not surprisingly, Tolkien, himself an inventor, privileged invention.

> To an inventor, that is, to a story-maker, the other two must in the end lead back … . At the centre of the supposed diffusion there is a place where once an inventor lived … . While if we believe that sometimes there occurred the independent striking out of similar ideas … we simply multiply the ancestral inventor, but do not in that way the more clearly understand his gift.
>
> (*EPCW*, 50)

Having dealt with Müller and Dasent, Tolkien turned to Lang, who was, after all, the occasion for his lecture. "Children's taste," Lang had declared, "remains like the taste of their naked ancestors thousands of years ago" (62). If anything, this outraged Tolkien even more than the solar theory, and he took strenuous exception to Lang's words. "[D]o we really know much about these 'naked ancestors,'" he inquired, "except that they were certainly not naked? Our fairy-stories, however old certain elements in them may be, are certainly not the same as theirs" (62). As an adult who read and wrote fairy-stories, he regarded it as both trivializing and patronizing to propose, as Lang did, that (1) the prehistoric period at which fairy-stories may be said to have arisen was analogous to "savage" cultures and (2) it was therefore the "childhood" of human development.

Tolkien rejected out of hand the notion that "children are the natural or specially appropriate audience for fairy-stories." The fact that fairy tales are "a natural human taste" does not necessarily mean, he declared, that this taste is natural to all humans, nor that it is more natural to children than to adults (57–58). Since his own taste for fairy-stories had been awakened in young manhood and quickened to full life by war, it followed that what fairy-stories had to offer was adult fare. The bowdlerized fairy tales being offered to children in his own time were sanitized versions with all the gore and mayhem excised. If they had to be edited down for children, it followed that they could hardly have been originally intended for them. He vigorously criticized Lang's own literary fairy-stories for their double vision – a patronizing attitude toward the child audience and a conspiratorial glance over the children's heads at any listening adults.

He praised "The Juniper Tree" precisely for its beauty and horror, for "its exquisite and tragic beginning, the abominable cannibal stew, the gruesome bones, the gay and vengeful bird-spirit coming out of a mist that rose from the tree" (56). Yet he found the story's chief attraction to be its immense antiquity, resident chiefly in the very elements that so disturbed the Victorians – the child murder and cannibalism. "I do not think," he declared,

> that I was harmed by the horror *in the fairy-tale setting*, out of whatever dark beliefs and practices of the past it may have come. Such stories have now a mythical or total (unanalysable) effect, an effect quite independent of the findings of Comparative Folklore and one which it cannot spoil or explain.
> (*EPCW*, 57)

The outbreak of World War I sharpened the sense of cultural nationalism even as it threatened to obliterate it. At the same time, it closed the golden century that had awakened that national sensibility. Its effect in both directions coincided with and may have spurred Tolkien's first efforts at a fictive myth for England modeled on the primary myths he was even then discovering. As an Oxford undergraduate he had written of *Kalevala*, "I would that we had more of it left – something of the same sort that belonged to the English" (*Biography*, 89). Distressed at the poor showing of England in the folklore stakes, he desired to remedy this deficiency by doing for England something similar to what Lönnrot had done for Finland. Out of this came the notion of a mythology for England, something that would give his own country a mythic (albeit, in his case, entirely fictive) identity of its own.

With World War II about to break as he gave his lecture, Tolkien revisited the subject, recapitulating and at the same time replying to the controversy by re-affirming myth's intrinsic value as story, not as source for extrinsic information. That Tolkien loved fairy-stories is plain to anyone who has read his work, and in a purely personal context perhaps we need look no further to explain his lecture. "When we have done all that research … can do," he said, "when we have explained many of the elements commonly embedded in fairy-stories … there remains still a point too often forgotten: that is the effect produced *now* by these old things in the stories *as they are*" (*EPCW*, 56; later emphasis added).[3]

But in a larger context, it is not unreasonable to speculate that, just as World War I had quickened his taste for fairy tales and aroused his ambition to create a mythology for England, so the shadow of World War II falling across his lecture moved him to rehearse the specific values he looked for and found both in fairy-stories and in his own mythology. Add to these the more intellectual background of the folklore controversy and the combination will point us back to Tolkien's own writing, deepening and widening the context in which this work can be understood.

And in this historical and intellectual context we should not overlook the folklore controversy as the whetstone that honed his own mythology at the same time that it sharpened his defense of the worth of fairy-stories "as they are": that is to say, as stories, not as rocks containing fossils more valuable than the matrix from which they may have been pried. He defended fairy-stories for their gift of enduring values to readers of any age. These values included recovery, escape, consolation, and *eucatastrophe* – the last a word of Tolkien's own coining to describe the sudden "turn" in fairy-story when victory is plucked from defeat, life is rescued from death, and joy triumphs over sorrow. And in an added context, those values cannot but have had a special and timely value not just to Tolkien but to his audience in relation to the two world wars – the one so recently over and the next about to start.

In both these contexts, it is easy to agree with Tolkien that it matters less where fairy-stories came from, or what they might originally have referred to, than what they have to give the reader in that *now* which he so strongly emphasized. For just as there will always be war, so, in Tolkien's view, there will always be fairy-stories, even if he has to write them himself. If we have the one, we surely need the other. We need fairy-stories to give us those very things that he listed so carefully – recovery of a more hopeful reality, escape from the imminent shadow of death, consolation for sorrow through the eucatastrophe that turns catastrophe to joy.

Without the fairy-story there will be just thunder, which no human ears will hear.

Notes

1 First published in *Essays Presented to Charles Williams*, published by Oxford University Press in 1947 but planned for publication before Williams's unexpected death in May of 1945. I have used this version as being closer in time and content to the original lecture than subsequent revised publications in *The Tolkien Reader* and *"The Monsters and the Critics" and Other Essays*, ed. Christopher Tolkien. Quotations from this work are cited in the text with the abbreviation *EPCW*.

2 See, for example, Jane Chance's *Tolkien's Art: A Mythology for England*, Carl Hostetter and Arden Smith's "A Mythology for England," Anders Stenström's "A Mythology? For England?" in *Proceedings of the J. R .R. Tolkien Centenary Conference*, and T. A. Shippey's "Long Evolution: *The History of Middle-earth* and Its Merits."

3 It is worth noting that this is precisely the argument he advances in his landmark 1936 Sir Israel Gollancz Memorial Lecture to the British Academy, "*Beowulf*: The Monsters and the Critics." Here he takes the critics to task for reading *Beowulf* as a historical document and not as a poem.

4 A kind of mid-wife

J. R. R. Tolkien and C. S. Lewis – sharing influence

Andrew Lazo

May 11, 1926, was a fateful day in the imaginative life of the English-speaking world. At 4:00 P.M., C. S. Lewis found himself at a tea for the English department at Oxford University, where he was a don. There he met J. R. R. Tolkien for the first time and had a talk with him afterwards. His diary for that day records his impression of Tolkien: "a smooth, pale, fluent little chap … [n]o harm in him: only needs a smack or so" (*All my Road*, 393). Thus began one of the most significant literary friendships of our time. The two became very close friends, and many of their most important works were forged in a crucible of both mutual criticism and mutual encouragement.

Although many are aware of the acquaintance that Lewis and Tolkien shared, fewer realize the extent of it or the importance their friendship had upon the work of both men. Soon after their meeting in 1926, they became fast friends. Indeed, in 1964, Tolkien told a correspondent that Lewis was "my closest friend from about 1927 [to] 1940, and remained very dear to me" (*Letters*, 349).

This friendship, however, cooled in later years for at least two reasons. The first was Lewis's devotion to the writer Charles Williams, whose writing Lewis discovered in 1936 upon reading Williams's novel *The Place of the Lion*. Ironically enough, Lewis made his discovery at the very moment that Williams, in his role as an editor for the Oxford University Press, was reading proofs of what was to become Lewis's landmark exploration of medieval love poetry, then called "The Allegorical Love Poem" (Hooper, 740–41). By Williams's estimation, Lewis's letter of admiration for *Lion* nearly crossed in the post with Williams's own letter admiring Lewis's book, which Williams later renamed *The Allegory of Love* (C. S. Lewis, *They Stand Together*, 479 n. 2). What followed was a friendship that, according to Lewis, "rapidly grew inward to the bone" (quoted in Hooper, 741) and that cemented itself when Williams, along with the press, moved to Oxford from London during World War II. On 20 May 1945, five days after Williams's death, Lewis called Williams "my great friend, my friend of friends … the most angelic man" (*Letters of C. S. Lewis*, ed. Hooper, 377). Indeed, if one may look to Lewis's poetry as any indication of his emotional history, Lewis makes a startling admission. In his poem "To Charles Williams," he addresses the late writer, lamenting that Williams's death was

A hard question and worth talking the whole night on. But with whom?
Of whom now can I ask guidance? With what friend concerning your Death
Is it worth while to exchange thoughts?

(*Narrative Poems*, 105)

While the poem must, of course, have been written after Williams's death in 1945, one cannot be certain exactly when. Although Walter Hooper judiciously warns about the paucity of evidence available for dating these poems (C. S. Lewis, *Narrative Poems*, vii), it may be safe to guess that Lewis wrote it sometime before 1954, when he began collecting his poems, published and unpublished, for a volume he intended to call *Young King Cole* (Hooper, 174). That Lewis would write a poem for Williams and not for Tolkien appears innocuous enough. But when one takes into account the fact that Tolkien wrote "Mythopoeia," his great poetic statement of myth theory, for Lewis, and – as Colin Duriez aptly notes in his Tolkien Centenary paper, "Tolkien and the Other Inklings" – even composed a humorous and affectionate poem for Williams, albeit declaring therein that he understood "not aught he said!" (Carpenter, *Inklings*, 126), then Lewis's omissions toward Tolkien make more sense in understanding the rift between the two.

While Lewis's question in "To Charles Williams" is rhetorical, intending both to eulogize and to acknowledge Lewis's great debt to Williams, it is certainly a signal that neither in verse nor in practice did Lewis apparently seek out Tolkien for the consolation that the dearest of friends could provide. One must not, however, draw the conclusion that their friendship was not extremely close. They met often and quite pleasurably. By 1931, it had become "regular custom that Tolkien should drop in … of a Monday morning and drink a glass," one of what Lewis called "the pleasantest spots in the week" (*Letters*, ed. Hooper, 292). The Inklings, a literary group who counted as members Lewis, Tolkien, and Williams, usually gathered on Thursday evenings in Lewis's rooms, "theoretically to talk about literature, but nearly always to talk about something better" (363). Inklings meetings began in about 1930, preceded by those of the Kolbítar Society, a group devoted to reading the Icelandic Sagas in Old Norse, which Tolkien had instituted in 1926. Present at these meetings were future Inklings Lewis and Neville Coghill, and in many ways these meetings solidified "the friendship between Lewis and Tolkien, which was the heart around which the Inklings grew," according to Duriez (*Encyclopedia*, 97). This same group met on Tuesday mornings in an Oxford pub, often at the Eagle and Child (Hooper, 765), and Owen Barfield mentions "annual spring walking tours" with Lewis, often including Tolkien (*Owen Barfield*, 22). Especially in light of the fact that late-night talks between Lewis and Tolkien were no rare occurrence, this omission points to the conclusion that Tolkien and Lewis shared no such intimacy as that which had sprung up between Lewis and Williams. As early as 1931 Tolkien was, by Lewis's own admission in a letter to lifelong friend Arthur Greeves, "one of my friends of the second class" (*They Stand Together*, 421).

By 1939, Williams, in Lewis's opinion, "had already become as dear to all my Oxford friends as he was to me" (quoted in Hooper, 741). It appears, however, that Lewis was not aware of the alienation that Williams engendered in at least one of those friends. Tolkien later said that he and Lewis "were separated first by the sudden apparition of Charles Williams, and then by his marriage" (*Letters*, 341). Although Tolkien in all likelihood did not mean that Williams's presence in Oxford was that of a ghost, his use of "apparition" does in fact point to the fact that Tolkien seemed to be haunted by Williams's influence on Lewis, to some degree at the cost of his own. Biographer Humphrey Carpenter records that, after Williams's transfer to Oxford made him suddenly a much greater participant in meetings with Lewis, including gatherings of the Inklings, "a little jealousy or resentment on Tolkien's part" began to spring up (*Biography*, 150–51). Ironically, while such bitterness was beginning to take root in Tolkien, Lewis saw the thing through different eyes, feeling as though he got more out of both men when both shared the same table with him. Although never apparently the dedicatee of a Lewis poem, Tolkien appears alongside Williams in one of Lewis's last great books, *The Four Loves*:

> In each of my friends there is something that only some other friend can fully bring out. By myself I am not large enough to call the whole man into activity; I want other lights than my own to show all his facets. Now that Charles is dead, I shall never again see Ronald's reaction to a specifically Caroline joke. Far from having more of Ronald, having him "to myself" now that Charles is away, I have less of Ronald. Hence true Friendship is the least jealous of loves.
>
> (Lewis, *The Four Loves*, 73–74)

At least, anyway, for Lewis.

Lewis's marriage to Joy Davidman in 1956 is a second reason that the distance widened between the two, for Tolkien found Joy's hold on Lewis nearly incomprehensible and the fact that Lewis married her "'very strange'" (quoted in Carpenter, *Inklings*, 243). To add insult to injury, Tolkien apparently had to find out about the wedding in the morning papers, a slight that he never forgot. In a draft of a letter to his son Michael, Tolkien mentions that Lewis never even told him of his marriage, and that he "learned of it long after the event" (*Letters*, 341). As Carpenter notes, Tolkien struck the line from the draft of the letter (*Letters*, 451 n. 1), which suggests that Lewis's death made him somewhat ashamed of the old resentment. Carpenter is certainly correct in suggesting that the marriage "profoundly injured" Tolkien (*Inklings*, 242), and possibly right in submitting that, had Joy not also appeared to puzzle and anger Tolkien, "he and Lewis might conceivably have preserved something of their old friendship" (*Biography*, 237).

It appears, however, as though Lewis's friendship meant more to Tolkien than the other way round, and that he was jealous of others who managed to get closer to Lewis. I have recently had these impressions confirmed to me in private correspondence with two men close to the situation: Douglas Gresham, Lewis's stepson, and Derek Brewer, former master of Emmanuel College, Cambridge, once a student of both Lewis and Tolkien. Brewer recently commented, "There was no doubt of the respect and affection with which Lewis regarded Tolkien, though I'm not so sure that Tolkien entirely reciprocated." One increasingly gets the impression that Tolkien was not entirely unaware of his position in the second rank, that the fact that he was not as close as he desired to be increasingly soured him toward the friendship, and that the frustrated desire to be closer to Lewis in actuality drove Tolkien further from him, contributing to the deepening silence between the two men. His jealousy of those who had gotten closer to Lewis was ironic, for Lewis's brother Warren, in many ways his closest friend, recorded in an unguarded moment in his diary the same sentiment about Tolkien. Hoping for some time with his brother one afternoon in 1933, Warren found Lewis engaged to go for a walk with Tolkien and lamented later in his diary, "Confound Tolkien! I seem to see less and less of J[ack] every day" (*Brothers*, 127).

Let me suggest that a third, less obvious reason for the cooling of their friendship arises from their reactions to each other's work. As I have said, both were for many years part of a literary gathering called the Inklings, which met twice weekly to discuss literature and read their own works in manuscript aloud to the group. It was there that many of Lewis's and Tolkien's books found their first hearing, and opinions there were honest and unstinting. Lewis, while certainly critical, was an ardent admirer of Tolkien's world. Tolkien, on the other hand, had no use whatsoever for Lewis's Narnian chronicles, whose charms always escaped him. He "disliked (them) intensely" (Carpenter, *Inklings*, 223), finding them hastily written and an incomprehensible jumble of too many mythologies, especially when he compared Narnia to his own painstakingly prepared world of Middle-earth. Lewis was certainly far more the critic than was Tolkien, who in a 1948 letter to Lewis examines the issue in depth:

> I am *not* a critic. I do not want to be one. I think that criticism … tends to get in the way of a writer who has anything personal to say. … Indeed (if I dare yet venture on any criticism again) I should think it gets in your way, *as a writer*. You read too much, and too much of that analytically. But then you are also a born critic. I am not. You are also a born reader.
>
> (*Letters*, 126)

Perhaps this lack of critical faculty in Tolkien contributes to the impression one increasingly gets from reading his comments: that he had little taste for modern fantasy literature other than his own.

Although these differences certainly divided the two over the years, it is important to remember that the distance between them was not nearly so marked as their closeness. Shortly after Lewis's death in 1963, Tolkien in a letter to his son reflected, "We owed each a great debt to the other, and that tie with the deep affection that it begot, remains" (*Letters*, 341). Their deep affection also begot their most famous work. Sometime in the 1930s, Lewis reportedly exclaimed to Tolkien, "[T]here is too little of what we really like in stories. I am afraid we shall have to write some ourselves" (Carpenter, *Inklings*, 65–66). I imagine the fruits of Lewis's suggestion have delighted many of us for years.

In an unpublished letter to a correspondent, located at the Marion E. Wade Center at Wheaton College, Illinois, Lewis wrote of the influences the two shared and talked of the influence he himself had on Tolkien, specifically, on the writing of *The Lord of the Rings*. In this letter, which for copyright reasons I may only paraphrase, Lewis claims that, by means of persistent encouragement almost to the point of harping, he acted more as a mid-wife for the books than as a parent. According to Walter Hooper, Lewis's former secretary and current trustee of the C. S. Lewis estate, Tolkien had already written up much of the background materials, such as genealogies and geographies, and was reading them to Lewis, known to his friends as "Jack" (C. S. Lewis, *On Stories*, xx). But Lewis was far from satisfied with the elaborate histories and source material that Tolkien had compiled. According to Hooper, Tolkien later recalled, "You know Jack. He had to have a *story*! And that story – The Lord of the Rings – was written to keep him quiet" (C. S. Lewis, *On Stories*, xx). Indeed, Lewis heard the whole of the trilogy, along with *The Hobbit* and *The Silmarillion* in manuscript form (Tolkien, *Letters*, 14, 21, 24, 34, 41, 58, 59, etc.) and offered criticism and incalculably great encouragement to Tolkien, at one point "putting the screw to [Tolkien] to finish" (Tolkien, *Letters*, 68). Although Tolkien did not always accept Lewis's criticism, he certainly heeded it; indeed, Tolkien often rewrote a passage purely because it did not sit well with Lewis. Tolkien later commented, "[W]hen [Lewis] would say, 'You can do better than that. Better, Tolkien, please!' I would try. I'd sit down and write the section over and over again" (*Letters*, 376). Evidently such efforts paid off, especially in the eyes of Tolkien's first and perhaps most formidable critic. According to a letter of 31 May 1944 to his son Christopher, Tolkien had been occupying his time before examinations

> by the desperate attempt to bring "The Ring" to a suitable pause, the capture of Frodo by the Orcs in the passes of Mordor before I am obliged to break off by examining. By sitting up all hours I managed it: and read the last 2 chapters (*Shelob's Lair* and *The Choices of Master Samwise*) to C.S.L. [who] … approved with unusual fervour, and was actually affected to tears.
>
> (*Letters*, 83)

This is just one example of the "sheer encouragement" Lewis gave Tolkien, who claims that Lewis "was for long my only audience. Only from him did I get the idea that my 'stuff' could be more than a private hobby" (quoted in Carpenter, *Inklings*, 32). In a letter to Clyde S. Kilby dated 18 December 1965, Tolkien goes on to assert, "[B]ut for the encouragement of C.S.L. I do not think that I should ever have completed or offered for publication the *Lord of the Rings*" (*Letters*, 366).

Let me suggest that Tolkien had an important fundamental and theoretic influence on the Narnian books, dislike them though he might. He had a hand in shaping many of Lewis's fundamental ideas, particularly about myth and Christianity. Perhaps the single most important point in Lewis's life was when he became a Christian in September of 1931. On the nineteenth of that month Lewis had invited Tolkien along with another future Inkling, Hugo Dyson, to dine, and afterward the three walked for hours around Addison's Walk on the Oxford grounds. The conversation centered on Christianity and the role of mythology.

Now, one of the things that Lewis and Tolkien held very much in common was a love of myth. In the paper "Is Theology Poetry?" delivered to the Oxford Socratic Club in 1944, Lewis claims, "If Christianity is only a mythology, then I find the mythology I believe in is not the one I like best. I like Greek mythology much better: Irish better still: Norse best of all" (*They Asked for a Paper*, 152). Tolkien shared this love of "Northerness," a passion that "engulfed" Lewis the moment he came upon a copy of *Siegfried and the Twilight of the Gods* illustrated by Arthur Rackham (C. S. Lewis, *Surprised by Joy*, 75). Lewis notes in a letter to Greeves an occasion (most likely in the autumn of 1929) when Tolkien came up to his rooms to talk of Asgard ("lit. the town of the Aesir … the home and habitual habitation of the [Norse] gods" [Boyle, *Everyman Encyclopedia*, 480]) for three hours, until 2:30 in the morning. "How could one turn him out," Lewis wondered; "the fire was bright and the talk good" (*They Stand Together*, 317). Their late-night talks were important to both men.

During that long, portentous night walk with Tolkien and Dyson in 1931, the conversation once more turned to myth. Tolkien challenged Lewis to see Christianity as another myth, only this time as a myth that actually happened. Before this time, Lewis and Tolkien had engaged themselves in the debate about "mythopoeia," a new word Lewis had coined to describe "the science of the nature of myths" (C. S. Lewis, *Letters of C. S. Lewis*, ed. Lewis, 163). In "On Fairy-Stories," Tolkien tells of "a man [doubtlessly Lewis] who … was kind enough and confused enough" to describe making a myth or a fairy-story as "[b]reathing a lie through Silver" (*TL*, 50).

Tolkien's long poem "Mythopoeia" arose from this debate as "a long answer to short nonsense" (*TL*, 6). Tolkien addressed the thirteen-stanza poem to "one who said that myths were lies and therefore useless, even though 'breathed through silver,'" and dedicated it from "Philomythus [myth lover] to Misomythus [myth hater]" (97). At the top of the fifth version (of seven), Tolkien wrote "J.R.R.T. for C.S.L" (7), thus drawing the battle lines and naming the combatants for this stage of the debate.

Three ideas in the poem particularly demonstrate the lasting effect the "long night talk" (C. S. Lewis, *They Stand Together*, 425) with Tolkien and Dyson had on Lewis. The most obvious effect is Lewis's conversion to Christianity nine days after the talk, on 28 September 1931, an event that gratified Tolkien deeply (cf. *Biography*, 148). Having presented in the poem and in the conversation the idea that myth could be at once story and truth, Tolkien suggested, and Lewis conceded, that Christianity was the truest of myth, which "draws some wisdom from the only Wise / and still recalls him" (*TL* 98).

Tolkien also planted in Lewis the seed of an idea that sprang to full bloom in the latter's thinking concerning the nature of evil. Tolkien asserts in the poem that "evil lies / not in God's picture but in crooked eyes / not in the source but in malicious choice / and not in sound but in the tuneless voice" (*TL*, 101).

The 1941 broadcast that Lewis published the next year as book 2 of *Mere Christianity* shows how Lewis's thinking had developed this idea in the succeeding ten years, for there he proclaims, "[B]adness cannot succeed even in being bad in the same way in which goodness is good. Goodness is, so to speak, itself: badness is only spoiled goodness" (35). He expounded this notion in his succeeding books, most notably in his fiction, especially *The Great Divorce.*

Tolkien affected Lewis most profoundly, however, by suggesting to him a twofold approach concerning the consideration and crafting of myth. The first part of this approach involved the fact that myth might have, at one time and in one place, become fact while still remaining myth. Tolkien suggests the idea in the lines

> I would with the beleaguered fools be told,
> that keep an inner fastness where their gold,
> impure and scanty, yet they loyally bring
> to mint in image blurred of distant king
> or in fantastic banners wave the sheen
> heraldic emblems of a lord unseen.
>
> (*TL*, 100)

Tolkien suggests a "distant king" about whom people try to make art. Though their inspiration may be as true as anything can be true, their art must on some level be myth. Lewis agrees with Tolkien's metaphor. In his poem "The Apologist's Evening Prayer," he claims, "Thoughts are but coins. Let me not trust instead / Of Thee, their thin-worn image of Thy head" (*Poems*, 129). The great statement of the development of this idea of Christ as both real figure and true myth comes in Lewis's 1944 essay "Myth Became Fact," wherein he concludes, "as myth transcends thought, Incarnation transcends myth. The heart of Christianity is a myth which is also a fact" (*Undeceptions*, 42). Ten years and more later, and, doubtless, after many discussions with Tolkien concerning such matters (see W. H. Lewis, 145–46, 194, etc.), Lewis has developed Tolkien's idea into a major tenet of his own thinking.

We have already heard Lewis echo a metaphor from "Mythopoeia." Elsewhere in the poem Tolkien suggests man as "sub-creator, the refracted light / through whom is splintered from a single White / to many hues" (*TL*, 98–99). Walter Hooper further confirms the influence of Tolkien's theory of man as "sub-creator," asserting that the idea "was immensely important to Lewis's understanding of Imagination" (566). Duriez notes that, although "Tolkien took the idea of sub-creation much further than C. S. Lewis," it nevertheless "deeply influenced" him (*Encyclopedia*, 192, 191). David Sandner perceptively comments that "[t]he very ability to write fantasy, to create a Secondary Realm, is, for both Tolkien and Lewis, derived from the same creative energy that made and moves all; to be a creative artist celebrates the Creation" (140). Indeed, the more one reads of and about both men, the more it becomes indisputable that one has to take the two together.

The notions arising from the late-night talk struck a deep chord within Lewis, and in many ways this was the turning point for him. Long an avowed and dogmatic atheist, with Tolkien's help he began to approach Christianity not only on a rational level, but on a mythic one as well. Tolkien was the author in many ways of the intellectual landscape Lewis subsequently occupied for the rest of his life.

Another element in Lewis's aesthetic and intellectual makeup that Tolkien provided for Lewis was the confirmation of the importance of fairy tales. Lewis said, "[W]hen I was ten, I read fairy tales in secret, and would have been ashamed if I had been found doing so … . [N]ow that I am fifty, I read them openly" (*On Stories*, 34). Tolkien shared his commitment to reading and enjoying fairy tales, claiming at the beginning of his famous essay "On Fairy-Stories" that he had "been a lover of fairy-stories since [he] learned to read (*TL*, 3). Tolkien voices an idea that Lewis later echoes: the opinion that enjoying fairy tales is far more a characteristic of one's taste than of one's age. And, based on the enduring popularity of their fantasy books, they were in all likelihood right. Their critical discussions regarding the medium, whether in Tolkien's "On Fairy-Stories" or in Lewis's several essays in *On Stories and Other Essays on Literature*, nearly all sound of a piece.

There are some apparent differences. Lewis, in writing about *The Lord of the Rings,* asserts that "no catchwords about 'escapism' … are in court" (*On Stories*, 85), seemingly contradicting Tolkien's statement that "[e]scape is one of the main functions of fairy-stories" (*TL*, 55). When we follow the seeming contradiction, however, not only do we find no such thing, what we in fact discover is Tolkien redefining the word "Escaping" in a fashion that seems almost Lewisian. Or, perhaps better, "Inklingian," for one may well imagine these meetings as the proving grounds for all manner of such ideas. Hooper declares that Tolkien's essay "was to have immense importance for Lewis" (732). So then, by allowing myth to become fact, Tolkien provided for Lewis an important piece of his imaginative landscape. By loving the same sorts of things, Tolkien supplied Lewis with a suitable traveling companion in that landscape at a crucial time in Lewis's intellectual development.

Having assessed the influence each had upon the other, let us now turn once again to the unpublished letter from the Wade Center in order to explore the influences they shared in common. One of the first things Lewis cites as a mutual influence was the way both men approached and appreciated nature. As noted above, Lewis was quite fond of walking and would take yearly walking tours with his friends, including Tolkien. On the sleeve of the first American edition of *Perelandra*, Lewis writes, "[M]y happiest hours are spent with three or four old friends in old clothes tramping together and putting up in small pubs" (quoted in Hooper, 794). Although their paces differed vastly (Tolkien's interest in botany and entomology prompted him to stop at nearly every rock or bush; cf.

Carpenter, *Inklings*, 57 and throughout), both men shared a deep and observant love of nature. A careful reading of the Narnia books will reveal to the reader an author very concerned with landscape: for example, at one point in *Prince Caspian*, the Pevensie children travel through a gorge in which they find "rumbling waterfalls, silver cascades, deep, amber-colored pools, mossy rocks … every kind of fern" (C. S. Lewis, *Prince Caspian*, 130). In *An Experiment in Criticism*, Lewis confesses that he is one of those who

> on a wakeful night entertain themselves with invented landscapes. I trace great rivers from where the gulls scream at the estuary, through the windings of ever narrower and more precipitous gorges, up to the barely audible tinkling of their source in a ford of the moors.
>
> (C. S. Lewis, *An Experiment in Criticism*, 52)

Certainly, even a cursory glance through Tolkien's writings provides the reader with several examples of Tolkien's extraordinary sense of natural places. Few who have ever visited Mirkwood, the Lonely Mountain, or the Elvish halls of Rivendell will ever forget them.

After citing their love of nature, Lewis next mentions to his correspondent several literary sources they had in common. Norse myth we have already touched upon. A Christian worldview also informed their writings, though certainly with more subtlety in Tolkien than in Lewis, for they were about different things.

Beowulf was another area of common ground. Tolkien's Royal Academy lecture "*Beowulf*: The Monsters and the Critics" was a groundbreaker for discussing that old poem, and even today the essay retains its vigor and yet poses questions we have not fully explored. Tolkien claimed that

> *Beowulf* is among my most valued sources; though it was not consciously present to the mind in the process of writing, in which the episode of theft arose naturally (and almost inevitably) from the circumstances. It is difficult to think of any other way of conducting the story at that point. I fancy the author of *Beowulf* would say much the same.
>
> (*Letters*, 31)

George Clark goes so far as to suggest that Tolkien's "description of the Beowulf poet and his work reads like Tolkien's idea of himself as a scholar" (*Tolkien and his Literary Resonances*, 44). His point that Tolkien may have not realized how deeply the poem worked on his own creative endeavors is well taken, but his charges that "Tolkien's readings mentally erased large portions of *Beowulf*" (41) perhaps go a bit too far in trying to assess the role of the poem in Tolkien's writing. Closer to the mark is Bruce Mitchell's evaluation of the worth of Tolkien's essay, which, he claims, "is fun to read. It is also a stylistic education, an intellectual challenge, a literary experience, and (for those who have ears to hear) a moral lesson" ("Tolkien and Old English", 209). One can imagine Lewis echoing all of these sentiments.

For his part, *Beowulf* deeply affected Lewis. As a social historian, Lewis claimed to be "sounder on … the court of Hrothgar … than on Oxford" (*On Stories*, 6). Derek Brewer mentioned to me in his e-mail that whenever Lewis and his students would reach a crux in translating the Anglo-Saxon poem, Lewis would always defer to Tolkien as the authority. There might have been many of those cruxes, for Lewis often hosted students in his rooms for "Beer and *Beowulf* Evenings," during which he "introduced his students to the mnemonic devices he had invented [for the learning of Old English], chanted *Beowulf* aloud, and passed around the beer jug" (Hooper, 749). In a letter to Greeves in 1916, Lewis mentions having already read the poem (*They Stand Together*, 106), and by 1922 he was hard at work translating it for himself as part of his work on Old English (*Road*, 135–37). He discusses *Beowulf* in all of his critical works: in his groundbreaking *The Allegory of Love*, at some length as "Primary Epic" in 1942's *A Preface to Paradise Lost* (12–18, 24, 25), in volume 3 of the *English Literature in the Sixteenth Century*, as well as in *The Discarded Image.*

Maybe the most direct fictive link, however, is between Tolkien's Beorn and Lewis's Lapsed Bear of Stormness. Beorn, "though a skin changer and no doubt a bit of a magician, was a Man" (Tolkien, *Letters*, 178) who turned into a bear and back again into a man. At the founding of Narnia, Aslan selects a few animals of each species to receive the gift of sentience and speech and at once sternly warns these Talking Beasts never to return to the ways of the Dumb Beasts lest they "cease to be Talking Beasts" (Lewis, *Last Battle*, 128). Of these, Lewis only mentions two examples of Talking Beasts who pay no heed to this warning and lose sentience, and of these two, the only one to return to sentience and regain speech is the Lapsed Bear. Thus, in Lewis we find a creature who wavers between being a sentient Talking Beast and a wild bear, a character that will very likely put readers in mind of Tolkien's Beorn, who undergoes a similar transformation. Paul Ford notes that creatures in Narnia, "are anthropomorphized to a high degree" (405), confirming the view that a Talking Bear is much like a man. Tom Shippey has recently noted that "Beorn … in Old English … means 'man': but it used to mean 'bear,' taken over and humanized" (*J. R. R. Tolkien*, 32). Even this detail describes a pattern of influence between Lewis and Tolkien wherein they discussed what they had read and were writing. It is hard to conceive of the work of either man reaching completion without the influence of the other.

Another important shared influence Lewis cites is Homer. At age sixteen, in 1914, Lewis recounted in a letter to Greeves that he had started reading the *Iliad* in Greek, which he found "stirring": he claimed that "those fine, simple, euphonious lines … strike a chord in one's mind that no modern literature approaches" (*Collected*, 71; see also n. 27). Three years later he recalled to Arthur a morning spent "on Homer whom I worship" (*They Stand Together*, 85). Indeed, at Oxford Lewis took a first class degree in Classical Honour Moderations, which included ancient Greek language and literature with particular emphasis on Homer (Hooper, 771), and his love of the mythic poet extended throughout his life. Owen Barfield tells of reading Homer with Lewis in the 1930s (*Owen*

Barfield, 21; see Pearce, 62 and n. 3), while Warren Lewis describes discussing the *Odyssey* with his brother in 1948 (222), and Barfield mentions that while Lewis lay bedridden shortly before his death in 1963, one of the things that "consoled him most [was] reading … the *Iliad*" (*Owen Barfield*, 106). In the 1950s, Lewis quite obviously had the *Odyssey* on his mind when he wrote the Narniad, especially *The Voyage of the "Dawn Treader,"* which contains as its central motif a sea quest and a journey toward a true home. John Lawlor notes that *Voyage* "draws upon the *Odyssey*" (78) and Paul Ford confirms his assertion (272), citing the passage in which Edmund mentions that the binding of King Caspian resembles what "they did with Ulysses when he wanted to go near the Sirens" (C. S. Lewis, *Voyage*, 239). We thus see Lewis approaching Homer, first as a school subject and then as a vehicle for literary inspiration and deep personal pleasure.

Tolkien shared Lewis's deep interest in Homer, saying that he "was brought up on Classics, and first discovered the sensation of literary pleasure in Homer" (*Letters*, 172). Carl Hofstetter and Arden Smith have suggested that as England's "greatest mythologer" (281) Tolkien attempted to resolve a distressing dilemma. Tolkien lamented that "there was Greek … Celtic [and] Scandinavian [myth], but nothing in English" (*Letters*, 144). Certainly one could only hope to meet this daunting challenge by crafting in England a towering myth like that of Homer, a feat that Tolkien may well have accomplished. Anders Stenström has claimed that Tolkien did not use the term "myth" in such a way (310). But by so doing, Stenström ignores discussions between Lewis and Tolkien about "the science of the nature of myth" that led to the composition of "Mythopoeia." Inexplicably, he makes no mention of the poem, which preceded by some seven years the essay "On Fairy-Stories," on which he bases much of his argument (*TL*, 7; *Biography*, 191), and which surely is germane to the discussion.

In the introduction to the recent collection he coedited with George Clark, Daniel Timmons asserts that "the literary aspects of Tolkien's work have been prominent in Western literature from Homer to the present day" (3). Brian Rosebury offers one such aspect, namely, the episodic construction of *The Lord of the Rings*, which may "remind one … of the *Odyssey*" (22), although he states that "the moral universe of Tolkien's mature work … is very different from Homer's" (86–87). Shippey agrees that there are important differences between Tolkien's work and Homer's, claiming that, although Tolkien had begun his Oxford education reading classics, he was "determinedly hostile to the Classical Tradition," and he points quite rightly to the "native and Northern tradition" which had far more influence on Tolkien's writing (*J. R. R. Tolkien*, 314). Although one may perceive Homer more in the foreground of Lewis's work and thought, by no means may one dismiss Homer's role in Tolkien's own work and thought, if for no other reason than to offer the possibility that one may yet write myth of such complex structure and enormous power.

Medieval romance was another enormously significant common love of both men. Tolkien's translations of *Sir Gawain and the Green Knight* and *Sir Orfeo* are still in print today and are still the subject of ongoing discussion and debate.

Recently, Shippey has pointed out how Tolkien accounted in his own work for the modern problem with the medieval idea of Westernesse, the Blessed Land, perhaps the Avalon to which Arthur was taken (*J. R. R. Tolkien*, 283). Anyone who spends much time in the continent to the west of England must surely conclude that, although Arthur somewhere awaits his eventual return, he can surely not be waiting somewhere in America. Shippey describes how Tolkien resolved this western dilemma in *The Silmarillion* by claiming that "'the Blessed Realm is shut'" (quoted in *J. R. R. Tolkien*, 284). Even so, such an explanation "continued to bother Tolkien into old age," and never really satisfied him (285). That such an attempted reconciliation should nag at him for so long demonstrates that, at least in part, some aspects of medieval romance worried him as much as some of those in his own writing.

Roger Schlobin has undertaken the "dangerous" task of attempting a source study of Tolkien's work using *Sir Gawain and the Green Knight*, and he suggests that the two works share at least "an intrinsic commitment to responsible virtue" (79). Shippey goes further, enumerating and illuminating the "ways the images of the *Gawain*-poet have been received and transmitted by Tolkien into living literary tradition" (*J. R. R. Tolkien*, 213). For his own part, Tolkien called a comparison of his books to Malory's Arthur "too much for my vanity" (*Letters*, 181).

The Arthur legends also deeply affected Lewis. On a walking tour in Cornwall in 1921, Lewis wrote to his brother, Warren, of spending the night in Tintagel, dispelling "the generally diffused belief that this place is connected with King Arthur: so far as I know from Malory, Layamon and Geoffrey of Monmouth, it is not: it is really the seat of King Mark and the Tristram story" (*Letters of C. S. Lewis*, ed. Hooper, 153).

One can trace Lewis's interest in Malory back to William Morris, for on 7 November 1914 Lewis writes to Greeves of sending off to Dent's for the Everyman version of Malory's *Morte D'Arthur*, naming Malory "the Master from whom William Morriss [sic] copied the style of his prose Tales" (*Collected*, 94). By January he had "nearly finished," finding himself "more pleased every day," for the *Morte* had "opened up a new world to me. I had no idea that Arthurian legends were so fine" (103). By May of the next year he had "read and finished 'The Green Knight' [Sir Gawain and the Green Knight]," finding it "absolutely top-hole … splendid … very impressive" (180). Shortly thereafter he ordered the "French prose romance of 'Tristan and Iseut'" (183) and, although he was not pleased with the binding, he found it "good beyond what I had expected," and upon finishing it he pronounced the book "really delightful: it is the saddest story on earth I think" (195–96, 207). Corbin Scott Carnell notes that Lewis's

> free-time reading during this period [1914–16] consisted chiefly of medieval literature or books which dealt with the Arthurian legend: Spenser, Malory, the *High History of the Holy Grail*, Chernier, Ronsard, *Sir Gawain and the Green Knight*, and nearly all of William Morris.
>
> (Carnell, 46)

Chrétien de Troyes's version he most likely found sometime in the late 1920s or very early 1930s, for he writes nothing of him to Arthur Greeves (letters to whom often serve as an invaluable Lewisian reading journal), nor does he mention Chrétien in the diary he kept sporadically from 1922 to 1927, but by Walter Hooper's estimation Lewis wrote his poem "Launcelot" in the early 1930s (C. S. Lewis, *Narrative Poems*, xii), which may suggest some encounter with Chrétien's "Lancelot." Chad Walsh notes that, in the poem, "Lewis has taken familiar Arthurian material and brought it alive" in a manner similar to Tennyson and Malory (51). What is certain is that Lewis knew Chrétien deeply by 1936, when he wrote his seminal *Allegory of Love*, devoting much of chapter 1 to a discussion of the development of Chrétien's ideas on the matter.

Arthurian romance pervades Lewis's work. The hero of Lewis's "interplanetary romances" embodies Arthurian tradition, for in the final book, *That Hideous Strength*, "besides being the 'Fisher King,' Professor Elwyn Ransom is also the 'Pendragon of Logres'" (Hooper, 234). It is here too that we have the wakened Merlinus Ambrosius, robed and anointed, roaring out authority and courtesy in fifth-century Latin (see *That Hideous Strength*, 318 and throughout). Walsh was one of the first critics to rightly acknowledge the "traces of Charles Williams's presence … specifically … in [Lewis's] use of the Arthurian legend in *That Hideous Strength* (13), a book Carnell calls "potent … in its reworking of Arthurian materials" (103; see also n. 9). Edward G. Zogby's claim that "the Arthurian elements in *That Hideous Strength* come more from Charles Williams than from Malory" (214 n. 5) is beside the point because it sets up a false opposition, like the suggestion that a certain chef's meal made of a particular cut of beef comes more from comparing notes with another chef than it does from the butcher.

The use of Merlin as a deus ex machina, owing something perhaps to Williams's influence on Lewis, troubles Walsh (119), an influence Tolkien termed "a pity" before going on to claim that he "was and remain[ed] wholly unsympathetic to Williams's mind" (*Letters*, 361). Perhaps this lack of sympathy had less to do, however, with Williams's Arthurian influence than with Tolkien's jealousy of Williams's seeming usurpation of Lewis's affections. Before Williams had exerted such a profound effect on the last book of the "space trilogy," Tolkien and Lewis had come up with a plan: according to a letter from Tolkien to publisher Stanley Unwin in 1938, the two had "meant each to write an excursionary 'Thriller': a Space-journey and a Time-journey (mine) each discovering Myth" (*Letters*, 29). That Williams now had far more influence in the last book of a series that he and Lewis had started together must have particularly rankled with Tolkien.

The Arthurian influence continued to operate throughout Lewis's writing. In 1947, Lewis reviewed Eugène Vinaver's three-volume compilation of the Arthur myths, *The Works of Sir Thomas Malory*, for the *Times Literary Supplement* (review published as "The 'Morte D'Arthur,'" C. S. Lewis, *Studies* 103–10). The year 1948 saw the posthumous publication of the fragment of Charles Williams's *The "Figure of Arthur"*, including Lewis's commentary on Williams's Arthurian poems. From 1950 to 1956, Lewis published the *Chronicles of Narnia*, which Lewis filled with literary allusions and structured with a medieval hierarchy and courtesy.

Paul Ford's *Companion to Narnia* is here a book of nearly inestimable value. Although he includes few explicitly Arthurian references, he does yeoman's work in collating and identifying references to such medieval themes as courtesy, hierarchy, chivalric orders, and quests. Medieval romance sets the tone for the entire seven books.

The next common source Lewis cites is the nineteenth-century fantasist George MacDonald. Although Tolkien was "not as warm an admirer of George MacDonald as C. S. Lewis was" (*Letters*, 351), he nevertheless acknowledged his debt, claiming to "owe … a good deal to the goblin tradition, especially as it appears in George MacDonald" (*Letters*, 178), which Tom Shippey has ably explored in the Clark–Timmons volume (183–98). Carpenter lists MacDonald among Tolkien's "childhood favourites" (*Tolkien*, 165).

Lewis's devotion was far more complete. He wrote, "I have never concealed the fact that I regard [George MacDonald] as my master; indeed I fancy I have never written a book in which I did not quote from him" (*George MacDonald*, 20). It is perhaps no surprise that both Lewis and Tolkien would hearken back to the Scottish clergyman who wrote both children's books (such as *The Princess and the Goblin*) and adult fantasy novels (such as *Phantastes*).

Lewis's unpublished letter then becomes a very accurate description of the basis by which the two influenced each other and of what also mutually influenced them. It becomes apparent that, in many ways, each owns a part of the other's creation, and we certainly have come to see that the importance of each to the other can scarcely be overstated.

5 "I wish to speak"

Tolkien's voice in his *Beowulf* essay

Mary Faraci

> Accordingly, with the sympathetic understanding of the Royal Society, the British Academy was established as an unincorporated society on 17 December 1901, for the purpose of promoting "Historical, Philosophical and Philological Studies."
>
> The Academy's first Secretary, (Sir) Israel Gollancz, energetically collected endowments for periodical lectures, and these, as published in the annual Proceedings, represent a formidable body of research.
>
> (Mortimer Wheeler, *The British Academy, 1949–1968*)

J. R. R. Tolkien, the Rawlinson and Bosworth Professor of Anglo-Saxon at Oxford, made a place for the *Beowulf* poet to stand with him on 25 November 1936 as part of the distinguished lecture series of the British Academy. Today, almost one hundred years after the establishment of the Academy, the Sir Israel Gollancz Memorial Lecture, "*Beowulf*: The Monsters and the Critics," counts as a great event in the history of the British Academy. As the scholar Professor Bruce Mitchell notes, "The Greenfield and Robinson *Bibliography* records seventy items on 'Literary Interpretations' of *Beowulf* before J. R. R. Tolkien's lecture and two-hundred-and-fifty between its publication and the end of 1972" ("J. R. R. Tolkien," 209).

According to Christopher Tolkien in the foreword to the collection of Tolkien's lectures, Tolkien's lectures were given to an audience who "could in no case … be presumed to have more than a general knowledge of or interest in the subject" (*Monsters*, 1). Published as an essay in the *Proceedings of the British Academy*, the lecture has continued to provide instruction and pleasure to new readers. Restored to his identities as a great critic and great writer, Tolkien can teach us what we still do not know about the dangers of "the best and most authoritative general criticism in English" ("*Beowulf*," 6). For an appreciation of the layered identities, among them great critic and great writer, emerging in the course of the lecture, we can borrow from the critical approaches to the discourse of power and choice in literary theory and criticism.[1] Reread in the light of speech-acts theory and discourse-analysis theory, the lecture becomes a work in progress, discovering new ways to rescue the *Beowulf* poet.

The influence of the *Beowulf* essay today speaks for the many worlds where Tolkien matters. Statements in the essay, situated in Middle-earth studies, have led us to new readings. Introducing the critical responses to Tolkien's Middle-earth tales, Daniel Timmons lets Tolkien's words from the *Beowulf* lecture speak for all critics:

> In his famous lecture on *Beowulf*, J. R. R. Tolkien states candidly, "I have not been a man so diligent in my special walk as duly to read all that has been printed on, or teaching on, this poem." These words could describe scholars of any subject, though I doubt many would be so frank. As Tolkien observes, critics often generalize on literary works without rigorous examination of the pertinent scholarship. Ironically this has been the case with much of the criticism on Tolkien.
>
> ("J. R. R. Tolkien: The 'Monstrous' in the Mirror," 229)

Taking on a life of its own in medieval studies and Middle-earth studies, the *Beowulf* essay has recharged syllabi, essays, and books. The essay continues to attract as much attention as the work of the *Beowulf* poet it managed to rescue from the critics. In the introduction to the Clark–Timmons volume, Daniel Timmons directs attention to "the shadowy guardians of the 'canon'" (3). Drawing on the images of dragons from Tolkien's essay that managed to win respect for dragons, Timmons attempts to win respect for the dragons in the Middle-earth tales: "The purpose of this volume of new essays on Tolkien is to recognize his stature in literary history and to examine his works afresh" (5). The readings of Tolkien's dragons and heroes in the Clark–Timmons volume work in and through the very words of the famous essay. George Clark even borrows the famous title to make the case for literary resonances in his essay, "J. R. R. Tolkien and the True Hero." Clark, furthermore, titles the first section, "Tolkien: The Heroes and the Critic" (39). In the same collection, Jonathan Evans directs Middle-earth readers to the famous essay: "Further insights into Tolkien's understanding of the narrative possibilities inherent in traditional medieval lore concerning dragons and their human opponents may be gleaned from his 1936 essay on *Beowulf*" ("Dragon-lore," 25).

In the 1979 work *Tolkien's Art: A Mythology for England,* Professor Jane Chance acknowledges the positive view of most medieval critics that the *Beowulf* essay "permanently altered our understanding of the Old English poem" (5). Chance moves beyond the critics to note in detail what else Tolkien was doing:

> In Tolkien's prose non-fiction, especially the lectures and forewords, the "monster" is the critic-scholar who prefers history and philology to art-for-art's sake, reflecting by his choice a ratiocination sterile, stale, and dead, in contrast to the alive and joyful imagination of the artist-hero with whom Tolkien identifies.
>
> (Chance, *Tolkien's Art,* 1979, 5)

As early as 1979, Chance captures a glimpse of the great writer playing hero:

> If Beowulf as the hero battles with monsters (Grendel and the Dragon) and the critics who have misunderstood him (W. P. Ker and R. W. Chambers), then, Tolkien fantasizes, the critics *are* the monsters – and Tolkien by defending Beowulf *is* the hero.
>
> (Chance, *Tolkien's Art*, 1979, 9)

She regrets that, "[a]s a work of prose non-fiction by a great writer, however, the article has been ignored" (8). In the revised version of *Tolkien's Art* (2001), Professor Chance writes,

> As a work of prose nonfiction by a great writer, however, the article has only recently begun to claim the attention of scholars interested in explaining the shape of Tolkien's mythology, although it has never been analyzed as a work of creative art in itself (a seeming non sequitur, given its prosaic and scholarly shape and form).
>
> (Chance, *Tolkien's Art* 2001, 13)[2]

Jane Chance's reading of the essay can reveal even more subtle distinctions through the discovery processes available today in literary criticism and theory, in particular discourse-analysis theory and speech-acts theory. In an age when the field of English studies is concerned with the subject as an effect of the discourse, one could not imagine a better place for the English major in colleges and universities today to begin a medieval course than in the drama underlying the lively relationship between Tolkien and the *Beowulf* poet in the lecture. Tolkien's "I" enters into a dramatic relationship with the verbs according to the lost rules of opposition belonging to the ancient grammatical inflections of active voice and middle voice. The lost distinctions of voice, restored to the lecture, oppose active-voice agents – critics who have covered up the poem – against middle-voice agents – critics who surrender to the poem. Reread in the context of the ancient opposition of middle voice and active voice, the lecture will attract new readers to follow Professor Chance's call to reconsider the *Beowulf* essay "as a work of prose non-fiction by a great writer." Reread as a middle-voice process, each "I" statement can be observed as it produces a new space for the poem, too long covered up by an active-voice agent.

Attempting to restore to grammars the lost category of middle voice, the French linguist Emile Benveniste, in an essay "Active and Middle Voice in the Verb," confronts the simplistic representation of the grammatical category of voice in grammars of present-day languages:

> The distinction between active and passive provides an example of a verbal category which seems designed to confuse our usual habits of thought … .

> In place of an opposition between active and passive, there was in historical Indo-European a triple division: active, middle, and passive.
>
> (Benveniste, "Voice," 145)

Benveniste continues to distinguish the ancient category of voice from the modern grammatical category of the verb:

> What characterizes the Indo-European verb in its own right is that it has reference only to the subject, not to the object … . [I]t does not include an indicator signaling the goal (or objective) of a process. It is thus impossible, in the presence of an isolated verb form, to say whether it is transitive or intransitive … . Everything is expressed and arranged with respect only to the subject.
>
> (Benveniste, "Voice," 146)

Benveniste summarizes, "It [voice] denotes a certain attitude of the subject with relation to the process – by which the process receives its fundamental determination" (146). Restored to a reading of modern verbs, the opposition of active voice against middle voice can account, for example, for the following sets: active: *I put (you) to sleep*, but middle: *I sleep* (Benveniste, "Voice," 149); "active: *attach*, but middle: *touch*; active: *put to vote*, but middle: *vote*; active: *put a rent on anything*, but middle: *lay a rent upon oneself*; active: *make to cease*, but middle: *cease*; active: *persuade*, but middle: *obey*" (Smyth, *Greek Grammar*, 393–94).

The language of the category of voice in present-day grammars presents only active voice and passive voice: active voice, *The boy threw the ball,* and passive voice, *The ball was thrown by the boy*. Considering that passive voice is merely a surface transformation of an active-voice verb and its agent, the readers of Tolkien's essay can see why the category of voice in grammars of present-day English is not adequate to begin to reveal the middle-voice relation of the speaker to the verbs in the lecture. The language of the grammars of ancient Greek presented Tolkien, the classical scholar, with the active-voice and middle-voice oppositions to distinguish the agent that remained outside the process of the verb from the agent that remained inside the process of the verb.[3] The "I" in the lecture draws effectively from the distinctions available in the category of voice in grammars of ancient Greek to employ a distinction lost in modern grammars. Restoring to Tolkien's English the lost category of the middle voice, the "I" of the lecture produces a drama between the critics' active-voice relationship to processes outside the world of the poem and the lecturer's middle-voice relationship to processes inside the world of the poem. With the benefits of the subject distinctions of active-voice and middle-voice opposition, the lecture reveals itself as Tolkien's dramatization of how the active-voice agents, the "authoritative critics" ("*Beowulf*," 6), had managed to cover up a poem revealing itself only to readers who would surrender in a middle-voice relation to the work of the *Beowulf* poet.

The views for the authoritative force of words were just beginning to take in the Oxford School of Philosophy in the 1930s. Developed as the theory of speech acts, the views of the performative force of words had their beginnings in the world of Oxford in that decade – a world that included Tolkien and J. L. Austin, the young leader of philosophical discussions. The theory of speech acts was first published in 1962 in *How to Do Things with Words* for a new audience, but the idea of the force of official words had begun in Oxford philosophy discussions in the 1930s: "In a short note, Austin says of the views which underlie these lectures that they 'were formed in 1939. I made use of them in an article on 'Other Minds'" (xi).

Looking back at the Oxford of the early 1930s when Tolkien, Rawlinson and Bosworth Professor of Anglo-Saxon, was attending the Inklings meetings on Thursday nights and Tuesday mornings with C. S. Lewis (*Biography*, 149), one finds an active young Fellow and tutor in philosophy at Magdalen College (Berlin, 7):

> The philosophical trend which afterwards came to be called "Oxford Philosophy" originated principally in weekly discussions by a small group of young Oxford philosophers – the oldest was 27 – which began sometime in 1936–37. They were suggested by J. L. Austin, who remained their leading spirit until the war brought them to an end.
>
> (Berlin, 1)

A colleague of the young Austin at this time, Sir Isaiah Berlin, in "Austin and the Early Beginnings of Oxford Philosophy," emphasizes Austin's philological interests:

> In this sense, Austin did not much believe in a specifically philosophical technology – the proliferation of gadgets to deal with difficulties. No doubt this insatiable interest in language and philology as such had something to do with this, and his superb classical scholarship fed his inordinate collector's curiosity, at times at the expense of genuinely philosophical issues.
>
> (Berlin, 14)

In *How to Do Things with Words*, Austin's students present their notes from the Harvard lectures in 1955. Austin was 44 – about the same age as Tolkien when he gave the *Beowulf* lecture. Tolkien proved in the 1936 lecture that, by the age of 44, he could deliver a full-blown grammar of the force of the authoritative speech acts of the critics. In the lecture, the acts of the *Beowulf* critics are represented in the active voice of agents acting out "archetypical performatives" in an "official capacity."[4] Exposing the history of arrogance of the active-voice agent behind each performative statement of critics in Anglo-Saxon studies, Tolkien, speaking as the Rawlinson and Bosworth Professor of Anglo-Saxon, begins the lecture with a defense of the Reverend Doctor Joseph Bosworth against the arrogant Reverend Oswald Cockayne:

> In 1864 the Reverend Oswald Cockayne wrote of the Reverend Doctor Joseph Bosworth, Rawlinsonian Professor of Anglo-Saxon: "I have tried to lend to others the conviction I have long entertained that Dr. Bosworth is not a man so diligent in his special walk as duly to read the books … which have been printed in our old English, or so-called Anglosaxon tongue. He may do very well for a professor."
>
> ("*Beowulf*," 5)

Immediately Tolkien represents the dogmatic critic as "unfair": "These words were inspired by dissatisfaction with Bosworth's dictionary, and were doubtless unfair" (5). Before Tolkien's remark, Professor Toller had suggested in the preface to the 1898 *Anglo-Saxon Dictionary: Based on the Manuscript Collections of the Late Joseph Bosworth*, "To compile an Anglo-Saxon Dictionary calls for so much in the compiler that some leniency towards shortcomings may perhaps be looked for by any one who attempts the labour" (ii). Tolkien begins the lecture by drawing attention to the "unfair" words of Cockayne. Impatient with the arrogance behind Cockayne's unfair words, Tolkien is prepared to expose the arrogance of the critics who have issued unfair words against the *Beowulf* poet, especially with the importance given to "books written about the books": "If Bosworth were still alive, a modern Cockayne would probably accuse him of not reading the 'literature' of his subject, the books written about the books in the so-called Anglo-Saxon tongue. The original books are nearly buried" ("*Beowulf*," 5).

Reading even more of Cockayne's remarks, one discovers the force of his arrogant attempt, from the beginning to the end of his essay, to warn the Oxford University Press not to publish the new edition of Dr. Bosworth's dictionary: "[A]ny new edition prepared by Dr. Bosworth can hardly be free from grave errors" (Cockayne, 1). He concludes,

> Against Dr. Bosworth I have no further grudge, than what one feels towards a man who has not done his work well … . But I find myself unable to stand by, silent, when the name of the University of Oxford is to be put on the title page of such a book as he will make.
>
> (Cockayne, 11)

Exposing the readings of the critics as acts outside the process of the poem, Tolkien dramatizes the arrogance of scholars who forgot even the event of the christening. Tolkien reminds us that Humphrey Wanley "christened" the poem as a poem: "*Beowulf* was christened by Wanley Poesis – *Poeseos Anglo-Saxonicae egregium exemplum*" ("*Beowulf*," 6). Wanley, the Saxonist and library-keeper (Hope, 84), "a valuable witness to original manuscript readings," had read the poem and copied down and published lines 1–19 and 53–73 "in 1705 before the fire took place" (Mitchell and Robinson, *Beowulf: An Edition*, 5). As one of the few who had read the original, Wanley counts in the lecture as a friend of the poem. Although "christened" as a poem by Wanley, the poem *Beowulf* found itself abused. Tolkien enjoys using a series of passive-voice structures to represent the acts of critics too arrogant to read the poem: "Poesis *was usually forgotten*; occasionally *admitted* by a side door; sometimes *dismissed* upon the door-step" ("*Beowulf*," 6; italics added). Statements in the passive voice serve – like active-voice verbs – to expose the agents as too far removed from the poem to even read it. Passive-voice verbs return: "The significance of a myth *is not easily to be pinned* down on paper by analytical reasoning" (15; italics added).

In active-voice verbs, Tolkien continues to expose the arrogance of critics who "swallow ... upon authority" even a paradox ("*Beowulf*," 11). Discovering the balance he admires in *Beowulf*, of a composition criticized because it "lacks steady advance" (28), Tolkien warns against the heretofore simplistic interpretation: "In any case we must not view this poem as in intention an exciting narrative or a romantic tale" (29). Tolkien returns again and again to expose the problems of simplistic summaries by critics who remain outside the process of the poem:

> [T]he shadow of research has lain upon criticism, The habit, for instance, of pondering a summarized plot of *Beowulf*, denuded of all that gives it *particular force* [italics added] or individual life, has encouraged the notion that its main story is wild, or trivial, or typical, *even after treatment* [Tolkien's italics] … . The comparison of skeleton "plots" is simply not a critical literary process at all.
>
> ("*Beowulf*," 14; italics added)

By remaining outside the world of the poem, critics had let the poem die: "For myth is alive at once and in all its parts and *dies* before it can be dissected" ("*Beowulf*," 15; italics added).

Tolkien enters in the middle voice to rescue the poet in the poet's world. At every turn, Tolkien draws attention to the force of the acts in the volume of discourse making up *Beowulf* criticism. Against that arrogant voice, each "I" statement in the lecture situates the speaker inside the process of the poem. In that relationship of subject to verb, the speaker returns in fresh ways to the problem of making a space for the poem to speak. For the subtle distinctions that the middle-voice relationship reveals, Tolkien, as if by second nature, speaks as storyteller. Avoiding the active-voice agent, "I" surrenders to the poem forgotten by the critics. In the middle voice, Tolkien seamlessly breaks away from the arrogance of the official capacity as British Academy guest lecturer. The speaker uses "I wish" to request permission to speak: "It is of *Beowulf*, then, as a poem that *I wish* to speak" ("*Beowulf*," 5; italics added). In the arrogance-free style that will emerge again and again throughout the lecture, the "I wish" situates the speaker inside the process of lecturing to the British Academy in an attempt to make room on the stage for the poem covered up for so long by historical reading. Later in the lecture, the "I wish" shifts to "I think" in an attempt to understand the critics' misunderstanding: "It is possible, *I think*, to be moved by the power of myth and yet to misunderstand the sensation" (15; italics added). The critics let "correct and sober taste" get in the way of admitting "that the monsters are anything but a sad mistake," but the speaker removes all obstacles: "*I have* the author of *Beowulf*, at any rate, on my side: a greater man than most of us" (16; italics added).

Later, in a balanced composition of "I think" statements, the lecturer surrenders to the work of revealing the poem as an expression of balance: "In this fundamental fact of poetic expression *I think* there is a parallel to the total structure of *Beowulf*" ("*Beowulf*," 30; italics added). Emerging again in "I think," the speaker, having admitted "defects of detail," is prepared to mount a fresh defense for the design of the poem: "The general design of the poet is not only defensible, it is, *I think*, admirable" (30; italics added). When "I think" enters again, the speaker brings the monsters into the design: "There is, *I think*, no criticism more beside the mark than that which some have made, complaining that it is monsters in both halves that is so disgusting; one they could have stomached more easily" (31; italics added). In "I agree," the subject again removes distance between the author and the speaker: "If the dragon is the right end for *Beowulf*, and *I agree* with the author that it is, then Grendel is an eminently suitable beginning" (32; italics added).

A middle-voice subject/verb relationship to the poem can see what the poet did: "Any theory that will at least allow us to believe that what he did was of design, and that for that design there is a defence that may still have *force*, would seem more probable" ("Beowulf," 14; italics added). Standing with both feet in the poem, early in the lecture, Tolkien begins to draw attention to the effects of the poet's "product of art":

> It is indeed a curious fact that it is one of the peculiar virtues of *Beowulf* that has contributed to its own critical misfortunes. The illusion of historical truth and perspective, that has made *Beowulf* seem such an attractive quarry, is largely a product of art.
>
> ("*Beowulf*," 7)

In "we," the lecture begins the work of revealing the poet for too long covered up by the arrogant acts of critics: "[*W*]*e have to deal* with a poem by an Englishman *using afresh* ancient and largely traditional material … . [We] might also now inquire what the poet *did* with it" ("*Beowulf*," 9; italics added). The speaker makes a space for the poetic force, "the total effect of *Beowulf*": "Higher praise than is found in the learned critics, whose scholarship enables them to appreciate things, could hardly be given to the detail, the tone, the style, and indeed *the total effect of 'Beowulf'*" ("*Beowulf*," 13; italics added). The earlier phrase, "using afresh," effective for dramatizing the special relationship of the poet to the process of inventing a world for us, returns in the words, "used them afresh": "[I]ts author, coming in a time rich in the legends of heroic men, has *used them afresh* in an original fashion, giving us not just one more, but something akin yet different: a measure and interpretation of them all" ("*Beowulf*," 17; italics added).

The lecture remains dedicated to restoring the creative aspects of the poet's relationship to the process of writing the poem:

> [T]here was available to a poet who set out to *write* [Tolkien's italics] a poem – and in the case of *Beowulf* we may probably use this very word – on a scale and plan unlike a minstrel's lay, both new faith and new learning (or education), and also a body of native tradition (itself requiring to be learned) for the changed mind to contemplate together.
>
> ("*Beowulf*," 21)

Understood as the subject inside the process of the middle-voice verb *to write*, the poet manages to break through the wall of "narrative or a romantic tale" ("*Beowulf*," 29) to emerge as poet, sculptor, and painter: "*We have* none the less in *Beowulf* a method and structure that within the limits of the verse-kind approaches rather to sculpture or painting. It is a composition not a tune" ("*Beowulf*," 30; italics added). In case the audience had not followed the distinctions between (1) active-voice agents of an authoritative force towering above objects and (2) middle-voice agents of an interpretative force in-between subjects, Tolkien invites the audience to surrender to the beginnings of the poem "in our northern world beneath our northern sky, and for those who are native to that tongue and land, it must ever call with a profound appeal until the dragon comes" ("*Beowulf*," 33–34).

At the time of the lecture, 25 November 1936, Tolkien was known as the Rawlinson and Bosworth Professor of Anglo-Saxon, author of the scholarly edition of *Sir Gawain and the Green Knight*, brilliant lexicographical work, and poems. *The Hobbit*, however, as Tolkien's biographer, Humphrey Carpenter, notes, had been submitted to the publisher in 1936 "by the first week in October" (*Biography*, 180), but it would not be published until "21 September 1937" (*Biography*, 182). Holding a research fellowship at the time of its publication, Tolkien confessed, "I shall now find it very hard to make people believe that this is not the major fruits of 'research' 1936–7" (*Biography*, 182). Today connections continue to be drawn between Tolkien's medieval sources and the Middle-earth tales. Jane Chance has continued to make a case for criticism connecting the great writer of *The Hobbit* with the great prose nonfiction writer of the *Beowulf* essay: "In this seminal essay in which Tolkien explains how he reads *Beowulf* there are many other ideas and concepts he fictionalises in *The Hobbit*, although critics have not generally recognized this" (*Tolkien's Art*, 1979, 32).

In the source studies, one passage often quoted from the lecture is Tolkien's criticism of the *Beowulf* dragon "for not being dragon enough, plain pure fairy-story dragon": "the conception [of Beowulf's dragon] […] approaches *draconitas* rather than *draco*" ("*Beowulf*," 17). He adds, "There are in the poem some vivid touches of the right kind – as *þa se wyrm onwoc, wroht waes geniwad; stonc aefter stane* (17)" "[When the dragon awoke, the strife was renewed, he crawled sniffing along the stone]" ("*Beowulf*," rpt. in Fry, 21). For his example, Tolkien quotes the line that includes the notorious *stonc*, a problem form for Fr. Klaeber, who notes, "See Gloss.: *stincan*. The verb form has been thought by various scholars to belong to *stincan* 'emit a smell' … and has been credited with the unusual sense of 'sniffed'" (Klaeber, 210). In the glossary to his edition of *Beowulf*, Klaeber gives "*stonc*" as a form derived from the verb *stincan* "move rapidly." When *The Hobbit* was published, its readers were privileged to get a full picture of what Tolkien considers "dragon enough": "He [Smaug] stirred and stretched forth his neck to sniff" (*H*, 215). In the Bosworth-Toller *Dictionary*, defended by Tolkien above, readers are directed to compare *stincan* with *stencan*. At the entry for *stencan*, the meanings "to pant, emit breath with effort" are given. In Fry's 1968 edition of the lecture, there is a translation following the Old English line immediately in brackets: "[When the *dragon* awoke, the strife was renewed, he crawled sniffing along the stone]" (21). Translating puzzling *stonc* of line 2288a as "crawled sniffing," Fry suggests that he might have gone to Smaug in *The Hobbit* for help. In recent works, Heaney translates *stonc* as "rippled," and Mitchell and Robinson gloss *stincan* as "sniff."

Carpenter's biography notes that, of the reviewers of *The Hobbit* in 1937, "some took delight in pointing out the ineptness of the publisher's 'blurb' that compared the book to *Alice in Wonderland* simply because both were the work of Oxford dons" (182). Perhaps it is the case that we can learn more about the contributions to the history of criticism and theory of the language in the respective disciplines of two Oxford dons, Tolkien and Austin. Indeed, both Austin and Tolkien would make room for the work of the Oxford mathematician and author Lewis Carroll. In the lecture, Tolkien imagines the state of *Beowulf* criticism in Lewis Carroll's words: "For it is of their nature that the jabberwocks of historical and antiquarian research burble in the tulgy wood of conjecture, flitting from one tum-tum tree to another" ("*Beowulf*," 9). As early as 1940, Father William from *Alice in Wonderland* appeared in Austin's "The Meaning of a Word" (*Philosophical Papers*, 59). Lines from "Jabberwocky" also turn up in Austin's *How to Do Things with Words* (96).

Although not always respected for their critical works, the Oxford English professor and Oxford philosophy professor continue to recharge their disciplines. Making a place for the criticism and theory of language begun in Oxford in the 1930s, the two share more than a respect for Carroll's words. In a middle-voice relationship to verbs similar to Tokien's voice in the *Beowulf* lecture, Austin attempts, sometime before 1939, to "exonerate" Aristotle from the active-voice arrogant misreading in the 1935 article of one philosopher-critic, Professor H. A. Pritchard: "I suppose it cannot be denied that Aristotle is capable of getting himself into pretty tortuous confusions; but this time, at least, *I think*, he can be *exonerated*" (*Philosophical Papers*, 25; italics added). There is in the voice of "I think" the sense that Austin produces a space for the great Aristotle to talk back to the critic like the space produced by Tolkien for the *Beowulf* poet, "a greater man than most of us" ("*Beowulf*," 16). The Oxford classical scholars left famous Latin examples. Echoing Tolkien's famous pair, *draconitas* and *draco*, Austin plays in the essay "Truth" (1950) with *veritas* and *verum* (Ricks, 34–35): "*In vino*, possibly, '*veritas*,' but in a sober symposium '*verum*'" (Austin, *Philosophical Papers*, 117). A history reflecting further on the critical contributions of the two Oxford professors would note that in 1956 Austin lectured on "Ifs and Cans" at the British Academy (Austin, *Philosophical Papers*, 205–32).

The two dons, considered unworthy of the adjective "Oxonian," are only grudgingly noticed in the 1975 work *Oxford in the History of England*. The author, a graduate of Oxford, A. L. Rowse, wonders about Tolkien, if "perhaps we may regard him [Tolkien] as the twentieth-century parallel to Lewis Carroll":

> An Oxford taste, much advanced by C. S. Lewis, Coghill and Auden, was for Tolkien's world of "hobbits," which has since gone round the globe. It is a taste I have not acquired; but there is no doubt that the Professor created a whole imaginative world. Perhaps we may regard him as a twentieth-century parallel to Lewis Carroll.
>
> (Rowse, 237)

He makes room, again only grudgingly, for Austin's theory of "speech habits":

> In a period of decline a certain scholasticism overtakes subjects, as at the end of the Middle Ages. One may take, for example, the so-much-advertised Oxford school of philosophy. J. L. Austin was a remarkable man – I knew him – and his analysis of linguistic usage, especially speech habits, of use [*sic*]. But what are we to think of the absurdly exaggerated cult of Wittgenstein, when the prophet himself had doubts of the possibility or value of the subject? In so far as this school has reduced the over-riding claims of philosophy to lay down the law for other disciplines – so intolerable in one's youth – it is welcome; and that much may be said for it.
>
> (Rowse, 252)

Until the real history of Oxford criticism and theory is written to include the *Beowulf* lecture and Austin's philosophical discussions of the 1930s, we will have to do with such critics.

As we begin today to read the *Beowulf* essay in the context of the general theory of speech acts and discourse analysis, we can discover that the lost category of middle voice can teach us how to approach Tolkien's rescue of the *Beowulf* poet from the critics who have not even read the poem. As new readers recognize Tolkien's identities as great writer and great critic working in the lecture, perhaps they will make room for him to say what he has been waiting to say about the 1936 event at the British Academy with the words that Austin used at Harvard:

> In these lectures [substitute "this lecture"] then, I have been doing two things which I do not altogether like doing. These are: (1) producing a programme, that is, saying what ought to be done, rather than doing something; (2) lecturing. However, as against (1), I should very much like to think that I have been sorting out a bit the way things have already begun to go and are going with increasing momentum in some parts of philosophy [substitute "literary criticism"], rather than proclaiming an individual mani-

festo. And against (2), I should certainly like to say that nowhere could, to me, be a nicer place to lecture in than Harvard [substitute "the British Academy"].

(Austin, *How to Do Things*, 164)

Notes

1 Writing contemporary cultural-political theory, in his review of the language of the "nature"/"history"/"culture" debate in feminist theory, Pheng Cheah offers the phrase "second nature" to name the acts of many women dedicating themselves to the laws of developing nations, even when to outsiders the acts do not necessarily serve women's rights. Those women, for whom feminist is one of many "layered identities," emerge as subjects of a nation. I am attracted to Cheah's application of the phrases "layered identities" and "second nature" ("Mattering," 135–36) for accounting for the several identities of Tolkien, among them, at the time of the lecture, the Rawlinson and Bosworth Professor of Anglo-Saxon at Oxford, the medieval critic, and the writer of *The Hobbit.*

2 Professor Chance's words in 1979, "As a work of prose non-fiction by a great writer, however, the article has been ignored," continued to be true for the field of *Beowulf* studies. Great medievalists at Oxford, from Kenneth Sisam in the 1960s to Bruce Mitchell in the 1990s, begin their discussions of the *Beowulf* essay in a statement or two in awe of Tolkien's storyteller gifts but move on in greater detail to discuss Tolkien's reading. Sisam begins, "As an account of what the poem means to Professor Tolkien, or of the way in which he, as a storyteller, would treat the plot, I have no criticism of it" (114). Sisam has more, much more to say about Tolkien's criticism, and nobody can stop him: "But I dissent on two matters which especially concern the structure of the poem" (114). Bruce Mitchell in "J. R. R. Tolkien and Old English Studies: An Appreciation," notes about the essay, "It is fun to read. It is also a stylistic education, an intellectual challenge, a literary experience, and (for those who have ears to hear) a moral lesson" (209). Mitchell interrupts his statement of support to begin his paragraph-long objection to parts of Tolkien's interpretation with the statement, "All this does not mean that I agree with every opinion he expressed" ("J. R. R. Tolkien," 209). Mitchell summarizes, "His 1936 British Academy Lecture had more influence than most of their [critics of his 'research responsibilities'] products" (210). Editors of the 1998 edition of *Beowulf*, Bruce Mitchell and Fred Robinson, acknowledge Tolkien's essay as "One Essential Essay" in a separate entry in the bibliography (235–36). In the introduction to his translation of *Beowulf*, Seamus Heaney makes room for praise for the essay's contribution to *Beowulf* studies:

> [W]hen it comes to considering *Beowulf* as a work of literature, one publication stands out. In 1936, the Oxford scholar and teacher J. R. R. Tolkien published an epoch-making paper entitled "*Beowulf*: The Monsters and the Critics," which took for granted the poem's integrity and distinction as a work of art and proceeded to show in what this integrity and distinction inhered.
>
> (Heaney, xi)

Perhaps it is to the introduction that Tolkien's followers can look for an unqualified reception for the *Beowulf* poet. Not only does Heaney acknowledge, as all medieval critics do, the force of the lecture, but he takes Tolkien's image of the *Beowulf* poet, "from the poet's Christianity and from his perspectives as an Englishman looking back at places and legends" (xvi), into Heaney's world of the "instability of the human subject:"

> In an age when "the instability of the human subject" is constantly argued for if not presumed, there should be no problem with a poem that is woven from two such different psychic fabrics. In fact, *Beowulf* perfectly answers the early modern conception of a work of creative imagination.
>
> (Heaney, xvii)

3 French linguist Emile Benveniste noted that

> they [the active-voice inflections and middle-voice inflections] always finally come down to situating positions of the subject with respect to the process, according to whether it is exterior or interior to it, and to qualifying it as agent, depending on whether it effects, in the active, or whether it effects while being affected, in the middle.
>
> (Benveniste, "Voice," 149–50)

Borrowing from Benveniste, Roland Barthes in the late 1960s seized the ancient distinction to serve the discourse of the literary critic for the subject of *to write* to be "effected" and "affected": "In the modern verb of middle voice *to write* the subject is immediately contemporary with the writing, being effected and affected by it" ("*To Write*," 143).

4 One of Austin's students, Mats Furberg, invents the name "archetypical performative" for acts performed in an "official capacity" (Furberg, 279): "Archetypical performatives are different. Their performer shoulders no obligations for the future. He has as it were pressed a button in a social machine" (280). Emphasizing the formal aspects of the "social machine," Furberg notes, "Austin's pet performatives – promises, warnings, etc. – are fairly informal compared to the archetypical ones" (282). Situating *Lord of the Rings* in the Foucauldian discourse of power and knowledge, Jane Chance notes that Tolkien in his fiction continued to expose as monstrous "the repressive speech-act" in the academy and other human communities because it threatened intellectuals in attaining the primary goal – the power of language in the pursuit of "truth" ("*Lord of the Rings*," 22).

6 Middle-earth, the Middle Ages, and the Aryan nation

Myth and history in World War II

Christine Chism

> I have in this War a burning private grudge – which would probably make me a better soldier at 49 than I was at 22: against that ruddy little ignoramus Adolf Hitler … . Ruining, perverting, misapplying, and making for ever accursed, that noble northern spirit, a supreme contribution to Europe, which I have ever loved, and tried to present in its true light.
>
> (J. R. R. Tolkien, Letter to Michael Tolkien, 9 June, 1941)

This chapter examines a conflict created in Tolkien's writing by his love for Germanic medieval sources and their (mis)appropriation by the Nazis before and during World War II, the period when Tolkien wrote *The Lord of the Rings*. These medieval languages, legends, and sagas (Icelandic, Germanic, Finnish, Gothic, and Anglo-Saxon) were close to the foundations of Tolkien's imaginative world-creating enterprise as well as of his scholarly career, and it is a fascinating topic to consider how he extends them from one area to the other. But I want to take seriously the "burning private grudge" that Tolkien describes in this 1941 letter to his son. In "ruining, perverting, misapplying, and making forever accursed" the "northern spirit" Tolkien had loved, Nordic race-mythology sharpened an ethical dilemma in the ambitions and costs of his creative writing.

This dilemma was already implicit in Tolkien's ongoing investigation of the power of imaginative writing. Throughout his career he melds the methodologies of scholar and author by thinking metaphorically in his essays and experimenting theoretically in his fiction to scrutinize the uses and powers of both (Ugolnik, 15–31; Chance, *Tolkien's Art*; Shippey, *Road*).[1] He castigates the textual judgmentalism of the literary criticism that places the critic above the text and often deafens her to it (Faraci).[2] He also questions the utility of fantasy writing, most notably in "On Fairy-Stories" and the playfully titled "A Secret Vice," and in allegories, especially *Leaf by Niggle* and *Smith of Wootton Major*. His theories of the autonomy (but not self-sufficiency) of created worlds have sparked comparison with those of Ernst Cassirer (Lentricchia, 66–67). But Tolkien questioned the work of created mythologies with a particularly self-consuming intensity during and after the war. I argue that he came to scrutinize his own world-creating enterprise because he had before him a parallel spectacle of world-creation gone wrong – in National Socialist Germany. Tolkien's wartime investigation of the uses of fantasy is driven by the realization that mythmaking is not innocent, that it can become a killing tool: most dramatically in the National Socialist politicization of art, fetishization of symbols, and cannibalization of medieval narratives and histories into pseudo-historical racialist mythologies.[3]

The Lord of the Rings is a tale of the renunciation of mythology and the willed return to history. The Ring – that weirdly empty, weirdly powerful object around which the narrative assembles itself – interrogates the imaginative capacity for world-creation itself. Middle-earth unfolds, grows more intricate, more peopled, more culturally diverse, more deep as we wander through it, but it blooms forth only in the shadow of its own immanent destruction. The loss of the Ring consigns Middle-earth to the joys and depredations of history – and this consignment to history is costly. It is no accident that the loss of the Ring maims Frodo forever and disenchants Middle-earth – it is also, possibly, no accident that *The Lord of the Rings* is the last long narrative this author completed. And, finally, I argue, it is no accident that the writing of this renunciatory narrative occupies dark night after dark night, during a time when Germany was mobilizing and recasting heroic "'Germanic' ideals" to articulate and impose its own terrifying new world.

Fantasies of power

Tolkien himself ferociously resisted any attempt to historicize his work in the light of the world wars and the progressive industrialization they accelerated. When critics and reviewers began to suggest analogues for *The Lord of the Rings* in the progress of World War II and modern industrialization (Blisset, 448–56; Fifield, 841–44; Fuller, 159–96; Giddings, 7–24), Tolkien dismissed such readings as "allegories" – a form he claimed to "cordially dislike" (in this context it connotes "reductive," "clunky," and "enslaved to mere events"; but elsewhere he is far more nuanced about allegories – they are one of his favorite ways to think about what fantasy writing does). He snarled that if *The Lord of the Rings* had really been an allegory, it would have ended with the "allies" of Gondor, Rohan, and Eriador claiming the Ring and setting themselves up as competing little Saurons all over Middle-earth (Tolkien, *FR*, 6–7). There is no compelling reason not to believe Tolkien when he says that his narrative wasn't influenced at all by the war, except that he made such a fuss about it. We have C. S. Lewis's word that "no one ever influenced Tolkien – you might as well try to influence a bandersnatch" (*Biography*, 201). But I would like to ease Tolkien out of his bandersnatchery and into the texture of the twentieth century and, simultaneously, to shift consideration of the Ring from "the will to mere power," which Tolkien asserted as its primary symbolism (J. R. R. Tolkien, *Letters*, 160) to a dark exploration of the powers of aesthetic production itself. Throughout his writing, Tolkien explicitly and persistently links the creation of fantastic and mythological worlds to the temptations of power, and never more so than during the war.

Myth and *mythology* can be understood both in formalist and sociological ways; a methodological point of this essay is that the two are inseparable.[4] In the first formalist sense, myths are "secondary worlds," autonomous textual entities, self-consistent, carefully formed and realized, drawing upon recognizable literary genres, but also strikingly differentiated from the "primary" world of the reader.[5] The point of using *myth* rather than *text* in this context is to gesture at largeness – the tendency to expand beyond the borders of one book and even one author. Fantastic mythologies are nothing if not ambitious, stretching easily into trilogies, quintilogies, open-ended multiauthored series. This burgeoning is where the first sense of mythology begins to press against the second. The second, sociological sense of *mythology* understands mythologies to be cultural productions – sometimes textual, sometimes dramatic, always performative – which are nurtured, cross-fertilized, and constantly reenacted to do social work: for example, the National Socialist construction of race war. Tolkien's textual mythologies grapple with the cultural mythologies produced in his time, not simply through what is represented or excluded, but also in how they meditate on the uses of myth-production (both textual and cultural) itself.

That Tolkien came to question the production of mythology in the shadow of World War II would not be surprising. National Socialist Germany had made myth-production into a political strategy. It mobilized myth into "a collection of themes … to spur crowds to action, themes that are always treated symbolically in speeches, images, and rituals" (Ayçberry, 65). Cultivating nationalism by drawing upon the lexicon of socialist mass-movement and symbolically adapting it for race war rather than class struggle (Lukacs, 104–10), the National Socialist Party appealed to its constituencies by symbolizing *Volksgemeinschaft* (the shaping of a people into a national community) and mythologizing a leader who could incarnate their collective longings, fears, and aspirations. This mythically fired popular legitimation differentiated mid-1930s' Nationalist Socialist government both from the totalitarianism of Stalin and from the fascism of Mussolini (Lukacs, 197–222; Schoenbaum, xi–xxii). National Socialism imparted a mythological unity to Germany's chaotic imperial and national history. The Third Reich – the Thousand-Year Reich for the next millennium – was to accomplish what the First Reich (under Charlemagne) and the Second Reich (under Bismarck) could only dimly envisage. Through spectacles and pageants, party rallies, and staged punishments, the party enacted these history-conquering mythologies as sovereign remedies for the perception (which it also nurtured) that Germany (and the modern industrial world in general) had been pressured to the brink of national, economic, and social disintegration.

These nationalist mythologies did terrifying social work, and they did it beautifully. They helped systematize atrocities so that they could appear to be business as usual – analogizable to the industrialization of slaughterhouses and other structural brutalities of civilization. They instrumentalized violence, demagoguery, and genocide as means to larger, better, more permanent ends. To Tolkien, however, militant nationalist mythologies were not being produced only in National Socialist Germany. Tolkien marked analogous strategies – he called them "war-hypnotism" – within wartime Britain and among the allied powers (*Letters*, 89). Late in the war, when his third son Christopher was stationed with the RAF, Tolkien condemned this "first War of the Machines" (*Letters*, 111): "Nothing can amend my grief that you, my best beloved, have any connection with it. My sentiments are more or less those that Frodo would have had if he discovered some Hobbits learning to ride Nazgûl-birds, 'for the liberation of the Shire.'"(*Letters*, 115). National Socialism was not the only problem – militant nationalisms were spreading all over the world.

However, if both Britain and Germany could use "war-hypnotism" to foster popular support for political imperatives, the politicization of art set Germany apart. To an unprecedented degree the Nationalist Socialist Party aggressively conscripted art, drama, film, and literature into state service. Brutality had to be institutionally nurtured (Theweleit, 142–269), but so did the dazzling ideals that drove it. Hitler, a would-be painter and architectural visionary, took care to nurture the work of artists who suited his aims and to purge those who did not (Ayçberry, 67–79). This mobilization of art to create a national mass culture raised crucial questions about the politics of the artistic imagination. Most famously, the Frankfurt School Marxists positioned themselves as critical theorists against National Socialist state formations and the aesthetics of mass culture (Jay, 113–218). Closer to home, Tolkien reflects the interests and even echoes many of the themes of a group of British writers and artists whom Stuart Sillers has described as twentieth-century Romantics: McNeice, Auden, Spender, and Britten.[6] Tolkien at once expresses and critiques a similar Romanticist strain when he develops a theory of the aesthetic that both dramatizes its own laborious production – rather than mystifying it as genius or sublimity – and relentlessly questions its own power to seduce.[7]

This investigation is not simply autobiographical. Tolkien undoubtedly engaged his own experiences and ambitions as he speculated about the production and power of art. However, the sheer amplitude of heroic, aspiring, entrapped, angelic, demonic, tragic, and triumphant artists and artifacts in Tolkien's worlds reveals them as wide-ranging thought experiments. Tolkien's explorations of the aesthetic production show it to be both powerful and terrifying: at times shaping and immortalizing formless natural beauty (as with the Silmarils), at times consuming artist and viewer alike with the blank ferocity of a black hole (as with, I will argue, the Ring). Each of Tolkien's created peoples opens a different set of ethical questions about the aesthetic. The angelic Valar help Eru (God) to create the world and then fall so deeply in love with their creation that they volunteer to be locked into it – a disaster for the world because the demonic Morgoth and Sauron are among them. The undying Elves "represent … Men with greatly enhanced aesthetic and creative faculties, greater beauty and longer life" (J. R. R. Tolkien, *Letters*, 176; 85, 236). The story of their "long defeat" puts the screws on aesthetic ideologies that propose the immortality of artistic power as a consolation for the transience of world and flesh. Orcs (as Morgoth's parody of Elves) represent art gone wrong, warped to military service, its immortality translated into invasive multiplication, perhaps (mischievously) a nightmare version of the work of art in an age of mechanical reproduction.[8] The Dwarves express the Vala Aulë's Frankenstein-like desire to bring insensate matter to life, and Dwarves continue to evoke Aulëin the life they pour into and draw from cold stone, gold, and jewels.[9] Through these invented peoples, Tolkien's mythologies theorize the work – both process and product – of art, as it calls forth, disciplines, and consumes the artist's imaginative and manual labor. Art becomes powerful through this labor, and it repays the labor lavished upon it by radiating a dangerous desirability; Silmarils, Arkenstones, Dwarvish halls, Elven sanctuaries, and Rings rivet anyone who strays into the field of their beauty.[10] Tolkien's artists founder less often in failure than in the dazzlement of a long-fought-for success.

These interrogations of literary and linguistic power intensify during Tolkien's most difficult and halting period of fantasy writing: the war and postwar years between 1938 and 1954; *The Lord of the Rings* was written from 1938 to 1949 and published in 1954–55. "On Fairy-Stories" was delivered as the Andrew Lang lecture at the University of St. Andrews on 8 March 1939 and worked up and published in a 1947 memorial collection dedicated to Charles Williams. "Leaf by Niggle" was written in 1940 and published in the *Dublin Review* in 1945. "English and Welsh" was delivered as the O'Donnell lecture at Oxford in October of 1955 (the day after *The Return of the King* was released).

Tolkien's power-wary war and postwar writings contrast instructively with a decisively prewar essay probably written in 1931: "A Secret Vice" (Carpenter, *Biography*, 265; Tolkien, *Monsters*, 3–4). This is a Victorian striptease of an essay. It delights in attributing guilt to the otherwise almost laughably pedantic hobby of creating private languages and mythologies. Tolkien makes it a pastime, an addiction, a deeply individualizing and pleasurable self-exploration, and a defense against an unspeakable world. His most affectionate anecdote of a fellow-addict is drawn from his army training in World War I, when in the middle of some interminable training lecture a man sitting next to him suddenly remarked dreamily, "Yes, I think I shall express the accusative case by a prefix!" (*Monsters*, 199). The essay relishes the prospect of the little man hugging his private grammar to himself through the tedium and furor of the Great War, only to dismiss him with a mordant acknowledgment of the indifference of the world to such delights: "Probably he was blown to bits in the very moment of deciding upon some ravishing method of indicating the subjunctive. Wars are not favorable to delicate pleasures" (*Monsters*, 200).

Here what is delightful – what compensates for loss of agency during the war – is power over language itself. Born into language, the language creator uses knowledge of the structures and strategies of many languages to create and lay claim to a tiny, personal, symbolic territory. The invented language reveals its creator's individualizing aesthetic explorations with a candor that becomes almost painful. Tolkien pleads indulgence as he reveals some snippets of verse in one of his own languages: "Their bare meaning is … not full of red blood or the heat of the world such as critics demand. Be kindly. For if there is any virtue in this kind of thing, it is in its intimacy, in its peculiarly shy individualism"

(*Monsters*, 213). The narrative stance here is at once intensely mannered and revealing, stemming more from a staged shyness than from any sense of genuine defensiveness. The essay ends with a jubilant Promethean call to linguistic creation; only Tolkien's early poem "Mythopoeia" is equally optimistic about the uses of literary power. Forget the prison-house of language: "You are the heir of the ages. You have not to grope after the dazzling brilliance of invention of the free adjective … . You may say *green sun* or *dead life* and set the imagination leaping" (*Monsters*, 219).

Eight years later, this same "free adjective" (even the same example: *green sun*) has become perilous, hedged round with suspicion and the longing for power. In "On Fairy-Stories" Tolkien theorizes how fantasy itself evolves from the free adjective. When storytellers learned to abstract the qualities from objects (the accidents from substances in medieval grammatical terms), they broke into a mother-lode both of incalculable power and potential abuse:

> But how powerful, how stimulating to the very faculty that produced it, was the invention of the adjective: no spell or incantation in Faërie is more potent … When we can take green from grass, blue from heaven, and red from blood, we have already an enchanter's power – upon one plane; and the desire to wield that power in the world external to our mind awakes. *It does not follow that we shall use that power well upon any plane.*
>
> ("OFS," 22; italics mine)

This passage links aesthetics to both politics and ethics. The fantastic secondary world is divided from the external primary world, but it also bleeds into it – through the author who exerts a sorcerous power over the textual world and longs to transfer it to the great, unheeding, life-giving, treacherous stream of history that he inhabits and must continually negotiate. This uncanny and somehow transgressive shiver of longing between what a writer creates and what is "external to his mind" is one of the most productive uncertainties in Tolkien's writing. It is deep-woven through "On Fairy-Stories," where he continually insinuates the independent (and sometimes cautionary) reality of elves, dwarves, dragons – intelligences completely unconcerned with humanity – into his discussions of their fantastic or metaphoric uses in literature. This desirous slippage provokes the wariness of the last sentence. The longing for power is there; it is enmeshed in the power of writing, and it can be misused.

How could we identify such misuse? Is such power to be mistrusted by definition? Tolkien positively relishes the fearsome power of fantasy within texts ("OFS," 22).[11] But while famously desiring dragons "with a profound desire," he doesn't necessarily want them in his neighborhood (20), and he does not pursue the question of how the power to reshape reality might be misused in the world "external to our minds." What would that look like? Delusion? Lunacy? What if the fantasy were powerful enough to convince others? What if it sought and found the ability to remake the world in its own image? How could its use or misuse be judged? Tolkien leaves such questions unexplored here. However, he opens a treacherous ethical no-man's land between literary and historical worlds, which his wartime writing at once patrols and irresistibly infiltrates.

Tolkien was conscious that he was sacrificing to Middle-earth his most productive years as a scholar, and that many of his colleagues at Oxford would take (and, judging from his rueful postpublication letters, did take) a dim view of his hobby gone wild (*Letters*, 278). Throughout his professional years at Oxford, during which he held two of the coveted university professorial chairs: Anglo-Saxon at Pembroke and Language and Literature at Merton College, Tolkien claimed rightly that he did not neglect his duties; indeed, he lectured, tutored, and examined more generously and conscientiously than many of his colleagues. However, his scholarly output remained slim. He grapples allegorically with this culpability in "Leaf by Niggle" (1940), ironically the only story that ever came to him, he claimed, without labor and need of revision. As Jane Chance and T. A. Shippey argue, "Leaf by Niggle" weighs fantasy (Niggle the painter) against scholarship and other duties (Parish the potato grower) (Chance, *Tolkien's Art*, 57–67; Shippey, *Road*, 39–41).[12] It is a story not of successful escape but of accountability. Niggle the artist finds justification only after death and not through his own merit. He niggles away his life (as his name suggests) and does not even complete his canvas, is freed from purgatory (the Workhouse) only through his appreciation of the fruits of scholarship (Parish's potatoes), and emerges beyond hope to find that a gorgeous and gratuitous mercy has renovated his painting into the landscape of Paradise. This gift humbles Niggle while subsuming his obsessive, painstaking, futile artistry into the work of the Creator itself. This subsumption doesn't simply justify Tolkien's fantasy-writing. More instrumentally during the 1940 intensification of the war in Britain, when his writing had stalled for over a year, it gave him the confidence to continue *The Lord of the Rings* (Carpenter, *Biography*, 196; Knowles, 32–141; Rosebury, 117).

If Tolkien's wartime explorations of fantasy-writing convey a more besieged sense of accountability, this intensified into even deeper questioning after the war ended and the vast 600,000-word *Lord of the Rings* (1954–5) was published. One of the darkest poems Tolkien ever wrote about fantasy was "The Sea-Bell" (1961), included in *The Adventures of Tom Bombadil*. If, as many critics have noted, Tolkien's early poem "Mythopoeia" expresses the pinnacle of his hopes for the divine nature of fantasy, "The Sea-Bell" correspondingly cries out from the depths (Rosebury, 109). It tells in first-person voice (very rare in Tolkien's poetry) the story of a traveler who finds "a white shell like a sea-bell" shining like a star on the wet shore. As he holds it, he hears "a call ringing over endless seas" and a boat slides up to him. He doesn't even hesitate: " 'It is later than late! Why do we wait?' / I leapt in and cried: 'Bear me away!' " (*Adventures*, 57). He is transported to a distant island where he wanders in isolation, haunted by the echo of fading music, retreating feet, and lurking terror, a sense of hidden life all around receding at his approach. Impatient with the denizens to show themselves, Ophelia-like, he assembles a madman's regalia from leaves, rushes, and flowers and addresses the silent land:

Here now I stand, king of this land,
with gladdon-sword and reed mace.
Answer my call! Come forth all!
Speak to me words! Show me a face!
(*Adventures*, 59)

The traveler's "gladdon-sword" recalls the finding of the Ring in the Gladden Fields (Shippey, *Road*, 250); his reed mace is no battle threat but a rudimentary pen. This is Tolkien's theory of fantasy in its most impatient and desperate guise: the hunger to encounter an animated world, to speak to it and to have it speak back in its own strange and wonderful languages. The traveler invokes it with flimsy majesty and commands an answer. What happens next is unclear: a black cloud shrouds him (or does he become blind?), he falls to his hands and knees and creeps into a desolate wood where he sits for a year and a day, "wandering in wit," amidst owls, beetles, spiders, and puffballs. Finally light returns, and he wakes from his stupor to discover that he has grown old. He has had enough of the eerie land: "Bent though I be, I must find the sea! / I have lost myself, and I know not the way, / But let me be gone!" After cold and hardship, he reaches the boat still waiting on the shore, to return home in it. But there he finds an even worse desolation, shuttered houses, empty roads, drizzling wind and rain, only grains of sand and a silent sea-shell recalling his journey. The traveler understands that he can never return.

Never again, as in sad lane,
in blind alley and in long street
ragged I walk. To myself I talk;
for still they speak not, men that I meet.
(*Adventures*, 60)

And there it ends. The sea-bell that rang with far-off echoes has become a dead shell, emptied down the drain with some grains of sand. This poem rewrites an earlier one, "Looney" (1934), where essentially the same thing happens, but with less provocation – the traveler simply wanders, without challenging the land to speak, and the black cloud comes upon him without warning. "The Sea-Bell" 's traveler is both more aggressive and more poignant – he transgresses in some way (pride?), but why is he punished so severely? Does the black cloud/blindness come from within or without? Can he be blamed for his insane claim to monarchy over the alien land when it dramatically refigures Tolkien's earlier recognition in "On Fairy-Stories" that fantasy-writing is inextricably enmeshed with longing for mastery? Tolkien is exquisitely aware, as Angela Carter muses, that "there is something odd about a grown man who devotes most of his time on the *qui vive* for the horns of elfland faintly blowing" (454). "The Sea-Bell" is Tolkien's imagined worst-case scenario: the romantic author-hero waving a fragile pen before an utterly mysterious world – and losing wits, life, and humanity for his bravado.

Shippey discusses "The Sea-Bell" as a sign of Tolkien's growing misgivings about his own tremendous investment in his fantasy worlds:

> One senses that Tolkien was doubtful … of the legitimacy of his own mental wanderings. For many years he had held to his theory of "sub-creation." … But by the 1960s he was not so sure. It is hard not to think that by then he saw himself (perhaps only at times) as a mortal deserted by the immortals and barred from their company. He no longer imagined himself rejoining his own creations after death, like Niggle; he felt they were lost, like the Silmarils.
>
> (Shippey, *Road*, 251)

This longing for a lost congress with a fantastic world (and was even that a delusion?) is perplexed even further by "The Sea-Bell" 's sense that the narrator should never have gone in the first place – or should have gone less hungrily. And, interestingly, the poem does not link itself most closely with the Silmarils as Shippey suggests but with something much darker: the Ring of power. We are told that in its fictional source, the Red Book of Westmarch, "The Sea-Bell" was annotated "Frodo's Dreme." This subtitle recalls the nightmares Frodo suffers in the last part of his life in Middle-earth, in which he mourns the Ring to which he has succumbed and which took his third finger – for weddings and bindings to other mortal creatures – with it. The empty shell cast away by the traveler in "The Sea-Bell" is what Frodo in his darkest moments feels he has become. Shippey suggests that Tolkien increasingly felt the same way – not only shorn of further ability to create but more and more radically questioning the legitimacy of such creation in the first place.

If the lost Ring haunts the traveler's narrative of the sea-bell, it shadows the longing for fantasy – so eagerly defended, so astonishingly pursued in Tolkien's writing – with the most powerful symbol of evil he ever came up with. This raises two questions: (1) How do we get from Promethean shaper of language to shadowy Ringbearer? – did anything ease the way for this darkening of the conception of fantasy? (2) Shouldn't we complicate our reading of the Ring accordingly? There has always been something mystified and frustrating about the emptiness of the Ring of power (what power? power over what?) – so obviously a magical symbol in a text so otherwise resistant to merely magical symbolism. What explains its allure? How does it grow on its owner even when it is not used – how can an unexercised and burdensome power corrupt? Why are Hobbits relatively immune when even Gandalf and Aragorn can't trust themselves to touch it? What, in short, makes it the Precious? The rest of this chapter treats each of these two questions in turn.

Worlds at war

Tolkien was acutely aware that the National Socialist *Weltanschauung* had mobilized and transformed the very medieval Germanic legends that he had studied all his life and that echoed through his own imaginative worlds. In the British wartime climate of blind hatred for Germans and all their works, he wrote to his son Michael, who was undergoing military training at the Royal Military College at Sandhurst:[13]

> There is a great more force (and truth) than ignorant people imagine in the "Germanic" ideal. I was much attracted by it as an undergraduate (when Hitler was, I suppose, dabbling in paint, and had not heard of it) … . You have to understand the good in things, to detect the real evil. But no one calls upon me to "broadcast," or do a postscript! Yet I suppose I know better than most what is the truth about this "Nordic" nonsense.
>
> (*Letters*, 55)

This letter crackles with the indignation of the territorial scholar. Tolkien claims a prior knowledge of "Germanic matters" to Hitler, the ignorant dabbler. He also claims a better knowledge than that of either the German ideologues who produced the "'Nordic' nonsense" or his British countrymen who cannot see "the good" in the Germanic ideals – let alone the "real evil." Tolkien goes on to define the heart of his animus, the "burning private grudge," quoted in the epigraph to this chapter. Tolkien's language is strong – "ruining, perverting, misapplying, and making for ever accursed" (*Letters*, 55). Long before the war, his fiction is obsessed with such tragic corruptions of noble and holy things: the poisoning of the two Trees, the cursing of the Silmarils, the treachery surrounding the Dwarves' treasure. Tolkien's imagination, tempered by Catholic belief in a fallen world and an Augustinian sense of historic mutability, is thoroughly primed to realize and mourn the intimacy with which cruelty and idealism, violence and beauty can come to interpenetrate.[14]

Tolkien's terminology in his letter to Michael ("'Nordic' nonsense") evokes the writings of Alfred Rosenberg, one-time editor of *Volkische Beobachter* (the National Socialist Party paper), ideologue of Nordic *Volkskultur*, race-theorist, anti-Semite, and anti-Catholic – and therefore noxious to Tolkien on at least four fronts.[15] His work both influenced Hitler and proved a useful instrument to him at an early stage in his climb through channels toward executive power in Germany. Rosenberg was sidelined (though not entirely silenced) once Hitler was ensconced in 1933; the influence of Rosenberg's wilder theories against Catholicism (and Christianity generally) needed reining in as Hitler successfully wooed opposing Catholic, Protestant, and neopagan factions to keep himself in place (Ayçberry, 117–22). Rosenberg's vast 1930 work, *Mythus des 20. Jahrhunderts* (*Myth of the Twentieth Century*), drew upon the dregs of German Romanticism, the grand gestures of *Kulturgeschichte*, and the pseudoscientific racialist theories of Arthur de Gobineau and Houston Steward Chamberlain to brew a weird draught of racialist idealist paranoia. He rewrote world history in the light of a mythology (*Mythus*) that elevated the Nordic race-soul as a fragile wellspring of positive, creative, artistic, masculine vigor against the stifling mass of southern subhuman race chaos exemplified by democracies, Jews, blacks,

Asians, Catholics, Pauline Christians, and urbanites. Rosenberg traces the etiology of Nordic honor back to primordial times. He speculates wildly about Atlantean or Hyperborean origins, but he lights on the Vikings as the oldest Nordic migration well-documented enough for him to sink his teeth into. In his hands they become freedom-fighting individuals motivated by honor (Rosenberg, *Race*, 102).[16]

Most apposite to Tolkien's concerns (especially his privileging of the virtues of pity and compassion in both *The Hobbit* and *The Lord of the Rings*) is Rosenberg's simplification of race war to an essential conflict between the organizing virtues of Nordic honor and race-chaotic love. Rosenberg shapes history into a perpetual mythological crisis in which honor must ruthlessly defend itself against the smothering flood of compassionate-seeming (actually hypocritical and dominance-seeking) race-chaos. This battle becomes both a "mythical occurrence" (101) and a constant danger: "The moment … in which love and pity (or, if one wants, compassion) become predominant, racial-*Volkish* and cultural degeneration begin to occur in all Nordic-conditioned states" (102).

Throughout his immense mythography, Rosenberg emblematizes particular historic moments as flashpoints of triumphant individualism and thus invigorates the Nordic with the force of those particulars. At the same time, any sense of historic accidence and atomization is projected onto the enemies of the Nordic life-creative force, who repeatedly emerge in a welter of cringing ferocity and overwhelm the Nordic.[17] The Nordic creative force thus emerges paradoxically as simultaneously vigorous and unbroken – and fragile and threatened, a very useful picture for provoking a crisis. To Rosenberg, this crisis comes to a head in World War I. Rosenberg drags out the heavy mythological artillery to make this clear.

> A new centre of our Being – sparkling, glorious and life-filled – has come into joyful activity. This new-and-yet-old *Mythus* … was threatened from within our own nation … when once again there dawned an age when the Fenris Wolf broke his chains, when Hel, exuding an odour of decay moved over the earth and the *Midgard-schlange* [Midgard serpent or serpent of Middle-earth] stirred the oceans of the world … . At the same time that *Mythus* of the blood, for which heroes had died, stirred anew in the bowed souls of those left behind by the departed warriors, until this *Mythus* was grasped and experienced in its final ramifications. The inner voice now demands that the myth of blood and the myth of soul, race and ego, *Volk* and personality, blood and honour; that this myth, alone and uncompromisingly, must penetrate, bear and determine all life.
>
> (Rosenberg, 96–97)

Rosenberg here forges a chain of linked mythologies of blood, soil, and racial essence to strangle the rest of the world, and he tempers it with the medieval Germanic writings that Tolkien loved, respected, and sought to realize, both imaginatively and academically.

Tolkien's response is quite clear. Although there is no evidence that he read Rosenberg (or Feden or any other folkish racialist apologists for National Socialism), he was intimately familiar with their philological antecedents. In "On Fairy-Stories," he dismisses the racialist strain in Dasent as "a mishmash of bogus pre-history founded on the early surmises of Comparative Philology" (20) – a description that fits Rosenberg just as well.[18] As a medievalist and a philologist exquisitely sensitive to the cultural and linguistic differences among Germanic peoples – the constant infighting between Huns and Lombards, Goths, Danes, Anglo-Saxons, and Vikings – Tolkien considered rampant lunacy the thoughtless agglomeration of even these Germanic people into a transcendent Aryan life force, let alone Rosenberg's Atlanteans, Greeks, Indians, Persians, Romans, Egyptians, and Nordic Jesus. And yet Tolkien, like Rosenberg, also wrote about the essential truth of mythology (Carpenter, *Biography*, 91–92, 147). How could Tolkien disinfect his own mythologies, his own scholarship, which drew from the same materials as Rosenberg?

This is where the philologist and scholar could come to the aid of the fantasist. In 1938 Tolkien wrote an incomparably pedantic and disingenuous letter to a German translator of *The Hobbit,* who inquired about Tolkien's own racial pedigree:

> I regret that I am not clear as to what you intend by *arisch.* I am not of *Aryan* extraction: that is Indo-iranian; as far as I am aware none of my ancestors spoke Hindustani, Persian, Gypsy or any related dialects. But if I am to understand that you are enquiring whether I am of *Jewish* origin, I can only reply that I regret that I appear to have *no* ancestors of that gifted people.
>
> (*Letters*, 37; italics Tolkien's)

And in his lecture "English and Welsh," delivered in October of 1955 as the last volume of *The Lord of the Rings* was being published, Tolkien furiously dismantles the whole mythology of racialism in successive steps that correspond closely to Rosenberg's discursive categories for assembling his definition of the Nordic: race, blood, soil, and unchanging essence. To Tolkien, Celts and Teutons alike, first, are people not races (*Monsters*, 167); second, they are to be defined by the languages they speak not the blood they carry (169); third, they are not unchanging essences or forces but historically, linguistically, and culturally heterogeneous and changing (171); fourth, they are not indigenous (tied to the soil) within any known region in which their languages are still spoken, in England as in Germany. All were invaders and all are products of Rosenberg's shibboleth, racial miscegenation (168–70). Tolkien ends this peroration – which is actually beside the point in an essay meant to inaugurate a lecture series about Celtic language influences on English – by half apologizing and half insisting upon its relevance: "My excuse must be that, though the dogs that I have been beating may seem … to be dead, they are still alive and barking in this land at large" (173). I would suggest that they are particularly loud to Tolkien because he is so appallingly close to them, grappling with the same problems of mythology and history, and driven by the same consciousness of crisis that had brought them forth.[19]

Rosenberg was not the only mythmaker mobilized by National Socialism who struck deeply at Tolkien's work as a medievalist and writer. There was also that other dabbler in medieval saga and poetry – Richard Wagner. Like Tolkien, Wagner had transformed Germanic medieval narratives into contemporizing dramas.[20] Much more than Rosenberg (though without Tolkien's scholarly expertise) he searched obsessively and imaginatively among both medieval source-texts and contemporary scholarship and fiction treating them. He ransacked widely, from *The Nibelungenlied* and *The Poetic Edda* to Jacob and Wilhelm Grimm's German folktales and their four-volume summa, *Teutonic Mythology*. Wagner drew upon the nationalizing *mentalité* of contemporary nineteenth-century philologists to stitch together medieval sources into a rich mythology for Germany.[21]

He had his work cut out for him. During its quarter-century composition, the *Ring* cycle underwent (but did not always synthesize) many revisions. Robert W. Gutman describes how, "especially in the two final dramas, fascinating stratas of the cycle's literary formation lie pell-mell like abandoned rock in an exhausted quarry" (Gutman, 156). A powerful experiential unity is imparted by Wagner's seamlessly textured music and a supple alliterative libretto whose lexicon is derived from exclusively Germanic roots. Yet as a text, the *Ring* is still pocked with the agglomerate of its medieval sources: *The Nibelungenlied*'s focus on the family feuds of medieval Austrian lordlings, the *Völsunga saga*'s uneven encyclopedic energy, the glittering, disjunct, story-nuggets of *The Poetic Edda* – including the solemn and prophetic *Völuspá* – the brisk reportage of Snorri Sturluson's *Prose Edda*, and the bumptious humor of *Thidreks saga* and the Grimms' story *The Boy Who Never Knew Fear*.[22] Like Siegfried grinding down the fragments of his father's shattered sword, Wagner with less success struggles to consolidate his medieval sources' intractable motley, the same motley that Rosenberg overlooked in his rush toward a totalizing *Mythus*, and that Tolkien spent his scholarly career relishing and expanding upon. Adding to the confusion, Wagner shaped these medieval sources to serve as contemporary imperatives that were themselves far from self-consistent, ranging from revolution to monarchism, salvation-through-love to the will-to-power, materialism to renunciation, triumphal epiphany to fatalist apocalypse.[23] Wagner's determined cannibalization of the old to bring forth the new undoubtedly recommended him to Hitler, whose programs also yoke reactionism to revolution, *Volk*-mythology to modern nationalist reformation.[24] In *Mein Kampf* Hitler credits Wagner with turning him into an artistic revolutionary (16).

Tolkien knew Wagner's *Ring* cycle – and perhaps in the early 1930s had enjoyed it.[25] His friend C. S. Lewis was a Wagner enthusiast who collected gramophone recordings of the *Ring* cycle, treasured a copy of the text illustrated by Arthur Rackham, and in his youth had begun collaborating with his musician friend Arthur Greaves on his own opera entitled "Loki Unbound." In the early 1930s C. S. Lewis, his brother Warnie, and Tolkien spent a long evening together reading *Die Walküre* aloud in the original German and then discussing it until almost midnight; Priscilla Tolkien remembers that Tolkien and Lewis also attended a performance of one of the *Ring* cycle operas at Covent Garden (Carpenter, *Inklings*, 5, 55–56). Despite Tolkien's curt later disavowals ("Both rings were round and there the resemblance ceases" [*Letters*, 306]), his evolving conception of his Ring's powers is arguably informed by Wagner (Shippey, *Road*, 297). Tolkien melds in his Ring the qualities that Wagner distributes between Alberich's ring and Mime's tarnhelm: like the tarnhelm, it confers invisibility, a fearsome aura, and expanded vision; like the Ring it corrupts through desire and signifies corrupted desire.

But Wagner is even more useful as a source for Tolkien to work against. Robert A. Hall, Jr., persuasively treats Tolkien's *The Hobbit* and *The Lord of the Rings* as a rejection of Wagner's *Ring* cycle ("Tolkien's Hobbit Tetralogy"). Tolkien attempts to wrest back from Hitler's Bayreuth the medieval matter of the Nibelungs and Volsungs, revealing the intensity of his dedication to these medieval sagas. In the late 1920s and early 1930s he actually recast them into his own rendition in an unfortunately unpublished poem he called "The New Volsung-Lay" (letter 295, n. 3, in *Letters*, 452; Shippey, *Road*, 277). And more generally throughout Tolkien's war and postwar writings, shadowy repudiations of Wagner's *Ring* lend a contentious vigor to his narratives. Aragorn, who explicitly rejects the chance to kill for the Ring, unwrites Siegfried, who doesn't hesitate; Wotan, the meddlesome All-Father who enslaves any creature he directly touches, is countered by the distant Ilúvatar of *The Silmarillion*, who enfranchises his creatures and leaves them, sometimes disastrously, to their own devices. In one other crucial area – the choice of pity over ruthlessness, compassion over vengeance – Tolkien makes his difference from Wagner a defining moment of his mythos.

This rejection gains contemporary urgency because Siegfried's dramatic ruthlessness had scripted for both Rosenberg and Hitler a foundational mythology for their own genocidal state-formation. Though it should not be underestimated, the Wagner–Hitler connection has been overdone.[26] For my purposes, Wagner provided a useful and gripping fantasy to Hitler without necessarily determining all his programs. A devotee from 1923 when he saw a performance of *Rienzi*, after his rise to the chancellorship in 1933, Hitler began sponsoring the Bayreuth festival, and under the directorship of Heinz Tietjen it expanded in scope to an official state event. Throughout the 1930s, international and Jewish conductors and performers were maneuvered out (or boycotted it) to make it a more exclusively German event. By the eve of the war, the festival saw itself as a nationalist teaching tool; its 1938 handbook states:

> Wagner's work teaches us hardness in the figure of Lohengrin … [T]hrough Hans Sachs, it teaches us … to honour all things German … . In *The Ring of the Nibelungs* it brings to our consciousness with unexampled clarity the terrible seriousness of the racial problem … [I]n *Parsifal*, it shows us that the only religion Germans can embrace is that of struggle towards a life made divine.[27]

When the war began in 1938 and the National Socialist Party was radicalized, the festival was functionalized even further: "It became the Führer's gift to audiences of convalescent soldiers, deserving munitions workers, nurses and others" (Grunberger, 412). Karl Ritter's wartime film, *Stukas*, tells the story of a shell-shocked pilot who is told by doctors that he needs a profound experience to bring him back to health. He goes to Bayreuth and is miraculously cured during the march from *Siegfried* (386). *Stukas* sanctifies Wagner's *Siegfried* as a cultural relic, whose "profundity" reinvigorates and cures even the most war-worn.

The choice of *Siegfried* for this sanctification is significant; in it Wagner's revolutionary artistry and Hitler's need to mythologize "the terrible seriousness of the racial problem" can march hand in hand. In *Siegfried*, Mime emblematizes Wagner's low opinion of nineteenth-century artists who timidly solder together pieces of past traditions into sterile reproductions.[28] The dwarf becomes a failed artist who can't forge a sword strong enough for Siegfried to wield. Conversely, Siegfried's reforging of Nothung dramatizes Wagner's conception of radical artistic creation: fearless, heedless of past forms, and ruthless. Siegfried begins by filing the fragments of his dead father's sword down to a powder so that he can see them "zersponnen … in Spähne" [spun into splinters] before melting them down completely and beating them out anew. This beating ["fegen"] is soon transferred to the body of Mime himself (*Wagner's Ring*, 206 n. 88). Just after Siegfried kills the dragon Fafnir and emerges from the hoard with the fatal ring on his finger, he hears a bird singing that Mime intends to kill him and steal both ring and hoard. A taste of the dragon's blood has given him the power to understand not only birds but also the thoughts of those who speak to him, and he questions Mime as to his intentions. In a gruesome and hilarious duet, Mime fawns upon his victorious hero-child, but what Siegfried hears is his plot to drug Siegfried and then murder him. Mime then offers Siegfried a drugged victory cup. Without a moment's hesitation, Siegfried kills him with Nothung, drags his body contemptuously onto the hoard he coveted, and never expresses any regret. He thus completes the demolition of his father's sword with the murder of his foster father.

This callous sacrifice of the old to the emergent is antithetical to Tolkien, both ethically and aesthetically.[29] Tolkien's writing, as Shippey argues, works to recover and imaginatively to reanimate past traditions, lost words, gap-ridden stories; it doesn't want to grind them down into splinters but wants to cherish the crippled fragments, and it justifies itself as it labors to represent them "in [their] true light" (J. R. R. Tolkien, *Letters*, 55; Shippey, *Road*, 26–50).[30] Thus, in *The Hobbit*, Tolkien rewrites the moment of Siegfried's murder of Mime, but he significantly alters the outcome. Just after Bilbo puts on the Ring for the first time, he, like Siegfried, is faced by a scrabbling, deceptive, dwarflike creature who wants the Ring and is willing to kill him to get it: Gollum. Bilbo is invisible and could easily dispatch Gollum with his sword, Sting, and he has a material reason to do so: Gollum is squatting across Bilbo's only escape route from the caverns. But Bilbo, unlike Siegfried, hesitates:

> Bilbo almost stopped breathing … . He was desperate. He must get away, out of this horrible darkness, while he had any strength left. He must fight. He must stab the foul thing, put its eyes out, kill it. It meant to kill him. No, not a fair fight. He was invisible now. Gollum had no sword. Gollum had not actually threatened to kill him, or tried to yet. And he was miserable, alone, lost. A sudden understanding, a pity mixed with horror, welled up in Bilbo's heart: a glimpse of endless unmarked days without light or hope of betterment, hard stone, cold fish, sneaking and whispering. All these thoughts passed in the flash of a second. He trembled. And then quite suddenly in another flash … he leaped.
>
> (*H*, 97)

The free indirect discourse investigates the difficulty of this decision. At first, like Siegfried, Bilbo feels repulsion for "the foul thing" and would genuinely like to kill and "put its eyes out." But a sense of fair play prevents him, and there isn't yet admissible evidence for Gollum's intentions. Then Bilbo is struck by "a sudden understanding" which leads not just to pity but to real compassion as he feels his way into the misery of Gollum's existence. Finally he leaps, not just over the lurking Gollum, but over the whole vicious Siegfriedian, Rosenbergian Nazi mindset that finds it more self-justifying to kill an enemy it views as threatening and contemptible than to try to understand him.

The Hobbit was written down from 1931 to 1937, but this scene was added in its 1947 revision in the light of developments in *The Lord of the Rings* – and, arguably, of World War II and the horrendous revelations that followed it.[31] Both the *Hobbit*-revision and *The Lord of the Rings* make this moment of pity pivotal to the design of Tolkien's Ring cycle. At the beginning of *The Lord of the Rings*, Gandalf tells Frodo Gollum's story and Frodo exclaims that Bilbo should have stabbed the vile creature while he had the chance. Gandalf gives him a significant glare and warns him that Bilbo's pity "may rule the fates of many – yours not least" (*FR*, 69). Later, when Frodo meets Gollum himself, he replays Bilbo's dilemma and attains the same sympathy. The repeated sparing of Gollum will eventually save Frodo's quest; Gollum will destroy the Ring, not Frodo.

By making this pity so significant, Tolkien negotiates the ethical dilemma that Wagner's devotees must still negotiate: how can one separate enjoyment of the complex artistic diagetic world from the political and cultural uses to which its power may be put. Can Wagner's *Ring* be experienced in quite the same way when we know that Hitler fantasized about Wagner, altered his hairstyle to evoke a picture of Wotan (Housden, 145), and spent his last days in his bunker fondling Wagner's precious holograph scores (later lost in the assault); that at the very end he scripted a Wagnerian love-death for himself? He and Eva Braun married and the next day committed joint suicide listening to *Gotterdämmerung*, and within a few hours radios throughout Germany were broadcasting Siegfried's funeral march (Köhler, 6–23). In short, can the work of art remain innocent in itself though cursed in its uses? This question beset Tolkien's writing throughout his life, but it is not until *The Lord of the Rings*, written between 1938 and 1949, that he fleshed out a negative answer.

Renouncing the Ring and returning to history

There is much to enjoy in Middle-earth: its polyglot diversity, its unexplored distances, its intoxicating sense of belatedness – all produced by the enticingly gap-ridden layering of mythological and narrative texts into which Tolkien poured his time and scholarly skills.[32] But amidst all this richness, the Ring hangs, empty, symbolic, and magical. In itself it is a mere form, or Form itself, abstracted from context, content, and narrative and refined to a blank tyranny.[33] From its first appearance when Tolkien had no idea what it would become, even stolid Bilbo is provoked to wonder, "What have I got in my pocket?" The Ring engenders the last riddle Bilbo asks Gollum, which Gollum couldn't guess – a true riddle after all, which Tolkien spent fifteen hundred pages explicating. It begs for narrative explanation, and that is precisely what it produces. Alberich's ring begets gold; Tolkien's begets stories. That is what makes it precious.[34]

Tolkien didn't know what the Ring was until surprisingly late in the process of composition (Shippey, *Road*, 259). He selected it as the link between *The Hobbit* and "The New Hobbit," his projected sequel. He gave it a capital initial. In 1938 it was still "not very dangerous, when used for good purpose. But it exacts its penalty. You must lose either it, or *yourself*" (*Shadow*, 42; italics Tolkien's). That doesn't sound dangerous at all! But up through the third draft, Tolkien was still weighing other motives for the protagonist's quest: lust for more dragon's gold, wanderlust, looking for Bilbo; ring-longing was still an afterthought. By late 1938, it was the single ring that Sauron was still missing but not yet the master Ring (*Shadow*, 227). By its fifth rewrite it was speaking its mastery with letters of fire (in the one-ring incantation that Tolkien apparently composed in the bath). By 1941 it was more or less settled. But questions continue to be asked about it all through the finished narrative. What is this Ring – "a little ring, the least of rings … a trifle that Sauron fancies" (*FR*, 254) – that it should be so questioned? – at Bag End, at Bombadil's house, at Bree, and at the council of Elrond, where its eventual exhibition, tiny and trembling in Frodo's hand, seems oddly anticlimactic after the great mountain of lore that has prepared its spectators for the view. Boromir is impressed, but what does the reader think?

This contrast between empty form and burgeoning narrative is precisely the point. Tolkien's text associates the Ring with the imagination – in its etymological sense – when it grants expanded vision and insight. Merely carrying it around sharpens Frodo's perceptions of Galadriel and Boromir, and his wound from a Ring-wraith's knife allows him to see more keenly in the dark. More instrumentally, the Ring is a productive mystery, opening a space for the generation of story. Tolkien's early drafts show that formulating questions (or mysteries) and then pursuing them kept his writing going even at the microlevel and became part of a process of ongoing discovery. He doesn't come to dark conclusions easily. He will often create a moment of suspense only immediately and reassuringly to close it again. Then he'll reconsider, reopen the question, and find some portentous way of keeping the question open – and productive.[35] But the questions are gradually answered, and those answers are determinative. The emptiness of the Ring calls forth the narrative, and the gradual definition of the Ring entices it into form. The form the Ring gradually takes in *The Lord of the Rings* becomes Tolkien's darkest, though still not hopeless, investigation of the powers implicit in the creation of mythologies.

In the plot to renounce the Ring, Tolkien negotiates the National Socialist poisoning of the sources of his mythology. It is not surprising that Tolkien, although no Marxist, comes to the same conclusion that Walter Benjamin does at roughly the same time. If mythology was being used by the National Socialists as the antidote to the perceived ravages of history, a return to history could counteract mythology. In *The Origins of German Tragic Drama* (1936), Benjamin castigates the mythologizing of history in order to critique the idealism of German Romanticism while ideologues such as Rosenberg were appropriating it for National Socialist purposes. In Benjamin's study, if Romantic idealism mobilizes life-giving, organic, and (delusorily) immutable symbols, then it can be counteracted by allegory, which is entwined with history and fixated upon the symbol's fragility, slippage, arbitrariness, proliferation, and mortality. Performing the mortal contingencies of history can help subvert the shining, antihistoricist idealism of the self-proclaimed Thousand-Year Reich. Tolkien similarly takes the empty symbol of the Ring as a producer of story, and he demythologizes it into a tool of dominion, an empty allegory of the will to power that draws attention to its own emptiness as a symbol. What seems to be an equalizer for a bourgeois Hobbit hero (Shippey, *Road*, 51–86) and a giver of long life and perpetual youth is revealed to be an instrument of dominion and death.

To bring about this demystification, Tolkien works against dehistoricizing tendencies within both the National Socialist inheritors of German Romanticism (among them Rosenberg and Wagner) and the traditions of English Romanticism that so profoundly imbue his own writing. Recent critics have gone so far as to argue that the English Romantic imagination is founded on an evasion of history. In popular Romantic fantasies, the imagination is produced, set apart, and given an otherworldly power. As genius or the apprehension of sublimity, it mystifies its own historical production; as negative capability or the capacity for intimate sympathetic exchange, it professes the power to renovate the relationship between writer, nature, and the world, regenerating each in the process (Liu, 32–40).[36] In *The Lord of the Rings*, Tolkien counteracts this Romantic imagination's evasion of history by returning to it a history that admits its own structural (and restructuring) violence. He demystifies the imagination's brooding, anchorless, force as an "unfathered vapor" (in Wordsworth's phrase) by giving it a demonic father who openly uses his artistry to spy and dominate. *The Lord of the Rings* transforms alluring romantic demons into monsters. Imagination degenerates to appetite; powerful speculation, to malignant dominion.

This degeneration from art to power is suggested by the circumstances of the Ring's forging in the Second Age. Sauron, a demiurge of many masks, for the first and only time poses as an artist interested in cultural uplift – and art in his hands becomes the most intimate form of domination. He seduces the Elven-smiths of Eregion by appealing to their creative ambition (*Silm*, 287–88). In the version in *Unfinished Tales*, Sauron finds an especially willing student in Celebrimbor, who "desired in his heart to rival the skill and fame of Fëanor," his grandfather and the creator of the Silmarils (*UT*, 236). Sauron exploits the Elves' creative ambition to claim the panoptical power of a writer over them – he hopes to make them his characters, transparent and manipulable. Like Wagner forging a master-*Ring* that cannibalizes his Germanic sources, or like Hitler forging a vicious nation-state that instrumentalizes a Wagnerian fantasy, Sauron's consummate artistry destroys what it engages, an irreversible destructive supersession. The Elves do the only thing they can do. They snatch off their rings and never use them again as long as Sauron holds his master-Ring.

The link back to the Silmarils through Celebrimbor is significant. Tolkien's conception of the Silmarils evolved as gradually as his conception of the Ring, and it darkened similarly as it evolved (Shippey, *Road*, 259–60).[37] As Derek Brewer says, "Tolkien is never afraid of a cliche" (in Salu and Farrell, 258) – part of his power as a writer is to reinvigorate them – and Fëanor is almost a pastiche of a fiery romantic genius. His shaping of the Silmarils gestures at Tolkien's theory of subcreation and prefigures the idea of the Ring as the tyranny of form. Fëanor takes light from the two Trees that illuminate the world and locks it into three crystals; his masterpiece transforms a brilliant, natural, perishable substance into an immortal, irresistible, and ultimately deadly work of art. Succumbing to their allure, the demonic Melkor poisons the two Trees and, unbeknownst to Fëanor, steals the Silmarils as he flees. Fëanor is begged by the Valar to break his Silmarils and give back the borrowed light in hope that it might revive the Trees. Fëanor refuses: "It may be that I can unlock my jewels, but never again shall I make their like; and if I must break them, I shall break my heart" (*Silm*, 78). This transformation of artwork into heartwork dooms Fëanor. When he discovers Melkor's theft of the Silmarils, he vows a terrible vengeance, and the rest of *The Silmarillion* tells how he and his sons destroy themselves and virtually all of the Elven kingdoms in the process of getting them back. In the meanwhile, until Melkor is finally tossed into the outer darkness by the Valar, the holy jewels adorn his iron crown – an implacable rape of the hallowed by the demonic.

The eventual fate of the Silmarils is an object lesson in the corruptive pursuit of art. Fëanor's last living sons become so debased in their bloody recovery that the jewels burn their hands. In despair, Maedhros flings himself and his Silmaril into a chasm of fire (foreshadowing Gollum); Maglor casts his into the sea and wanders bereft and singing on the shore (foreshadowing the narrator of "The Sea-Bell"). The last Silmaril, stolen from Melkor's crown by Beren and Lúthien and bequeathed to Elwing and Ëarendil, becomes the evening star, a message both of loss and hope to Middle-earth, safe because it is untouchable. Similar degenerations of art preoccupy Tolkien's later work. Silmarils, Arkenstones, mithril, Rings – all come to stink of power, desire, and doom. The problem is they also provoke good stories; there's something delectable in the fear and longings they stir. It is not high and sublime. It is an appetite.

The Lord of the Rings brings that message home, deromanticizing Fëanor's fierce longing for his lost (he)artworks into Gollum's more homely greed.[38] Even Gollum's name is a spasmodic gulp, and by the time Frodo meets him, his single remaining delight is eating fish. This delight links him revealingly to a character from the *Völsunga saga* and Snorri Sturluson's *Prose Edda*: Otr. Otr is the middle brother of Fafnir the future dragon and Regin the smith who will rear Sigurd, urge him to kill Fafnir, and be killed by him. Hreidmar, a wealthy man, is their father. Otr spends his days in otter shape, catching fish, which he eats (with wonderful vividness) "alone with his eyes shut, because he could not stand seeing his food diminish" (Byock, 57).

In a brilliant gesture of corporeal demystification, the *Völsunga saga* places the self-enchanting fondness of Otr's greed at the heart of Fafnir's ring-crowned hoard; Otr's death and burial in the hoard instigates the curse of the ring and the whole ensuing tragedy. Hreidmar demands a large wergild for his son's death: to stuff Otr's skin with yellow gold and then cover it entirely with red gold. Loki steals Andvari's hoard including the ring, incurring Andvari's curse in the process. He returns with the hoard and Odin claims the ring for himself. They stuff the otter skin until it stands upright and then cover it with red gold, but when they are finished, one whisker is still protruding. Odin is forced to give up the ring to hide the whisker, thus sating Otr's now mythically expanded greed and dooming Hreidmar, Fafnir, Regin, and eventually Sigurd himself.

When Wagner adapts the incident, he gets rid of Otr and substitutes Freia, a goddess of love and immortality whose burial within Alberich's stolen hoard figuratively prostitutes her. Tolkien does something equally interesting; he transfers Otr's oral greed to Gollum, the ring's most craving seeker. He thus demystifies the lure of the ring from a Romantic urgency to a helpless creaturely hunger. Gollum's power fantasy wonderfully disenchants the sublimities of mastery:

> Perhaps we grow very strong … Lord Sméagol? Gollum the Great? *The* Gollum! Eat fish every day, three times a day, fresh from the sea. Most Precious Gollum! Must have it. We wants it, we wants it, we wants it!
>
> (*TT*, 241)

The longing for mastery thus darkens into addiction but also becomes more understandable and – it has to be said – terribly appealing.[39]

Attraction to the Ring is not Gollum's only defining hunger; he catches even more intimately at his author's writerly self-conception as a myth-creating philologist. Before Gollum was Gollum he was Sméagol, "the most inquisitive and curious minded" of his family, "interested in roots and beginnings … his head and his eyes were downwards" (*FR*, 51–52). "Sméagol" is derived from the

Anglo-Saxon *sméagan* (to scrutinize, investigate, penetrate, examine), and its adjectival form *sméah* (sagacious, sharp, crafty, subtle). When Gandalf reconstructs Gollum's origins, he discovers a significant darkness within the seemingly innocent name. Sméagol had a friend aptly enough named "Déagol" (Anglo-Saxon *diegol, digol* [secret, mystery, deep, profound]). In Anglo-Saxon writing *diegol* has a wide semantic range: from the mysteries of God to the dark viscosities of Grendel's mere, from the angelic to the demonic.

Déagol is the finder of the Ring – it belongs to mystery before it falls into the clutches of investigation. Tolkien's first idea was that Déagol should find the Ring at the roots of a riverside thorn tree, thus associating the Ring with roots and also with magic (thorn trees and magic are associated in Anglo-Saxon charms and in Kipling's *Puck of Pook's Hill*, where the leaf of the thorn tree is one of the three leaves for working an enchanted forgetfulness). It also recalls the Anglo-Saxon rune *thorn* (Þ), of which *The Rune Poem* sententiously cautions "anfeng ys yfyl" [grasping is evil/painful] (*Rune Poem*, l. 8, in Dobbie). This is a nice shadowy origin story complete with a hint of sorcery and warning against possessiveness (seizing). But Tolkien decides against this. The published version is less realistic and more inspirational. Déagol is fishing in a boat in the river (while Sméagol roots profitlessly about on the banks). Suddenly a great fish grabs his line and drags him to the bottom. There he sees something glinting in the mud, and grabbing blindly, he makes his way back to the surface. Washing away the river slime he finds the beautiful Ring in his hand. The fish who leads to treasure evokes one of the helping creatures in folktales or Jonah's fish who acts as the terrifying instrument of God. There is a sense of triumph – to bring up brilliance in a handful of mud – that would appeal to a philologist or historian sifting patiently through the detritus of ancient writing to come up with a single crucial connection. It is a much more heroic origin story and smacks of epiphany.

Sméagol murders Déagol for the Ring. This original murder of "mystery" by "investigation" makes deadly the need to search into visibility (imagine) what is lost or hidden. It moves toward the ravenous imagination that takes its darkest shape in the visible form of Sauron himself: condensed to a single devouring Eye and a grasping hand. Yet it is clear that this investigation of mystery drives Tolkien's own artistic production. Sméagol expresses the consuming curiosity about origins that Tolkien shares with many medieval scholars; the philologist incessantly searching for roots upon which to graft imaginative reconstructions (Ugolnik, "Wordhord," 15–31; Shippey, *Road*, 53). Glimpsing the distant splendor of the Misty Mountains, Gollum surmises that "the roots of those mountains must be roots indeed; there must be great secrets buried there which have not been discovered since the beginning." But when he "worm[s] his way like a maggot into the heart of the hills," revealing another etymological affiliation with A-S *smugan* [to creep through a hole] and thus a strange brotherhood to the dragon Smaug of *The Hobbit* [Shippey, *Road*, 82], he finds that "all the 'great secrets' under the mountain had turned out to be just empty night: there was nothing more to find out, nothing worth doing, only nasty furtive eating and resentful remembering" (*FR*, 53, 54). The Ring itself both catalyzes and signifies this disenchantment of curiosity into appetite, the artistic (or crafty [*sméah*]) investigation of mystery into its murder, and Sméagol into Gollum.

This is a cautionary transformation for any writer who harnesses the skills of philological inquiry to an appetite for fantastic production. It accomplishes more self-questioning disenchantment in one stroke than the tragic rape of the Silmarils does in several hundred pages. Yet Tolkien does not lose his sympathy for his Ring-devoured creature. Instead, Gollum becomes the most incessantly spared and forgiven creature in *The Lord of the Rings*. The narrative treasures Gollum, treats him like the precious creature he names himself, puts off discarding him, tracks his consumption to its bitter end along with Frodo's. Gollum's death with the Ring imagines a suicidal end not only for imaginative production but also for its ongoing scrutiny, the yoked team of fantasy and scholarship that drives Tolkien's continued investigation of the uses of the aesthetic. The pitying disavowal that ultimately makes Gollum's fortunate fall into the Cracks of Doom both inadvertent and self-inflicted is an act of faith (or individual despair) that the Ring can be given up at all.

Gollum thus plays out not only the vicious potential of the fantastic imagination but also the cruelty of its renunciation. For Tolkien to give up mythology would be tremendously difficult – even a poisoned mythological imagination was still precious in its origins and in the labor that had gone into it. Tolkien was profoundly invested in his own mythologies – and for many of the same reasons that Rosenberg was; they had both been galvanized by crisis and the traumas of World War I. Tolkien writes of the genesis of his own love of fantasy: "A real taste for fairy-stories was wakened by philology on the threshold of manhood, and quickened to full life by war" ("OFS," 42). He had begun inventing Middle-earth during his recovery from trench warfare at the Somme in World War I, and he had been nurturing a proliferating legendry from his own philological skill and a reimagination of medieval eddas and sagas since 1917. Even if these sources were "ruined, misapplied, perverted, and rendered forever accursed," it would be horrific to relinquish them.

But one pivotal scene makes it clear why it is crucial to do so. The most suggestive association of the Ring with imaginative vision comes aptly on the summit of Amon Hen (the Hill of the Eye). Frodo, as he looks out over the world, wearing the Ring, sees

> a world of mist in which there was only shadows: the Ring was upon him. Then here and there the mist gave way and he saw many visions: small and clear as if they were under his eyes upon a table, and yet remote. There was no sound, only bright living images.
>
> (*FR*, 416)

The Ring makes its wearer invisible and dematerializes the world into a pliant mist, but it also refines its wearer's vision: we see Frodo learning to see through the mist, drawing the whole of known Middle-earth into the compass of his gaze. This intimates the shaping power of the imagination as it turns chaos into world. The affect of this scene, however, banishes ambitions of world-mastery to the faintest biblical echo of Christ's temptation by Lucifer on the heights. For Frodo, this is a world not for the taking but rather in imminent danger of being occupied by someone else. Frodo's vision shows him the extent to which this little, clear, remote, table-top world – which lies like an open manuscript before him – is under siege:

> Everywhere he looked he saw the signs of war. The Misty Mountains were crawling like anthills: orcs were issuing out of a thousand holes … .The land of the Beornings was aflame … . Horsemen were galloping on the grass of Rohan; wolves poured from Isengard. From the havens of Harad ships of war put out to sea; and out of the East Men were moving endlessly: swordsmen, spearmen, bowmen upon horses, chariots of chieftains and laden wains … . Mount Doom was burning, and a great reek rising.
>
> (*FR*, 416–17)

This apocalyptic panorama is at once the text's widest vision of a world overrun by war and Frodo's closest encounter with Sauron. It is also a crux where the text works through the impacts of its own cultural moment. Alan Liu appositely suggests that such moments of apocalyptic imagination offer both an escape from and an incomparably intimate encounter with history:

> Apocalyptic imagination was that which suffered firsthand the most brutal facts of history and then dipped itself in the blood of those facts to etch the handwriting on the wall – the writing that says, "No, this should not be," by means of fantastic figurations saying, in essence, "No, this *is* not." That such figuration denies history is indisputable. But surely such denial is also the strongest kind of engagement with history.
>
> (Liu, 35)

Tolkien's introduction to *The Lord of the Rings* denies direct allegory and strives hermetically to seal his diagetic world into a "No, this *is* not" – and I actually trust those denials: Sauron does not "equal" Hitler; Frodo does not "equal" Tolkien – both figures are more extendable than that. But I think that the scene of near apocalypse on Amon Hen admits to the bright, remote world of Middle-earth an oblique engagement with contemporary history that becomes more gripping for its obliquity.

In this scene, the terrifying intimacy of this pressuring history becomes a call to action and resistance. As Frodo looks out over the world that undeniably evokes the widening sweep of a world war, his gaze is drawn to the center of occupation, the black tower of Barad-dûr, a distillation not just of Hitler's Germany but of all the inexorable forces of industrial depredation at work in the twentieth century, from before the Great War forward: "wall upon wall, battlement upon battlement, black, immeasurably strong, mountain of iron, gate of steel, tower of adamant … . All hope left him" (*FR*, 417). At that point he feels the searchlight sweep of Sauron's Eye, looking for him personally, stripping away his anonymity, and, worst of all, despite his denials, finding an answering assent in his heart: "Verily, I come, I come to you" (417). Frodo writhes between the pressure of Sauron's hunger and an acerbic countervoice (who later turns out to be Gandalf): "Take it off! Take it off! Fool, take it off! Take off the ring." Then in a moment of free will, he is aware of himself again: "Frodo, neither the Voice nor the Eye: free to choose and with one remaining instant in which to do so" (*FR*, 417). He takes off the Ring and from this moment pursues the road to Mordor with suicidal single-mindedness. Frodo thus transforms his whisper of compliance to Sauron into the means of his destruction: Frodo will come to Sauron but as an infiltrator, not a slave.

This scene rescues Frodo as an agent amidst terrible historical forces. It is not a rebirth of a self essentially free from these forces; it is not a version of Rosenberg's triumphal Nordic individualism. It doesn't deny determinative pressures and penetrations; rather they inform Frodo's choice as they drive him from within. Nonetheless, it pries open a tiny, valiant middle space between historical determinism and romantic subjectivism. The subsequent narrative is unflinching in showing that this tiny space left for agency will not be enough to save Frodo – the pressures are simply too great, and Frodo will succumb to the Ring and never recover from its loss.[40] But it will help in overthrowing Sauron. This space of choice wrested from the seething trauma of war becomes exemplary, implicating not only Tolkien and his own struggle with the poisoning of the imagination but Tolkien's readers and all who, in Gandalf's terms, live to see such times. Tolkien's *The Lord of the Rings* is thus not a reflection or allegory of the war but a responsive defiance against the war and against war-hypnotism wherever it might be found. The narrative not only registers but also strategizes against the impact of the National Socialist corruption of mythology, its state conscription of aesthetics, its deft manipulation of sublimity.

And it is alert to the costs of its own strategies. They are bespoken most immediately in Frodo, who after the Ring's destruction is left crippled and will-less, worn from without and eaten from within: a tiny image of collateral damage. But Frodo is only the beginning – Middle-earth itself fades from mythology to history. After the dizzying joy of the Ringbearers' recovery at Cormallen Fields, which brought Tolkien to the point of tears in 1949 when he finally reached it (Tolkien, *Letters*, 321), Middle-earth gradually succumbs to temporality, stills, grays, and etiolates.[41] We feel the force of Gollum's final long-ago riddle in *The Hobbit*: "This thing all things devours," of which the answer is Time. Every last-ditch immortality finally relinquishes its hold: Lorien fades; Rivendell is abandoned. After one celebratory summer, we seem to be perpetually in autumn. Companions are left behind; the Elves, who distill and incarnate the immortal aesthetic and creative aspects of humanity, pass away to the West. Any observer of the last conversations of Gandalf, Celeborn, Galadriel, and Elrond would have seen "grey figures, carved in stone, memorials of forgotten things now lost in unpeopled lands" (*RK*, 263). Finally, we are brought to the

Grey Havens, as wan a refuge as their name suggests. Frodo doesn't die; he goes west – but as the phrase suggests, it might as well be death. His healing will be possible only beyond the circles of the world in the last imaginary refuge, a glimmer of consolation that remains remote. Sam returns to the poignant embrace of family life and generation.

I don't know how I can convey the power of this ending; scholars seem to be coded at the genetic level for receptiveness (or its lack) to Tolkien. But I believe it partly comes from the intensity of *The Lord of the Ring*'s engagement with its own historic moment – which doesn't reduce the story or make it derivative but rather shows why it matters. It is a fantasy that wills its own disenchantment into history, a mythology that (unlike National Socialist visions of the Thousand-Year Reich or other nationalist mythologies) assents to its own mortality and agrees to fade.[42] Unlike Wagner, it refuses apocalypse, laboriously carves out history's costs, pressures, and fragile delights, drags its remaining fingers through the blood and brings itself in the end to write: *This shall be.*

How does one return to mythology after that? For several years Tolkien attacked the *Silmarillion* manuscripts with enormous energy, attempting to reenvision its entire framework as the tale of Morgoth's corruption of the creation-wide artwork of the world itself – "the whole of 'Middle-earth' was Morgoth's Ring" (*Morgoth's Ring*, 400) – a tremendous task which seemed to grow larger at every turn. He involved himself in maneuvers to get *The Silmarillion* and *The Lord of the Rings* published together – like one long narrative journey – but *The Silmarillion* manuscripts were neither in good order nor consistent with their sequel. Tolkien was unsuccessful in playing Collins against Allen & Unwin, and so *The Lord of the Rings* was issued alone. Afterwards, revision of the many competing, inconsistent, experimental narratives of *The Silmarillion* to a single authoritative version may have seemed like a step backwards in more ways than one – though he spent a lot of time expanding the annals, genealogies, cartographies, and etymologies of his fourteen invented languages; in other words, his revisions often accentuate historical divergence and accidence rather than mythological unity.

Eighteen years went by between the publication of *The Lord of the Rings* and Tolkien's death, and while he managed to produce some long-expected scholarly projects, his capacity to bring his longer literary projects to completion seemed short-circuited. He started a sequel, "The New Shadow," but soon abandoned it; after the destruction of the greater demons of the *Ring*, Aragorn's regime "would contain no tales worth recounting" (J. R. R. Tolkien, *Letters*, 419). The valedictory *Smith of Wootton Major* is the only work of literature Tolkien completed subsequently, and it nostalgically glances through Tolkien's central themes from a graceful distance (Helms, *Tolkien's World*, 118–25). However, no mastery is possible in Smith's Faery; the landscape is too surreal, projectional, and expansive even for its attempt, and Smith gives up his imaginative star with a melancholy sense both of benison and defeat. In a 1967 letter to Roger Lancelyn Green (who reviewed it), Tolkien himself describes *Smith* as "an old man's book, already weighted with the presage of 'bereavement'" (*Letters*, 388). Humphrey Carpenter, Tolkien's excellent biographer, writes of Tolkien's awareness during his last years of "a perpetual discontinuity, a breaking of threads in his work which delayed achievement and frustrated him more and more" (Carpenter, *Biography*, 240). In a letter dated a month before his death, Tolkien thanks a generous reader, Lord Halsbury, for the warmth of his appreciation and the offer of his future help with manuscripts, writing of his own seeming inability to finish, "Over and above all the afflictions and obstacles I have endured since *The Lord of the Rings* came out, I have lost confidence" (*Letters*, 431). This may have paradoxically resulted from his dazzling success and his depression at his cult status. But I think also that Tolkien's war-driven, self-questioning investigation of the uses of mythology had brought him to a point with no energy to move forward and yet had worn away at the enabling presuppositions for going back.

But Tolkien did not disavow his own mythological labors just because he could not finish them. For the rest of his life he treated Middle-earth not as an allegorization of twentieth-century events but as a key to them – applying his characters' names to historical developments with gusto in letters and interviews. Subsequent readers have followed suit; Tolkien's characters exemplify recognizable tendencies and character types that are still around us. We could see Adolf Hitler as the silver-tongued Saruman, spellbinding a country with his speeches, but we could also choose to hear echoes of Winston Churchill or even George W. Bush. So used, the fantasy world bleeds into the external world in a way that is wonderfully undetermined and provocative. Its fantastic sprawl becomes shapely and exemplary, and the world of history with which it grapples becomes the strangest, shiftiest, most fantastic and mysterious world of all.

When his wife, Edith Bratt Tolkien, died in 1971, Tolkien had a name from his *Silmarillion* mythologies carved upon her tombstone: Lúthien, the intrepid Elf who gave up immortality to wed the mortal Beren. Together they steal a Silmaril from Morgoth's crown and, even though they die for it, their love provides one of the few bright interludes in *The Silmarillion*'s ever-darkening mythology. When Tolkien himself died two years later, he instructed that the name "Beren" be written upon his own stone. This could be read in a number of ways: a final wishful rift between fantasy and history, a delusion of heroic significance, an act of faith in the immortality of his bond to his wife throughout their sometimes troubled marriage and beyond death. But as a self-chosen appellation, "Beren" has an additional resonance. Foreshadowing the crippled and nine-fingered Frodo, Beren had lost his right hand. It was bitten off by Morgoth's devouring wolf as Beren waved the Silmaril before it in defiance. Given *The Lord of the Ring*'s exploration of the costly ethics of renunciation, its willingness to question creativity to the point of disablement, it seems fitting that Tolkien should claim the mantel of a hero maimed as he defied a ravening wolf with his half-rescued Silmaril.

Notes

1 The famous tower metaphor in "*Beowulf*: The Monsters and the Critics" is one instance, while *Smith of Wootton Major* began as the introduction to a new edition of George MacDonald's *The Golden Key*. Tolkien often showed up at meetings at which he was expected to present an essay only to read a poem or story instead.

2 Mary Faraci's contribution to this volume (chapter 5) was initially presented at the Thirty-sixth International Congress on Medieval Studies, Kalamazoo, MI, May 2001.

3 Recent scholars have suggested other profitable ways to historicize Tolkien. T. A. Shippey's exemplary study, *The Road to Middle-earth*, draws him down from the pedestal of fantasy *ex nihilo* (or out of its ghetto) by linking him to other British writers of the postwar period such as George Orwell, William Golding, and T. H. White (Shippey, *Road*, 288). Sebastian D. G. Knowles historicizes "Leaf By Niggle" as a war text that enables Tolkien to write *The Lord of the Rings* (132–41). Brian Rosebury also convincingly situates Tolkien within twentieth-century literary history, linking him to the lost generation of World War I writers but also showing his affinities with modernism and its critical aftermaths (133–52). Lee D. Rossi attributes "a literature of political despair" to both C. S. Lewis and Tolkien but he exonerates their pessimism granted the difficulty of the historical problems with which they were faced (1–6, 89–134).

4 There are, of course, other useful directions to take myth in Tolkien. Anne C. Petty delineates a Lévi-Straussian structural anthropological "mythic impulse" at work in Tolkien in *One Ring to Bind Them All*; both Helms and Kocher sensitively read the Christian mythic structures and oppositions within Tolkien's work in, respectively, *Tolkien's World* and *Master of Middle-earth*.

5 Randel Helms carefully delineates the aesthetic principles that distinguish Middle-earth in *Tolkien's World*, 76–108.

6 Stuart Sillars gives Tolkien a single dismissive citation as a popularizer of one of the symbolic reflexes of twentieth-century British Romanticism ("unity with the natural world" [150]), but I think Tolkien is actually much closer to the center of Sillars's definition of this group's defining concerns, which include nature as a refuge from industrialism and a questioning of the uses of creativity in the modern world.

7 Daniel Hughes shows how Tolkien grapples with neoclassical and romantic theories of art; he outlines the different romanticist influences in Tolkien's fantastic writing, from Blake's mechanistic Urizen to Coleridge's linking of the imagination and the will in the *Biographia Literaria* (81–96).

8 About which Walter Benjamin was writing in 1936.

9 The most vivid example is Gimli's longing to garden the unfolding recesses of the Glittering Caves.

10 "On Fairy-Stories" makes this link between fantasy-production and desire very clear: "Fairy-stories were plainly not primarily concerned with possibility but with desirability. If they awakened *desire*, satisfying it while often whetting it unbearably, they succeeded" ("OFS," in *Monsters*, 40).

11 Jane Chance explores the centrality of monsters to Tolkien's writing in *Tolkien's Art*.

12 Helms reads it persuasively as staging the conflict between pursuit of art and duty to community (*Tolkien's World*, 109–18).

13 In letters Tolkien inveighed against the anti-German prejudice endemic in English radio broadcasts and printed media, noting the same genocidal inflections at home as abroad, especially as the prospect of victory brightened (*Letters*, 93).

14 An arresting instance is Galadriel's terrifying vision of herself as the beautiful Lady of the Ring culminating in "All shall love me and despair!"

15 Tolkien's respect for particular Jews and Jewish cultures emerges sharply in his private letters: *Letters*, 37–38 (1938), 67 (1944), 394–95 and 410 (1971) (where he considers the possible Jewish ancestry of the source of Sam Gamgee's name).

16 I am citing from the excerpts of *Myth* translated and collected in *Race and Race History*, which anthologizes a broad range of Rosenberg's writings

17 It is easy to see why H. P. Lovecraft, with his visions of invasive, tentacled, chthonic chaos, found Rosenberg so very gripping.

18 Verlyn Flieger beautifully contextualized Tolkien's address to fantasy's philological, anthropological, and racialist scholarly antecedents in her address at the Thirty-sixth International Congress on Medieval Studies, Kalamazoo, MI, May 2001.

19 Many readers are, in fact, quite critical of the fascism implicit in Tolkien's creation of "good" and "bad" races (divisions he complicates), his fantasizing of historical transcendence (they don't see the critical questioning that accompanies it), and even his use of light and dark imagery (which he also complicates deliberately – Aragorn's standard is mostly black; Saruman's is white, etc.). Robert Plank addresses these issues cogently and ends with a provocative speculation about Tolkien's address to the twentieth-century growth of fascism: "Tolkien's View of Fascism," in Lobdell, *Tolkien Compass*, 107–15. Jane Chance's *Mythology of Power* contextualizes *The Lord of the Ring*'s appeal to 1960s' counterculture, and outlines how Tolkien systematically undercuts fascist, authoritarian, and normalizing ideologies of power in favor of the gradual evolution of democratic mutual respect, service, and humility. For a contesting view of Tolkien's appeal as an antirevolutionary, escapist "safe trip" for 1960s' adolescents, see Walmsley, "Tolkien and the 60s," in Giddings, 73–86. I'm delighted to point out from twenty years later that Walmsley's report that Tolkien had his moment and then died a not undeserved cultural death has been exaggerated.

20 Ruth Noel discusses Tolkien's very different usages of ancient and medieval mythological texts in *Mythology of Middle-earth.*

21 Tolkien's own longing to create an English nationalist mythography is discussed at length in Jane (Nitzsche) Chance's study of Christian and medieval sources and influences in *Tolkien's Art.* More briefly, in *Road* (268–72) Shippey urges a distinction between nationalism and patriotism, making Tolkien a patriot rather than a nationalist. However, I think that Tolkien's construction of Englishness in his characterization of the Shire is to be distinguished from Hitler's Nordic nationalism, chiefly by its self-positioning as always already tiny, precarious, and half-lost. It emerges in the shadow of a destruction so inexorable that nothing could recover it – neither a triumphant political, cultural, and military nationalist program (which would destroy it further as Saruman shows) nor a past-sanctifying politics of heritage. The Red Book that Frodo bequeaths to Sam ends in blank pages open to subsequent narration. We are continually reminded that the Shire is a part of Middle-earth and that the parochialism of Hobbits is both delusory and idiotic. An open-bordered country, an open-ended history book, and a need to open the minds of parochial inhabitants to the larger world they inhabit – all offer interesting resistances to traditional nationalisms. I am grateful to Frank Grady for the trenchant questioning that prodded me toward this reading.

22 Elizabeth Magee outlined the scope of Wagner's problem in trying to reduce this mass of sources into a gripping narrative form:

> From north to south across the spectrum he found versions of events which tallied nowhere except for Siegfried slaying the dragon, winning a hoard and marrying Gunther's sister … . What was Wagner to make of a hero who appears now as valiant champion, now as superman, now as a kinsman of Dennis the Menace and Desperate Dan?
>
> (Magee, "In Pursuit of the Purely Human," in Wagner, 29–32; also Gutman, 35, 43, 62, 121–22, 159–60)

23 Over its twenty-five-year gestation, Wagner revised the text in the light of every philosophy he found elucidating in his progress from revolutionary republican to tragic renunciate: socialist, Romanticist, anarchist, utopian, Hegelian, Proudhonian, and Feuerbachian – all bound together with (but not quite synthesized through) a massive dose of Schopenhauer (Roger Hollinrake, "Epiphany and Apocalypse in the Ring," in Wagner, 41–47).

24 Martyn Housden makes the most systematic and documentary case for Hitler as revolutionary; John Lukacs sees him as imaginatively combining conservative and utopian impulses (76–112).

25 He came to dislike it later, when critics persisted in likening his Ring to Wagner's or to the Nibelungen ring in Wagner's medieval sources. An acerbic letter complains about his Swedish translator's wheeling and dealing in Nibelungen lore; he attacks not only the translator's assumption about the Ring's derivation but also his scholarly expertise (*Letters*, 306–7).

26 Joachim Köhler recently went so far as to reduce Hitler to a self-deluding instrument of the obsessive, anti-Semitic, failed-revolutionary, Wagnerian vision. Even aside from essentializing Wagner's self-conflicted and disparate corpus to an internally coherent program and giving him a sinister posthumous agency mediated unproblematically through his Bayreuth descendants, this reading seems a little romantic (even Wagnerian) in itself.

27 Cited in Grunberger, 412; Köhler discusses how, as early as 1925, the festival approvingly forecast Hitler's rise to power (191–94).

28 In Wagner's medieval sources, Mimir or Regin forges the sword instead of Siegfried (367 n. 11).

29 This is one of Wagner's inconsistent moments – he retains Siegfried's revolutionary triumph even after he comes to a darker recognition of the futility of any real break with the past.

30 This imaginative search for a lost past engendered by a fragment or ruin is another place where Tolkien connects powerfully with English Romanticism. This gesture of recreation from loss can be as underhandedly innovative as Wagner himself, but in centralizing the gap between past and present rather than hastening to smooth it over with powerful continuities, it defines itself very differently. Its movement is toward heritage, a tragic investment in the lostness of history even as it works toward the past's reanimation.

31 Bonniejean Christensen compares initial and revised versions of "Riddles in the Dark" to argue that Tolkien systematically deepened the nastiness of Gollum's character – which makes Bilbo's restraint more dramatic (9–28).

32 Rosebury beautifully discusses the "meticulously depicted expansiveness" (9) of Middle-earth as a sensuously effective aesthetic strength (7–53); his argument counters Christine Brook-Rose's frustration at the hypertrophic realism and redundancy she sees as weighing down the narrative (233–55).

33 I am grateful to my colleague Colin Jager for suggesting this reading.

34 It's also why Hobbits, immured in the everyday and the pragmatic, are relatively immune to the Ring, while Elves, Dwarves, Men, and Wizards, all endowed with stirring powers of inquiry and craft, don't dare touch it or are quickly consumed if they do.

35 One example (of many) is the first appearance of the Black Rider, which could be paraphrased thus: "Who is this Black Rider who just rode up out of nowhere? Oh, just Gandalf being dramatic. Wait, no. We don't know who he is. *Or should that be* what *he is*?" (J. R. R. Tolkien, *Shadow*, 47–48).

36 Alan Liu's excellent study, *Wordsworth: The Sense of History*, is the most powerful statement of this thesis (32–40). I am oversimplifying Liu's discussion and turning it inside out by foregrounding the imagination rather than nature and history.

37 Randel Helms explores *The Silmarillion*'s Christian and theological contexts in *Tolkien and the Silmarils*; Clyde Kilby gives a revealing account of its author's attitude toward it and struggles with it in *Tolkien and the Silmarillion*.

38 Tolkien's 1952 recording of the Gollum passages from *The Hobbit* should not be missed. In a letter to his publisher, he boasts with justice that "I do a very pretty Gollum" (*Letters*, 164).

39 Shippey discusses it as the modern trope of addiction in *Road* (126–27) and at greater length in *J. R. R. Tolkien: Author of the Century.*

40 In a letter to a reviewer, Tolkien links Frodo's situation – subjected to pressures beyond his resistence – to "sacrificial situations" possible throughout history but becoming more common during and after the wars:

> I did not foresee that before the tale was published we should enter a dark age in which the technique of torture and disruption of personality would rival that of Mordor and the Ring and present us with the practical problem of honest men of good will broken down into apostates and traitors.
>
> (*Letters*, 234)

41 Verlyn Flieger eloquently discusses Tolkien's experiments in temporality in *Question of Time.*

42 It thereby follows the example of Galadriel, a character who dramatizes with particular intensity Tolkien's incessant attempts to wrest an innocence from the urge toward creative mastery – the making of eternal realms within the world as bastions against historical senescence and change. In successive versions she is variously (1) implicated in Fëanor's exile but not guilty of blood-letting, (2) stained by ambitions toward dominion (which she dramatically relinquishes in *The Lord of the Rings*), and (3) wholly innocent of anything but the bad timing with which she abandons Valinor. When Galadriel finally relinquishes Middle-earth, the reverberations of her surrender adumbrate Tolkien's own final concession to history in the narrative.

Part II

J. R. R. Tolkien's *The Lord of the Rings* and medieval literary and mythological texts/contexts

7 Tolkien's Wild Men

From medieval to modern

Verlyn Flieger

The form and subject matter of J. R. R. Tolkien's major fiction clearly derive from the medieval genres of epic, romance, and fairy tale. This said, it should also be noted that Tolkien puts a modern spin on many of his characters, reconfiguring the contexts and situations in which they play a part while at the same time keeping faith with the medieval types from which they derive. Of the many elements that make his work both classic and unclassifiable and energize his stories with a life of their own, this must be counted not the least important. His medieval roots are plain to see – from the surface texture of costume, custom, battle-gear, and speech to the deeper borrowings of theme and pattern from *Beowulf*, Malory, and the *Gawain* poet. His modernity of treatment is less clearly obvious, largely because it is so seamlessly integrated into the medieval structure.

One of the areas in which his medievalism and his modernism join most fruitfully is in his handling of one of the less-imitated medieval character types – the Wild Man. A familiar figure in the literature and folklore of the Middle Ages, he was called *wudu-wása* in Anglo-Saxon, *wodwos* in Middle English, *sylvestre* in Old French. His proper title is Wild Man of the Woods. A refugee from civilization, he is a prowler lurking both actually and metaphorically on the borders of society. His home is the forest, the wilderness outside the boundaries set by civilization. The word *forest* apparently originates from the Latin *foris,* meaning "outside" (Saunders, 1). The Wild Man is the archetypal outsider, the prowler on the borderlands between the wild and tame, exiled either by his fellow men or by his own misanthropy. The prototype is Enkidu, the hairy buddy of the eponymous hero in the Babylonian epic of *Gilgamesh,* or perhaps Nebuchadnezzar of biblical fame, crawling on all fours, gnawing grass and letting his fingernails grow. But these are only the precursors of a whole crew of medieval manlike monsters from the Grendel of *Beowulf* to Glamr, the walking dead terror of *Grettissaga.*

In his book *Wild Men in the Middle Ages*, Richard Bernheimer gives a general description of the type. The Wild Man is

> a hairy man curiously compounded of human and animal traits, without, however, sinking to the level of an ape. It exhibits upon its naked human

> anatomy a growth of fur, leaving bare only its face, feet, and hands … . Frequently the creature is shown wielding a heavy club or mace, or the trunk of a tree; and since its body is usually naked except for a shaggy covering, it may hide its nudity under a strand of twisted foliage worn around the loins.
>
> (Bernheimer, 1)

Bernheimer elaborates this picture with phrases culled from European folklore: "Huge, hairy, and mute," "so large that his legs alone have the size of trees," "a creature of woods and rocks" (113–14). He observes that, "[t]he creature itself may appear without its fur, its club, or its loin ornament. Any one of its characteristics may be said to designate the species" (2). The type, then, is a convention, and as Bernheimer notes, individual specimens vary.

A representative example might be the Wild Man in Chrétien de Troyes's *Yvain* who appears to Calogrenant, a knight of Arthur's court, near the opening of the poem. Riding through the wood of Broceliande in search of adventure, Calogrenant comes upon a prototypical specimen. First, he is huge.

> si vi qu'il ot grosse la teste
> plus que roncins ne autre beste,
> chevox mechiez et front pelé
> s'ot pres de deus espanz de lé.
>
> [I saw his head's size was enormous,
> a huger head than any horse's
> or other beasts, with tufts of hair.
> His forehead was completely bare
> and measured more than two spans wide.]

He is also a sort of cross between flora,

> oroilles mossues st granz
> autiex com a uns olifanz,
> [a huge ear filled with mossy plants,
> just like the ears of elephants]

and fauna:

> les sorcix granz et le vis plat
> ialz de çete, et nes de chat,
> boche fandue come lous,
> dans de sengler aguz et rous
> [His brows were full, his face was flat,
> with owlish eyes, the nose of a cat.
> His wolfish mouth was split apart
> by wild boar's teeth, bloodred and sharp.]

He is hairy,

> Barbe rosse, grenons tortiz,
> [His beard was red; his whiskers in
> great knots]

and misshapen:

> Et le manton aers au piz,
> longue eschine torte et boçu;
> [His chest merged with his chin.
> His long spine twisted in a hump.]

He carries a club,

> Apoiez fu sor sa maçu
> [The creature sat upon the stump and leaned upon his club]

and dresses in skins:

> qu'il n'avoit ne lin ne lange,
> einz ot a son col atachiez
> deus cuirs de novel escorchiez,
> ou de deus tors ou de deus bués.
> [He wore
> no wool or linen clothing, for
> instead the fellow was arrayed
> in two wild bulls' hides, newly flayed.]

Calogranant ends his quasi-comic description by reiterating the Wild Man's size:

> Et fuz montez desor un tronc,
> S'ot bien dis et set piez de lonc;
> [He leaned against a fallen tree,
> and then I realized that he
> was seventeen feet tall, at least.]
> (Lines 291–320; Cline trans., lines 271–99)

And yet when Calogrenant asked him what he was, the creature replied, "qu'il ert uns hom" [that he was a man] (line 328).

An equally conventional, but considerably briefer, appearance of the Wild Man occurs in *Sir Gawain and the Green Knight*, where the *wodwos* harry the bewildered Sir Gawain as he rides through the winter forest on the way to his meeting with the Green Knight.

> Sumwhyle with wormeȝ he warreȝ, and with wolves als,
> Sumwhyle wyth wodwos, þat woned in þe knarreȝ.
> (Tolkien and Gordon, 23)

[At whiles with worms he wars, and with wolves also,
at whiles with wood-trolls that wandered in the crags.]
(*Sir Gawain and the Green Knight, Pearl, and Sir Orfeo*, 43)

The paradigm is roomy enough to hold a number of variations from the Grendels and Glamrs, bestial or uncanny but clearly related to humanity, to the outright shape-changers, the were-beasts who can assume either human or animal form and whose animal shape is most often that of wolf or bear. Best known, perhaps, are the Norse hero Sigmund and his son Sinfjotli from *Völsunga saga*, who, when they find and put on wolf skins to hunt in, are trapped in the wolf shape, and come close to killing one another before they get free. Such werewolf stories abounded in the Middle Ages and seem to be equally popular today, if Stephen King is anything to go by.

Another example is the battle-mad berserkers, whose reputation is explicit in their name, derived from "bear-sark," or "bear-shirt." The exemplar here is Böðvar Bjarki of *Hrolfs Saga Kraka*, whose *fylgja*, or "fetch," appears and fights as a bear while Böðvar sleeps. But such man-beasts were not always seen as men transformed into beasts; they could be beasts elevated above ordinary humanity. The Celtic horned god Cernnunnos is of this type, a supernatural figure, man-shaped but with the antlers of a stag. All these testify to the fearsomely close connection between human and animal that haunted the pagan mind and that the Christian church worked so hard to eradicate.

A more refined use of the Wild Man figure supplies us with a psychological variation on the type. Neither the medieval version of the missing link that Bernheimer describes nor the were-beast of myth and legend, this Wild Man is simply a man with what we would now call a severe personality disorder. The psychological Wild Man is not born wild but has wildness thrust upon him by some shock or trauma that produces bizarre but usually temporary aberrant behavior. One example of this type is the Merlin of Geoffrey of Monmouth's *Life of Merlin*. When his brothers are killed in battle, Merlin goes mad, forsakes civilization, and runs wild in the woods with only the beasts for company. A better known example is Sir Thomas Malory's Lancelot, who falls into a similar madness, but for a slightly different reason – he too has lost a loved one, Queen Guinevere, who in a jealous rage has banished him from her sight. He first swoons and then runs mad.

> And whan Sir Launcelot awooke oute of hys swoghe, he lepte oute at a bay-wyndow into a gardyne, and there wyth thornys he was all to-cracched of his vysage and hys body, and so he ranne furth he knew nat whothir, and was as wylde [woode] as ever was man. And so he ran two yere, and never had man grace to know hym.
>
> (Malory, 487)

Lancelot and his malady exemplified one of the most popular literary treatments of the Wild Man, a malady to which medieval lovers were particularly susceptible, and to which Malory's Tristram and Chrétien's Yvain also succumbed. Indeed Richard Bernheimer describes this madness as almost an "occupational disease of knight-errantry," explaining that,

> When they believe they have been slighted in love, these warriors have a way of breaking all bonds, sometimes stripping themselves naked, and invariably repairing to the woods, expressing their sadness and degradation by leading the life of the wild man.
>
> (Bernheimer, 14)

Yet another variation on the conventional Wild Man type is the medieval outlaw, the masterless man. As his name implies, the outlaw is on the run from society not because of his primitive nature or as the result of a psychotic break but because of some legal transgression. He too is a prowler on the borderlands, a lurker in the woods. His avoidance of society is no irrational aberration but a quite reasonable fear of the law. At its best this outlaw type is personified in Robin Hood, living merrily in the greenwood and occasionally drawing a bow against some stuffy bureaucrat.

But this is rare. In life, which tends to be scruffier than literature, the outlaw type shows up in England as the brushwood men, in France as the Jacquerie, escaped serfs with nothing to lose, desperate men living wild because they could not risk a return to civilization. By those more fortunate, wealthier, and on the right side of the law, they were seen as very low on the scale of humanity, hardly better than the standard Wild Man. A fourteenth-century tale, *Le Despit au Vilain*, says of them, "They are a sorry lot. Should they eat meat? Rather should they chew grass on the heath and go naked on all fours" – phrases which make the comparison plain (Joly, 461, quoted in Tuchman, 175). In all his guises, then, the Wild Man was to the Middle Ages just what he is to the twentieth century – an ever-present threat to our thin veneer of socialized behavior, the image of what we fear, of what we all might become.

Like their medieval counterparts, Tolkien's Wild Men come in all varieties. He has forest trolls, wood-elves, outlaws, and shape-changers, all of whom fit more or less comfortably into the general category. His first attempt at taking the convention and updating it may be Beorn, the man-bear of *The Hobbit.* Beorn is described as "a huge man with thick black beard and hair, and great bare arms and legs with knotted muscles. He was clothed in a tunic of wool down to his knees and was leaning on a large axe" (*H*, 128). He towers above Gandalf, and the Hobbit Bilbo "could easily have trotted through his legs without ducking his head" (128). So far, though he is certainly better dressed, he closely approximates the Wild Man of Bernheimer's description, including the massive legs and the weapon. But Beorn is a modern version, friendly, hospitable, fully capable of speech, and possessed of a house, farm animals, and a sense of humor. He is a twentieth-century children's Wild Man, hearty and jolly and not really frightening, just mysterious. True, he seems to be a shape-changer, and it is strongly implied that he has a habit of occasionally turning into a bear. Nevertheless, he is never actually seen as a bear, and the character and the episode in which he figures are treated with disarming jocularity.

A more typically medieval Wild Man is Ghân-Buri-Ghân, one of the aboriginal Drúadan, who makes a cameo appearance late in *The Lord of the Rings*. In that civilized society he is seen by the other characters as a leftover, a prehistoric figure surviving in a modern world, a "remnant," as one of them says, "of an older time … wild and wary as the beasts" (*RK*, 105). Viewing Ghân-Buri-Ghân from the darkness outside Theoden's tent, Merry Brandybuck is reminded of the Pukelmen, the primitive stone figures he saw on the road to Dunharrow. Borrowing straight from the Gawain poet, Tolkien calls him a "Wose," and glosses this in the text as "Wild [Man] of the Woods" (105).

Ghân-Buri-Ghân is "a strange squat shape of a man, gnarled as an old stone," with the "hairs of his scanty beard" straggling "on his lumpy chin like old moss." He is "short-legged and fat-armed, thick and stumpy, and clad only with grass about his waist" (105–6), all of which brings him pretty close to the standard type of Bernheimer's description. Still, though Tolkien clearly wanted to give the standard Wild Man a place in his pseudo-medieval world of Middle-earth, this one, too, is not wholly typical. Like Beorn, he also talks, though his dialogue sounds like that of a Hollywood Tarzan: "Wild Men live here before Stone-houses," "fight not," "kill orc-folk," "we help" (106). For another thing, he is not a menace but a good guy, guiding the Men of Rohan to Gondor for the battle and asking no reward except to be left alone.

Tolkien's more complex versions of the figure exceed the convention by their lengthier treatment and fuller development as characters. I will offer three and a half examples. My first example is an unlikely one: Strider, the guide and rescuer of the Hobbits who becomes Aragorn, the uncrowned king. As one of the two major heroes of *The Lord of the Rings*, Strider seems an odd candidate for Wild Man status. But a close look shows that he has the requisite characteristics to fit him into the outlaw type. He is first introduced to Frodo and the reader as a figure both actually and metaphorically on the edge of society, sitting alone in the corner of the common-room at Bree among "vague figures difficult to make out in the shadows and corners" (*FR*, 167). Thus introduced, he is made to seem just one among many strangers, men on the move, "squint-eyed, ill-favoured" types. "One of the wandering folk – Rangers we call them," says Butterbur the innkeeper (168), and it is clear that the word "ranger" carries its own suspicion, suggesting someone too much at home in the wild, living rough and sleeping out, not like civilized folk who live in houses.

Others have the same opinion. "That's Stick-at-nought-Strider," Bill Ferny tells the Hobbits, "though I've heard other names not so pretty" (193). Even after the Hobbits meet and talk with him, Strider seems too tough-looking a character for their Shire-bound sensibilities to accept. Frodo suspects uneasily that he has "fallen in with a rascal" and reflects with considerable anxiety that he has very little money with him. "All of it would hardly satisfy a rogue," he thinks, and moreover "he could not spare any of it" (175). He clearly expects that such a suspicious-looking character must be a robber of the highway variety. Sam's opinion is no better. "He comes out of the Wild," says Sam, "and I never heard no good of such folk" (178). With grim humor Strider consciously plays up this side of himself. "I have a rather rascally look, have I not?" he asks the Hobbits, with a "queer gleam in his eye" (177).

It seems clear that our first view of Strider is intended as a deliberately negative picture of the outlaw or brushwood Wild Man. Tolkien has purposely presented him in the worst light in order to make his transformation all the more effective when he is subsequently revealed, first, as a kind of Robin Hood figure – from the greenwood, not the brushwood – and then, as the noble Aragorn, the crownless who shall be king. Tolkien is playing variations on the medieval variation itself and playing mind-games with the reader as he does it. He takes Strider from rascal to forest ranger to king, progressively peeling away the layers that have concealed his identity until we see this Wild Man as in some ways the most civilized man in the book – certainly the one with the longest lineage, the most distinguished heritage, and the most brilliant future.

The next example is Túrin Turambar, the hapless protagonist of one of the most poignant episodes in Tolkien's mythology, "The Tale of the Children of Húrin." As a character, Túrin is based on Kullervo, an equally hapless character from the Finnish *Kalevala*, which Tolkien much admired. Kullervo is a mixture of outcast and misanthrope, and Túrin is another. Both are orphaned; both are social misfits. Their energies cannot be harnessed to civilized pursuits, and their affinities are with the wild rather than with the human world. Both exist on the fringe of society, always solitary, always on the outside looking in. In the line of Tolkienian Wild Men, Túrin is a greater mix of types than Strider, combining outlaw and psychological Wild Man. Tolkien's modernity comes into play here, and Túrin is presented as a civilized man paving his own road to self-destruction and betrayed at last by his own wrong-headedness. Thus the character is more sympathetic, his story more tragic because he is the architect of his own defeat.

What gives Túrin a special poignance as a Wild Man is that his tragedy need not have happened. What he becomes makes us constantly aware of how different he might have been. Tolkien has made Túrin a paradigm of modern alienation, a self-exiled outsider driven by emotions he does not understand, willful and conflicted, coming to painful self-awareness only at the end of his life. Moreover, Tolkien supplies a greater than medieval range of causes for his Wild Man behavior. For example Túrin, like Merlin or Lancelot or Tristram, suffers attacks of madness, but these come not from loss of relatives or from disappointment in love but from shock and horror at his betrayal of those who love him. When he discovers the death of Finduilas, the Elf-maiden whose unrequited love for him has led her to her death, he swoons, and when he finds that he has unknowingly killed Beleg, his best friend, he becomes truly mad, catatonic. He suffers loss of speech and memory, and must be led about by others while his madness lasts.

Also extra-medieval is Túrin's habitual appearance, although it too supports his Wild Man identity, for he is in a sense "hairy," that is, unshaven, untrimmed, and uncombed. But unlike his medieval counterpart, this is not from natural inclination but rather because he is a guerrilla warrior with little opportunity to attend to his appearance, to shave or get his hair cut. Though his foster-father, Thingol, offers him a place among his knights, Túrin chooses "the north-marches" (*march* = "borderland") and walks "far and wide in the wild woods" (*UT*, 79). There he cares "no longer for his looks or his attire, but his hair [is] unkempt, and his mail covered with a grey cloak stained with the weather" (79). Coming into Thingol's hall one day from the wild, unkempt and with ragged garments, he is taunted by a jealous Elf, Saeros, who with ironic solicitude offers him a comb for the "thicket of brambles" that is his hair, describes him as "wild and fell," and explicitly calls him a "woodwose" (80). In revenge, Túrin ambushes Saeros, strips him naked, and chases him through the woods to his accidental death.

This incident provides yet another aspect that links Túrin with the Wild Man: nakedness. But again, the motif is reworked, and the context changed. Instead of being himself naked, he imposes nakedness on someone else, in revenge for his insults turning Saeros into a kind of inadvertent Wild Man running naked in the wild wood. But the episode has other Wild Man repercussions, for it is this incident that sends Túrin into the woods for good, so to speak. He flees to the forest at first out of fear of apprehension, but stays out of stubbornness and wounded pride. Tolkien has made Túrin's affinity for the wild at once practical, psychological, and archetypal. He chooses the forest over Thingol's hall first, as refuge and, then, because he cannot bring himself to be judged, or to sue for a pardon he feels he does not need. It is a conscious choice, a clearly rhetorical gesture, intended as a reproach to those he leaves behind. Both the act of choosing and the choice of venue recall the meaning for "forest" cited earlier, "outside." Feeling himself an outsider, alienated, Túrin has made metaphor into fact and put himself beyond the pale.

A telling clue to Túrin's psychological Wild Man status comes with his most exasperating and revealing quirk. He keeps changing his name as if he had no real sense of self, taking on a succession of abstract identities, each of which is a marker of his alienation from himself and the world around him. After the naked-chasing episode, convinced that his motives have been misconstrued, he calls himself Neithan, "the Wronged." Refusing to apologize or explain, he exiles himself to the woods and joins a band of outlaws, themselves recognizable Wild Man types. But these outlaws are not Robin Hoods. They are true brushwood men, thieves, and rascals, and Túrin finally leaves them in disgust.

Once more on the side of right, given a chance to reform himself, he takes the battle-name Gorthol, "Dread Helm," thus dehumanizing his own and everyone else's view of him. When by tragic accident he kills Beleg Strongbow, his best friend, he again takes a new name, calling himself Agarwaen son of Umarth, "Bloodstained, son of Ill-fate." Next he takes the name Mormegil, the "Black Sword," another dehumanization. Most telling of all, when asked his name he says only, "I am Wildman of the Woods" (*UT*, 110). If that does not make it clear, nothing will. It is Tolkien' s gift, however, that he makes us see this Wild Man as all too human and therefore tragic, as a real Wild Man could never be. Treating a medieval character with twentieth-century psychological insight, Tolkien shows us in Túrin an existential man, creating meaning out of his own perception, searching for his identity, yet unwilling to accept it.

My next example is the most complex and both the most and the least typical. It is, as may be guessed, Gollum, Tolkien's most brilliant creation, a medieval Wild Hobbit with distinctly modern overtones. Gollum is an amalgam of all the types. Readers of *The Lord of the Rings* first encounter him offstage, so to speak, described to Frodo by Gandalf as being "of Hobbit-kind; akin to the fathers of the fathers of the Stoors" (*FR*, 62). He is thus an aboriginal. He is the murderer of his friend Déagol, the original finder of the Ring, and is thus an outlaw, shunned by his relatives, expelled from his family, and driven into the wild. We are told that

> He wandered in loneliness, weeping a little for the hardness of the world, and he journeyed up the River, till he came to a stream that flowed down from the mountains, and he went that way. He caught fish in deep pools with invisible fingers and ate them raw . . . . So he journeyed by night up into the highlands, and he found a little cave out of which the dark stream ran, and he wormed his way like a maggot into the heart of the hills, and vanished out of all knowledge.
>
> (*FR*, 63)

Like the conventional medieval Wild Man, Gollum becomes a degenerate, feral figure, constantly associated with animal images. But Gollum's animals are from the bottom of the evolutionary scale. The passage quoted above compares him to a maggot. Other animal images include spider, squirrel, and frog. At his first appearance, crawling down the cliff-face of the Emyn Muil, he is repeatedly referred to as "it," as if he had no humanity. He is "a small black shape" whose "clinging hands and toes were finding crevices and holds that no hobbit could ever have seen or used, but it looked as if it was just creeping down on sticky pads, like some large prowling thing of insect-kind" (*TT*, 219). Like an animal, Gollum goes on all fours. Like an animal's, his eyes gleam green when caught in the light. Like an animal, he is naked. Nowhere in the narrative is there any mention of clothing, as if, like a real animal, he does not need to be provided with covering.

Gollum is also psychotic, driven mad by his obsession with the Ring. It is just here, however, that Tolkien's modernity takes over, for Gollum's madness is distinctly of the twentieth century rather than of the Middle Ages. Gollum's split into the dual personae that Sam calls Slinker and Stinker is a psychological division into conflicting, even opposing selves, the kind of division that the Middle Ages regularly treated allegorically, often personifying the split as Soul and Body. In Tolkien's hands it becomes a paradigm of the twentieth century, the age of anxiety. More than just a psychological Wild Man in the Merlin–Lancelot tradition, Gollum is a case study, a textbook example of what the popular psychoanalytic terminology of the mid-twentieth century called a split or multiple personality, a schizophrenic.

Gollum hears voices, and is haunted by their demands. Not only does he talk to himself, but his two voices/selves are in deep conflict with one another. In addition, his madness has skidded him backwards down the developmental scale. Where the conventional Wild Man is evolutionarily regressive, slipping from a civilized town-dweller or court habitué to a hunter-gatherer, Gollum is psychologically regressive. He is infantile. Ghân-Buri-Ghân talks like a Hollywood Tarzan. Gollum talks baby-talk: "Nice little hobbitses … they jumps on us like cats on poor mices … cruel little hobbitses" (221). And like the brushwood men he is a refugee from civilization, indeed, it is his experience as a fugitive that qualifies him as a guide for Sam and Frodo on their way to Mordor.

But I promised three and a half examples. My half example, part of Gollum and yet separate from him, is Tolkien's most modern, most moving depiction of the Wild Man. It is, of course, the least likely Wild Man in the book – Frodo Baggins. When we see Gollum and Frodo side by side, day after day, we see also the potential Gollum in Frodo as well as his struggle against being wholly taken over by the madness that has wasted and destroyed that lost creature. As the narrative progresses, the two characters move nearer to one another. One by one, Gollum's Wild Man characteristics are transferred, albeit sometimes only momentarily, to Frodo.

First he is stripped of his clothes. In the Tower of Cirith Ungol Sam finds him lying naked on a heap of filthy rags. Then he is temporarily reclothed, which should make him more human but instead makes him more animal-like, for like Calogrenant's Wild Man he is clothed in orc garments of animal skin, "long hairy breeches of some unclean beast-fell" (*RK*, 189). Finally, on Mt. Doom, too weak to stand erect, he is reduced to crawling up the mountain on his hands and knees like an animal. And at the last, as they go up Mt. Doom, Frodo's nakedness becomes symbolic, a metaphor for his loss of self: "I am naked in the dark," he tells Sam, "and there is no veil between me and the wheel of fire" (215).

The reference to the wheel of fire – the Ring – is the final evidence of another Wild Man characteristic, madness, the madness that has been growing on Frodo since the Ring came into his possession. Though its visits are fitful, it increasingly takes possession of him, altering his behavior and lessening his humanity. Approaching the Tower of Minas Morgul, Frodo feels "his senses reeling and his mind darkening. Then suddenly, as if some force were at work other than his own will, he began to hurry, tottering forward, his groping hands held out, his head lolling from side to side" (*TT*, 313).

It is an ugly picture of a creature bereft of rational mind, and both Sam and Gollum have to run after him and turn him around to bring him to his senses. When Sam finds Frodo in the Tower of Cirith Ungol, his confession that he has the Ring and his offer to carry it cause Frodo to turn on him like a maddened beast. Later, on the slopes of Mt. Doom, when Sam again offers to carry the Ring, Frodo tells him with sad self-knowledge, "If you tried to take it I should go mad" (*RK*, 214). At that moment he is sane, for self-knowledge is sanity. In the ensuing moments he loses that self-knowledge, and then he does go truly mad. He is mad when, having come to Mt. Doom to destroy the Ring, he instead puts it on and claims it as his own. At that moment he becomes the most possible, the most persuasive, the most modern of all Tolkien's Wild Men – the madman who thinks he is sane, who has had self-knowledge and has lost it.

In medieval literature the Wild Man is a stock character, sometimes a figure of fear, sometimes a figure of fun – as with Calogrenant's Wild Man – sometimes a figure of sympathy, as is the case with Merlin and Lancelot. But he is not often a figure who shows us something of ourselves, something essential, pitiable, and typical of the human condition. In Gollum and Frodo, and in Túrin as well, Tolkien has made the medieval Wild Man into a figure at once medieval, modern, and timeless.

8 The valkyrie reflex in J. R. R. Tolkien's *The Lord of the Rings*

Galadriel, Shelob, Éowyn, and Arwen

Leslie A. Donovan

Since the first publication of *The Lord of the Rings* in 1954–55, many readers have considered the paucity of female characters in J. R. R. Tolkien's trilogy not only a disappointment but also a serious flaw in his work. Edith L. Crowe sums up this response when she writes, "The most problematic aspect of Tolkien is indeed the disappointingly low percentage of females that appear in his best-known and best-loved works, *The Hobbit* and *The Lord of the Rings*" (272). Other critics interpret the lack of women in *The Lord of the Rings* as indicative of weak technical craft or a latent misogyny[1] in Tolkien's character. An early writer, Catherine Stimpson, states such a position with her criticism that Tolkien's women are built on "the most hackneyed of stereotypes" (*J. R. R. Tolkien*, 18). More recently, Patrick Curry notes *The Lord of the Rings* would be "seriously impoverished" without its women characters, but he concedes that Tolkien's presentation of women represents a "paternalism if not patriarchy [that is] unmissable" (127). In contrast, attempting to justify Tolkien's portrayals of women, scholars like Crowe insist "he was only reflecting his sources and his times" (272). Those with similar perspectives argue that, as women played central roles in few medieval texts, it would have been inappropriate for Tolkien's modern reweaving of traditional materials to emphasize or substantially expand female roles. Such scholars reason that, since most of Tolkien's life predated advances in contemporary women studies and gender theory, his works cannot be expected to reflect feminist approaches in women characters.

Focusing on the significance of Tolkien's existing women characters rather than their infrequency, Helen Armstrong, however, asserts that "Despite the conventionally, even doctrinally, male-centred aspects of Tolkien's world, he also bucked that same system … by creating active heroines" (250). In accord with such views, Lisa Hopkins writes that "Power in the works of Tolkien is often to be found in the hands of a woman" and that "women in Tolkien are not portrayed solely in the light of their relationships to men" (365). Although Crowe admits readings of Tolkien as a "hidden feminist" are untenable, she contends "Tolkien exhibits attitudes toward power that are quite compatible with, if not identical to, the attitudes of many who define themselves as feminists" (272). Studies from similar feminist perspectives perceive that Tolkien's

> small number of women have a range of parts to play whose importance is remarkably disproportionate to their numbers. Their very scarcity seems to invest them with an air of uniqueness and of almost talismanic status, and in some cases their very femininity … is in Tolkien the very source of their strength.
>
> (Hopkins, 365)

Seeking to support readings of Tolkien's women as strong, authoritative characters with pivotal narrative importance, some writers situate Tolkien's works within the contexts of classical epics, Christian typology, psychological archetypes, or contemporary gender constructs. For example, Mac Fenwick has found echoes of Homer's Circe and Calypso in Tolkien's Galadriel and parallels between Shelob and Homer's Sirens, Scylla, and Charybdis. As evocative as such classical connections are, by limiting his only study to these two diametrically opposite female characters, Fenwick cannot account for the motif throughout Tolkien's trilogy of women as empowered forces. In addition, although convincing analogies may be made between Galadriel and the Virgin Mary,[2] such applications of Christian typology hold little promise for explaining the authority of other women in Tolkien's trilogy. Peter Goselin uses Jung's mythic archetypes to describe the polar relationship between Tolkien's women characters as a manifestation of the female anima, but again uses only Galadriel and Shelob to exemplify this dimension of women's power in the trilogy. Other studies analyze the ways in which Tolkien's women operate within a larger gender construct of masculine and feminine principles. From this viewpoint, Melanie Rawls explains that

> his Feminine Principle is not the negative of the Masculine Principle, but is another kind of being, equal yet other, in stature and power. This diversity adds dimension and complexity to his characters, as they dance the dance of complementarity.
>
> (Rawls, "The Feminine Principle," 13)

Yet, valuable as these examinations are for comprehending the variety of resources, allusions, and narrative functions of women in Tolkien's works, their discussions are peripheral to Tolkien's primary interests and goals, and none explore fully the multiply rendered features of women's power within Tolkien's most famous work, *The Lord of the Rings*. The extraordinary strength of women characters in the trilogy can be explained, however, within a context of specific relevance to Tolkien's background – that of the medieval Germanic heroic literatures that played such a crucial role in Tolkien's personal and professional consciousness.[3] Despite Tolkien's own frequently recorded distaste for scholarship seeking to identify the original sources for later works,[4] not only Tolkien's women characters but all his Middle-earth fiction has its heritage in the literature and culture of the Middle Ages. Many studies have acknowledged with C. W. Sullivan that Tolkien's "traditionally patterned narrative" may be better understood "not through the lenses of modern critical methods but through lenses developed for the study of earlier works" (11). Confirming such views, Evans writes that Tolkien's Middle-earth fiction reflects "a dependence upon medieval developments of the motif and narrative type that preserves and highlights aspects of the tradition and at the same time extends them" ("Dragon-lore," 22), and Marjorie Burns summarizes the medieval origins that enrich the texture of Tolkien's narratives by stating that "Behind every setting and every character in J. R. R. Tolkien's writings on Middle-earth, lies a history of literary, mythological, and linguistic complexity" (219).

Beyond such general acknowledgments of the medieval backgrounds for Tolkien's work is a recognition of his particular debt to medieval Germanic texts. While it would misrepresent Tolkien's accomplishments to speak of texts from the Old Norse, Old Icelandic, and Anglo-Saxon cultures as direct sources for *The Lord of the Rings*, few scholars deny that literary resonances from such cultures infuse Tolkien's trilogy. As is well attested by his professional scholarship as well as by his personal letters, Tolkien possessed an abiding appreciation for medieval literature from northern Europe. Early in the history of Tolkien scholarship, Charles Moorman even went so far as to assert that "The greatest single influence upon Tolkien's work is the eddas and the sagas of the North" (212), a statement echoed by Lynn Bryce's later remark that "Throughout his life works of Old Norse continued to have a profound appeal to Tolkien's imagination" (113). Even when arguing Tolkien's debt to classical literature, Fenwick acknowledges the validity of an earlier statement by Auden when he admits "There can be no denying that for Tolkien North was indeed a sacred direction and that the bulk of his imaginative enterprise is based upon a lifetime's intimate acquaintance with the literature of the ancient North" (17). Attesting specifically to the relevance of Old Norse material to Tolkien's literary aesthetic, T. A. Shippey identifies a Germanic "combination of pride, ferocity and sadness" as a "note that Tolkien often aimed at" in his works on Middle-earth ("Tolkien's Sources," 155). More recently, Gloriana St. Clair has commented:

> The concept of fate in Northern works, the need for courage, a conception of evil, the tragedy of mortality, the doom of immortals, and the paradox of defeat are themes common to Northern literature and *The Lord of the Rings*.
>
> (St. Clair, "Overview," 66)

The cumulative voice of such scholarship confidently asserts Tolkien's legacy to medieval Germanic traditions, especially those of Old Norse and Old English literature. None of these studies, however, offers detailed scrutiny of the female analogues in medieval Germanic literatures that serve as likely patterns for Tolkien's strong women characters.[5] In particular, as independent individuals, personally responsible and socially empowered to affect change on a global scope, Tolkien's primary women characters in *The Lord of the Rings* – Galadriel, Shelob, Éowyn, and Arwen[6] – are narrative agents charged with the authority of distinct heroic women figures from Old Norse mythology and literature called the valkyries.[7]

In their varying emphasis on the themes of light, prophecy, physical prowess, self-sacrifice, cultural leadership, unwavering will, public ceremony as a binding commitment, and the support of a chosen hero, the heroically rendered characterizations of Galadriel, Éowyn, and Arwen partake of the conventions common to medieval valkyrie figures.[8] Through valkyrie-associated imagery, these women function as emblems for the often conflicting Germanic motifs of grievous loss and glorious fulfillment, individual will and community responsibility, determined constancy and unlooked-for revitalization so central to Tolkien's fictional vision. Providing a contrast to these positive figures, Shelob's dark inversion of such themes punctuates their epic significance. As relief images carved from heroic tableaux featuring Germanic valkyries, Galadriel, Shelob, Éowyn, and Arwen stand out from the narrative's background as more than secondary, incidental literary figures. In them, Tolkien seeks his own contemporary response to medieval traditions by establishing his valkyrie-indebted women as elemental forces whose presence in the trilogy allows the possibility of human and heroic completion. For example, unlike medieval valkyrie counterparts such as Sigrún and Sváva, Arwen's choice of mortality results not in Aragorn's tragic death but in a life lived with her beloved. Similarly, Éowyn realizes a full human potential that joins both her masculine and feminine selves, which was impossible for other valkyrie antecedents such as Brynhild and Hervör.

Yet, the valkyrie-associated figures of Wealhtheow, Sváva, Sigrdrífa, Brynhild, and Hervör that so peopled Tolkien's imagination are not simply plucked from the pages of medieval manuscripts and inserted whole into *The Lord of the Rings*. Rather, as with all the medieval sources from which he drew material for his secondary world fiction, Tolkien reshapes the valkyrie tradition to suit his own purposes and the needs of his culture. Specifically, the heroically situated Galadriel, Éowyn, and Arwen are built from those valkyrie characteristics that held the most potency for Tolkien's Christian, post-World War II, prefeminist vision of modern epic. By eliminating from his primary women figures the concept common in valkyrie typology of the female inciter and her accompanying vengeance for kin or personal insult,[9] Tolkien constructs them as reflective of moral good, heroic ideals, noble behavior, and responsible leadership by means of a female identity concordant with contemporary perceptions of women as significant forces within society and the world. Although admittedly idealized, his construction of strong women characters results most likely from Tolkien's personal admiration of women such as his mother and his wife, Edith, as well as the historical climate of his times. After World War II, the professional, religious, and societal cultures to which Tolkien belonged both continued to emphasize traditional roles for women while simultaneously recognizing the possibilities of new familial models, employment opportunities, and social as well as political importance for them. Like medieval valkyrie figures, it was more socially possible for post-World War II women to maintain independent identities without sacrificing their expected cultural validity, a concept the morally conservative but broad-thinking Tolkien may have found attractive.

Other women in *The Lord of the Rings* occasionally behave in ways suggestive of the medieval valkyrie tradition, but their valkyrie associations are less developed than those of Galadriel, Shelob, Éowyn, and Arwen. For example, Goldberry is a shining, radiant, otherworldly figure who serves food and drink, but she exhibits no ceremonial function, no loss of a central element of her life, and no martial abilities. Ioreth speaks words that indicate foresight or a prophetic knowledge of events, but her words, inherited from oral tradition and gossip, never suggest the character herself has prescient abilities. In her independent personality and her willingness to strike a physical blow for her people near the end of the trilogy, Lobelia Sackville-Baggins may be valkyrie-like but her greediness and covetousness early in the texts are not common valkyrie traits. Although Rosie Cotton's teasing of Sam may be vaguely reminiscent of the inciter functions of medieval valkyrie figures,[10] her wholesome ordinariness has no relationship to Odin's battle goddesses. Appropriately, it is not in the rural setting of these Hobbits, in the urban city-dwellers of Minas Tirith, or in the spirits of nature's woodlands that the valkyrie figure finds her place in Tolkien's work. Instead, Tolkien situates his version of the valkyrie figure in Middle-earth's heroic sphere, where battles and legends, prophecies and heritage, nobility and courage lead to difficult, even painful, choices, with large-scale consequences for the future.

Belied by their apparent marginality in Tolkien's text, the significance of Galadriel, Shelob, Éowyn, and Arwen resides primarily in the heroic choices each makes based on the necessities that drive their valkyrie-associated wills. The individual wills of valkyries are conceptually equivalent to the mode of desire frequently discussed in contemporary feminist and gender theory,[11] in that the choices they make determine the fate of both the women characters themselves and their world's history. Evocative of a similar process by which the wills of Tolkien's women influence events in *The Lord of the Rings*, but in the context of women's actions in Old English literature, Gillian Overing writes

> we see how marginal desire, whether this is monstrous, feminine, or even heroic, continually intrudes upon and deflects the progress of dominant desire … [by presenting] us with a polyphony of voices, an interplay of desires, which contribute to its [the text's] restless complexity and dynamic irresolution.
>
> (Overing, 220)

Tolkien's Galadriel, Shelob, Éowyn, and Arwen are characters whose words and actions in *The Lord of the Rings* provide a similar polyphony of motives that shift the plot's course of events as well as the reader's expectations of an appropriate outcome.

Galadriel, Shelob, Éowyn, and Arwen partake of the same Germanic or northern themes found throughout the larger trilogy by means of character traits patterned on standardized, stereotypical attributes of benevolent valkyrie figures such as Wealhtheow, Sváva, Brynhild, Sigrún, and Hervör. These characteristics commonly include: (1) divine or semidivine origins or ancestry; (2) noble social status; (3) superior wisdom, intellect, or acumen; and (4) exceeding beauty. As many women in early literature and mythology possess these same qualities, it is no surprise that in *The Lord of the Rings* Tolkien incorporates these conventions into his portrayals of Galadriel, Éowyn, and Arwen. However, other attributes specifically connoting valkyrie traditions offer greater significance for Tolkien's women characters. The dominant valkyrie-specific traits of women in heroic settings relevant to *The Lord of the Rings* are that such figures (1) exhibit an otherworldly radiance, sometimes associated with the glittering shine of armor or with the fractured illumination linked to battle fires; (2) possess physical prowess equaling or exceeding that of male heroes; (3) serve ceremonial functions within the hall such as ritual cup-bearing at official occasions, gift-giving to heroes, and sewing or preserving special heroic garments, which challenge heroes to fulfill their destinies; (4) perform prophetic acts or engage in other speech acts that determine some future fate; (5) choose actions based on the operation of their own strong wills; and (6) undergo the loss of something central and precious to their lives. Illustrated by Shelob in *The Lord of the Rings*, the obverse valkyrie aspect, which incorporates many of these same characteristics in a negative chroma, is typified by baleful, vengeful, destructive female figures such as Grendel's mother in the Old English *Beowulf* and Hrímgerth in the Old Norse *Helgi Lays*.

The word "valkyrie" comes from the Old Norse *valkyrja*, meaning "battle-determiner" or "chooser of the slain." It refers to a semidivine female figure whose pagan religious associations derive from her position as a battle maiden under Odin's command. Like the *dísir*, other closely allied Old Norse female figures, the valkyries are characterized as "armed, powerful, priestly. They function as arrangers of destinies and intermediaries between men and the deity" (Damico, "Valkyrie Reflex," 176). Jenny Jochens describes the traditional mythological function of the valkyries when she writes:

> At Óðinn's bidding they select the men who are destined to fall in battle and they reward victory to the survivors. As such they form an important link between the divine and the human world. Having withdrawn the heroes from human life, the valkyries continue to look after them in the divine world, where they serve them drink.
>
> (Jochens, 39)

In heroic Germanic poetry, some valkyrie women also form compelling relationships with male heroes that alter the course of events in the human world. Helen Damico explains the authority to establish such relationships resides in the valkyrie's

> acts of choosing the hero in battle, of laying upon him the task that will shape his heroic identity, of investing him with an unwearying, heroic energy that will secure victory in battle, and then, if necessary, of accompanying him to the afterlife.
>
> (Damico, "*Beowulf*"'*s Wealhtheow*, 67)

Further, through her archetypal interaction with warriors slain in battle, "The valkyrie offers death, embodies contact with death; her semi-religious, priestess function gives her tremendous power as the repository of men's fears and ambivalence" (Overing, 229).

In Old Norse literature, valkyrie figures are commonly presented in two distinct aspects, either as "fierce, elemental beings," who sometimes "require sacrificial appeasement," or as "benevolent guardians," who serve the hero in "the court as well as the battlefield" (Damico, "Valkyrie Reflex," 176–77). The grim, malevolent aspect of the valkyrie is generally considered a remnant of an earlier mythic conception, while the benevolent figure is considered a development of later Germanic mythology and literature. Although the Old English term *wælcyrge*, linguistically equivalent to Old Norse *valkyrja*, appears consistently only in references to "creatures who are malevolent, destructive, corrupt, and associated with slaughter" (Damico, "Valkyrie Reflex," 177), Anglo-Saxon writers tended to depict women in heroic texts using conventions associated with both benevolent and malevolent Old Norse valkyrie figures. In his seminal article "*Beowulf*: The Monsters and the Critics," Tolkien expresses his acute awareness of such parallels between Old Norse and Old English literary practices when he remarks on the "fundamentally similar heroic temper of ancient England and Scandinavia" (25). A product of this common Germanic legacy shared by Anglo-Saxon and medieval Scandinavian peoples, this valkyrie reflex[12] allows benevolent Old English women characters, such as *Beowulf*'s Wealhtheow, Judith, and Juliana, to be considered valkyrie-indebted figures. Just so, through their inherited associations with valkyrie traditions, Tolkien's women take their models from these same heroic Germanic women. Whether his presentations of Galadriel, Shelob, Éowyn, and Arwen are based on his direct response to valkyrie figures in Old Norse literature, to the valkyrie reflex he recognizes in portrayals of women in Old English literature, or to a combination of these, is irrelevant. What is relevant for the purposes of this study is that Tolkien's women inherit valkyrie-like characteristics carrying medieval cultural connotations, which Tolkien adapts to the modern heroic, cultural, and moral attitudes promoted in his texts.

Like the valkyrie-associated Wealhtheow in *Beowulf*, Tolkien's Galadriel is "the ideal queen, [who] reigns over a hall resplendent with light" (Damico, "*Beowulf*"*'s Wealhtheow*, 9). Galadriel rules her Elven environment with similar composure and resplendence, enhanced by allusions to light and radiance common in valkyrie imagery. Constantly referenced by terms connoting radiant or shining qualities, Galadriel's name itself means "lady of light" in Tolkien's invented Sindarin language.[13] Although her radiance is not derived from the metallic brightness of armor, arm-rings, or necklaces typical in the portrayals of Old English and Old Norse valkyrie figures, Galadriel's external brilliance is described in terms related to a general heightened intensity of color, especially the whiteness of her dress, her shining eyes, her fair physical features, and her blonde hair. The first time we see Galadriel, she is "clad wholly in white" (*FR*, 369), echoed later by "clad in simple white" (*FR*, 381). At the close of the trilogy,

Galadriel appears "robed all in glimmering white, like clouds about the Moon" (*RK*, 308). Throughout his descriptions of Galadriel, Tolkien uses the term "white" to suggest the illuminative qualities of starlight, moonlight, and sunlight so strongly associated with her character. Further associating the Elven queen with visual intensity, Tolkien consistently identifies Galadriel as "tall and white and fair" (*FR*, 376) and later as simply "tall and white" (488). Whether these references refer to the whiteness of the Lady's raiment or to the white flawlessness of her skin, also described by "her white arms" (380), they establish her overall brightness and indicate an intensity of hue that is an inseparable part of her physical nature.

In Eddic literature, several valkyrie figures are described, like Galadriel, as *hvít* (white) (*HHv*, 28), *fögr* (fair) (*Völ*, 2), and *lióśa* (shining) (*Sigsk*, 53). In addition, Galadriel's white clothing echoes the "álptarhamir" (swanskin cloaks) of the valkyries in *Völundarkviða* (*Vl*, prose before 1). Similarly, Galadriel's appearance in her Elven swan barge (*FR*, 388–89) echoes the Eddic descriptions of the *Völundarkviða* women, who are identified as both valkyries and swan-maidens. Another Old Norse valkyrie, Brynhild, is presented through swan imagery as "álft af báru" (a swan upon a wave) (*VS*, 177). Galadriel's white features and her swan barge link her to these valkyries in images formed from the brightest naturally occurring color. Through such references, Tolkien establishes his visual treatment of the Elven queen to reflect the uppermost extreme on the spectrum of light. Thus the whiteness of Galadriel's own physical form, combined with the external trappings of her dress and her ship, equates the Lady with lightness and, by extension, moral goodness in its most saturated form.

In addition to using the color white and a fair appearance to establish the visual intensity of Galadriel's physical presence as indicative of a heightened moral state, Tolkien highlights the Lady's supremacy of form and nature by including references to shining eyes and gold in his portrayal of the Elven queen. When first introducing Galadriel and her husband, Celeborn, Tolkien writes, their eyes "were keen as lances in the starlight" (*FR*, 369). Such an identification of the Lady's eyes as one of her shining features suggests a similar brightness in the eyes of many valkyries. For example, the skaldic poem *Hrafnsmál* describes a valkyrie with "gloegghvarmr" (gleaming eyes).[14] Galadriel's "deep gold" hair (*FR*, 369) further accentuates her identification with heightened expressions of light as well as links her portrayal to descriptions of the valkyries' physical features. Recalling Old Norse valkyries whose hair is generally described as pale or golden, Gimli eloquently addresses the shining, golden qualities of Galadriel's hair, when he claims a strand of it "surpasses the gold of the earth as the stars surpass the gems of the mine" (*FR*, 392). Illustrating this same principle of brightness associated with light-colored hair, the same *Hrafnsmál* valkyrie with gleaming eyes also features "hvíta haddbjarta" (brightly light hair). These additional visual motifs of radiant eyes and golden hair serve to emphasize the brilliance inherent to Galadriel's character as reflective of her enhanced physical and moral state.

Further concordant with Eddic descriptions of valkyries, Galadriel's radiance is an innate part of her very being. When the Company leaves Lothlórien, the "white form" of Galadriel "shone like a window of glass upon a far hill in the westering sun, or as a remote lake seen from a mountain: a crystal fallen in the lap of the land" (*FR*, 393). At the end of *The Lord of the Rings*, the Lady's innate radiance is summarized in the statement that "she herself seemed to shine with a soft light" (*RK*, 308). Like the valkyrie in the *Helgi Lays*, who is "biartlituð" (bright of form) (*HHv*, 17), such a description presents Galadriel as the very image of the Old English term "ælfscīnu" (Elf-shining) (*Judith*, line 14), a term that appears in connection with the heroine Judith.[15] The immanent brilliance of this Elf-shining light so central to the Elf queen's nature is later emphasized in the tunnels of Cirith Ungol, when Frodo sees "a light in his mind, almost unbearably bright at first, as a sun-ray to the eyes of one long hidden in a windowless pit … he saw the Lady Galadriel" (*TT*, 329). In this image of Galadriel, sun imagery offers an additional connection to valkyrie-associated figures whose brightness is also often likened to the sun. To cite two examples, the Old English Juliana is described as "sunscīene" (sun-shining one) (*Juliana*, line 229), and the Old Norse Sigrún as "sólbiört" (sun-bright) (*HH II*, 45).

Enlarging upon the gold motif as well as incorporating the illuminative qualities typical of valkyrie figures, Galadriel's concealed Elven ring of power, Nenya, provides another piece of evidence that links her to the medieval valkyries. When Frodo first sees Galadriel's ring, "it glittered like polished gold overlaid with silver light, and a white stone in it twinkled as if the Even-star had come down to rest" (*FR*, 380). While Nenya's magical power makes the ring different in nature from the gold rings of adornment and currency that frequently bedeck Germanic valkyries, its effect as part of Galadriel's external brilliance associates her with other ring-wearing valkyrie figures, such as Judith, who is "bēahhrodene" (ring-adorned) (*Judith*, line 138), and Sigrún, who is "baugvarið" (ring-wearing) (*HH II*, str 35) and "gullvarið" (gold-wearing) (*HH II*, 45). Much as the medieval valkyrie's actions are typically motivated by the woman's strong will, Nenya responds to Galadriel's will by intensifying the Lady's own inherent light at moments of import. Illustrating this property, at Galadriel's consideration of Frodo's offer to her of the One Ring, Nenya "issued a great light that illumined her alone and left all else dark" (*FR*, 381).

Accentuating the valkyrie-like emphasis on light in Tolkien's characterization of Galadriel is the phial of light she gives Frodo as a parting gift. Like Galadriel, so, too, medieval valkyries are sometimes recorded as bestowing on their heroes special gifts of power with properties of brightness or glittering. For example, the valkyrie Sváva grants Helgi an especially illustrious sword described as "varið gulli. / Hringr er í hialti" [adorned with gold, ringed on the hilt] (*HHv*, 8–9). In *Beowulf*, Wealhtheow, another valkyrie-associated figure, gives the hero "wunden gold / ēstum geēawed, earm[h]rēade twā, / hrægl ond hringas, healsbēaga mæst" [wrought gold, granted in good will, two arm-bands, mail and rings, and the greatest neck ring] (Klaeber, ed. *Beowulf*, lines 1193–95). Like these brightly gleaming gifts from valkyrie-associated women, Galadriel's phial

> glittered as she moved it, and rays of white light sprang from her hand. "In this phial," she said, "is caught the light of Eärendil's star .... It will shine still brighter when night is about you. May it be a light to you in dark places, when all other lights go out."
>
> (*FR*, 393)

Serving just such a purpose, the phial provides Frodo and Sam not only illumination but the strength of Galadriel's spirit necessary for them to battle the darkness and malice of Shelob and Cirith Ungol. Although Galadriel's gift of magically captured starlight has no direct parallels in medieval Germanic texts, Tolkien's inclusion of this phial in his text echoes gifts to medieval heroes in its qualities of illumination.

While the main narrative of *The Lord of the Rings* never shows Galadriel wielding valkyrie-like martial skills or physical prowess,[16] she is portrayed through the valkyrie-associated act of ceremonial cup-bearing at occasions of narrative import. Such occasions typically involve either the welcoming of heroes, as in the case of the valkyries who welcome fallen warriors to Valhalla, or the departure of heroes, as in the case of Sigrún's farewell to Helgi (*HH II*, 46–47). As Jane Chance describes this activity of valkyrie-associated women in human halls, "The mead-sharing ritual and the cup-passer herself come to symbolize peace-weaving and peace because they strengthen the societal and familial bonds between lord and retainers" ("Grendel's Mother," 254). Like the Old English Wealhtheow and other Eddic women[17] who participate in official court ceremonies involving the sharing of ritual drink as a means of establishing loyalties and commitments from heroes, Galadriel enacts this valkyrie function at the Company's departure from Lothlórien. As Tolkien describes,

> Now Galadriel rose from the grass, and taking a cup from one of her maidens she filled it with white mead and gave it to Celeborn.
>
> "Now it is time to drink the cup of farewell," she said. "Drink Lord of the Galadrim! ..."
>
> Then she brought the cup to each of the Company, and bade them drink and farewell.
>
> (*FR*, 390)

The sequence here in which Galadriel offers the ceremonial "cup of parting" (*FR*, 390) filled with a special drink, first to the king and then to the heroes, parallels the process by which other valkyrie figures in medieval literature serve their ceremonial function of official cup-bearing. To cite one example from *Beowulf*, Wealhtheow, seeking to establish public bonds of loyalty between her sons and Beowulf, first takes the ceremonial cup to her lord Hrothgar, then to Beowulf, and then to the rest of the warriors (Klaeber, ed. *Beowulf*, lines 1162–233). Like the specially noted "white mead" in Tolkien's text, the "wīn" [wine] Wealhtheow serves also has specific ritual implications. In *Beowulf*, the term "wīn" is used rather than the more common drink of mead or beer primarily to denote the ceremonial drink served by Hrothgar's queen.[18] In similar fashion, the "vín" [wine] in *Eiríksmál*[19] Odin calls the valkyries to bring is a special drink for it must be such "sem vísir come" [as if a prince were coming] (1).

Immediately following her cup-bearing scene, Galadriel's ritual aspect further resembles the court functions of valkyrie figures when she grants gifts to each member of the Company. Much as the gifts awarded by medieval valkyries strengthen the commitment of the hero to both the woman and his heroic destiny, Galadriel's gifts are chosen to aid each individual hero's quest as well as to confirm their commitments to the Lady and her world of honor, beauty, and peace. Gimli's three golden hairs from the Lady's tresses, Sam's box of gardening soil from Lothlórien, and Aragorn's Elfstone brooch of ancient heritage from his beloved – all speak to those desires deepest within these heroes' hearts in an effort to inspire them to future action, while reminding them of the bonds forged to Galadriel and Lothlórien, bonds associated with the mythological past that the Elven queen, like the valkyries, embodies. By assuming such ceremonial functions at this point in the narrative, Galadriel acts as a force that unifies conflicting motives and desires among the Company. Although the members of the Company will be later separated from each other, their intensely powerful personal experiences of Galadriel and Lothlórien, coalescing in the combined cup-bearing and gift-giving ceremony, establish a commonality that continues to join the individuals to each other and to their larger purpose throughout the trilogy.

An important adjunct to Galadriel's gift-giving function is her preparation of special garments for Tolkien's heroes. The grey Elven cloaks, given at the Company's parting from Lothlórien, show that the heroes are "indeed high in the favour of the Lady! For she herself and her maidens wove this stuff; and never before have we clad strangers in the garb of our own people" (*FR*, 386), as one Elf explains. Galadriel's construction of these cloaks with properties that conceal the heroes from detection underscores her relationship to medieval Germanic valkyrie figures not only in her giving of such magical gifts, but also in the weaving motif. In medieval literature, valkyrie figures frequently prepare special garments or weavings intended to assist, inspire, or incite the hero's quest. The valkyrie's association with sewing, embroidering, or weaving may be a literary remnant of an earlier attribute that linked such figures with other Old Norse mythological women called the *dísir* or *norns* who wove the tapestried fates of humans. Examples of the weaving or sewing skills associated with valkyrie-like women include the *Völundarkviða* valkyries who "línn spunno" (spin flax) (*Völ*, 1); Signy who gruesomely tests her sons' courage by stitching their shirts to their skin (*VS*, 122); and Brynhild who "kunni meira hagleik en aðrar konur. Hún lagði sinn borða með gulli ok saumaði á þau stórmerki, er Sigurðr hafði gert" [was more skilled in handwork than other women. She adorned her tapestry with gold and embroidered on it the great deeds, which Sigurd had accomplished] (*VS*, 166).

Galadriel's ability to assess and test the Company's motives is another powerful attribute connecting her to the traditions of the Old Norse seers, *norns*, or *dísir*. While normally these prophetess figures are not rendered as valkyries, the valkyrie Brynhild foretells future events (*Sigsk*, 52–63), and Skuld is identified as both a valkyrie and a norn (*PrE*, 44 and 61). Galadriel's prophetic perceptions of the heroes' inner thoughts is summarized in Gimli's comment that she reads "many hearts and desires" (*RK*, 49) and Sam's description of her searching look at their first meeting as "looking inside me" (*FR*, 373). In addition, Galadriel has prescient abilities that allow her to "perceive the Dark Lord and know his mind" (*FR*, 380), while hiding her own power. Like the valkyrie-norn Skuld, Galadriel's prophetic abilities also involve a special relationship to a sacred body of water. Her prescience is partly a result of her involvement with the magical water of a well, her Mirror, in which Frodo and Sam are allowed to look for information about the future. While her command of it is somewhat limited,[20] Tolkien's description of Galadriel's actions and words regarding her Mirror show it functions only through her interaction. The ritual process by which Galadriel invokes the prophetic powers of her Mirror is described thus:

> With water from the stream Galadriel filled the basin to the brim, and breathed on it, and when the water was still again she spoke. "Here is the Mirror of Galadriel," she said. "I have brought you here so that you may look in it, if you will."
>
> (*FR*, 377)

When the Hobbit heroes look into the water, they see visions of an apocalyptic future evocative of the Old Norse Ragnarok, which the valkyrie-norn Skuld prophesies by looking into her own magical well. Although these foretellings from Galadriel's Mirror both trouble their souls and warn them of potential dangers, the visions also allow Frodo and Sam to understand and accept more fully the hazards of their quest.

Like the valkyries who intercede with Odin on behalf of exceptional heroes for the world's sake, Galadriel wields her personal and prophetic power in a battle of universal impact. In Galadriel's case, her refusal of the One Ring (*FR*, 380–81) is valkyrie-like in that it is an action undertaken as the result of a supreme exertion of the character's will. Both her Elven nature and prophetic abilities make Galadriel acutely aware of her responsibility to her culture. By refusing Frodo's offer of the One Ring, Galadriel exhibits her concerned awareness not only of herself and her people but also of a universe in which good and evil struggle for supremacy. Galadriel's prophetic powers enable her to recognize that her acceptance of the One Ring would be the destruction of herself, her Elven people, and the larger world of Middle-earth, for by doing so she would become a tool of evil, "beautiful beyond enduring, terrible and worshipful" (*FR*, 381). Like Sigrún, Brynhild and other valkyrie figures who choose to aid a hero rather than battle against him, Galadriel exerts the force of her will to turn away from a choice that would make her a vehicle for violence and destruction.

Further linking her to Odin's battle maids, Galadriel's choice to sacrifice the paradisiacal haven of Lothlórien in order to save her world alludes to the theme of the valkyrie's sorrow precipitated by extreme personal loss. As Damico describes the Old Norse analogues' treatment of this theme, the medieval valkyrie figure "is touched with sorrow [that] follows convention, for the quality appears as a consistent attribute of the female figures in Eddic and Anglo-Saxon heroic poetry" (*"Beowulf"'s Wealhtheow*, 20). For Germanic valkyries such as Brynhild and Sigrún, grief results from a choice made by the valkyrie herself which leads to giving up her immortality, to the betrayal of a lover, or to the death of a beloved hero. Similarly, Galadriel's choice to reject the One Ring seals the already apparent fate of Lothlórien's disappearance from the world. After the destruction of the One Ring, she acknowledges her "power is diminished, and Lothlórien will fade, and the tides of Time will sweep it away. We must depart into the West, or dwindle to a rustic folk of dell and cave, slowly to forget and to be forgotten" (*FR*, 380). It is this loss eternal, which can be neither denied nor succumbed to, that Tolkien himself has identified as the "real theme" of *The Lord of the Rings*.[21] In his study of the loss-eternal theme, Len Sanford identifies the impact of this theme on Germanic literature and mythology when he writes, "Northern mythology takes a darker view – that the struggle between man and monster must end in man's defeat, yet he continues to struggle; his weapons are … naked will and courage" (17). Galadriel's most profound expression of this loss-eternal theme[22] finds voice in her song about Lothlórien's fading. Resonant with the *ubi sunt* motifs commonly found in Old English elegiac poetry,[23] Galadriel laments:

> Ah! like gold fall the leaves in the wind, long years numberless as the wings of trees! The years have passed like swift draughts of the sweet mead in lofty halls beyond the West, beneath the blue vaults of Varda wherein the stars tremble in the song of her voice, holy and queenly. Who now shall refill the cup for me? For now the Kindler, Varda, the Queen of the Stars, from Mount Everwhite has uplifted her hands like clouds, and all paths are drowned deep in shadow; and out of a grey country darkness lies on the foaming waves between us, and mist covers the jewels of Calacirya for ever. Now lost, lost to those from the East, is Valimar!
>
> (*FR*, 394)

While the *ubi sunt* motif in Old English poetry is not associated specifically with valkyrie figures, its definitive connection to heroic themes and its presentation by Galadriel, a female speaker, provides a matrix of personal loss, the heroic world, and women's power highly evocative of valkyrie literature.

Providing a thematic antithesis to Galadriel, Shelob typifies the inverse image of the benevolent valkyrie reflex in *The Lord of the Rings*. As Tolkien's only example of the baleful, malevolent valkyrie figure found in Germanic mythology and literature, Shelob represents an opposition that serves to intensify Tolkien's emphasis on the benevolent valkyrie motifs reflected in his other women characters. While Joe Abbott closely examines Shelob's affinity to monstrous female figures in Old Norse and Old English literature, his study omits exploration of

Tolkien's spider creature as indicative of the medieval valkyrie figure in her negative, perverted aspect. His recognition, however, of Shelob as reminiscent of Old Norse and Old English giantess figures – who live in geographically liminal spaces, are associated firmly with darkness, and are begotten from ancient races of beings – parallels the themes and conventions commonly attached to the malevolent forms of the valkyrie.

An emblem of unconquerable evil will, Shelob's gigantic, dark, bloated presence establishes an extreme contrast to Galadriel's humanly proportioned qualities of light, beauty, and heightened moral goodness. As Shelob offers a parodic inversion of the benevolent valkyrie aspects of Tolkien's Elven queen whose maternal virtues guide and protect her people, so too has the valkyrie-associated Grendel's mother been described as "a parodic inversion, both of the Anglo-Saxon queen and mother, the ideal of which was embodied in the Virgin Mary" (Chance, "Grendel's Mother," 252–53). Like Galadriel, Shelob is a force with mythological associations beyond Middle-earth, a creature with the ability to affect conflicts in the scope of the larger world (*TT*, 332). But, while Galadriel, like the benevolent valkyries, interacts extensively with her community of Lothlórien and serves as a responsible leader of her people, Shelob operates in isolation, devoid of community, "unabated in malice" (*TT*, 333). Unlike, Galadriel who cares for other beings and races outside her scope of direct influence, Shelob broods only on herself. As Tolkien explains,

> Little she knew of or cared for towers, or rings, or anything devised by mind or hand, who only desired death for all others, mind and body, and for herself a glut of life, alone, swollen till the mountains could no longer hold her up and the darkness could not contain her.
>
> (*TT*, 333)

Her insatiable desire to continue her monstrous existence is, as Jane Chance remarks, "the embodiment of the primordial desire for survival" (*Mythology of Power*, 114). Further, Shelob's will is enacted not as Galadriel employs the power of her will to preserve other peoples of Middle-earth, but to satisfy her ultimately selfish greed for the meat she acquires by destroying those same peoples. For Rawls, "Shelob is what happens when the feminine concern with the individual and with the inner life is taken to the extreme" ("Feminine Principle," 10). Similarly, Fenwick explains Shelob is "a force that denies all ends except her own gloom and hunger" (23). Her kinship with baleful, valkyrie-associated figures is based on such destructive purposes. Unlike Tolkien's other primary female characters, but very like the malevolent valkyrie figures who are almost always bent on the hero's destruction, Shelob always seeks to destroy rather than to preserve or create.

Complementing the destructive aspects of her nature, the malevolent valkyrie figure is most often presented as an unnatural version of heroic appearance and behavior. Because the excessive strength of such valkyries is portrayed generally as monstrous in its inversion of medieval ideals of femininity, the malevolent valkyrie is often portrayed as the hero's most physically specific and powerful opponent. Just so, in his trilogy, Shelob is Tolkien's most vivid, terrifying force of evil and the most substantial of the physical threats Frodo encounters. In Tolkien's vision, the Orcs are foul and powerful but conquerable, while battles with the Ringwraiths and the Ring itself are more properly conflicts of the spirit than they are of the body. Not even Sauron, that preeminent force of evil whose most explicit description is rendered as a large baleful eye, can match the overwhelmingly visceral vision of evil found in the spiderlike Shelob. Her evil nature, like the monstrous valkyrie-associated Hrímgerth of the *Helgi Lays* and Grendel's mother of *Beowulf*, is evidenced in her inhuman form. As Hrímgerth and Grendel's mother are unnaturally formed humans in their immense size and sea-monster connotations, Shelob is not a naturally evolved spider, as indicated by her hugeness as well as by Tolkien's statement that she is not precisely a spider, but rather "an evil thing in spider-form" (*TT*, 332). Shelob's unnaturalness is emphasized by her claws as well as by her size. In addition, while neither creature takes Shelob's spiderlike form, both Grendel's mother and Hrímgerth have claws,[24] just as on Shelob "at each leg's end there was a claw" (*TT*, 334). Odd additions for a spider-like creature, Shelob's claws may be derived from Tolkien's knowledge of Hrímgerth and Grendel's mother. If so, this detail of Shelob's anatomy, which has no direct purpose in Tolkien's plot development, offers additional acknowledgment of this character's valkyrie roots. Other evidence linking Tolkien's spider creature to the inhuman qualities of such grim battle demons is that her hide resembles Grendel's mother's skin or body covering in that it is tough enough to deflect weapons (Klaeber, ed. *Beowulf*, lines 1518–29), much like the armor commonly worn by valkyries. Describing this nearly impenetrable quality of Shelob's "age-old hide," Tolkien writes that it was "ever thickened from within with layer on layer of evil growth. The blade scored it with a dreadful gash, but those hideous folds could not be pierced" (*TT*, 337).

Further, in Old English and Old Norse literature, the fierce battle-demon type of valkyrie character reverses the weaving or sewing motif related to the benevolent valkyrie in that the monstrous woman is often presented as destroying warriors by fettering or binding them.[25] Functioning in much the same way, Shelob "bound in cords" (*TT*, 337) her victims as a precursor to eating them. Similarly, Modthrytho in *Beowulf* weaves bonds especially designed to destroy warriors, described as "wælbende weotode tealde / handgewriþene" [slaughter-bonds woven by hand, reckoned and ordained] (Klaeber, ed. *Beowulf*, lines 1936–37). Shelob's binding cords resemble not only Modthrytho's bonds but also the fetters used by warrior women in the *First Merseberg Charm* whom Damico has identified as associated with the valkyrie tradition (*"Beowulf" 's Wealhtheow*, 43). In addition, the cords with which Shelob binds Frodo and her other victims are closely related to the webs with which she seals the opening to her den. Her web of "countless cords" (*TT*, 331) further recalls the weaving or sewing traditions of the Germanic valkyrie figures. As Tolkien describes his spider creature's web, "Across the width and height of the tunnel a vast web was spun, orderly as the web of some huge spider, but denser-woven and far greater, and each thread was as thick as rope" (*TT*, 331). While the weaving motif in Old Norse texts is not generally suggestive of violence, in one skaldic poem, *Darraðarljóð* in *Brennu-Njáls saga*, women specifically identified as valkyries use their own weapons and the body parts of dead warriors to weave a garment that determines the deaths of warriors.

Shelob also exhibits the typical valkyrie trait of unusually intensified eyes. Unlike the shining eyes of the benevolent valkyries, malevolent valkyrie figures commonly display terrifying and baleful eyes, as in the "ötul augo" [fearsome eyes] (*HH II*, 4) of one Eddic valkyrie. Just as terrible, Shelob possesses "two great clusters of many-windowed eyes" that are "Monstrous and abominable" (*TT*, 329). Her eyes also shine, but with "fell light" (*TT*, 334) and "pale deadly fire" (*TT*, 329). The terror of Shelob's eyes reflects her unnatural origins and responses for they are "bestial and yet filled with purpose and with hideous delight" (*TT*, 330). Like Shelob, *The Wonders of the East*, an Old English travelogue preserved in the *Beowulf* Codex, describes one of its female monsters as having "wælcyrian eagan" [valkyrie eyes] and "eahta fet" [eight feet] (Orchard, 186). While we cannot be certain Tolkien had this specific monster in mind when he created Shelob, the cluster of imagery referring to a terrible-eyed, eight-footed, valkyrie-associated creature, in a text Tolkien must have known, suggests more than a casual connection between Shelob and *The Wonders of the East* monster.

Yet as closely as the monstrous and malevolent Shelob parallels baleful valkyrie figures, the most direct and compelling evidence for the valkyrie tradition in Tolkien's texts resides in the character of Éowyn. Like Tolkien's Éowyn, the figures in Germanic literature and mythology most clearly identified as valkyries are martial maidens, helmeted women, armored for battle[26] who are sometimes garbed as men. Such medieval women participate in ambiguous definitions of their gender roles, which reject traditional binary definitions of gender.[27] While the attributes elaborated earlier are significant elements in representations of Germanic valkyrie figures, it is the warrior aspect that most securely identifies a woman character's debt to Odin's battle maids. Tolkien's Éowyn is modeled explicitly on such benevolent warrior women as Brynhild, who "fór með hjálm ok brynju ok gekk at vígum" [took up helmet and mail and went to battle] (*VS*, 165), and the two Hervörs in *Heidrek's saga* who wage war alongside men. Like these medieval valkyrie antecedents, Éowyn has been trained not only for battle but also has martial abilities equal to those of the most heroic men, as is typical of such cross-gendered valkyrie figures. As Gandalf tells Éomer, she possesses "a spirit and courage at least the match of yours" (*RK*, 143). By showing Éowyn armed for battle several times in his text, Tolkien insists on her martial abilities as a major facet of her character's identity. Her martial depiction is founded on the fact that she is "a shieldmaiden" (57; 239; 243), a term cognate with the Old Norse *skjaldmeyjar*, used frequently to describe valkyrie figures. As a shield-maiden, Éowyn is part of an order of nobly born women warriors who appear "clad like a Rider and girt with a sword" (58), who "ride and wield blade" (58), and who do "not fear either pain or death" (58).

Paralleling such descriptions in both word choice and conceptual content, the Old Norse valkyrie Brynhild identifies herself by saying, "Ek em skjaldmær, ok á ek með herkonungum hjálm, ok þeim mun ek at liði verða, ok ekki er mér leitt at berjast" [I am a shield maiden. I wear a helmet and ride with the warrior kings. I must support them, and I am not averse to fighting] (*VS*, 168).

As with other valkyrie-identified women, Éowyn's female identity does not preclude her from wielding power, regardless of whether Tolkien presents her character gendered as a courtly princess or as an armored warrior. Gifts suitable for a warrior rather than a courtly woman, Éowyn's arms are awarded to her by her king. As Tolkien writes, "Éowyn knelt before him [Théoden] and received from him a sword and a fair corslet" (*TT*, 128). By accepting these gifts, Éowyn accepts not only arms but an obligation as defender of her people. This valkyrie-like obligation is evident as the warband sets off to Helm's Deep in the image of Éowyn standing outside the doors with a sword "set upright before her, and her hands … laid upon the hilt" (*TT*, 128). Continuing this martial imagery, Éowyn later wears "a helm and was clad to the waist like a warrior and girded with a sword" (*RK*, 68). Such a description closely echoes that of the valkyrie Brynhild who "hefir sverð í hendi ok hjálm á höfði ok var í brynju" [had a sword in her hand and a helmet on her head and was in mail] (*VS*, 177). Part of her martial aspect requires Brynhild to assume the role of military leadership at times of need, as indicated in her statement "Ek mun kanna lið hermanna" [I must review the troops of warriors] (*VS*, 168). Just so, Éowyn's training for battle grants her the authority to lead her people, govern them, and provide for their welfare in the absence of Théoden. Hama validates her right to such authority when he asserts, "She is fearless and high-hearted. All love her. Let her be as Lord of the Éorlingas, while we are gone" (*TT*, 128). Although her desire physically to engage in battle is rejected by Théoden, Éowyn has the valkyrie's personal power and social obligation to take up arms herself as a means of protecting her people. Where some critics view Éowyn's character as either reflective of the powerlessness inherent in traditional female roles that trap women in their femininity or as indicative of her rejection of femininity through her warrior trappings, Hama's words indicate instead her authority to be simultaneously a woman and a warrior. Her personal courage, martial skill, innate virtue, and noble genealogy make her a suitable leader of the Rohirrim, illustrating that in Tolkien's world other factors "are often more important than gender in legitimizing female political power" (Crowe, 275).

Not only is Éowyn related to Old Norse and Old English battle maidens in training and leadership within her culture, she also resembles valkyries in her psychological configuration. Recognizing the formidable nature of this woman's spirit at their first meeting, Aragorn notes "strong she seemed and stern as steel" (*TT*, 119). Like the medieval valkyrie figures Brynhild and Sigrún, Éowyn is a character whose nature houses a will that must be satisfied by physical action. She articulates this aspect of her psychology when she tells Aragorn, "I am weary of skulking in the hills, and wish to face peril and battle" (*RK*, 57). What Éowyn fears most is that, by fulfilling her duty to remain at home to protect her people, her shield-maiden spirit will remain caged until "all chance of doing great deeds is gone beyond recall or desire" (*RK*, 58). To gain her freedom and to achieve her desire of serving her people honorably in battle, Éowyn, like the Old Norse Hervör and Thorbjörg,[28] disguises her female identity with male clothes and an assumed male name. Éowyn's desire to ride into battle as a male warrior named Dernhelm is an effort to fulfill her shield-maiden training and heritage, while maintaining her personal honor. Her disguise is not an attempt to hide the fact that she is a woman, for her training verifies that in the culture it is acceptable that women engage in battle, but rather her disguise is necessary to conceal the fact that she is Éowyn, the niece whom Théoden has forbidden to ride to this particular battle with him.

Yet, in Tolkien's medieval analogues, the valkyrie's will often results in tragedy, death, and destruction. In *Beowulf*, the valkyrie's desire for violent action, accomplished through the female form, is represented by Modthrytho's actions that reveal a "death-centred masculine desire versus female as life-giver" (Overing, 254). In the *Helgi Lays*, Sigrún's love for the hero leads to his death. Echoing the tragic results common to such valkyrie counterparts, Éowyn's choice to don male garb in order to fulfill her role as shield-maiden arises from her expectations of heroic failure as well as her own death. These expectations are foregrounded in Merry's recognition that, disguised as Dernhelm, hers "was the face of one without hope who goes in search of death" (*RK*, 76). Éowyn's act of volition, however, results not in tragedy but in unforeseen victory. Although Théoden and Aragorn attempt to thwart her desire to engage in physical battle, Éowyn fulfills this desire by clothing herself as Dernhelm, an act of her own volition and determination. As she whispers in Merry's ear, "*Where will wants not, a way opens*" (77). Like her brother Éomer, when Éowyn rides to battle as Dernhelm, she embodies what is best and most heroic in the Rohirrim. Where he recalls the image of the great warrior of Rohan's past, the shield-maiden Éowyn is the very form of her people's continuing history, a symbol of Rohan's living heritage, its recent struggle against disintegration and hopelessness, as well as the potential transformation of its future. As such, her shield-maiden's skill and courage, intensified by the extremity of her need, join with the force of her valkyrie will to accomplish one of the trilogy's most heroic deeds, the prophesied battle impossible for anyone else to win, the killing of the Ringwraiths' Black Captain. Yet, it is not simply her strength of will that enables Éowyn to vanquish the Black Captain; her victory also owes much to the tension between the masculine and feminine gender roles inherent in the valkyrie reflex that Tolkien has appropriated for her characterization. Like Eddic valkyries who wield their physical power to aid beloved heroes, Éowyn's blows against the Black Captain are struck to aid Théoden, for "on the battlefield, it is love, a feminine attribute which motivates her and gives her the power to act – again, an interplay of feminine and masculine attributes" (Rawls, "Feminine Principle," 10).

Éowyn's connection to the valkyrie reflex, however, is founded on more than her role as a warrior maiden and the exertion of her strong will. As with Galadriel, Éowyn is portrayed in terms of the intensification of light common to the benevolent Germanic valkyrie figures. Éowyn resembles the Elven queen in that she too is "clad in white" (*TT*, 117; *RK*, 57) or "a white robe girt with silver" (*TT*, 119). Also similar to Galadriel's, Éowyn's "long hair was like a river of gold" (119), and "her bright hair, released from its bonds, gleamed with pale gold" (*RK*, 116). The gold of her hair in such passages is associated with treasure, but its shining qualities contribute to her valkyrie-like radiance in descriptions of her "long braided hair gleaming in the twilight" (68) and the "light fell about her, and her hair shone in the sunrise" (117). Like other valkyrie figures in Tolkien's texts and in Germanic literature, Éowyn's illumination is featured in her eyes as well as in her hair. Two particular passages highlighting this element of her radiance comment that "her eyes were shining" (*TT*, 127) and "her eyes were on fire" (*RK*, 57). But, as in Galadriel's characterization, Éowyn's valkyrie radiance is also a generalized facet of her physical nature, for she appears as "a glimmer in the night" (57) and "golden as the sun and white as snow" (255). Unlike Tolkien's other primary women characters, however, Éowyn's brilliance is sometimes associated with battle gear, as his statement "clad now in mail … [she] shone like silver in the sun" (*TT*, 128) makes clear. The glittering qualities imparted by her armor are identical to the medieval valkyries' most-often identified source of radiance.

Further, Éowyn functions in the valkyrie's court aspect by bearing both female witness and a ceremonial cup at moments of social significance. In her role of court princess, the Germanic valkyrie commonly attends a king and, like Éowyn in her first appearance in the trilogy (*TT*, 117), is often presented standing beside or behind the king's chair during occasions of sociocultural import. In Tolkien's text, Éowyn is present not only at the Company's entrance to Meduseld's hall, but also at Gandalf's initial rejuvenation of Théoden. While she is not shown at Théoden's address to his people, Éowyn presides at the king's board and attends his subsequent arming of the heroes. In this scene, Éowyn performs the traditional court valkyrie act of ritual cup-bearing. Like Wealhtheow in *Beowulf*, as well as the other valkyrie figures discussed in connection with Galadriel's cup-bearing aspect, Éowyn, in what can only be described as a ritualistic ceremony, brings a cup of wine to her king as a means of confirming the verbal commitments made previously by the heroes. Blessing Théoden's reaffirmed heroic leadership through this ceremonial act, she uses the ancient language of her people,[29] "*Ferthu Théoden hál.* … Receive now this cup and drink in happy hour." (127). Éowyn then offers the cup to each guest in much the same ritual common to medieval valkyrie court figures such as *Beowulf*'s Wealhtheow.

At her first appearance in Tolkien's text, Éowyn, like Rohan, is a diminished power, helpless to do more than stand behind the king. Nonetheless, after fulfilling the valkyrie role of ceremonial cup-bearer at the king's board, Éowyn has become an image of Rohan in the process toward rejuvenation, and represents its urgent need to reestablish appropriately healthy social bonds. Later, Éowyn again serves the cup in a formal fashion; but this time she serves it to Aragorn before he sets off on the Path of the Dead. As Tolkien writes,

> In her hand she bore a cup, and she set it to her lips and drank a little, wishing them good speed; and then she gave the cup to Aragorn, and he drank, and he said: 'Farewell, Lady of Rohan! I drink to the fortunes of your House, and of you, and of all your people. Say to your brother: beyond the shadows we may meet again!' "
>
> (*RK*, 58)

In this instance, the cup ceremony establishes Éowyn's authority publicly to sanction the venture as well as providing Aragorn with an official opportunity to show her appropriate honor and to offer her heroic hope. Since Éowyn is dressed as a warrior in this scene, her blessing also carries martial connotations in keeping with the Company's needs at this moment. Her final ritual offering of the shield-maiden's cup occurs near the end of the trilogy as a fulfillment of her people's past and an affirmation of their future. As part of the Mark's custom to honor the memory of Théoden by including him in their list of former kings, Éowyn "bore a filled cup to Éomer" (255), which then initiates the ceremony by which Éomer formally assumes his rightful place as Rohan's new king. Like Wealhtheow and other valkyrie-associated queens who preside over ceremonies by bearing ritual cups, Éowyn's formal actions and female presence acknowledge her culture's debt to an honorable past and its equal responsibility to an heroic future.

While Éowyn is not associated with the usual valkyrie motif of sewing or weaving heroic garments, like other benevolent valkyrie figures, she is responsible for arming Merry with heroic battle gear and for bestowing special heroic gifts. Although it is at Aragorn's request that she arms Merry, the choice of gifts is clearly Éowyn's responsibility, as indicated in her words to him, "I will show you the gear that I have prepared for you" (*RK*, 75), and then, "I have granted it [selecting arms for Merry] as I could" (75). In gratitude for Merry's achievement in helping to destroy the Black Captain and as a "memorial of Dernhelm" (256), Éowyn later performs the traditional valkyrie role as the giver of heroic gifts when she awards Merry "an ancient horn, small but cunningly wrought" (256).

Éowyn's final relationship to medieval valkyrie figures is that, like them, she struggles with a loss which is not only deeply personal, but has societal implications. For Éowyn, her loss involves the common valkyrie theme of conflicting loyalties to herself and her society. In Éowyn's case, the division she combats is a battle between her individual needs and her cultural responsibilities. Dogged and "haunted" (*TT*, 124) for years by Wormtongue, whose desire for her was ignoble and unwholesome, Éowyn sacrificed her own self-esteem and dreams of a fulfilling future in order to tend the ailing Théoden. As an individual woman and a representative of the governing class of her people, Éowyn is desperate for the healing and hope a noble liberator can offer both her and her Rohirrim culture. Even though the Company's efforts free Rohan from the progress of Wormtongue's evil, Éowyn and her Rohirrim culture in fact have been only partially rejuvenated. Mirrored by Éowyn's considered and thoughtful reaction after Théoden's response to Gandalf (119), the despair and hopelessness of her people have been stayed by the dismissal of Wormtongue but have not yet been obliterated. In Aragorn, Éowyn recognizes the heroic potential to revive the health of her failing self and people. Yet Aragorn's different destiny cannot allow him to function as the complete answer to Rohan's needs. For Éowyn and her people, the definitive rejection of their despair comes only after the incomplete image of freedom and hope Aragorn represents is replaced by a corrected vision which stimulates social growth and healing, while preserving the independent spirit of Rohan represented by Éowyn.

Like Old Norse women who disarm themselves after falling in love with a hero,[30] Éowyn's corrected vision effects her transformation from an ambiguously gendered valkyrie whose sole desire is to perform the functions of a warrior into a valkyrie who gains human fulfillment as a wife. Until she meets Faramir, Éowyn's individual and cultural needs are confused; she wants to engage in physical combat, but she also desires Aragorn because of the hope he has inspired in her and her people. Although both needs are aspects of the same desire made manifest in different forms of her awareness, her dual nature wars against itself. For Rohan, the heroic measure of its culture and history, represented by Théoden, is only partially revived by Wormtongue's removal. Full restoration of cultural health rests on Théoden leading his warriors to battle and on the promotion of Éomer, both emblems of a past glory's unstained heroism. For Éowyn, however, the public standard of heroism in Aragorn that she interprets as the ideal salvation for her culture offers no possibility for the restoration and reintegration of her personal needs. Aragorn becomes an imperfect image of rejuvenative heroism for her people and for herself. Although Aragorn as the returned king can motivate the recovery of Éowyn's body from the wound inflicted on her by the Black Captain, her true "recuperation transcends merely physical healing" (Chance, *Mythology of Power*, 99). Requiring a "psychological bridging of her despair" (97) as much as her body's health, Éowyn's complete restoration relies on the new possibility of love as the foundation for her future. Despite his appreciation of her personal strengths and public efforts, Aragorn cannot love Éowyn as an individual woman. In contrast, Faramir loves the public and private aspects of Éowyn's identity, thereby enabling a resolution between her individual and cultural needs. Although in a different context, Jane Chance suggests the significance of emotion as the basis for such resolution, when she writes that for Éowyn "hope as the remedy for despair arises from love" (97–98). Yet despite the answers love provides, Éowyn, like her valkyrie counterparts, retains her shield-maiden spirit, "tamed" (*RK*, 243) to be sure, but not diminished. Rather, with her marriage to Faramir, she commits her public and private selves to a union that satisfies both aspects of her nature. Although she says, "I will be a shield maiden no longer, nor vie with the Great Riders, nor take joy only in the songs of slaying. I will be a healer and love all things that grow" (243), the use here of the word "only" insists that in the future she will not simply reject but transcend the limitations of her shield-maiden role. Her new awareness acknowledges the effects of healing as well as of battle, of growth as well as of death. In this, Éowyn integrates her dual nature by joining her valkyrie-identified public goal of restoring her people to their previous cultural glory to her newly perceived individual needs of pursuing love as well as battle. By not permitting the former to dominate, however, her transformation allows both to coexist and draw strength from each other. To live with Faramir in Ithilien is not a rejection but an extension of Rohan, for her cultural identity as a valkyrie is still authoritative, though it is now completed by her personal, emotional fulfillment as well. In this unified state, her character becomes more than a lord's second-in-command. Instead, Éowyn's future suggests her ruling side by side with Faramir through her personal volition and with cultural purpose, each individual completing the other.

Although Arwen's character is less developed than Tolkien's other primary heroic women characters, she too is consistently described in terms of valkyrie typology, including physical radiance. Unlike Galadriel, whose valkyrie-like radiance is metaphorized in a variety of astronomical images, Arwen's radiance is consistently identified with starlight, as her Elven epithets Undómiel and Evenstar emphasize (*FR*, 239). The association of Arwen's physical presence as a light in the dark is illustrated when Frodo sees her "glimmering in the evening, with stars on her brow" (*RK*, 251). Further connecting her to the valkyrie topos, the motif of shining light residing in the eyes is also attached to Arwen. At Frodo's first sight of her in Rivendell, he sees "the light of the stars was in her bright eyes" (*FR*, 239). Later, the motif of the valkyries' intensified eyes is compounded by light imagery as an element of her personal power, when Tolkien writes of Arwen that "the light of her eyes fell on him [Frodo] from afar and pierced his heart" (250).

Arwen is not only radiant in her person, but she also partakes of the courtly attributes of Germanic valkyrie figures by bestowing gifts of inspiration and reward with illuminative properties to heroes. Reminiscent of Brynhild's tapestry in the *Völsunga saga*, Arwen's gift to Aragorn of the banner standard she prepared herself reminds him of his rightful heritage and offers a talisman of hope that inspires the despairing warriors at its unfurling. Once revealed in all its glorious implications, upon the standard

> flowered a White Tree, and that was for Gondor; but Seven Stars were about it, and a high crown above it … . the stars flamed in the sunlight, for they were wrought of gems by Arwen daughter of Elrond; and the crown was bright in the morning, for it was wrought of mithril and gold.
>
> (*RK*, 123)

When Halbarad presents this standard to Aragorn, he highlights Arwen's role in its making by telling Aragorn, "It is a gift that I bring you from the Lady of Rivendell … . She wrought it in secret and long was the making" (48). By emphasizing Arwen's role as the maker of this potent, radiantly shining, heroic standard, the half-Elven woman becomes further linked to the valkyrie women who sew, weave, or otherwise prepare garments and other textile objects for heroes. But it is not only Aragorn on whom Arwen bestows a shining gift of heroic implications: Frodo also receives from her the gift of her own necklace. In a formal setting, evocative of the gift-giving scenes of Galadriel and other valkyrie figures that use imagery associated with weaving, Arwen tells Frodo,

> "wear this now in memory of Elfstone and Evenstar with whom your life has been woven!" … And she took a white gem like a star that lay upon her breast hanging upon a silver chain, and she set the chain about Frodo's neck. "When the memory of the fear and the darkness troubles you," she said, "this will bring you aid."
>
> (*RK*, 253)

By virtue of its close association with Aragorn's queen, Arwen's gift grants Frodo heroic reward, while her words concerning how it may serve him in the future hint at the possibility of Arwen as a prophetic figure as well.

In addition, Arwen's characterization evokes the Germanic valkyrie reflex in more than the superficial actions of gift-giving and banner embroidery. She also gives up the shining otherworld, that rightful part of her cultural heritage. In awarding her Elven birthright to Frodo, Arwen says,

> A gift I will give you. For I am the daughter of Elrond. I shall not go with him now when he departs to the Havens; for mine is the choice of Lúthien, and as she so have I chosen, both the sweet and the bitter. But in my stead you shall go, Ring-bearer.
>
> (*RK*, 252)

In contrast to Éowyn's characterization as a woman whose love for Faramir allows her to reconcile her personal and political obligations, Tolkien presents Arwen as the type of valkyrie who must forsake obligations to her race and family in order to realize the power of love as part of her identity. St. Clair remarks that Tolkien's late addition to the text of Arwen as Aragorn's spouse may reflect Tolkien's desire to highlight the theme of an immortal's love for a mortal, which so interested him in *The Silmarillion* ("Tolkien as Reviser," 148). However, this theme of divided loyalties, which prompts the valkyrie-like loss of Arwen's immortality in order to gain her fulfillment in romantic, human love, also places her alongside the tradition of Germanic literary figures such as Brynhild, Sigrún, Sváva, and Sigrdrífa. Like Sigrún and Brynhild, Arwen can achieve personal fulfillment as Aragorn's wife only by rejecting the immortality that comes with her Elven heritage. Hers, like her Germanic predecessors, is a bittersweet choice in which joy and tragedy intertwine. The profound consequences of Arwen's renunciation of her birthright result in the bitterness of her final interaction with her father, Elrond. At their farewell, Tolkien writes that "they went up into the hills and there spoke long together, and bitter was their parting that should endure beyond the ends of the world" (*RK*, 256). The common motif of the valkyrie's loss of something precious and central to her life is obvious. Unlike Éowyn's marriage to Faramir, Arwen's marriage to Aragorn establishes no newly forged alliance between the woman's individual and cultural selves. As appropriate and fulfilling as their marriage is described in Tolkien's text,[31] it represents the beginning of a different Arwen standing at the head of a changed society, whose new self and new culture are gained only at the cost of her own individual heritage. What she gives up of her own volition in order to help initiate the coming of the New Age remains as important in the reader's mind as what she has gained. Necessary though her break with her cultural heritage might be for the purposes of Tolkien's final resolution, it reverberates with a pathos that cannot be ignored, a pathos that resonates at the same frequency as the Germanic valkyrie-brides' rejection of their divine heritage for the love of a human hero.

Representatives of heroic modes and motivations, women characters in *The Lord of the Rings* are most appropriately understood as agents of power and influence who develop their empowered literary contexts from that pivotal perspective through which Tolkien asks us to look fully into the future only by gazing intently into the medieval past. Shaped by Tolkien's admiration for and desire to transcend the conventions of medieval heroic literature, valkyrie-associated themes transform the characters of Galadriel, Shelob, Éowyn, and Arwen from mere literary accessories to figures whose words and actions carry intrinsic importance in the trilogy. In his treatment of women characters by means of traditional valkyrie typology, Tolkien appropriates, as he does throughout his epic fantasy, "an established element from the Old Germanic past, accepts what is useful in it and constructs something greater in its place" (Boenig, 12). Without these heroically rendered women, Tolkien's texts would lack the epic completion only truly possible through the union of heroic oppositions: male and female, good and evil, life and death, joy and grief, individual and community, hope and despair.

By recasting medieval valkyrie analogues as his own contemporary models of heroism and sacrifice in *The Lord of the Rings*, Tolkien establishes what he considers the most appropriate narrative purpose for a fairy tale: that happy fulfillment he defines elsewhere as the accumulated power of Recovery, Consolation, and Eucatastrophe.[32] The "good catastrophe" or "joyous 'turn'" ("OFS," 86), which Tolkien sees as the most potent ending for a fairy-story, comes not without grief and sorrow. So the actions of Galadriel to save Middle-earth cause the fading of Lothlórien, and the choice Arwen makes to construct a New Age results in her eternal separation from her Elven kindred. Although Éowyn, like Arwen, gains the joy of love, she must leave behind the singular independence of her shield-maiden identity in order to express the full potential of romantic union. The valkyrie resonances from which Tolkien builds these heroic women enhance the eucatastrophic fulfillment at the trilogy's close. Enabling that end to be "Far more powerful and poignant," the characters of Galadriel, Éowyn, Arwen, and even Shelob, like the Eddic valkyries on whom they are patterned, serve to establish "a piercing glimpse of joy, and heart's desire, that for a moment passes outside the frame, rends indeed the very web of the story, and lets a gleam come through" ("OFS," 87). Reinforced by the antithesis represented in Shelob, Tolkien's modern benevolent valkyries – Galadriel, Éowyn, and Arwen – are preservers of tradition, defenders of their culture, bearers of the future, and forces for moral good. But, most of all, shining with the radiance of their valkyrie forebears, their images and names flame like candles in the dark for his heroes. The memory of Arwen inspires Aragorn to reclaim his kingship, the sight of Dernhelm revealed as Éowyn battling the Black Captain kindles Merry's hobbit courage, and the name of Galadriel calls forth Sam's extraordinary effort outside Shelob's lair. Finally, this is the true heritage of the valkyrie reflex in *The Lord of the Rings*. Like their medieval counterparts, whose heroic qualities form a bridge between the divine and human worlds, so Tolkien's valkyrie women weave together both the humble and the sublime in the same pattern of Middle-earth's heroic history.

Notes

1 A recent study by Candice Frederick and Sam McBride examines biographical evidence in an attempt to discern rationale and patterns for what they see as the idealized, stereotypical, even to a degree antifeminist, presentations of women in Tolkien's works as well as the works of Lewis, Williams, and other members of the Inklings.

2 For readings of Galadriel's resemblance to the Virgin Mary, see Michael W. Maher, chapter 14 in this volume, and Sly, "'Weaving Nets of Gloom.'"

3 Although his works contain many female figures indebted to medieval Germanic literatures, *The Lord of the Rings* provides a particularly rich context for such an examination and is representative of this tendency in all Tolkien's creative works. Because of this and the constraints of this chapter, this study restricts its discussion only to these female characters in Tolkien's trilogy.

4 See, for example, J. R. R. Tolkien's discussion of origins in his essay "OFS," in *TL* in *TR*, 45–57.

5 Although none discuss in detail the specific relationships of Tolkien's women characters to medieval Germanic sources, some studies mention briefly the debt of characters such as Galadriel, Shelob, and Éowyn to Old English and Old Norse texts. See, for example, Lynn Bryce, "Influence of Scandinavian Mythology," 113–19; and T. A. Shippey, *Road to Middle-earth.*

6 While *The Lord of the Rings* contains other notable women characters, space limitations make it necessary to restrict discussion to those women characters most central to the trilogy's narrative development and most distinctly evocative of Germanic valkyrie traditions – Galadriel, Shelob, Éowyn, and Arwen.

7 For general discussions of valkyrie figures in Old Norse literature and culture, see Jochens, *Old Norse Images of Women*, and Davidson, *Roles of the Northern Goddess.*

8 The body of Germanic mythological and heroic literature dealing most explicitly with valkyrie figures and cited in this study include the following medieval Old Norse texts: *Hervör's saga* (in C. Tolkien, ed., *Saga of King Heidrek*); *The Poetic Edda* (in Neckel, *Edda: Die Lieder des Codex Regius)*; *The Prose Edda* (in Sturluson, *Edda: Prologue and Gylfaginning*, abbreviated here as *PrE*); and *Völsunga saga* (in Jónsson, *Fornaldar sögur Norðurlanda*, abbreviated here as *VS*). Texts commonly collected as part of *The Poetic Edda* are cited by strophe number and abbreviated as follows: the *Helgi Lays* – *Helgakviða Hjörvarðssonar* (*HHv*), *Helgakviða Hundingsbana* I (*HH* I), *Helgakviða Hundingsbana* II (*HH II*); *Fáfnismál* (*Fáf*); *Sigrdrífomál* (*Sigrd*); *Sigurðarkviða en skamma* (*Sigsk*); *Völundarkviða* (*Völ*); and *Völuspá* (*Vsp*). In addition, due to close affinities between the Old Norse and Anglo-Saxon cultures, Old English texts such as *Beowulf*, *Judith*,

and *Juliana* include women frequently characterized in terms of valkyrie attributes. References to these Old English poems are made by line number from the following sources: Klaeber, ed. *"Beowulf" and "The Fight at Finnsburg,"* 3rd ed. with 1st and 2nd; Timmer, ed. *Judith*; and Woolf, ed. *Cynewulf's Juliana.* All Modern English translations of Old Norse and Old English material are my own.

9 See, for example, Hervör in *Heidrek's saga* and Brynhild in *VS.* While Lobelia Sackville-Baggins eventually takes action for the insults to herself and her Hobbit community by striking a physical blow against the Shire's enemies, I have restricted this study to those women characters who play a major or primary role in the text's narrative development.

10 Inciting the hero to action is one of the most frequently discussed characteristics of Old Norse women characters, especially those portrayed in the valkyrie tradition. However, since Tolkien basically eliminates this characteristic from his valkyrie-associated women, the inciter role is not discussed in this study. For discussion of medieval inciter figures, see Jochens.

11 Thorough explorations of Tolkien's women in *The Lord of the Rings* using feminist or gender theory approaches (such as those of Hélène Cixous, Julia Kristeva, Judith Butler, or Luce Irigaray) would be valuable additions to contemporary studies of Tolkien's work. However, as such studies are outside the scope of this chapter's primary focus, discussion of such concepts will be featured here only briefly.

12 For further discussion of the Old English valkyrie reflex, see Damico, "Valkyrie Reflex" and *"Beowulf"'s Wealhtheow.*

13 Since the "Galadhriel" variant form of her name, meaning "tree-lady," is used only in *The Silmarillion*, it is clear that Tolkien made a conscious choice in *The Lord of the Rings* to emphasize the qualities of light associated with this Elven queen.

14 References to *Hrafnsmál* are taken from Kershaw, *Anglo-Saxon and Norse Poems*, 76–87.

15 Although she is a biblical figure, Damico discusses the Old English Judith as characterized through the valkyrie reflex ("Valkyrie Reflex," 185).

16 That Galadriel possesses physical prowess equal to or superior to that of a male is suggested by the comment in appendix B that "Galadriel threw down its [Dol Goldur's] walls and laid bare its pits" (*RK*, 375).

17 See, for example, Sigrdrífa (*Sigrd*, 2–4) in *The Poetic Edda*, and Brynhild in *VS*, chap. 21.

18 Of the three times this word appears in *Beowulf*, twice it is associated with Wealhtheow's cup-bearing ritual and its only remaining occurrence is used to describe Unferth as "wīne druncen" (line 1467). Even the later reference may reflect the wine's ritual connotation, for it recalls a scene in which Unferth in his officially sanctioned role of thyle bestows a special sword of ancient heritage on Beowulf.

19 References to *Eiríksmál* are taken from Kershaw, *Anglo-Saxon and Norse Poems*, 93–99.

20 Expressing her limited control of the Mirror, Galadriel explains,

> Many things I can command the Mirror to reveal … and to some I can show what they desire to see. But the Mirror will also show things unbidden, and those are often stranger and more profitable than things which we wish to behold. What you will see, if you leave the Mirror free to work, I cannot tell. For it shows things that were, and things that are, and things that yet may be. But which it is that he sees, even the wisest cannot always tell.
>
> (*FR*, 377)

21 See J. R. R. Tolkien's letter to Joanna de Bortadano in *Letters*, 246–47.

22 Another detailed discussion of Tolkien's loss-eternal theme may be found in Senior, "Loss Eternal in J. R. R. Tolkien's Middle-Earth."

23 Among the Old English elegiac poems containing the *ubi sunt* or loss-eternal theme are *The Wanderer* and *The Seafarer*, in Pope, *Seven Old English Poems.*

24 See Grendel's mother's "atolan clommum" [terrible claws] (Klaeber, ed. *Beowulf*, line 1502), and Hrímgerth's "klymmor" [claws] (*HHv*, 22).

25 See *The Poetic Edda*'s valkyrie Herfönðr [warrior-fetter] (*Vsp*, 30) and the *First Merseburg Charm*'s warlike women who "hapt heptidun" [fastened fetters] in Barber, 65.

26 Examples include the valkyries in *Hákonarmál*, who are described as "hjalmaðar sátu / ok höfðusk hlífar fyrir" [helmeted they sat and they carried shields before them] (Kershaw, 106); the "mey und hiálmi" [woman under the helm] (*Fáf*, 44); and the "hiálmvitr" [helmeted-spirits] (*HH II*, 54).

27 For more extensive discussions of gender roles in relation to Old English women, see Overing, "Women of *Beowulf*," 219–60; and Mary Dockray-Miller, "The Masculine Queen of *Beowulf*," 31–38.

28 Thorbjörg appears in *Hrólfs saga Gautrekssonar*, ed. Jónsson.

29 "*Ferthu Théoden hál*" is Old English meaning "Go you Théoden whole/healed." In *The Lord of the Rings*, Tolkien uses Old English as the native language of the Rohirrim. It is the only language in the trilogy he did not create, suggesting the close relationship between the Riders and the Anglo-Saxon culture so important to Tolkien's professional life.

30 Brynhild in *Völsunga saga* as well as Sigrdrífa and Sigrún in *The Poetic Edda* are examples of such valkyrie figures.

31 Tolkien describes the joyousness of their marriage when he writes, "together they went up into the High City, and all the stars flowered in the sky. And Aragorn the King Elessar wedded Arwen Undómiel … and the tale of their long waiting and labours was come to fulfillment" (*RK*, 251).

32 For discussion of his views on the appropriate structural elements of fairy tale literature, see Tolkien's "OFS."

9 Exilic imagining in *The Seafarer* and *The Lord of the Rings*

Miranda Wilcox

> In the disappearance of small things, I read the tokens of my own dislocation, of my own transiency. An exile reads change the way he reads time, memory, self, love, fear, beauty: in the key of loss.
>
> (André Aciman, *Letters of Transit: Reflections on Exile, Identity, Language, and Loss*)

In his letters, Tolkien commented on Old English, Old Norse, Finnish, and Celtic influences in his creative work.[1] Those familiar with the plots of *Beowulf* and *The Hobbit* will recognize the similarity between a Hobbit and a thane who each steals a cup from a dragon, thereby provoking attack, whereas readers of *Beowulf* in Old English will recognize the golden roof of Edoras (*eoderas*, "dwelling" or "precinct" in Old English) in Rohan as the gleaming roof of Heorot (*FR*,131; Klaeber, ed. *Beowulf*, lines 308a, 311). On a more subtle level, an elegiac tone persists through *The Lord of the Rings* and is reminiscent of the lyric-elegiac quality, a sadness of time and change deeper than melancholia, present in much Old English poetry.

One Old English poem, *The Seafarer*, has more than tonal resonance with Tolkien's fiction. Tolkien's association with *The Seafarer* undoubtedly began when he read the poem as a student. But his formal engagement with the poem began while he taught with E. V. Gordon at Leeds University in the 1920s. Tolkien and Gordon planned on publishing a critical edition of *The Seafarer* and *The Wanderer* after their successful publication of an edition of *Sir Gawain and the Green Knight*. Not only was Tolkien critically engaged with *The Seafarer* text; he also incorporated *The Seafarer* into his creative realm by means of linguistic manipulation. He reworked a passage of *The Seafarer* in Old English in two unpublished stories – "The Lost Road" and "The Notion Club Papers."[2] By the time Tolkien began working on *The Lord of the Rings*, *The Seafarer* emerged as an established element in his fictive world. I propose that the sequence of influence of *The Seafarer* on Tolkien was the same as the well-documented influence of *Beowulf* and the *Battle of Maldon*; this sequence of influence begins with scholarly textual engagement followed by creative linguistic manipulation resulting in fictive integration.

The Seafarer is one of a group of Old English elegies found in the Exeter Book.[3] In lines 1–64a, the Seafarer recounts his suffering on sea voyages, his discontent with life on land, and his decision to make a significant sea journey.

These lines are characterized by vivid and detailed descriptions of winter weather and stormy seas, though the lyric spontaneity of the verse diminishes thereafter and assumes a homiletic tone (lines 64b–124). The poem expands from the initial natural realism to a reflective lament for mortal transience resolved by the expectation of heavenly joy.

Tolkien's formal engagement with *The Seafarer* began when Tolkien left Oxford to join the staff at Leeds University as Reader in English Language in 1920.[4] Two years later, E. V. Gordon joined the staff at Leeds, and he and Tolkien began to collaborate on critical editions of Old and Middle English texts. Together they published in 1925 a critical edition of *Sir Gawain and the Green Knight*, a fourteenth-century poem written in the difficult Northwest-Midlands dialect. They also worked on an edition of *Pearl*, a poem in the same manuscript as *Sir Gawain*, and a joint edition of *The Seafarer* and *The Wanderer*, another elegiac Old English poem (Ida Gordon, *Seafarer*, vii). A new edition of *The Seafarer* was needed to replace that in Thorpe's 1842 *Codex Exoniensis*, which lacked a critical apparatus discussing textual and interpretative problems. Tolkien and Gordon's edition was even listed as forthcoming in the facsimile edition of the Exeter Book in 1933 (Chambers *et al.*, 40). However, their efforts were hampered by distance when Tolkien was elected Rawlinson and Bosworth Professor of Anglo-Saxon at Oxford in the fall of 1925. Neither project was completed when E. V. Gordon unexpectedly died in 1938.

Scholarly debates regarding *The Seafarer* changed dramatically before 1949, when Tolkien finished his 600,000-word book (the first two volumes of *The Lord of the Rings* were not published until 1954; the third volume would follow in 1955). Trends in scholarship shifted away from textual difficulties to thematic and interpretative concerns and can be characterized as fluctuating between two methods of interpretation: the literal and the allegorical.[5]

As early as 1909, G. Ehrismann suggested reading the sea voyage as an allegorical representation of man's life. Ehrismann considered lines 64b–124 a direct continuation in which the poet explained the conclusions that can be drawn from the Seafarer's experience: the transient joy and pain of life in contrast to heavenly joys. In 1917, L. L. Schücking endorsed and expounded Ehrismann's theory: the sea voyage represents life as a road to eternity or death. O. S. Anderson continued the allegorical tradition in 1937–38, but his reading was generally considered too extreme (Timmer, "Elegiac Mood," 40). Although it was too late to affect Tolkien's use of *The Seafarer* in *The Lord of the Rings*, the allegorical method reached its height in G. V. Smithers's two-part article in 1957 and 1959, which details the patristic and vernacular metaphor of *peregrinus*, symbolic of man in exile from Paradise.[6] An alternative to reading the poem as allegory was based on the literal and often involved the symbolic or some midpoint between realism and allegory.

In 1936, C. W. Kennedy offered a literal interpretation of *The Seafarer* in *Old English Elegies*, reprinted in 1943 as a chapter in *The Earliest English Poetry*. He described the Old English elegies, *The Seafarer* being one, as lyrics with contemporary freshness and a timeless quality, and he considered the faithful depiction of nature in *The Wanderer* and *The Seafarer* as evidence of real seafaring experience rather than as stylized elegiac evocations (1, 9, 13). Kennedy argued that the subjective mood and realistic detail in the first half of the poem seem "incompatible with the theory that a general idea is there clothed in the conventions of allegory" (16). Dorothy Whitelock offered an influential literal interpretation in 1950 when she proposed that the Seafarer literally forsakes society for loneliness and exile as a *peregrinus*, or "pilgrim/hermit." Ida Gordon similarly refuted allegorical claims for an interpretation of *The Seafarer* and argued that the poem was written in the form of a secular stylized elegy colored by Christianity ("Oral Tradition", 3). She shifted from a literal to a symbolic interpretation in her introduction to *The Seafarer* edition in 1960, which I will discuss in greater detail later in this chapter (p. 138). E. G. Stanley tried to resolve the tension between realism and allegory by interpreting the "imagined situation" of the poem in terms of poetic diction.

Both *The Seafarer* scholarship and Tolkien's writing reflect the aesthetic debate between allegory and symbol during the first half of the twentieth century. Responding to the Romantic method of interpretation, early twentieth-century scholars described allegory in pejorative terms as an artificial fabulous metaphor, external and arbitrary in contrast to symbol, an inward figural metonymy, and elevated as an intrinsic means of representing truth (D. L. Madsen, 121–22). In *The Allegory of Love*, C. S. Lewis clearly divides symbolism as a "mode of thought" and allegory as a "mode of expression" (48). D. L. Madsen interprets Lewis's demarcation: "So allegory takes an intangible fact and invents *visibilia* with which to express it; symbolism, however, records the attempt to see a spiritual archetype through or within our material world" (122). Tolkien is likely to have been sympathetic to Lewis's division of allegory and symbol because he read parts of *The Allegory of Love* before its publication (Lewis, 1) and expressed a similar "topical" view of allegory in his letters.

> I dislike Allegory – the conscious and intentional allegory – yet any attempt to explain the purport of myth or fairytale must use allegorical language. (And, of course, the more "life" a story has the more readily will it be susceptible of allegorical interpretations: while the better a deliberate allegory is made the more nearly will it be acceptable just as a story.)
>
> (*Letters*, 145)

Despite this statement, Tolkien did write allegorically. His well-known lecture "*Beowulf*: The Monsters and the Critics" allegorizes scholars reading *Beowulf*, and his short story "Leaf by Niggle" is an allegory for the creative process or, as Tolkien would say, "sub-creation."[7] Criticism of *The Seafarer* between the 1930s and 1950s was mixed, partly new critical and partly patristic-allegorical, and Tolkien reflects both these positions at various times in his criticism and fiction.[8]

Although it is difficult to conjecture what Tolkien's interpretation of *The Seafarer* would have been since Tolkien's criticism and fiction reflect both symbolist and allegorical positions, it is possible that E. V. Gordon and Tolkien's interpretation may have influenced Ida Gordon's symbolist interpretation of *The Seafarer* in the introduction to her edition published in 1960. Ida Gordon, E. V. Gordon's widow, indicates in her foreword that she used notes by her husband and Tolkien as the basis for her edition. She rejects allegory as an explicit genre since the tone of lament instead suggests elegy. She interprets the secular seafaring imagery in the first half of *The Seafarer* as mirroring the Christian associations in the second half (7). Gordon traces the themes of exile and wandering in terms of the Old Irish and Old Welsh secular lyric elegy characterized by personal lament and gnomic utterances (15–21), the plaint for the brevity of life in Latin scholastic poetry (14), and the vocabulary of the Germanic heroic poetry (26–27).

Linguistic manipulation is the second stage of Tolkien's assimilation of *The Seafarer* into his own work. Although Tolkien did not complete an edition of *The Seafarer*, the poem remained in his consciousness. In addition to lecturing and other professorial duties, Tolkien continued working on his mythology *The Silmarillion*, which he started while convalescing from trench fever in 1917. The earliest drafts were called "The Book of Lost Tales,"[9] in which Eriol, a mariner of close kin to the Northwestern legendary figures Hengest and Horsa, sails west to Tol-eressëa, an Elvish island, and becomes a witness to Elvish history. In later revisions, Tolkien changes Eriol's name to Ælfwine, who sails west from Anglo-Saxon England to find the Elves (*BLT1*, 13–20; *BLT2*, 278–334). In the 1930s, Tolkien started a new story, "The Lost Road," in which the Eriol/Ælfwine figure reappears as a dreamer, sailor, and time traveler from northern Somerset *c.* 915, who most literally embodies the Seafarer as a character.[10] In several drafts of this story, Ælfwine chants a poem in Old English derived from *The Seafarer* at the court of King Edward the Elder (*Lost Road*, 83–104).

> Monað modes lust mid mereflode
> forð to feran, þæt ic feor heonan
> ofer hean holmas, ofer hwæles eðel
> elþeodigra eard gesece.
> Nis me to hearpan hyge ne to hyringþege
> ne to wife wyn ne to worulde hyht
> ne ymb owiht elles nefne ymb yða gewealc.

> [The desire of my spirit urges me to journey forth over the flowing sea, that far hence across the hills of water and the whale's country I may seek the land of strangers. No mind have I for harp, nor gift, nor delight in women, nor joy in the world, nor concern with aught else save the rolling of the waves.]

(*Lost Road*, 84)

Tolkien's version alters some phrasing and omits five lines from the original *Seafarer* text. He situates not only the language of his rewritten text but also his character Ælfwine in a setting reflecting the contemporary scholarly opinion regarding the text and date of the Exeter Book.[11]

Tolkien further incorporated *The Seafarer* into a creative linguistic form in a later story, "The Notion Club Papers." He abandoned "The Lost Road" after several chapters and revisions, but the themes and characters reappear in "The Notion Club Papers," a story written in 1945 during the later stages of the composition of *The Lord of the Rings*. Both "The Lost Road" and "The Notion Club Papers" were conceived as projects addressing the question of time and myth, especially in relation to developing a comprehensive English mythology. In "The Notion Club Papers," two Oxford dons, members of an informal literary society called the Notion Club, travel back in time to the mythic past of *The Silmarillion*. One of the dons, Lowdham, has a dream: he hears and sees Old English lines similar to those chanted by Ælfwine in "The Lost Road," and which Lowdham believes were derived from *The Seafarer*, "that strange old poem of longing" (*Sauron*, 243).

> Monath modaes lust mith merifloda
> forth ti foeran thaet ic feorr hionan
> obaer gaarseggaes grimmae holmas
> aelbuuina eard uut gisoecae.
> Nis me ti hearpun hygi ni ti hringthegi
> ni ti wibae wyn ni ti weoruldi hyct
> ni ymb oowict ellaes nebnae ymb ytha giwalc.
>
> [My soul's desire over the sea-torrents
> forth bids me fare, that I afar should seek
> over the ancient water's awful mountains
> Elf-friends' island in the Outer-world.
> For no harp have I heart, no hand for gold,
> in no wife delight, in the world no hope:
> one wish only, for the waves' tumult.]
>
> (*Sauron*, 243–44)

Lowdham analyzes his dream as an "echo of some older lines that are not found at all among the preserved fragments of the oldest English verses . . . . I think mine is probably the older and better text" (*Sauron*, 244). Tolkien archaizes the orthography and inflection of *The Seafarer*.[12] He also shifts the voice from third person to first. Christopher Tolkien comments that his father probably made alterations to *The Seafarer* because he felt that the preserved text was corrupt (*Sauron*, 287–88 n. 50). In this version, Tolkien substitutes *aelbuuinna eard* (*ælfwina* in later spelling), meaning the "land of the Ælfwines, the Elven-friends," for *The Seafarer* text's *elþeodigra eard*, "land of aliens or foreigners," to more specifically fit his narrative purpose (*Sauron*, 244). Tolkien extends the historical tradition of Old English seafaring in general and of the literary tradition of *The Seafarer* in particular into his own writing (Flieger, *Question of Time*, 162).

Since Tolkien studied and wrote about *The Seafarer* for approximately twenty years before beginning *The Lord of the Rings*, it is not surprising that thematic and verbal echoes of the former reverberate through the latter. One of the similar themes and narrative strategies in both *The Seafarer* and *The Lord of the Rings* is exile, a state characterized by loneliness, bereavement, and deprivation. In the first half of the poem, the Seafarer describes himself as journeying across the *wræclastas*, "the paths of exile," on the sea estranged from land and kin (line 57). The Elves in *The Lord of the Rings* describe themselves to Frodo as being exiles tarrying on Middle-earth for a while before they follow their departed kindred and return over the Great Sea (*FR*, 89). The underlying Christian symbolism regarding the exile of a fallen people establishes a deeper figural association between the two texts.

Exile is also a pertinent metaphor for Christian exegetes: human beings are *peregrini*, or "wanderers," in exile from Paradise and estranged from God. Several biblical passages define the dimensions of man's mortal exile: *peregrinamur a Domino* [we are wandering from the Lord] in 2 Corinthians 5:6 and the influential imagery of the *peregrini et hospites sunt supra terram* [they are wanderers and strangers on the earth] in Hebrews 11:13.[13] The exilic imagery of the New Testament looks back to the cause of human exile, the expulsion from the Garden of Eden, described in Genesis. Further elaborations of the Christian metaphor of exile occur in patristic writing, Christian Latin elegies, and Latin and Old English homilies (Ida Gordon, *Seafarer*, 13–14, 22–27; Smithers, 137–53). In her introduction to the *The Seafarer*, Ida Gordon indicates symbolism between the traditional lyric-elegiac theme of exile and the ecclesiastic metaphor of "exile" for man's life on earth; she also draws symbolic association between the "homeless wanderer" of elegy and the *peregrinus*, the "alien" in this world who seeks his heavenly home (22).[14]

Tolkien, as a devout Catholic and professional medievalist, was very aware of the Christian theme of exile: "Certainly there was an Eden on this very unhappy earth. We all long for it, and we are constantly glimpsing it: our whole nature at its best and least corrupted, its gentlest and most humane, is still soaked with the sense of 'exile'" (*Letters*, 110). Since Tolkien believed that exile was a fundamental human experience, there seems to be correlation in his fictive world where exile is a recurring theme. Tolkien specifically indicates that a sense of a fall and consequent "mortal" estrangement is crucial in both the process of sub-creation (*Letters*, 145) and Elvish history, particularly the Noldorin exile from the Valar (*Letters*, 147–48).[15] But certainly Tolkien's *The Silmarillion* and *The Lord of the Rings* cannot be reduced to a mythological retelling of Christian theology.

Verbal echoes and thematic concerns from *The Seafarer* surface subtly in *The Lord of the Rings*. Images of crying seabirds, sailing, and the arrival of spring occur in both the Old English poem and Tolkien's works with similar thematic implications. Elegiac poignancy characterizes the exilic imaginings of the Seafarer and the Elves.[16] The Seafarer and the Elves are prompted to leave their exilic state and sail in search of eternal existence in a Christian or mythological paradise, with the sea as the bridge between their mortal existence and eternal existence. Nevertheless, these seafarers cannot travel between states of existence regardless of their anticipation of future joys until they reconcile their memories of the past and forsake their earthly materiality. I will examine the three levels of exilic dislocation the Seafarer and the Elves experience, and then I will focus on the process of departure from the exilic abode or the return to the true homeland where there is greatest verbal resonance between the two texts.

Exile

In their exilic imagining, both the Seafarer and Tolkien's Elves experience a juxtaposition of two time dimensions: the past and future. The exiles must prepare themselves to relinquish the past before embarking into the unknown future. At the moment of decision, the exiles do not simply experience time linearly as a journey toward paradise but as a dynamic fusion of memories and expectations in the present (Ricoeur, 21–22). Essentially, both the Seafarer and the Elves must confront mortality to a certain degree in preparation for their movement from the mortal plane of exile to an exalted or redeemed state. This blurring of passage through time and preoccupation with loss heighten the elegiac tone in both the Old English poem and *The Lord of the Rings.*

Exile involves dislocation on several levels: temporal, spatial, and spiritual. The intensity of the exilic experience increases with the combination of estrangements. On a temporal level, the memory of a more pleasant past conflicts with the sorrow of the present exilic experience. The limitations of the body govern the spatial level. On a figural level, a spiritual exile is estrangement from the divine, a rupture between an ideal state and a fallen state. These three levels often function in complex combinations unique to a particular individual's exile. However, complex experiences cannot always be labeled in terms of artificially discrete categories; often the boundaries among temporal, spatial, and spiritual levels blur since time is frequently expressed in terms of space and spiritual abstraction is described in terms of the concrete.

On a temporal level, memory of a past time is essential for the perception of exile; if no tension existed between past and present, the exilic experience would not be painful and laden with loss. The Seafarer is much preoccupied with remembering his physical discomforts and loneliness on past sea journeys (1–33a), and he laments the general decay of mortal life. The Elves, too, are burdened with memories of two long ages of strife and sorrow in Middle-earth in contrast with their long treasured memories of the beauty in Valinor, the earthly paradise, from which they were exiled. Tolkien describes the Elvish anguish: "Their temptation is different towards a faint melancholy, burdened with Memory, leading to an attempt to halt Time" (*Letters*, 267).

The Seafarer suffers hardship, pain, and sorrow while sailing the harsh seas. The first thirty lines of the poem, filled with images of icy hail and stormy waves, create the mood of bleak isolation. The description of physical and emotional trials at sea represent the spiritual hazards of earthly life (Ida Gordon, *Seafarer*, 10).

> siþas secgan, hu ic geswincdagum
> earfoðhwile oft þrowade,
> bitre breostceare gebiden hæbbe

gecunnad in ceole cearselda fela,
atol yþa gewealc, þær mec oft bigeat
nearo nihtwaco æt nacan stefnan,
þonne he be clifum cnossað.

[I relate trials, how often I suffered days of affliction in times of hardship; I have endured bitter breast-care, experienced many abodes of sorrow on the ship: terrible tossing of the waves, the oppressive night watch held me there often at the boat's brow since it dashes by cliffs.]

(*Seafarer*, lines 2–8a)[17]

The cold blasts of wind and piercing hailstorms in lines 29b–33a intensify the realistic, vivid portrayal of the winter environment. The Seafarer suffers cold, hunger, loneliness, and danger on the stormy seas, while the Elves suffer hardships in the long war against Morgoth in the northernmost reaches of Middle-earth. The Elves assume the position as leaders in the *nihtwaco* against foul beings of all sorts, and experience sorrow when their kingdoms and heroes are ravaged.

Both the Seafarer and the Elves lament the lost golden past; they dwell on the desirability of that irretrievable past. Tolkien describes the pull of memory on the Elves in one of his letters:

> But the Elvish weakness was in these terms naturally to regret the past, and to become unwilling to face change: as if a man were to hate a very long book still going on, and wished to settle down in a favourite chapter. Hence they fall in a measure to Sauron's deceits: they desired some "power" over things as they are (which is quite distinct from art), to make their particular will to preservation effective: to arrest change, and keep things always fresh and fair.
>
> (*Letters*, 236)

However, the Elves must confront the fact that their preserving power is vulnerable to mortal mutability. Their handiwork, although beautiful and marvelous in relation to other races in Middle-earth, is ultimately temporary. The Seafarer poignantly expresses this acceptance of the transitory uncertainty of material possessions and social institutions.

Dagas sind gewitene,
ealle onmedlan eorþan rices;
nearon nu cyningas ne caseras
ne goldgiefan swylce iu wæron,
þonne hi mæst mid him mærþa gefremedon
ond on dryhtlicestum dome lifdon.

[Days are soon over, all the glories of the kingdom on earth; now there are no kings, nor caesars, nor gold-givers, such as there were once before, when they accomplished most fame with them, and lived in most lordly glory.]

(*Seafarer*, lines 80b–85)

This passage echoes the *ubi sunt* section in *The Wanderer* (lines 92–98) and the theme of general decay in *The Ruin* (lines 21–41a). Political stability within an Anglo-Saxon kingdom rarely lasted more than several generations, hostility between kingdoms contributed to political turbulence, and encroaching Viking raids resulted in loss of Anglo-Saxon life and property (Loyn, 45–72).

Tolkien made such political and social instability a part of Elvish kingdoms. Many Elvish heroes – Fëanor and his sons, Fingolfin, Fingon, Celebrimbor, and Gil-galad, to name a few – were lost in the wars of Middle-earth, and the beautiful lands and cities of Gondolin, Nargothrond, Beleriand, and Eregion were laid waste. After the Silmarilli were lost, many of the Eldar sailed west and "never came back to the lands of weeping and of war" (*Silm*, 315). Other Elves, like the Nimrodel and her lover Amroth, were lost while seeking the havens (*FR*, 355). However, some Eldar leaders – Cirdan the Shipwright, Celeborn and Galadriel, and Elrond – remained in Middle-earth with their households. By the end of the Third Age, when *The Lord of the Rings* begins, four Elf kingdoms linger: the West Havens, Rivendell, Greenwood (Mirkwood), and Lothlórien, where the Elves struggle to preserve the beauty they love.

The limitations of the body govern exile on the spatial level. The Seafarer desires to be in the *elþeodigra eard*, "the country of foreigners" (line 38), which some scholars have interpreted as the land of the *peregrini*, "the pilgrims," or in other words, the heavenly homeland of the righteous (Smithers, 6). The sea is a spatial symbol of the division between mortality and immortality. To cross this division, the Seafarer must do more than alter his position in space: he must change his mode of existence through the death of his body. On Middle-earth, the immortal Elves experience a degree of mortality when they become more susceptible to being killed in battle. But since their bodies are capable of being immortal, many Elves must confront mortality by means of their transitory environment rather than by death.

A fundamental theme in both *The Seafarer* and *The Lord of the Rings* is the relationship between mortality and immortality. In *The Lord of the Rings*, Tolkien must negotiate the interactions of immortal and mortal beings. He summarized his thematic intentions in a letter:

> The real theme for me is about something much more permanent and difficult [than war]: Death and Immortality, the mystery of the love of the world in the hearts of a race "doomed" to leave and seemingly lose it; the anguish in the hearts of a race "doomed" not to leave it, until its whole evil-aroused story is complete.
>
> (*Letters*, 246)

Although immortal, the Elves must come to terms with mortality since they interact with mortal beings and are inhabitants of a world in constant flux. The Seafarer also must confront death because of the uncertain length of his own life. He lists three causes for the cessation of life: old age, battle, and sickness (lines 68–71). As the Seafarer comes to terms with his own death, he realizes that, regardless of whether he leads a life of hardship or ease, he will die. He is consoled with the hope that after death his life of hardship will be rewarded.

> Gedroren is þeos duguð eal, dreamas sind gewitene;
> wuniað þa wacran ond þas woruld healdað,
> brucað þurh bisgo. Blæd is gehnæged,
> eorþan indryhto ealdað ond searað,
> swa nu monna gehwylc geond middangeard.
> Yldo him on fareð, onsyn blacað,
> gomelfeax gnornað, wat his iuwine,
> æþelinga bearn, eorþan forgiefene.
>
> [All the host has fallen, the joys are passed away, the weaker ones remain and hold fast this world, use it through labor. Glory is bowed down, the honor of the earth grows old and withers, as does each man throughout middle-earth. Old age sets on him, his face turns pale, the gray-haired one mourns, knows his lost friends, sons of nobles, have been laid in earth.]
>
> (*Seafarer*, 86–93)

The Seafarer evokes death; death depends on time and time upon death. If there is no time, there can be no death. The progression of time emphasizes the brute facts of human biology: aging and death follow birth. Things of the mortal world are mutable; the only true permanence and security exist in God.

It is on Middle-earth that the exiled Elves experience a degree of mortality. The Noldor would never have passed the ice that marked the boundary of Valinor if they had yet been subject to the "weariness, sickness, and the many weaknesses that after became their lot dwelling far from Valinor," but "still was the blessed food of the Gods and their drink rich in their veins and they were half-divine" (*BLT1*, 166). The Noldor were "but new-come from the Blessed Realm, and not yet weary with the weariness of Earth," according to *The Silmarillion* (90). But they become more susceptible to being killed in battle, live in a transitory environment, and watch everything else die. The Curse of Mandos specifies the limitations of the Noldorin immortality: "Eru appointed you to die not in Ea … , and no sickness may assail you, yet slain ye may be, and slain ye shall be" (*Silm*, 88). The Doom of Mandos for the kin of Fëanor and all those Elves who refused to turn back to Valinor is repeated in "The Lost Road":

> A measure of mortality should visit the Noldor, and they should be slain with weapons, and with torments, and with sorrow, and in the long end they should fade upon Middle-earth and wane before the younger race. Much else he foretold darkly that after befell, and he warned them that the Valar would fence Valinor against their return.
>
> (*Lost Road*, 116)

In this unhappy state, the Noldor establish themselves on Middle-earth and begin their long years of sorrow. *The Silmarillion* tells of the long Elvish struggle against Morgoth for the Silmarilli and later against Sauron, the next dark lord, after his treacherous creation of the One Ring. By the end of the Third Age, when *The Lord of the Rings* begins, the Elves remaining in exile on Middle-earth harbor a long memory of grief and loss.

Not only did the Elves suffer the loss of their own kinsman; they are saddened because they must watch in grief as generations of their mortal friends pass away (*Silm*, 178). In Middle-earth, the Elves perceive their immortality to be a tragedy because, as the constants in the midst of flux, they have to relinquish precious objects and individuals. This conflicts with their natural possessive instinct. It is men and Hobbits in *The Lord of the Rings* who model the necessity of letting go and dealing with the subsequent pain of loss while trusting in the unknown future (Flieger, *Question of Time*, 114). The Elves envy man's death because, as immortals, they are doomed to live through all time in weariness and watch the other inhabitants of Middle-earth pass away.

> Nay, time does not tarry ever, but change and growth is not in all things and places alike. For the Elves the world moves, and it moves both very swift and very slow. Swift, because they themselves change little, and all else fleets by: it is a grief to them. Slow, because they do not count the running of years, not for themselves. The passing of seasons are but ripples ever repeated in the long stream. Yet beneath the Sun all things must wear to an end at last.
> (*FR*, 404–5)

Tolkien twists mortal sadness by portraying the opposite situation – immortality and the related inherent difficulties. The timeless Elves and temporal men live in the world at different speeds, and their intersecting paths must involve a shift from "time to timelessness" (Flieger, *Question of Time*, 107–8). Each race desires what the other has: One must let go of life and the world and the other cannot relinquish its hold. Verlyn Flieger concludes, "Human as we all are, it is hard to face death, hard to accept loss, hard, therefore, to find consolation in the Escape from Deathlessness" (114).

On a figural level, a spiritual exile is an estrangement from the divine: a rupture between an ideal state and a fallen state. In Christian terms, the Seafarer is in spiritual exile from God as a mortal being on earth. The Elves on Middle-earth are removed from the wisdom and power of the divine Valar. Spiritual exiles seek to bridge the spatial and temporal dislocation that separates them from the divine.

In *The Seafarer*, the abstract qualities of heaven and earth are polarized in the homiletic section: "Blæd is gehnæged, / eorþan indryhto ealað and searað, / swa nu monna gehwylc geond middangeard" (lines 88–90) [the glory, the honor of earth, is curbed, grows old and withers, just as every man now throughout middle-earth] is juxtaposed against the "ecan lifes blæd, / dream mid dugeþum" [glory of eternal life, bliss among the noblest] available with the angels (lines 79–80). Transience, the limitations of the body, and the flaws of mortality cannot compare to the timelessness, sanctification, and redemption of eternal glory in heaven.

Tolkien incorporates an estrangement from the divine in his cosmogony; the exiled Elves are physically absent from the Valar and thus they experience temporal and spiritual dislocation as well. Tolkien explained in a letter that Elvish history is about the

> fall of the most gifted kindred of Elves [the Noldor], their exile from Valinor (a kind of Paradise, the home of the Gods) in the furthest West, their re-entry into Middle-earth, the land of their birth but long under the rule of the Enemy, and their strife with him, the power of Evil still visibly incarnate.
>
> (*Letters*, 148).[18]

At the end of the Third Age, the Elves are suddenly faced with the future, either fading or leaving Middle-earth forever. Both options are painful, and both will involve a great deal of loss. The Seafarer is also faced with the decision of whether to remain in familiar complacency or to seek his lost homeland. The seeking will involve sacrifice of familiarity, separation, and hardship.

The greatest textual similarities between *The Seafarer* and *The Lord of the Rings* occur during the process of decision-making the Seafarer and the Elves must complete before they embark on their journey from exile. Caught between static familiarity and the unknown, the exiles must confront the past and future. The inevitable passing of time propels the Seafarer and the Elves into the future, but their memories pull them back into nostalgic melancholy as they dwell on their loss. This blurring passage through time creates a particularly poignant elegiac moment that André Aciman eloquently describes as exilic imagining.

> With their memories on overload, exiles see double, feel double, are double. When exiles see one place they're also seeing – looking for – another behind it … . Exiles see two or more places at the same time not just because they are addicted to a lost past. There is a very real, active component to seeing in this particularly heightened retrospective manner: an exile is continuously prospecting for a future home.
>
> (*Letters*, 13)

In response to specific external influences, the Seafarer and the Elves experience the doubleness inherent in exilic imagining when they feel tension between their desire to journey home and their possessive hesitancy.

Sea birds and desire

Two passages in *The Seafarer* and two passages in *The Lord of the Rings* depict the Seafarer's and Legolas's desire for a sea journey. The *modes lust* [heart's desire] (line 36) prompts both the Seafarer and, I would argue, the Elves to leave their homes, possessions, and communities for the divine. The sea becomes a conduit between the mortal and spiritual plane for both the Seafarer and the Elves.

The Seafarer and Legolas juxtapose their present locations in Anglo-Saxon England and Middle-earth with their desired destinations: *elþeodigra eard* [country of foreigners] and Valinor, the Elvenhome, in the doubleness of exilic imagining. The Seafarer's and Legolas's psychic instability between past and future is paralleled in the physicality of the crashing waves and the tossing birds in all of the textual examples.

> For þon cnyssað nu
> heortan geþohtas, þæt ic hean streamas,
> sealtyþa gelac sylf cunnige –
> monað modes lust mæla gehwylce
> ferð to feran, þæt ic feor heonan
> elþeodigra eard gesece –
>
> [Therefore now thoughts press my heart, that I, myself, in the deep flood, tumult of the salt-wave, come to knowledge, the spirit's desire admonishes the soul to travel every occasion, so that I seek a country of foreigners far from here.]
>
> (*Seafarer*, 33b–38)

This contemplated voyage is different from the seafaring experience already described. The *elþeodigra eard* has been interpreted as the heavenly home of the *peregrini*, men exiled on earth (Ida Gordon, *Seafarer*, 38). *Elþeodigra* is specifically used metaphorically in the Blickling homily for Quinquagesima Sunday.

> Forþon we habbaþ nedþearfe þæt we ongyton þa blindnesse ure ælþeodignesse; we send on þisse worlde ælþeodignesse; we synd on þisse worlde ælþeodige, & swa wæron siþþon se æresta ealdor þisses menniscan cynnes Godes bebodu abræc; & forþon gylte we wæron on þysne wræc-siþ sende, & nu eft sceolon oþerne eþel secan, swa wite, swa wuldor, swe we nu geearnian willaþ.
>
> [Therefore it is needful for us to perceive the blindness of our pilgrimage; we are in the foreign land of this world – we are exiles in this world, and so have been ever since the progenitor of the human race broke God's behests, and for that sin we have been sent into this banishment, and now we must seek hereafter another kingdom, either in misery or in glory, as we may choose to merit.]
>
> (Morris, *Blickling Homilies* 2: 23.1)

The manuscript of the *Blickling Homilies* is dated to the tenth or eleventh century.[19] It is plausible that a common audience would recognize the imagery of Blickling homilies in *The Seafarer*: a Christian desires to return to his *eþel*, his heavenly homeland that is foreign to this mortal world.

Legolas describes the Elvish desire to return to their homeland in the far west with the Valar. This desire is manifest in the sea-longing inherent in Elves: sailing west on the straight trajectory to the Valar is their literal passage from the mortal-like life on Middle-earth to the divine. The Valar gave the High Elves who still lingered in Middle-earth grace, so that when they at last wearied of the mortal lands, they could take a ship from the Grey Havens and pass into the Uttermost West; and this grace continued after the change of the world (*RK*, 351). A *palantír* remained in the Tower of Emyn Beraid at the Gulf of Lune. Unlike the other stones, this stone looked only to the sea. Elendil set it there so that he could look back with "straight sight" and see Eressëa in the vanished west. Cirdan puts it on Elrond's ship when he leaves (*FR*, 74, 154; *RK*, 361). The journey across the western sea on the straight way from Middle-earth to Valinor corresponds to a mortal's physical death and a soul's journey to heaven.

Elvish sea-longing is an innate desire tied both to the music of Illuvatar heard in water and to their desire for their western home, Valinor (*Silm*, 19–20). For example, Galadriel warns Legolas, Frodo's Elf companion, that he will no longer feel peace once he hears sea waves. When Legolas hears the crying gulls at the mouth of the Audain he cries:

> Look! … Gulls! … A wonder they are to me and a trouble to my heart. Never in all my life had I met them, until we came to Pelargir, and there I heard them crying in the air as we rode to the battle of the ships. Then I stood still, forgetting war in Middle-earth; for their wailing voices spoke to me of the Sea. The Sea! Alas! I have not yet beheld it. But deep in the hearts of all my kindred lies the sea-longing, which it is perilous to stir. Alas! For the gulls. No peace shall I have again under beech or under elm.
>
> (*RK*, 149)

The journey over the sea represents the end of the Elvish exile from their immortal peers and the end of the Seafarer's mortal exile. The Seafarer is "longing to leave the cliffs and rocks of time and set out for the distant glories of eternity" (Anderson, 15).

The second passage in *The Seafarer* describes the psychological change that precedes physical movement. The verbs of journeying, wandering, and roaming with the spirit foreshadow the physical movement of the ship that will bear the Seafarer and the Elves away.

> Þæt se beorn ne wat,
> sefteadig secg, hwæt þa sume dreogað
> þe þa wræclastas widost lecgað.
> For þon nu min hyge hweorfeð ofer hreþerlocan,
> min modsefa mid mereflode,
> ofer hwæles eþel hweorfeð wide,
> eorþan sceatas, cymeð eft to me
> gifre ond grædig.

> [That man, the warrior in luxury, does not know what some suffer, those who journey the most vast paths of exile. Because now my spirit wanders from the body's chest over the sea-flood, roams wide over the country of the whale, the regions of the earth, the lonely flier yells, calls also to me desirous and hungry.]
>
> (*Seafarer*, lines 55b–62a)

The spirit flying over the sea represents the Seafarer's spiritual journey necessary to find earthly paradise in anticipation of the soul's release from the body and journey to heavenly paradise. The mind/spirit wandering far and wide recalls the awakening of Legolas's desire to follow the birds across the sea.

> To the Sea, to the Sea! The white gulls are crying,[20]
> The wind is blowing, and the white foam is flying.
> West, west away, the round sun is falling.
> Grey ship, grey ship, do you hear them calling,
> The voices of my people that have gone before me?
> I will leave, I will leave the woods that bore me;
> For our days are ending and our years are failing.
> I will pass the wide waters lonely sailing.
> Long are the waves on the Last Shore falling,
> Sweet are the voices in the Lost Isle calling,
> In Eressëa, in Elvenhome that no man can discover,
> Where the leaves fall not: land of my people for ever!
>
> (*RK*, 261)

Legolas cannot escape the fate of his race: to depart from Middle-earth or remain and fade. Like the Seafarer, Legolas suffers heart-wrenching pain at the thought of leaving Middle-earth, but the desire to seek the land beyond the lapping sea waves burns bright in his breast. The passage over the sea is not death for the Elves. According to Tolkien's mythology, there was first an actual Earthly Paradise, the home and realm of the Valar, as a physical part of the earth (*Letters*, 237). The Elves leave Middle-earth in ships built in the form of great white birds to sail west beyond the global limits of the ocean in a literally straight trajectory more akin to bird flight than a ship sailing on the curvature of the globe. Although human death involves the separation of the soul from the body, the Elves simply board a ship to sail to another state of existence.

Possessive hesitancy

In the second example, both quotations depict the pull of the possessiveness of materiality resulting in the Seafarer's and the Elves' hesitancy to leave, even though the departure has the promise of a greater reward. Their longing to depart on the journey home is great, but they sorrow because of the precious things left behind. The Seafarer must leave his family, society, and familiar daily life for the uncertainty of a journey into the unknown. Although he holds the *wen*, "expectation," of bliss, his faith is not as tangible a source of strength as experience in the face of the unknown.

For þon nis þæs modwlonc mon ofer eorþan,
ne his gifena þæs god, ne in geoguþe to þæs hwæt,
ne in his dædum to þæs deor, ne him his dryhten to þæs hold,
þæt he a his sæfore sorge næbbe,
to hwon hine Dryhten gedon wille.
Ne biþ to hearpan hyge ne to hringþege –
ne to wife wyn ne to worulde hyht –
ne ymbe owiht elles nefne ymb yða gewealc;
ac a hafað longunge se þe on lagu fundað.

[There is no man over earth so proud spirited, nor so good of his gifts, nor so bold in youth, nor so valiant in his deeds, nor his lord so loyal to him, that he will not always feel anxiety over his voyage, as to what is the Lord's purpose for him. Nor is there any thought for the harp, nor for receiving rings, nor for joy in a woman, nor for hope in the world, nor for any thing else outside the thrash of the waves, yet he who starts a journey always has yearning.]

(*Seafarer*, lines 39–47)

It is human nature to make attachments to one's environment; however, these bonds made with the exilic abode amplify the split the exile experiences upon returning to his or her real home.

In *The Seafarer*, the harp metonymically evokes the music and heroic tales in the mead hall, the gift of rings evokes the reciprocal relationship between the lord and his retainers, and the "wife" evokes family. All three metonymies refer to a different aspect of communal Anglo-Saxon society in contrast with the loneliness evoked by the tossing of waves. The Seafarer declares that he will go forth, with no thought for past pleasures in the mead hall or joys of family, with his mind steadfast on his sea journey. In other words, the Seafarer claims he has no regrets about leaving, though his staunchness is negated by line 47, translated by Nora Kershaw as "yet there is never any peace of mind for him who goes to sea" (169). Ida Gordon also suggests "yearning" as a possible interpretation for *longung*: "yet he who begins a journey always has yearning" (*Seafarer*, 39 n. 47). The Seafarer yearns for familiar social interactions and suffers the bittersweet pangs of loss even with the promise of a greater reward.

Although the Elves feel a growing desire to return to the Valar and be exiles no more, they feel torn by great possessiveness with regard to their handiwork on Middle-earth. The Elvish possessiveness is especially manifest in the Elven Rings wielded by Elrond and Galadriel, who strive to maintain sanctuaries of timeless peace and beauty. The Elves struggle to maintain their traditions and face the imminent fading of their race. Tolkien further elucidates the Elves' nostalgia as a sin of pride and avarice:

> They wanted peace and bliss and perfect memory of "The West" and yet to remain on the ordinary earth where their prestige as the highest people, about wild Elves, Dwarves, and Men, was greater than at the bottom of the hierarchy of Valinor. They thus became obsessed with "fading," the mode in which the changes of time (the law of the world under the sun) was perceived by them. They became sad, and their art antiquarian, and their efforts all really a kind of embalming – even though they also retained the old motive of their kind, the adornment of earth, and the healing of its hurts.
>
> (*Letters* 151–52, see also 197)

Ultimately, the more pressing concern for fading – physically diminishing and intellectually regressing to ignorance – surpasses their hesitancy to leave Middle-earth.

Spring as stimulus

Despite recognizing the necessity for action because of inevitable death or fading, the Seafarer and the Elves remain indecisive until the arrival of spring stimulates them to leave their exilic state. *The Seafarer* lyrically describes the changing of seasons that intensifies the contrast between the earthly transience the exiles experience and the spiritual permanence the exiles seek. As the Fourth Age begins, the Elves know that spring will never come again to their homes and forests because the power of the Elven Rings diminishes.

Like the Elves, the Seafarer contemplates his journey, and his state of mind fluctuates between faith and fear. His inner desire, *modes lust*, and external prompting, *bearwas blostmum nimað*, conflict with his internal trepidations and the external bodings of the cuckoo (Greenfield, 105). There is *sorge* [sorrow] for the materiality left behind. The arrival of spring only indicates the inevitability that winter will return in the endless cycle of seasons. The passage focuses on the transitory nature of earth's beauty; flower blossoms and tree foliage suggest the brevity of earthly life.

> Bearwas blotsmum nimað, byrig fægriað,
> wongas wlitigað, woruld onetteð;
> ealle þa gemoniað modes fusne
> sefan to siþe, þam þe swa þenceð
> on flodwegas feor gewitan.
> Swlyce geac monað geomran reorde
> singeð sumeres weard, sorge beodeð
> bitter' in breosthord.

> [Groves take on blossoms, cities become fair, meadows are beautiful, the world hastens on, all these things urge the spirit eager in mind to journey, to him who thus plans to travel on flood-ways. Likewise, the cuckoo admonishes

> in sorrowful speech, the guardian of summer sings, forebodes grief, bitter into his breast-hoard.]
>
> (*Seafarer*, lines 48–55a)

Like the blossoms and foliage, the cuckoo, a herald of summer, brings only sorrow to the Seafarer; the cuckoo's cry speaks of the inexorable passage of time. The Seafarer recognizes that the *woruld onetteð* [world hastens on] just as his life hastens toward death. Linking springtime beauty with the hastening world cues the reader to a symbolic situation (Cross, 104). Yet the rebirth of nature can also parallel a spiritual awakening. The powerful springtime reminder of both deterioration, which provokes eschatological meditation, and creation, which stimulates spiritual rebirth, prompts the Seafarer to embark on a "spiritually significant journey" (Whittier, 408–9).

The Elves also feel *bitter in breosthord* [bitter in mind/spirit] concerning the arrival of spring. Galadriel tells Frodo that the Elves can only sadly look back from their deepening winter existence in Middle-earth (*FR*, 443). Galadriel laments further: "Do you not see now wherefore your coming is to us as the footstep of Doom? For if you fail, then we are laid bare to the Enemy. Yet if you succeed, then our power is diminished, and Lothlorien will fade, and the tides of Time will sweep it away. We must depart into the West, or dwindle to a rustic folk of dell and cave, slowly to forget and to be forgotten" (*FR*, 431). Her sorrow is best expressed in song; she knows that, whether or not Frodo successfully completes his quest, the golden blossoms will not bloom on the mallorn trees (*FR*, 396).

> I sang of leaves leaves, of leaves of gold, and leaves of gold there grew:
> Of wind I sang, a wind there came and in the branches blew.
> Beyond the Sun, beyond the Moon, the foam was on the Sea,
> And by the strand of Ilmarin there grew a golden Tree.
> Beneath the stars of Ever, eve in Eldamar it shone,
> In Eldamar beside the walls of Elven Tirion.
> There long the golden leaves have grown upon the branching years,
> While here beyond the Sundering Seas now fall the Elven-tears,
> O Lorien! The Winter comes, the bare and leafless Day;
> The leaves are falling in the stream, the River flows away,
> O Lorien! Too long have I dwelt upon this Hither Shore
> And in a fading crown have twined the golden elanor.
> But if of ships I now should sing, what ship would come to me,
> What ship would bear me ever back across so wide a Sea?
>
> (*FR*, 439–40)

Tolkien writes in a later essay, "Shibboleth of Fëanor," that Galadriel's lament "harks back to the days of her youth in Valinor and the darkness of the years of Exile while the Blessed Realm was closed to all the Noldor in Middle-earth" (*Peoples*, 338–39). The "Sea" is used metaphorically for Valinor in contrast to "Hither Shore," representing Middle-earth. Despite Galadriel's sorrow for her beloved mallorn trees, she eventually accompanies Elrond, Gandalf, and Frodo onto the gray ship at the Havens. She realizes, as do the other Elves, that change is inevitable as a result of time's fluid progression and that time cannot be stopped or circumnavigated.

All of the Elvish songs in *The Lord of the Rings* juxtapose Valinor and Middle-earth in the doubleness of exilic imagining. Galadriel's lament polarizes Aman and Lorien just as Legolas standing on the shores of Middle-earth hears the waves falling on the Last Shore in Eressëa, the Elvenhome. Frodo identifies High-elves by their singing another song: "O Elbereth! Gilthoniel! / We still remember, we who dwell / In this far land beneath the trees, / Thy starlight on the Western Seas" (*FR*, 108; *RK*, 344). Even the last stanza of the Elbereth song, sung several times through *The Lord of the Rings*, reflects the gulf between Middle-earth and Valinor.

A similar doubleness is evident in the very format of *The Seafarer*: the initial natural realism followed by a generalized mediation on mortal transience with gnomic and homiletic tones. Together the sections provide a mirror reading of the other; the Seafarer wants to move from the *iscealdne sæ* [ice-cold sea] to the *elþeodigra eard*, and the Christian exile seeks heaven, the *dryhtnes dreamas* [joy of the Lord]. Imagery of spring and the cuckoo prompt the Seafarer to action, and the knowledge that spring will not come impels the Elves to seek the Havens.

Ultimately, both the Seafarer and the Elves must come to terms with a world that is *læne* [loaned], the Old English word for the "temporary nature of things in the world," and with an *ece*, or "eternal," world before they can make the final commitment to embark on their journeys:

> gielleð anfloga,
> hweteð on hwælweg[21] hreþer unwearnum
> ofer holma gelagu, for þon me hatran sind
> Dryhtnes dreamas þonne þis deade lif,
> læne on londe.
>
> [The lonely flier yells, irresistibly, the heart sharpens on the whale-way over the surface of the water. Because the joy of the Lord is far warmer to me than this life in death lent on land.]
>
> (*Seafarer*, lines 62b–66a)

This pivotal passage is the culmination of the previous realism and an elaboration of the theme in more general terms (Whitelock, 266–67). C. W. Kennedy eloquently describes lines 64b to 66a as the moment in *The Seafarer* where "details of past experiences, vividly remembered and sharply reproduced, set the tone of the poem, and lead naturally to the elegiac and Christian passages" (*Elegies*, 18). Just as the Seafarer contemplates the limits of mortality in contrast to the everlasting joy in heaven within the context of his final journey, the Elves, too, anticipate arriving at an eternal destination without the impermanence and mortality of Middle-earth.

The last few lines of *The Seafarer* make the final summary of exile and return. Although men live on earth, a land far away from God, they have hope of reconciliation and returning to God after death. The only way to reverse the consequences of the Fall is to live faithfully and seek God's mercy.

> Uton we hycgan hwær we ham agen,
> ond þonne geþencan hu we þider cumen,
> ond we þonne eac tilien, þæt we to moten
> in þa ecan eadignesse,
> þær is life gelong in lufan dryhtnes,
> hyht in heofonum.
>
> [Let us ponder where we are going home and then think how we came thither and then we each strive that we may arrive into the everlasting happiness, which is the long life in the love of the Lord, hope in heaven.]
>
> (*Seafarer*, lines 117–22a)

It is this exilic imagining between earth and heaven that offers the final explanation of *The Seafarer* and, specifically, the movement of the spirit from the body in search of the *dryhtenes dreamas* [joys of the lord {or band}]. Tolkien incorporates the Seafarer's preoccupation with transience in relationships and the losses and suffering in mortality into *The Lord of the Rings* as a result of a progression of influence beginning with scholarly textual engagement, followed by linguistic manipulation, and culminating with fictive integration.

In danger of losing hope in the face of mortal transience, both the Seafarer and the Elves opt figuratively and literally to set sail to their eternal home. The sea becomes a transcendent bridge between the mortal and the divine. However, the journey is bittersweet with the pain of loss. In neither account do the seafarers reach their journey's end and verify their paradisiacal expectations; their destination remains but a vision. They remain caught in a poignant gap between the past pains of mortality and future expectations of joy. Reflecting on such texts helps us to capture a brief glimpse of the essence of exile.

Notes

I am very grateful to Katherine O'Brien O'Keeffe for her guidance and helpful advice. I would also like to thank Diego Bartholomew and Daniel Perett for their Tolkien expertise and their encouragement. However, any errors are my own.

1 Other scholars have further documented Tolkien's use of linguistic forms and images from medieval literature. See Chance (Nitzsche), *Tolkien's Art*, and Shippey, *Road to Middle-earth*, for more information about Tolkien's literary sources. Also see St. Clair, "Overview of the Northern Influence on Tolkien's Works," in Reynolds and GoodKnight, 63–67, and "*Volsunga Saga* and Narn," 68–72; Mitchell, "J. R. R. Tolkien and Old English Studies," in Reynolds and GoodKnight, 206–12; Andy Orchard, "Tolkien, the Monsters, and the Critics: Back to *Beowulf*," in Battarbee, 73–84; Verlyn Flieger, "The Green Man, the Green Knight, and Treebeard: Scholarship and Invention in Tolkien's Fiction," in Battarbee, 85–97; Clive Tolley, "Sægde seþe cuþe: J. R. R. Tolkien as Anglo-Saxonist," in Battarbee, 99–110, and

"Tolkien the Unfinished," in Battarbee, 151–64; and also Jonathan Evans, "The Dragon-Lore of Middle-earth," in Clark and Timmons, 21–38.

2 Christopher Tolkien edited J. R. R. Tolkien's "The Lost Road," in *The Lost Road and Other Writings*, and "The Notion Club Papers," in *Sauron Defeated: The End of the Third Age*.

3 Manuscript no. 116 in Ker.

4 The dates regarding Tolkien's life are taken from Humphrey Carpenter's biographical appendix B in *Biography*, 264–67. See also chapters 3 and 4 for more details concerning Tolkien's scholarship.

5 *Seafarer* scholarship before 1920 was dominated by three difficulties: the translation of *forþon* in lines 27a, 33, 39, 58a, and 64; the interpretation of the poem as a dialogue between an experienced seafarer and a young mariner; and identification where the text was corrupt as a result of scribal error and/or Christian interpolation. These three difficulties were first suggested by German scholars in the late nineteenth century and early twentieth century. The German arguments are summarized in 1902 by Lawrence in "*The Wanderer* and *The Seafarer*," and by Krapp and Dobbie in *The Exeter Book*. By the time Kershaw's *Anglo-Saxon and Norse Poems* was published, the dialogue theory was out of favor, *forþon* could be translated as a colorless adverbial phrase "assuredly" without controversy, and only the integrity of lines 103–24 remained in question (16–19). The dialogue theory was later to be reargued by Pope in "Dramatic Voices in *The Wanderer* and *The Seafarer*."

6 Even though Smithers's interpretation in "The Meaning of *The Seafarer* and *The Wanderer*," has been labeled allegory, Smithers himself qualified his argument: "The human figure used to introduce *The Seafarer* and *The Wanderer* is not straightforwardly or solely allegorical. In building up two imaginary human beings from the typical and therefore abstract *peregrinus* and 'exile,' the author(s) have to some extent translated these two notions back into terms of ordinary reality" (6). The Anglo-Saxon poets were able to turn type-figures into human beings because the connections would be clear to the contemporary audience without explicit mention.

7 See *Tolkien's Art* by Chance (Nitzsche) (57–67) for an allegorical interpretation of "A Leaf by Niggle." See also Shippey's *Road to Middle-earth* (33–42).

8 Since "acts of interpretive allegory are transactions between fluctuating critical communities and formative texts," postmodern theorists with revised interpretations and definitions might read *The Seafarer* and *The Lord of the Rings* in terms of allegory (Whitman, 6; C. Madsen, 109–10). Seidel describes the "implicit allegory of exilic imagining" (15). Seidel believes the notion of difference and distance in the exilic situation lends itself to allegorical reading "because [of] the doubleness implicit in exilic positioning" (14).

9 Christopher Tolkien edited J. R. R. Tolkien's "The Book of Lost Tales" in two volumes.

10 See Flieger's essay "Footsteps of Ælfwine," for a detailed analysis of the progression of the Eriol/Ælfwine figure in Tolkien's fiction.

11 Tolkien matches his word forms to those characteristic in the Exeter Book. Förster describes the vocabulary and phonology in the Exeter Book as being West Saxon with an archaic flavor of an Anglian dialect (Chambers *et al.*, 66–7). Flower concludes by dating the manuscript to 970–90 with composition in west Wessex (Chambers *et al.*, 90). Contemporary scholarship is considerably less confident about using evidence in the verse for purposes of localization.

12 Tolkien uses consonant symbols found in the earliest Old English texts (A. Campbell, 54): "th" for "þ and "ð" (55, 57), "b" for "f" (57), lowering of "i" to "e" and "o" (123), double consonants (63, 65), and "-un" weak case ending for "-an" (617).

13

> Iuxta fidem defuncti sunt omnes isti non acceptis repromissionibus sed a longe eas aspicientes et salutantes et confitentes quia peregrini et hospites sunt supra

terram. Qui enim haec dicunt significant se patriam inquirere et si quidem illius meminissent de qua exierunt habebant utique tempus revertendi nunc autem meliorem appetunt id est caelestem ideo non confunditur Deus vocari Deus eorum.

(Heb. 11:13–16)

Augustine further elaborates the distinction between a heavenly and an earthly existence in *De civitate Dei* 15.1–2. In *Enarratio in Psalmum CXXV* 1, 3, Augustine extends the *peregrinus* figure to all men: "Homo civis est Ierusalem, sed venitus sub peccato, factus est peregrinus" [Man is a citizen of Jerusalem but having come under sin, he was made alien].

14 Ida Gordon summarizes her interpretation of *The Seafarer* and *The Wanderer* as being concerned "with the commonplaces of universal truths, their approach is an oblique one. They give poetic reality to those commonplaces by setting them in terms of personal experience, imaginative and lyrical, against the background of ancient poetic heritage" (*Seafarer*, 29).

15 "There cannot be any 'story' without a fall – all stories are ultimately about the fall – at least not for human minds as we know them and have them" (J. R. R. Tolkien, *Letters* 147).

16 The use of the term "Elves" in this paper is limited to those living in Middle-earth at the end of the Third Age. These Elves are described in appendix F of *The Lord of the Rings* as being Eldar (West-Elves) composed of two groups: the High-elves, who "had returned in exile to Middle-earth at the end of the First Age," and the Grey-elves, who had not sailed for Valinor but lingered on the shores of Middle-earth. The Exiles adopted the Sindarin language of the more numerous Grey-elves and intermarried. Tolkien concludes the summary by describing the longing explored in this paper: "In the hearts of the Exiles the yearning for the Sea was an unquiet never to be stilled; in the hearts of the Grey-elves it slumbered, but once awakened it could not be appeased" (*RK*, 468).

17 I cite the text from Ida Gordon's edition, *The Seafarer*, instead of from the standard Anglo-Saxon Poetic Record, vol. 3, because Gordon specifically indicates that she incorporates the text and notes produced by her husband and Tolkien (*Seafarer*, vii). All translations are my own unless otherwise noted.

18 See the description of the Noldorin exile in Tolkien's *Silmarillion*, 91–102, and *Letters*, 147–48.

19 Ker manuscript number 382.

20 *The Seafarer* has numerous sea-birds making sounds: "*ylfete song*" [wild swan song] (19); "*ganetes hleoþor*" [gannets cry] (20); "*huilpan sweg*" [curlew melody] (21); "*mæw singende*" [seagull singing] (22); "*stearn isigfeþera*" [tern, ice-feathered one] (23–24); "*earn bigeal, urigfeþra*" [eagle screamed, dewy-feathered one] (24–25).

21 Gordon follows Krapp and Dobbie in emending "*wælweg*" in the manuscript to "*hwælweg*" in favor of meter. However, Smithers suggests that "*wælweg*," a word of uncertain meaning, would be more appropriate. He conjectures that "*wælweg*" means "road to the abode of the dead, road taken by the dead" from the component parts "*wæl*" [corpse, dead body] and "*weg*" [way, road] (Smithers, "Meaning," 137–40; 1959, 99–103). See now Muir, 2:511.

10 "Oathbreakers, why have ye come?"

Tolkien's "Passing of the Grey Company" and the twelfth-century *Exercitus mortuorum*

Margaret A. Sinex

> The Dead awaken;
> for the hour is come for the oathbreakers:
> at the Stone of Erech they shall stand again
> and hear there a horn in the hills ringing.
> Whose shall the horn be? Who shall call them
> from the grey twilight, the forgotten people?
> The heir of him to whom the oath they swore.
> From the North shall he come, need shall drive him:
> He shall pass the Door to the Paths of the Dead.
>
> (J. R. R. Tolkien, *The Return of the King*)[1]

The "Passing of the Grey Company" occupies a crucial place in the long war against Sauron and in the fortunes of the dynasty of the Númenoreans.[2] In this episode, the Lord Aragorn leads a small company beneath the mountains in Rohan to gather the Army of the Dead to fight under his command against the forces of the Dark Lord. Aragorn and his companions choose to walk the Paths of the Dead following the spectacular military victory at Helm's Deep in western Rohan, but only a few days before Sauron openly lays siege to Gondor, the City of Kings. While Gandalf and Pippin ride directly to the High City, and while King Théoden of Rohan musters his army in Edoras to ride to the relief of his beleaguered allies in Minas Tirith, Aragorn learns of a previously unsuspected force sent northwards by the Dark Lord along the Anduin to the siege. So overwhelming is the threat posed by this unforeseen host of reinforcements that Aragorn fears the city of Gondor will fall to Sauron's army unless this new peril is met quickly. Encouraged by Elrond's counsel and the prophecy of an ancient seer, Aragorn chooses to risk gathering the Army of the Dead beneath Rohan's *Dwimorberg* (the "Haunted Mountain"), to ride with them to the banks of the Anduin, and there to cut off Sauron's secondary host before it ever reaches the siege of Minas Tirith.

Within *The Lord of the Rings* as a whole, the episode focuses on Aragorn as a leader, illuminating those traits that justify his destiny as King of both Gondor and Arnor. Again, the positioning of this episode within the larger narrative is quite significant. He leads the Grey Company on the Paths of the Dead *after* he proclaims his title in Rohan and wrests control of the Stone of Orthanc from Sauron, but *before* he displays his standard at the siege of Gondor and enters his own city. Walking the Paths of the Dead is a transitional moment for the future King Elessar. And the episode not only celebrates those traits that make him worthy of kingship but also offers readers glimpses of perils he avoids and temptations he rejects.

Reading the "Passing of the Grey Company" in the context of selected twelfth-century Latin narratives can illuminate many of the episode's crucial features. This "Shadow Host" shares many defining characteristics of the Armies of the Dead we find in twelfth-century accounts, in particular their prolonged spiritual suffering, their restless physical roaming, and of course their appearance. These prescholastic treatments of the *Exercitus mortuorum* highlight two elements of particular relevance to Tolkien's creation: the military threat posed by the troop of the wandering dead and its penitential purpose.

Twelfth-century authors wrote their accounts before the concept of purgatory had fully crystallized and before the ghostly troop became thoroughly "diabolized" and plainly equated with infernal powers (Schmitt, 118). In these early texts, the ultimate spiritual fate of the troop's members is not altogether clear, and as selected examples will illustrate, tormented souls still hope for salvation under certain circumstances. As we shall see, those special circumstances require the cooperation of the living. Consequently, the spiritual meaning assigned to the hosts is more ambiguous, a bit murkier, than it became in later scholastic treatments. Further, a soul's hope of salvation is often intertwined with some very mundane political and familial (even financial) concerns. That is, as Jean-Claude Schmitt notes, "In earlier tales, the theme participated simultaneously in secular strategies for power and in monarchic ideology," whereas later, in the hands of the scholastics, "[t]he framework of reference is no longer monarchic ideology but moral theology" (120). Similarly, as we shall see, Tolkien's Shadow Host is very much involved in "secular strategies for power" in the long struggle against Sauron. And the leader of this valuable fighting force had to make a crucial *political* choice – whether to ally himself with the Dark Lord or with Gondor.

These early Latin narratives are somewhat more plastic and malleable in their meanings and consequently better suited to Tolkien's own artistic purposes than subsequent accounts. Indeed, Schmitt observes that these early texts offer a variety of kinds of "apparitions" sometimes commingled: one, "a procession of the penitent dead, an army of pitiful shadows that raised its lamentations and begged for prayers"; the other, "the furious army [that] traveled through the air in the din of weapons, horses and dogs" (101). Tolkien's creation draws on both types.

The Anglo-Norman monk Orderic Vitalis (1075–1142) is credited with assigning the name of Hellequin's Hunt to the ghostly armies said to trouble the living in the twelfth century (Schmitt, 93). His description and those of others stress the threatening military might of Hellequin's Hunt and the penitential purpose of the troop of the wandering dead. Three features from this early group contribute to Tolkien's fashioning of his episode: first, the relationship of exchange between the living and the dead; second, the powerful ties between lord and vassal, so demanding that they bind man to man even after death; and third, the theme of the misuse of military power.

We find one of the most detailed descriptions of the Army of the Dead in book 8 of Orderic Vitalis's *Ecclesiastical History*, written between 1133 and 1135 (Schmitt, 94). Not only is Orderic's one of the longest accounts, but it dramatizes the crucial relationship of exchange between the living and the dead in several texts from this period. We frequently see an exchange made between a living witness to the sight of the Army of the Dead and a member of that army. Typically the dead ask the living to perform some service to alleviate their suffering. Orderic's witness is a priest, Walchelin, who observes an enormous procession containing three groupings, each representing one of the medieval estates. The last is the imposing army of knights itself, numbering in the thousands: "Ecce ingens exercitus militum sequebatur et nullus color nisi nigredo et ignis in eis videbatur. Maximis omnes equis insidebant, et omnibus armis armati velut ad bellum festinabant, et nigerrima vexilla gestabant" [Behold a vast army of knights was following and no color was seen in them except blackness and flame. All of them were astride very large horses and equipped with every kind of armament as if they were rushing to battle, and they were carrying the blackest standards] (*Orderic*, 240, 242).[3] Further, like the members of this army, we will see that the ghosts of Tolkien's Shadow Host are also impressively equipped for battle and are visible chiefly as blackness and flame.

After several incidents, including Walchelin's two ill-conceived attempts to seize one of the "very blackest" (*nigerrimi*) horses as proof of his experience, the first of two ghostly suppliant knights accosts him. Identifying himself as William of Glos, he reveals that he is tortured by his sin of usury in life. He entreats the young priest to set right the wrongs he perpetrated by acting as a messenger. Would the priest order his wife and son (still living) to return property (a mill offered as a pledge) that he had seized when the impoverished owner proved unable to repay the loan? Compounding his own sin, William had failed to relinquish the mill to the poor man's heir and left it to his own instead. But the priest Walchelin proves a tough case, and after first agreeing, he then refuses to perform the service the dead knight requests.

Again, this was perhaps an injudicious choice on Walchelin's part, since the rejected ghost begins threatening and throttling him until the priest is rescued by a second ghostly knight, who also has a bad conscience and a task for him to perform. The second suppliant proves to be his own brother Robert. He is burdened by what may be considered his own war-making potential in life. Like the thousands who ride with him, Robert is tortured by the arms he bore while living: "Arma quae ferimus ignea sunt et nos foetore teterrimo inficiunt, ingentique ponderositate nimis opprimunt, et ardore inextinguibili comburunt" [The arms we bear are on fire and poison us with the foulest stench, and they crush us with their great heaviness and consume us with an unquenchable heat] (Orderic, 246, 248). Yet, he hopes that his brother will be the agent of his spiritual release.

And he begs the priest to perform suffrages on his behalf: "Obsecro memento mei precibusque piis et elemosinis succurre michi. Nam a Pascha florum usque ad unum annum spero salvari, et clementia creatoris ab omnibus tormentis liberari" [I beg you remember me and with devout prayers and alms help me. For one year from Palm Sunday I hope to be saved and freed from all torments by the mercy of Our Creator] (248).

But before he can even ask his brother Walchelin to perform these suffrages, he must first convince the priest to hear his request. And Walchelin (a true twenty-minute egg) holds out for quite some time. The ghostly Robert wins his younger brother over by recalling many details of their shared boyhood together and by angrily rebuking him for his ingratitude. Robert reminds him sharply that, following their parents' death, he took on the role of parent himself, bankrolling his young brother's education in France and providing money for clothes and books. Confronted by the undeniable ties of family and the "service" (love, nurture, education) provided by Robert in life, the tough young priest is persuaded.

After a fit of sobbing, Walchelin acknowledges his fraternal ghost and now agrees to return the favor (as it were) to provide the service his dead brother requests. He agrees to perform the suffrages as asked, to liberate the suffering Robert forever from his spiritual agonies. In his reading of this passage, Schmitt stresses the reciprocal nature of the transaction; the priest acquiesces "in return for the services rendered by Robert while he was alive" (98). Here, the living brother provides service to relieve the spiritual burden of the penitent dead. What Tolkien has done in "The Passing of the Grey Company" is to reverse this traditional direction of service found in the narratives of Oderic Vitalis and others. In Middle-earth, to achieve their own enduring spiritual peace, the Army of the Dead must serve the living one last time.

Who are the members of Aragorn's Shadow Host? They are the shades of the King of the Mountains and his army, who in the dawn of the reign of Gondor had sworn an oath to Isildur to fight as his allies in any future war against Sauron. Their king swore his formal allegiance to Isildur at the great black Stone of Erech. Yet when the Dark Lord threatened again and Isildur called upon his allies, the King of the Mountains refused to fight (either for Isildur or Sauron), earning himself and his people a binding curse from Isildur:

> "Thou shalt be the last king. And if the West prove mightier than thy Black Master, this curse I lay upon thee and thy folk: to rest never until your oath is fulfilled. For this war will last through years uncounted, and you shall be summoned once again before the end." And they fled before the wrath of Isildur, and did not dare go forth to war on Sauron's part; they hid themselves in secret places in the mountains and had no dealings with other men, but slowly dwindled in the barren hills.
>
> (*RK*, 55)[4]

The service these ghosts must provide the living is their military might, once wrongfully withheld from Isildur years before and now properly directed at long last by Isildur's heir, Aragorn. While the direction of service has been reversed, we find in Tolkien's Shadow Host all the defining features of the early *Exercitus mortuorum*: their spiritual affliction, their restive roaming, and their appearance. And, when we examine the diction attentively, we even detect traces of the language of Hellequin's Hunt.

Like the priest's brother Robert and the thousands who ride with him in Orderic's text, Tolkien's "Sleepless Dead" are trapped in a kind of purgatorial wasteland for many generations. They have gained enough spiritual insight to understand their past misdeeds and are indeed anguished by that knowledge, but they are apparently unable to atone for them through their own efforts alone. This spiritual torment manifests itself outwardly in their compulsion to roam the landscape. Compare Robert's words to his brother to those of the ghostly spokesman (the King of the Mountains) who stands forth from the Host to address Aragorn. Referring to the great fiery globs on his heels, Robert explains:

> [E]t quia preciosis et acutis utebar calcaribus ut festinarem ad effundendum sanguinem iure sarcinam in talis baiulo enormem, qua intolerabiliter gravatus nulli hominum depromere valeo penae quantitatem … . Plura michi non licet tecum frater fari quia miserabile agmen festinanter cogor prosequi.
>
> [And because I used my pointed and expensive spurs as I hastened to waste blood now justly do I bear huge burdens on my heels, whereby weighted down intolerably I am able to reveal to no man the amount of my suffering … . It is not permitted that I speak more with you brother since I am forced to rush after this wretched troop.]
>
> (Orderic, 248)

Similarly, in answer to Aragorn's question "Oathbreakers, why have ye come?" the ghostly spokesman (the King of the Mountains), demonstrating comparable spiritual insight, replies, "To fulfil our oath and have peace" (*RK*, 63). However brief his answer, the king comprehends his disastrous error committed years ago and still hopes to make restitution, thereby winning lasting spiritual peace for himself and his subjects.

Just as Robert is propelled to ride with the others by his horrible compulsion, to keep moving as it were, Tolkien's Shadow Host has long terrorized the small hamlets in the mountain valleys with its own compulsive movements. And, in times of unrest, the Host gathers at the Stone of Erech, the site of their original oath: "[I]t was a trysting-place of the Shadow-men and there they would gather in times of fear, thronging around the Stone and whispering" (*RK*, 63).[5] Tolkien's own epithet "the *Sleepless* Dead" (emphasis mine) suggests that these shades are spurred into an unwelcome, never-ending motion. Walter Map's description of King Herla and his troop (a version of Hellequin's Hunt written in the 1180s) also evokes this compulsive, itinerant movement. Herla's host is said to hold to its "*circuitus … vesanos sine quiete vel residentia*" [raging circuit without calm or settled rest] (Map, 30). This note of madness or frenzy is reiterated in Map's other account of the Wild Hunt, in this version led by King Herlethingus. He describes the King's retinue pursuing their "*erroris infiniti*" [never-ending wandering] and their "*insani circuitus*" [mad circuit] (370).[6] The restive wandering of Tolkien's Sleepless Dead mirrors outwardly the internal spiritual agonies from which they cannot free themselves, unless they are liberated by the living – in this case, by Isildur's heir.

Aragorn's command of the Dead permits his future subjects and Tolkien's readers to imagine him (really for the last time) in alternative roles before he is finally revealed to his own people as the true king at the bittersweet victory in defense of Minas Tirith. This episode of the "Passing of the Grey Company" offers us glimpses of darker, alternative destinies Aragorn might have pursued. However briefly, others perceive him as both "The King of the Dead" and as a rival of the Dark Lord himself.

Aragorn is actually acclaimed as the "King of the Dead" temporarily in addition to his many other titles (the Dúnadan, the Elfstone) and names (Longshanks, Elessar, Stick-at-nought-Strider). As the Grey Company (now including the Dead) emerges from beneath the *Dwimorberg* and rides through the Morthond Vale, the fleeing inhabitants assign Aragorn his new title: "Ever there rose the same cry in the gathering night; 'The King of the Dead! The King of the Dead is come upon us!'" (*RK*, 62). And when they reach the shores of the river Gilrain, Aragorn is literally hailed as the "King of the Dead" by both his terrorized allies (the men of Lamedon) and his enemies (the men of Umbar and Harad) as they clash at the fords: "But defenders and foes alike gave up the battle and fled when we came [Legolas reports], crying out that the King of the Dead was upon them" (151).[7] Just as he assumes the title and certainly the function temporarily, both are returned to the Shadow Host's leader (King of the Mountains) once he has fulfilled his obligations at last: "And thereupon the King of the Dead stood out before the host and broke his spear and cast it down" (153). The breaking of his spear symbolizes the cessation of his military career, the fulfillment of his oath, and his spiritual redemption.

Not only is Aragorn perceived by all mortals in his path as the King of the Dead during the wild ride down the Morthond Vale to the Anduin, but he is also imagined even more darkly as an avatar of Sauron by the Elf Legolas. Observing him commanding the Army of the Dead at Pelargir, Legolas imagines his friend taking on the name and the function of the Dark Lord himself: "In that hour I looked on Aragorn and thought how great and terrible a Lord he might have become in the strength of his will, had he taken the Ring to himself. Not for naught does Mordor fear him" (*RK*, 152). Aragorn rejected both title and role long years ago, of course, but the Elf's momentary, dark vision and especially his phrase "how great and terrible a Lord" recall the temptation of Galadriel in her garden and especially her choice of words as she projects herself as the new "Queen." After Frodo offers her the One Ring, she imagines herself as "beautiful and terrible as the Morning and the Night ... dreadful as the Storm and Lightning," and she adds, "[A]ll shall love me and despair" (*FR*, 381). We should remember the extraordinary power of the temptation the One posed, since even the Lady of Lórien confesses to having fantasized (as we would say) more than once about ruling in the Dark Lord's place.

Like the Lady of the Golden Wood and unlike Boromir, Aragorn "pass[es] the test" (*FR*, 381), but other lesser temptations and distractions remain. Tolkien crafted "The Passing of the Grey Company" to sharpen our sense of Aragorn's powers, to offer an example of another temptation he avoids, and to establish his worthiness to become not only Captain of the Host of the West but King Elessar. As he walks the Paths of the Dead, Aragorn displays his self-control and his command of others, what the text terms "the strength of his will." When Aragorn and his companions attempt the path, they themselves become like the Dead, and yet the future king holds to his purpose.

As they approach the passage beneath the Dwimorberg, Elf, Dwarf, Man, and horse pass into the Netherworld of Men, the domain of human ghosts, those of the King of the Mountains and his unfortunate people. Nearing the daunting threshold dividing the living from the Dead, the Company assumes some of the Shades' characteristics, such as color. In a sense, we can understand the "Grey Company" literally. Even those who simply *hear* of Aragorn's intention to risk the passage drain of color: "Éomer turned and gazed at Aragorn, and it seemed to Merry that the faces of the Riders that sat within hearing turned pale at the words" (*RK*, 52). His announcement has a similar effect on the shield-maiden Éowyn: "[H]er face blanched, and for long she spoke no more" (56).

The Company is hard to see, and they themselves have increasing difficulty seeing. The Rohirrim they leave behind are associated with dawn, light, and sight, whereas they themselves are associated with night, darkness, and sightlessness. The Company "dies" to mortal sight as Éowyn's eyes darken: "When they were lost to view, she turned, stumbling as one that is blind" (59). Her people hide themselves until sunrise, refusing to witness the Company's departure: "[T]hey hid themselves in fear and would not come forth until the day was up" (59). And facing the forbidding entrance in the failing light, the Company cannot read the inscriptions above it: "Signs and figures were carved above its wide arch too dim to read" (59). Further, once he has passed the threshold, Gimli is virtually blinded inside the passage: "[A]nd at once a blindness came upon him, even upon Gimli Glóin's son who had walked unafraid in many deep places of the world" (60).

The description of the portal to the world of the Dead is marked with strong suggestions of the infernal. It is a strange locus possessing enervating properties that sap the vitality of the living, and the Company discovers that more than one of their senses are affected. As they draw near, sounds are stifled and killed. Gimli speaks: "[B]ut the others were *silent*, and his voice *fell dead* on the dank fir-needles at his feet" (*RK*, 59; emphasis mine). They experience disturbing tactile sensations as their bodily warmth leaks away; the Dwarf volunteers, "My blood runs chill" (59), and "his knees shook" and his feet feel "like lead" as he forces himself over the liminal boundary (69). To their sight as they stand in the

Dimholt all color seeps away, leaving only black ("black ridges," "black trees") and gray ("the light was still grey," "fear flowed from it [the Dark Door] like a grey vapour") (59).

The topography itself is simplified, reduced to primordial shapes – a "hollow" and a tall upright rock: "[T]hey found a hollow place opening at the mountain's *root* [emphasis mine] and right in their path stood a single mighty stone like a finger of doom" (*RK*, 59). "[A]nd in the wall the Dark Door gaped before them like the mouth of night" (59). The similes used of these geographical features – "finger" and especially "gaped" and "mouth" – recall the medieval Hell Mouth. In its determination to walk "The Paths of the Dead," the Company appears to be on the verge of being swallowed alive.

Both Elf and Dwarf attest to the acute disorientation, both spatial and temporal, often associated with visiting the Netherworld. Gimli expresses confusion about the amount of time that has passed during their journey beneath the *Dwimorberg*, and he confesses bewilderment about their physical location when the Company emerges into the domain of the living once again.

> Yet as Gimli after learned it was still two hours ere sunset of the day on which they had set out from Dunharrow; though for all that he could tell it might have been twilight in some later year, or in some other world.
>
> (*RK*, 61)

The Dwarf is completely "turned around," as we would say, and requires a geography lesson from a companion, Elrond's son Elladan. "'Where in Middle-earth are we?' said Gimli and Elladan answered: 'We have descended from the uprising of the Morthond'" (62). Even Legolas acknowledges that, during his exposure to the Shadow Host, he seemed to have entered a state of altered consciousness. He confesses that, with the final departure of the Shadow Host after their service at Pelargir, he seemed to return to ordinary waking consciousness – his experience of the Dead was like a dream vision: "[A]nd swiftly the grey host drew off and vanished like a mist that is driven back by a sudden wind; and it seemed to me that I awoke from a dream" (153).[8]

Besieged by these sensations and by increasing disorientation, members of the Company are gripped by a terror, which, significantly, they share with their animals.[9] I say "significantly" because this shared emotion emphasizes their mortality and their vulnerability. They are very much alive, very much made of flesh and blood, as they are about to plunge into the realm of the Dead. Interestingly, no member of the Company is immune except for Legolas, who does not fear the ghosts of Men. The terror is overcome in two ways: through the power of Elven magic[10] and through the power of love, both the love the horses feel for their Rangers and the love Elf, Dwarf, and Men feel for their Lord and leader, Aragorn. It is at this moment, at the passing of the "Dark Door," that the function of the entire episode of the Grey Company is clearest. Aragorn is worthy of his high destiny because of his ability to command and his power to elicit the love of others:

> Then Aragorn led the way, and such was the strength of his will in that hour that all the Dúnedain and their horses followed him. And indeed the love that the horses of the Rangers bore for their riders was so great that they were willing to face even the terror of the Door, if their masters' hearts were steady as they walked beside them.
>
> (*RK*, 60)

It is unfortunate perhaps that Legolas did not see fit to comfort his friend Gimli as he did his horse, because the Dwarf needed it. Walking the Paths of the Dead is Gimli's worst ordeal in many respects, and shame prods him over the threshold.[11] Once the Company is inside, Tolkien inverts a familiar narrative pattern in Norse literature for his own literary purposes. Typically, in Scandinavian texts, living men enter the underground realm of the dwarfs, often hoping to filch some of their hidden gold. Yet here, the Dwarf Gimli is the interloper in the underground world of dead Men, and it is he who narrates the Company's journey. The Dwarf begins by "stumbling" and finds "that he could scarcely walk" (60). In the end, he becomes a lesser creature than the horses who walk quietly with their "steady" Rangers and the enchanted Arod: "He stumbled on until he was crawling like a beast" (60). He is wholly "un-dwarfed," so to speak. What better way to highlight Aragorn's strength of will and unwavering purpose than to "see" it through the eyes of the most thoroughly crushed and terrorized member of the Company?

In keeping with the Norse narrative pattern, the temptation presented to Aragorn on the Paths of the Dead is the lure of gold. The Men of the Mountains hid it beneath the Dwimorberg originally, and Baldor of Rohan once entered the Dark Door on a quest to retrieve it but never returned to the land of the living. The human remains that Aragorn turns aside to view in the torchlight are his. Gimli marvels at Aragorn's calm, yet he too approaches the corpse in his leader's company: "'Does he feel no fear?' muttered the Dwarf. 'In any other cave Gimli Glóin's son would have been the first to run to the gleam of gold. But not here! Let it lie!'" (*RK*, 60). After pondering Baldor's fate, Aragorn very explicitly rejects the search for the ancient, hidden gold as an unworthy quest and loudly and clearly names his object:

> "For that is not my errand!" he cried, turning back and speaking to the whispering darkness behind. "Keep your hoards and your secrets hidden in the Accursed Years! Speed only we ask. Let us pass, and then come! I summon you to the Stone of Erech!"
>
> (*RK*, 61)[12]

Significantly, it is after his forthright summons that the Shadow-men begin to follow, to "fall in" behind the heir of Isildur. Gimli, the last of the living, seems to hear their footfalls: "And a rumour came after him like the shadow-sound of many feet" (61). Isildur's heir will neither be deterred nor distracted from his goal.

Just as this Army of the Dead can be heard whispering inside the passage, its members can also be seen at times by those with gifted sight once the Grey Company returns to the lands of the living. And, like the medieval *Exercitus mortuorum*, Aragorn's Shadow Host is fully equipped for battle. Legolas reports: "The Dead are following … . I see the shapes of Men and horses, and pale banners like shreds of cloud, and spears like winter-thickets on a misty night. The Dead are following" (*RK*, 63). We find a similar specificity about armaments in the description of a ghostly troop in the *Expugnatio Hibernica* of Gerald of Wales (Giraldus Cambrensis). He describes the Army of the Dead assailing the English forces by night at the siege of Osraighe:

> [E]cce virorum quasi milia milium infinita undique in illos irruencium, at tanquam in impetu furoris sui cuncta devorancium, cum armorum sonitu et securium collisione non modica, necnon et clamore terribili celum replente. Cuiusmodi phantasma in Hibernia circa expediciones frequens esse solebat.
>
> [Behold countless thousands of thousands of men assaulting them from all sides, as if swallowing them up in the vehemence of their fury with the ringing of weapons and no small clashing of axes and also filling the heavens with a fearful clamor. Apparitions of this sort were usually frequent around campaigns in Ireland.]
>
> (Gerald of Wales, 38)

We might also compare the aural quality of Gerald's account – the sharp sounds of weapons colliding and of voices crying in the foreground – with the muffled distanced tumult of Gimli's account of the Shadow Host's final assault in Tolkien:

> And suddenly the Shadow Host that had hung back at the last came up like a grey tide, sweeping all away before it. Faint cries I heard, and dim horns blowing, and a murmur as of countless far voices; it was like the echo of some forgotten battle in the Dark Years long ago. Pale swords were drawn; but I know not whether their blades would still bite, for the Dead needed no longer any weapon but fear.
>
> (*RK*, 153)[13]

And fittingly, the Mirk of Mordor that Sauron sends northward with his forces to the siege of Minas Tirith both obscures and illuminates the Shades of Men. The emphasis on blackness and fire recalls Orderic's description. Gimli recollects the scene: "[T]he Shadow Host withdrew to the shore. There they stood silent, hardly to be seen, save for a red gleam in their eyes that caught the glare of the ships that were burning" (152). Walchelin reports of the passing procession: "[N]o color was seen in them except blackness and flame" (Orderic, 242).

In the language describing the grueling, frantic ride to the banks of the Anduin, we detect traces of the frenzied whirlwind Hellequin's Hunt, "the raging circuit," "the mad circuit" of Walter Map's account. Aragorn's Army of the Dead scatters the mountain dwellers (his future subjects) as so much frantic prey:

> Lights went out in house and hamlet as they came, and doors were shut, and folk that were afield cried in terror and ran wild like hunted deer. Ever there rose the same cry in the gathering night: "The King of the Dead! The King of the Dead is come upon us!"
>
> Bells were ringing far below, and all men fled before the face of Aragorn; but the Grey Company in their haste rode like hunters, until their horses were stumbling with weariness.
>
> (*RK*, 62)[14]

Aragorn can compel the Dead to serve him in a desperate hour because he is Isildur's heir. His power to enforce their military cooperation derives from the strength of the vassalic ties that once bound the King of the Mountains to his liege Lord Isildur. Aragorn's lineage and the "strength of his will" are the sources of his authority. And when we look at these twelfth-century narratives we can also find instances in which death does not end the obligations of vassal to lord. A curious tale, *De fundatione monasterii S. Fidis Sletstatenis*, appended to the *Book of Miracles of Saint Foi of Conques* in the first half of the twelfth century, illustrates the binding nature of a vassal's oath beyond the death of his master (Holder-Egger, 996–1000).

In this narrative, a knight named Walter of Diebolsheim is visited by his dead lord, Count Conrad, and entrusted with important messages.[15] The ghostly count must first prove his identity. He must also prove that God has sanctioned his visitation to his vassal Walter. And again we see the relationship of exchange as in the earlier example of the two brothers Robert and Walchelin. Here, Count Conrad reminds Walter that in life he had promoted and rewarded him above all his other vassals. In death he requires further service from his knight and holds him to it "per fidei sacramentum" [by his oath] (998). Walter must ask Conrad's still living brother, Bishop Otto of Strasbourg, to bequeath the count's portion of his inheritance to Saint Foi. This gift as well as Bishop Otto's "prayers" and gifts of alms will help to alleviate Conrad's penitential torments. The ties that bind are transcendent in this tale about the support and protection of the monastery of Saint Foi of Sélestat. And although Tolkien again reverses the direction of service, these ties are equally transcendent in Middle-earth.

As we have seen, the particular service Aragorn requires of the Dead is military. As Jean-Claude Schmitt and others have noted, a number of these twelfth-century narratives used the theme of the furious, ghostly troop to criticize the second estate for misdirecting their formidable war-making power. (The texts chastized the aristocracy for directing its violence inwards, for targeting other European Christians, for example.) Schmitt writes,

> Undoubtedly, in the twelfth century there was a relationship between the increasing prevalence of the furious army of the Dead and all the contemporary measures being taken to rein in the feudal system and to limit its wars and devastation.
>
> (Schmitt, 100)

Returning to Orderic's text for a moment, we recall that Robert and his fellow knights are tortured by the weapons they had carried into battle. Robert himself is forced to wear agonizingly heavy flaming weights on his heels "because I used my pointed and expensive spurs as I hastened to waste blood" (248). He was in life, he confesses, overly zealous in killing, too eager. Tolkien's King of the Mountains may also be said to have misdirected his military might, not by traitorously fighting against his Lord Isildur, but by "opting out," as we would say. He misuses his potential by refusing to use it at all in a just war against the Dark Lord. (He chose to sit out that round.) Within its own moral framework, Tolkien's text criticizes this king's misuse (or non-use) just as clearly as some twelfth-century texts criticize a heavily armed aristocracy for victimizing the "wrong" populations too close to home.

And finally, if some authors of the period used the *Exercitus mortuorum* to rebuke the second estate in this manner, the Army of the Dead participated in twelfth-century political ideology in another way as well, for often the service the dead perform for the living helps to found a dynasty or to ensure its survival and protect its possessions. In these instances, the service is frequently in the form of crucial information. Returning to Count Conrad for a moment, we discover that he also has some quite secular dynastic issues on his mind. He entrusts his loyal knight with a prediction about the family's glorious destiny that he must deliver to his brother Duke Frederick. If the duke follows his instructions to the letter, his own son will become king of the Staufen dynasty (Conrad III, in 1138), and, subsequently, another male relative will become a great emperor (Frederick I, in 1155) (Schmitt, 105).

Unlike Count Conrad, the members of Tolkien's Shadow Host render long-delayed military service rather than offer information to the living. Yet that service is no less essential in preserving a dynasty – that of King Elessar of the line of Valandil, Isildur's son, Elendil's son of Númenor. And like their ghostly medieval counterparts, the Shadow-men's aid at the shores of the Anduin proves decisive in defending property: in this instance, Aragorn's most valuable possession, the City of the Kings. And lastly, while the intervention of the Dead under Aragorn's leadership does not, strictly speaking, found a dynasty, it does participate in bringing the Third Age to a close, and in inaugurating the Fourth Age – "the Time of the Dominion of Men." Tolkien's Shadow Host functions within the "monarchic ideology" of Middle-earth as surely as the *Exercitus mortuorum* did in many twelfth-century texts.

The Shadow Host also has a secondary function within *The Return of the King*, for the episode helps to justify Aragorn's elevation from his early status as the chieftain of the Dúnedain of Arnor to that of king of both Gondor and Arnor, "the greatest that now is" (*RK*, 242). As we have seen, he is justified by virtue of his lineage and by his "strength of will," but also by the love he elicits from members of all the races. It is surely significant that much of the debate about the proposed journey beneath the Dwimorberg stresses the need for every member of the Company to make the choice freely. Aragorn tells his friends, "Therefore, only of your free will would I have you come, for you will find both toil and great fear, and maybe worse" (55).[16] Elf, Dwarf, and Man all assert their desire to follow him on the Path, despite their very imperfect understanding of its perils: " 'I will go with you even on the Paths of the Dead, and to whatever end they may lead,' said Gimli. 'I also will come,' said Legolas, 'for I do not fear the Dead.' " (55). And standing at the entrance to the Path itself, Halbarad, Ranger of the North, states: "This is an evil door, … and my death lies beyond it. I will dare to pass it nonetheless" (*RK*, 59).

"The Passing of the Grey Company" contrasts the right choice made willingly, without coercion, by Aragorn's companions, motivated by their love and loyalty, with the wrong choice (also made freely) years ago by Isildur's ally the King of the Mountains. In addition, the episode dramatizes *the state* of being free to choose and opposes this to the Shadow-men's penitential existence, bound as they are by Isildur's oath and shackled by his curse, unable to expiate fully their failure until redeemed by Isildur's heir. Just as the Shadow Host is compelled to wander the landscape they inhabited while living, they are compelled to obey Aragorn's commands. It is very different for the living members of the Grey Company, as Éowyn observes: "They go only because they would not be parted from thee – because they love thee" (58).

Notes

1 These verses of the epigraph were spoken by "Malbeth the Seer, in the days of Arvedui, last king at Fornost," prophesizing the passing of the Grey Company.
2 The episode comprises chapter 2 of Tolkien's *The Return of the King*.
3 All translations from the Latin are my own.
4 The king's failure to honor his alliance should be contrasted with the elderly King Théoden of Rohan's willingness to answer Gondor's call.
5 The Shadow-men's tendency to appear in times of crisis is paralleled by both Gerald of Wales (Giraldus Cambrensis) and Walter Map in their accounts of the Army of the Dead. In his *Expugnatio Hibernica*, Gerald relates that the ghostly army appears to the English troops laying siege to Osraighe, a military conflict that would certainly qualify as a "time of fear." And Map sets the coming of the "Wild Hunt" in the first year of Henry II's reign following a prolonged period of political instability, often called the Anarchy. Similarly, Aragorn rides with the Army of the Dead just months before he is crowned King.
6 Map, of course, is at great pains to highlight this restless wandering because he wishes to emphasize its pointlessness for his own literary purposes. Cheekily, he claims that the court of Henry II actually *replaces* the Wild Hunt, thus casting his own king in the role of Herlethingus and himself as a worn and weary courtier compelled (like brother Robert in Orderic Vitalis) to follow his lord the length and breadth of late twelfth-century England. When we consider the uncertain spiritual fate of those who traditionally ride in the ghostly troop, Map is making a risky joke about his lord and king.

7 The Shadow Host's appearance at the river Gilrain has a secondary function as well, and that is to separate the truly noble leader from his followers. The Dead's arrival furnishes supernatural proof of a man's heroism. In this case, the Lord of Lamedon, Angbor, stands his ground undeterred while his men break and flee: "Only Angbor, Lord of Lamedon, had the heart to abide us; and Aragorn bade him gather his folk and come behind, if they dared, when the Grey Host had passed" (*RK*, 151). (Subsequently, the faithful Angbor does lead his troops north to the siege of Gondor.) We find a parallel in Gerald of Wales's use of the ghostly troop that surrounds the English army at the siege of Osraighe in his *Expugnatio Hibernica.* The terror this nocturnal force inspires highlights the bravery of two men, Robert de Barry in particular, who not only rushes to the defense of his leader, FitzStephen, but also labors to secure his prize sparrowhawk amidst the chaos (Giraldus, 37).

8 Of course, the temporal dislocation experienced by King Herla is far greater (quite shocking in fact) in Walter Map's account of this king's journey to the netherworld to visit the pygmy king's home. Herla and his retinue also face a cavern in a high cliff and a long dark passage: "Cauvernam igitur altissime rupis ingrediuntur, et post aliquantas tenebras in lumine, quod non videbatur solis aut lune sed lampadarum multarum, ad domos pigmei" [Therefore they entered a cavern in a very tall cliff and after considerable darkness they reached, in a glow that seemed neither of sun nor of moon but of many lamps, the palace of the pygmies] (Map, 28). When Herla and his band return to the living world, he believes that three days have passed, when in fact several centuries have elapsed.

9 The sensitivity of horses to the shades of men is also well attested in classical antiquity. See Felton's discussion of domestic animals' "sixth sense" in her *Haunted Greece and Rome*, 5–6 and 80. I would note here that this time-honored motif (domestic animals *always* sense the presence of evil and death long before their owners do) is still with us in horror fiction of the twenty-first century.

10 Legolas soothes the agony of his horse:

> But Arod, the horse of Rohan, refused the way, and he stood sweating and trembling in a fear that was grievous to see. Then Legolas laid his hands on his eyes and sang some words that went soft in the gloom, until he suffered himself to be led.
>
> (*RK*, 60)

11 "[A]nd he was wroth with himself. 'Here is a thing unheard of!' he said. 'An Elf will go underground and a Dwarf dare not!' And with that he plunged in" (*RK*, 60).

12 Galadriel warns against distractions or falling from the path as she tries to comfort Sam, who is distressed by the visions he has seen in her Mirror.

13 A number of classical authors also describe ghostly armies drawn to particular battlefield engagements, and, like the fighters Gerald reports, they are often sighted in the air. See Felton's account of reports by Pliny the Elder, Tacitus, and Lucan (36). Interestingly, the ghostly troop survived into the twentieth century with Arthur Machen's short story "The Bowmen," set in World War I. See Felton, 89–90.

14 The following description also implies that Aragorn and his followers are in an uncharacteristic state of frenzy. Legolas's words evoke a certain recklessness and a temporary disregard for the living that is quite out of character: "[T]rampling unheeded the grass and the flowers, we hunted our foes through a day and a night" (*RK*, 151).

15 See Schmitt's discussion of this complex narrative, 103–7.

16 Aragorn again stresses freedom of choice when he discusses his intentions with Éowyn: "But those who follow me do so of their free will; and if they wish now to remain and ride with the Rohirrim, they may do so. But I shall take the Paths of the Dead, alone, if needs be" (*RK*, 57).

Part III

J. R. R. Tolkien

The texts/contexts of medieval patristics, theology, and iconography

11 Augustine in the cottage of lost play

The *Ainulindalë* as asterisk cosmogony

John William Houghton

In his classic study *The Road to Middle-earth*, T. A. Shippey introduces the term "asterisk-reality" in order to discuss the tendency of philologists to reconstruct not only the forms of lost words (typically marked by a prefixed asterisk) and lost languages, but also the world-views that those words and languages described; the difficulty, he says, is that such reconstruction shades off quickly into pure imagination (15–17). He goes on to treat Tolkien's creative process as the production of asterisk-realities, whether in the form of reconstructions, like Elves, or, like Hobbits, that of imagined things that fit indistinguishably amongst real ones. In the opening section of *The Silmarillion*, and one of the earliest to have been drafted (cf. *BLT*1, 61–62), Tolkien gives what he later called the Elves' "cosmogonical myth," the *Ainulindalë* (*Letters*, 146). It is an asterisk-cosmogony, an imagined account of the creation of an asterisk-reality: and as the Hobbits fit neatly into the historical world, down to the level of having a respectable Old English etymology (*LR*, 1172), so (though we might not on first reading expect it to) the *Ainulindalë* fits neatly amongst the real cosmogonies known to early medieval Europe.

Latin Christian thinkers in the actual early medieval period inherited two cosmogonies, representing the disparate beginnings of their tradition in Jerusalem and Athens: on the one hand, they had the Hexameron, the story of the six days' work of Creation in Genesis; on the other, they had the *Timaeus* of Plato, the only one of the dialogues to have been translated into Latin (and thus their only direct source for Platonic thought). As Tolkien first conceived of the materials that eventually became *The Silmarillion*, the asterisk early medievals would have received in the *Ainulindalë* a third account of Creation. Tolkien's fictional auditor of the Elvish creation myth represents early moments of English history: first, as Eriol, he is an Angle from before the time of that people's migration to Britain, and then in a revision, as Ælfwine, he is an Anglo-Saxon mariner (*BLT*1, 24–25; *BLT*2, 302, 330).

The modern reader, finding the *Ainulindalë* very different from Genesis, might reasonably expect that if Eriol/Ælfwine had passed the Elvish story on to medieval thinkers, they would have found it equally strange, if not completely irreconcilable with their Christian faith. In fact, however, the commentary tradition – and particularly the work of Saint Augustine of Hippo – allows Tolkien's myth to consort with Genesis at least as easily as the *Timaeus* does. While early medieval thinkers had access to various late-antique Christian and pagan commentaries on the *Timaeus* (all of them more or less reflecting the doctrine of the Neoplatonist philosopher Plotinus)[1]and to various patristic writings on the Hexameron, their primary resource for cosmological reflection lay in Augustine's writings. Had medieval theologians encountered the *Ainulindalë*, they would have found its picture of a double creation – creation as music in the song of the Ainur and then as fact in the word of Ilúvatar – reassuringly easy to fit into the schema of Augustine's Christian-Neoplatonist synthesis.

Saint Augustine

The tale of Creation in the opening chapters of the book of Genesis held a particular fascination for Augustine – in large part because he saw in it refutation of Manicheanism, the religion he had followed as a young man. For a modern audience, the last part of Augustine's *Confessions* is probably his most familiar discussion of the subject, but he also considers it in *De civitate Dei* [The City of God] and in three biblical commentaries: *De Genesi contra Manicheos* [On Genesis against the Manicheans], *De Genesi ad litteram imperfectus liber* [An incomplete book on the literal sense of Genesis], and *De Genesi ad litteram libri duodecim* [Twelve books on the literal sense of Genesis; cited hereafter simply as *De Genesi*]. The last of these presents Augustine's definitive word on the subject (even though, being written between 401 and 415, it antedates *De civitate Dei*) and was widely circulated in the Middle Ages, not only in its own right but also as excerpted in Saint Bede the Venerable's *In Genesim* [On Genesis], such Bedan successor-texts as Alcuin of York's *Interrogationes Sigeuulfi in Genesim* [Sigewulf's questions on Genesis], and the Old English *Hexameron* of Ælfric of Eynsham.

For the typical modern reader, the most striking feature of Augustine's various commentaries on Genesis is what he means by "literal." When people today talk of taking Genesis literally, we usually understand them to mean that the surface sense of Genesis, with God creating the world over the course of six days and resting on the seventh, is a historical account as it stands. Augustine has in mind a more complex sense of "literality": in this literal reading, he understands key words of Genesis such as "day," "heaven," and "earth" in a symbolic sense, rather than in their ordinary meanings. Citing the example of Saint Paul's applications of the stories of Hagar and Sarah (1 Cor. 10:11) and Adam and Eve (Eph. 5:32) – both of which he takes to be literal, historical accounts – Augustine argues that, whether or not a particular biblical narrative is a historical record, it can be allegorical, that is, it can refer to something else in sacred history. What he proposes to discuss in Genesis is the nonallegorical sense, and he sees that sense in this case as historical (*De Genesi*, 1.1.1–2). This seems like backing into the topic, treating the derivative – allegorical – sense before the primary – literal – meaning; but Augustine wants to rule out figurative, allegorical meaning from the beginning precisely because the *literal* sense he finds in the opening of Genesis is itself *expressed* figuratively. That is to say, when Moses (whom

Augustine accepts as the author of Genesis) tells the story of Sarah and Hagar, he does so in reasonably matter of fact prose; it is Paul who sees the story as an allegory prefiguring two covenants. But when Exodus says that God led the people of Israel through the Red Sea with a strong "right hand" (Ex. 15:6), Moses is using poetic imagery, without expecting anyone to think that God actually has a physical body. The *literal*, historical sense of the text is that the author is using a figure of speech to refer to God's divine power, whereas one common *allegorical* reading is that crossing the Red Sea prefigures baptism. Thus Augustine calls his symbolic interpretation the *literal* sense of Genesis because he is convinced that Moses deliberately used symbols in writing about real historical events of the Creation.

For Augustine, then, the creation story in Genesis is a historical record that the author has chosen to express, not simply through a single figure of speech such as "right arm," but through a whole symbolic narrative. This is, certainly, a highly rhetorical distinction, but Augustine, born in North Africa in 354, received the late-antique world's standard education in rhetoric, which included close study of the great texts of pagan culture; he later went on to become a professor of rhetoric himself. We know from the *Confessions* that the young Augustine wept over the death of Dido in Virgil's *Aeneid* (*Conf.* 1.13), and that one of his reasons for rejecting his mother's Christian beliefs was dissatisfaction with the literary style and content of the Christian Scriptures (*Conf.* 3.5.9). One factor in Augustine's conversion to Christianity was reading the "books of the Platonists" (presumably the *Enneads* of Plotinus [*Conf.* 7.20.26]); another was hearing the sermons of Saint Ambrose, bishop of Milan. Ambrose's allegorical method of interpretation made virtues of what Augustine had previously seen as flaws (*Conf.* 6.4–5.8); it opened the way for Augustine to apply his own considerable talent, and his formidable grasp of rhetorical technique, to the task of biblical interpretation.

One time when Augustine would have heard Ambrose preach was the week before his own baptism at Easter of 387 (*Conf.* 9.6.14); tradition has it that the set of sermons on Genesis collected as Ambrose's *Hexameron* were delivered on that occasion. Ambrose's account of Creation is closely based on an earlier set of sermons by Saint Basil of Caesarea. Both Ambrose's Hexameron and Basil's were known in the early Middle Ages, the latter in a Latin translation by Eustathius; Bede cites each of them in *In Genesim*. Basil uses relatively little allegory in his exposition; his emphasis falls mostly on answering the objections of pagan philosophers and on feeling a sense of awe at the marvels of Creation. Ambrose's *Hexameron* spends less time on the philosophers than Basil's original; whereas Basil will offer a detailed refutation of Aristotle or Plato, Ambrose is more likely to say that God's will, as Moses reports it in Genesis, is sufficient explanation for anything. Ambrose uses more allegory in his interpretation than Basil – for example, he says that the sun and the moon prefigure Christ and the Church (bk. 4, Hom. 6.2.7) – but his allegories are more occasional set-pieces than a connected chain of interpretation. When Augustine himself comes to the interpretation of Genesis, however, he applies Ambrose's methods to Basil's concerns, giving a connected figurative interpretation that shows that Genesis agrees with the theories of the philosophers.

Allegorical interpretation can seem a highly arbitrary procedure: Ambrose's teaching that the sun symbolizes Christ and the moon the Church at best provokes in us admiration for his cleverness. Augustine's interpretation of Genesis, however, grows out of a very careful attention to the exact words of the text, and we should note again that he does not regard his method as allegorical. His concern in *De Genesi* is not (like Ambrose) to find ways in which Moses's story prefigures later events but rather to explain Moses' literal historical meaning, as Moses expressed it in symbolic language.

This interpretation begins with the first words of Genesis: "In the beginning, God created the heavens and the earth. And the earth was invisible and formless. And darkness was over the abyss."[2] Ambrose had dwelt on the various senses of "in the beginning." The phrase could refer to a beginning in time, or it could mean that heaven and earth were first in the sense of being the elements out of which everything else was to be made. Or the phrase may indicate an overview: in Greek, "in the beginning" is expressed as "at the head," a phrase which can also mean "in sum." All of these are possible literal senses of the text; according to the mystical sense, "in the beginning" could be a reference to the Second Person of the Trinity, who is the "Alpha and the Omega, the first and the last, the beginning and the end" (Rev. 21:13). Augustine sums up all of this in a sentence in the opening chapter of *De Genesi*; then he moves to the point that really interests him. Ambrose had assumed that "heaven and earth" refers straightforwardly to the physical world; explicitly rejecting the philosophers' discussions of the four elements, his interpretation confined itself to the Scriptures, citing Isaiah on the nature of the heavens and Job on the position of the earth (bk. 1, Hom. 1.6). Augustine, in contrast, interprets the phrase in light of questions from the larger Christian tradition and from philosophy as well.

Augustine begins (1.1.2) from an obvious (though unstated) question: "What about the angels?" These creatures of pure spirit certainly exist, but Ambrose's reading of heaven and earth leaves Genesis with no mention of their creation. Possibly, then, "heaven" refers to the spiritual Creation, and "earth" the corporeal. But if this were the case, the passage might seem to be a needless duplication of the detailed account of corporeal Creation in the later verses of the chapter. Or perhaps (taking the philosophers into account) "heaven and earth" refers to the unformed matter that will later be shaped into spiritual and corporeal creatures; but then we again have the problem that there is no account of the shaping of spiritual creatures. Hence, Augustine concludes (1.1.3) that "In the beginning God created heaven and earth" means that spiritual creatures were created in a state of perfection, and corporeal creatures were created as unformed matter, in accordance with what follows, "The earth was invisible and formless."

This brief glimpse may be enough to give a sense of the meticulousness with which Augustine approaches the text, a greater care even than that of his two predecessors. Indeed, the key points of his reading start with a textual element to which Basil and Ambrose pay little attention. That element is the way Moses's formulaic account includes certain phrases that seem at first glance to be redundant. The account of each of the six days of Creation begins, "And God said, 'Let there be made' … and so it was made." On four of the six days, this formula is followed by a statement that "God made" something. Then God names the thing that has just been created, and God sees that it is good. Finally, each account but the last concludes, "There was evening and there was morning, the [*n*th] day." Augustine worries at the overlap of "let there be made," "so it was made," and "God made." As we have already seen, he is not willing to ascribe any redundance to mere rhetorical style; rather, he assumes that each element in the formula has its own individual significance. Moreover, Augustine notes that Moses did *not* use this formula in the first verses of Genesis (that is, we never read, "And God said 'Let there be made heaven and earth'"), and he points out the significance of the change.

Augustine sets out his complex analysis of all this in a rather tentative way, putting forward and retracting various possible interpretations before settling on the one that seems to him to offer the best fit. His argument can be considered in summary, as its form has little relevance to our present study. The phrase "And God said" refers to the fact that God calls things to form through the Second Person of the Trinity, the Word who is the form of all Creation.[3] Thus, "Let there be made" refers to the creation of things as ideas in the Word. "And so it was made" refers to the creation of things as ideas in the minds of the angels; for when God causes these spiritual beings to understand what it is that God is creating, the concept in the angelic minds is itself something that God has made.[4] "And God made," in turn, refers to the creation of things in their own proper existence, creation in the ordinary sense of the word. Finally, "God saw that it was good" refers to the Holy Spirit brooding over Creation – not passively approving of what is made, but actively holding it in being.

Augustine's analysis of the repetitions in the story of Creation thus leads him to conceive of a four-step process, one that we would think of as repeated (with small variations) on each of the six days. But Augustine goes on to show that this temporal language of four steps and six days is also, for the most part, symbolic. The formula runs, "And there was evening and there was morning, one day." Augustine points out that this formula cannot refer to the ordinary sequence of evening and morning, for that sequence is only a local effect – when it is evening in one place, it is morning in another, half the world away (4.30.47). To summarize again: Augustine, having already determined that "Let there be light" refers to the creation of intellectual creatures, now goes on to combine that insight with his four-stage process of Creation in order to interpret "evening" and "morning." "And so it was done" means that God creates in the angels knowledge of what God is about to create; "There was evening" refers to the angels' direct knowledge of the created things in themselves; and "There was morning" means that the angels turn back from seeing created things to contemplate, praise the source of the Creation in God, and receive revelation of further new creatures.[5] Thus the "day" to which Genesis refers is in fact the angelic host, the intellectual light that understands, perceives, and gives praise for God's Creation (4.24.41–28.45). God's activity in Creation does not take place over six chronological days (of whatever length), to be followed by rest on the seventh; rather, God creates everything simultaneously, in an eternal moment. Nor does the sequence in angelic knowledge indicate a passage of time; the angels themselves are temporal creatures, but in their direct contemplation of God, they observe the simultaneity of divine action. There is, Augustine says, a true six- or sevenfold repetition in the act of Creation, but that repetition takes place in one single moment. This sixfold singularity may seem a difficult concept, Augustine says, but that is precisely why Moses chose to express it in terms of six days, making the difficult simple enough for a child to understand (5.3.6).

Yet even if creation is, generally, simultaneous, some elements of the Creation narrative clearly do refer to events that must take place in time – such as the earth bringing forth plants with their seeds. The meaning, Augustine says, is that God's simultaneous Creation included both the creation of some things in their actuality and the creation of the "causal reasons" of other things. Augustine likens these "causal reasons" to seeds, and for this reason often calls them "seminal reasons" (*rationes seminales*). The concept, which comes to Augustine either directly from the Stoics or else via Plotinus, refers to a real material element that will bring about some phenomenon at a later point in time, after a sort of dormancy. When Moses says that the earth brought forth plants or fish or birds, he means that God created in the world the physical-ontological potential that led the earth in due time to bring forth flora and fauna. These causal reasons, like DNA, may be expressed in more than one way: the child may grow to adulthood or may die in adolescence; water may become wine through the growth and fermentation of grapes or through the words of the Word made flesh. The working out of the potentials of causal reasons is subject both to the effect of secondary causes and to the explicit will of God; both the ordinary course of nature and miracles express the causal reasons (6.14.25–18.29). This is not to say, however, that God places the causal reasons of all things within Creation: Augustine grants that God may have reserved some causal reasons in God's self, so that they are not subject to the necessity of other causes and take effect only when God chooses. But even these reserved causal reasons, with their immunity to ordinary causation, fall within the necessity of God's will: miracles may surprise us, but one part of God's plan does not contradict another (6.18.29).

Augustine's picture of Creation, then, is a single moment of divine action with a five-part internal structure:

1 God's eternal intention to create, enunciated in the Word;
2 God's Creation in the minds of the angels of a knowledge of what is to be made;
3 God's creation of things, some of them (like the angels) in full existence, but most of them (like trees, plants, and human beings) in the potentials called "causal reasons";

4 the angels' perception of the created things; and
5 God's eternal support of the Creation through the Holy Spirit.

These points address only the original moment of Creation and God's internal management of the cosmos – God's underlying support of beings. Other sections of *De Genesi*'s twelve books deal with the actual creation of human beings from the slime of the earth and with God's external management of the universe. In regard to this latter question, Augustine says at one point that the angels are God's agents for carrying out the design of providence (8.24.45); at another, he compares angels to gardeners – they do the work, but God gives the increase (9.18.35). He even considers (without accepting it) the proposition that the angels were created in two varieties, the heavenly and the mundane, only the latter being involved in the Fall (11.17.22). He also toys with the idea that Satan lived for a while among the angels (11.26.33; it is a position he adopts in the later work, *On Correction and Grace*).

The Ainulindalë

Readers of *The Silmarillion* will have already recognized in this account of Augustine's thought elements that would have allowed the reader in Tolkien's imagined Middle Ages to reconcile the *Ainulindalë* with Genesis; but it may nonetheless be helpful to summarize Tolkien's myth. "Ainulindalë" means "the Music of the Ainur" (*Silm*, 314), and music is the overriding symbol of the whole cosmogony. In the beginning, there was Eru (the One, translated in the back matter of the book more precisely as "he who is alone," 328, 358), who is called Ilúvatar ("Father of the All," 336, 356, 360). Ilúvatar "made first the Ainur, the Holy Ones, that were the offspring of his thought" (15).[6] Ilúvatar proposed musical themes to the Ainur, and they sang, individually at first, reflecting the individual parts of Ilúvatar's mind from which they came; but as they began to discover harmony, Ilúvatar called them together and propounded the theme of a Great Music, for each of them to adorn. The symphony began; but after some time, Melkor, the mightiest of the Holy Ones, began to introduce themes of his invention. As others followed him, discord spread, until at length Ilúvatar introduced a second theme of his own. The discord grew yet more violent, and Ilúvatar brought in a third theme, which drew together his earlier two, even as the discord moved toward its own unity. Finally, there seemed two separate musics, until Ilúvatar arose a third time and drew all into one final chord.

When the music had ended, Ilúvatar, in order to demonstrate that Melkor's discord only served his own higher purpose, gave the Ainur a vision of what till then had only been Music. Taking them to the edge of the home he had made for them, he showed them a world sustained in the void: their Music, he explained, was its design and history. From this vision, and their memory of the music and of Ilúvatar's comments, the Ainur had much foreknowledge of the world's development; but the knowledge of some things Ilúvatar reserved to himself. The vision itself contained surprises: in particular, the third theme referred to the creation of Elves and human beings. Ilúvatar had designed the world as a home for these his Children, yet the Ainur had had no hint of their existence until they saw the vision. The vision lasted only a short time and ended before the Music had fully unfolded. When it had passed away, the Ainur for the first time perceived Darkness. Ilúvatar then gave the world real existence, creating it with the single word *Eä*, "Let these things be."[7] Many of the Ainur then entered into Creation, only to find that it was not yet developed according to the shape of the Great Music; time, the unfolding of that Music, had begun only with their entry into the world. The Music itself, the vision, and all the other events of which the story tells had taken place in the timelessness of the presence of Ilúvatar.

In the original context of the *Book of Lost Tales*, the Ainur are seen as gods, and aspects of that view survive even into the *Lord of the Rings*, where, for example, "A Elbereth Gilthoniel" looks very much like a hymn to their star-kindling Queen.[8] A medieval Christian reader of *Ainulindalë* could certainly have taken them as angels (as Tolkien suggests and as modern readers commonly do); even the Hebrew Scriptures sometimes refer to the angels as gods, for example in Psalm 82:1 (Vulgate Ps. 81:1, *Deus stetit in synagoga deorum* [God stands in the assembly of the gods]). Taking the Ainur as angels and, accordingly, Eru Ilúvatar as God, the reader would find the *Ainulindalë* strikingly similar to the scheme set out in *De Genesi*. In both cases, God first creates the angels and then reveals to them the further elements of Creation; the angels' own knowledge reflects ideas in the divine mind. In both cases, as well, after the revelation, God gives real existence to what the angels have perceived, upholding that existence in the void; yet that real existence has only the undeveloped potential of what it will become in the unfolding of time, and God reserves to God's self the introduction of elements unanticipated in the basic design.

Granted these similarities, however, the two schemata do contrast in two ways. First is the fact that the predominant musical images function in the *Ainulindalë* in the way that speech and light, taken together as intellectual illumination, do in Augustine's reading of Genesis. Second is the way the Ainur act as sub-creators, developing the themes proposed to them by Eru Ilúvatar, whereas Augustine focuses on God as the sole creator. As to the first of these points: while it is true that Augustine does not use musical images in any significant way in *De Genesi*, he employs them extensively in other writings. In letter 166, discussing why some people are born only to die almost immediately, Augustine compares the lengths of various lives in Creation to the lengths of various tones in music: as a skilled composer uses rhythm, so also "in hoc labentium rerum tamquam mirabili cantico" [in this wonderful song of succeeding events] God follows the same laws, granting the lifespan the "quam deus dispositor temporum nouit universitatis moderamini consonare" [which God, distributor of time, knows to be in harmony with the control of the universe] (*Epistulae*, 566; *Letters*, 19). Another source of musical imagery is the scriptural statement that God disposed Creation in accordance with number, measure, and weight (Wisdom 11:21): because Augustine understands music to be principally a matter of number, his references to this text can lead him to musical imagery. More specifically, the numbers of music give it rhythm, and rhythm serves Augustine as one of several favorite images with which to describe the place of evil in the universe. He often points out that, as a brief silence gives form to a song or speech, so also the nothingness of evil in fact plays a role in the larger pattern of creation.[9] In the *Ainulindalë*, Ilúvatar makes precisely this point in showing Melkor the results of his rebellion:

> Thou shalt see that no theme may be played that hath not its uttermost source in me, nor can any alter the music in my despite. For he that attempteth this shall prove but mine instrument in the devising of things more wonderful, which he himself hath not imagined.
>
> (*Silm*, 17)

The idea expressed in this passage, common in Augustinian writings, would fit easily with *De Genesi*; indeed, though he does not use the musical imagery, Augustine does specifically say (while discussing the temptation of Adam and Eve) that God will bring good from Satan's actions, despite what the devil intends (11.22.29).

On the second point, that of the Ainur as sub-creators, we have already noted that Augustine describes the angels as God's gardeners and as agents to whom all Creation is subject. For Augustine, the angels are free, rational, and immensely powerful spiritual beings, and in this sense they play a role in the unfolding of Creation, as do human beings on a lesser scale. This is a wide sphere of influence, but it seems to be more restricted than that ascribed to the Ainur: the *Ainulindalë* does not picture the other rational creatures as contributing to the Great Music, even on a smaller scale. On the other hand, the *Ainulindalë* does insist that the Children of Ilúvatar are somehow distinct from the rest of the Music – not only in that they come from the third theme, Ilúvatar's theme, in such a way that the rest of the Music merely prepares their habitation, but also in the specific insistence that Men, at least, are free and both Elves and Men reflect parts of the mind of Ilúvatar that the Ainur would not otherwise have known (*Silm*, 18). The Music of the Ainur develops the themes of Ilúvatar, but it is not the full tale of Creation; and the Children of Eru have a part in that tale, as they will have in the music at the end of days (15). Thus there is in the *Ainulindalë* itself implicit evidence that the Ainur differ from the Children in power but not in the basic character of sub-creators.

All this being said, however, the fact remains that the *Ainulindalë* gives far more attention to the Ainur's development of the divine design than Augustine does to the work of the angels (and in terms of space, at least, more attention than it gives to the divine work of Creation itself). The role of the Ainur harmonizes with Tolkien's interest in sub-creation, his declaration (years after the first versions of the *Ainulindalë*) that "we make still by the law in which we're made" ("Mythopoeia," 99). While Augustine's philosophy would have room for this idea of Tolkien's, the actual text of Genesis focuses rather determinedly on the primary creative activity of the one God, leaving little room for more reflection on sub-creation than we have already seen. Moreover, the late-antique world in which Augustine wrote also militated against a Christian author giving too much attention to angelic sub-creation. The idea of sub-creators was common among the competing philosophies and religions of the day; but unlike the Ainur or Augustine's angels, these sub-creators, often lesser gods in a pantheon, typically figure in a scheme that sees the created world as flawed, unworthy of the original intentions of the primary Creator. Some such ideas were held by the Manicheans.[10] In Augustine's day, too much talk of angels as contributors to Creation could seem to contradict not only the belief in one God but also the declaration that the Creation is good. The anti-Manichean Augustine would do neither.

The language of myth

Given Augustine's reading of Genesis, then, the asterisk-cosmogony of the *Ainulindalë* would fit alongside the other cosmogonies known to the early medieval West – an asterisk Bede or Ælfric, stumbling across Eriol/Ælfwine's report, would have been able to assimilate it to the scriptural account. To the degree that Tolkien's myth strikes its real reader as different from Genesis, it represents a particularly ironic twist on the philologically inspired creative process Shippey finds in Tolkien: not only can he imagine things for which we easily find a place in the primary world, he can also imagine things that fit in ways we would not expect.

It may be that Tolkien knew of *De Genesi* before he began his own work; I have not been able to find any evidence that Tolkien had studied the commentary, but the text is not particularly obscure, and Tolkien may have seen it. He may also, of course, have read Plotinus directly (as Laurence Pittenger of the University of Toronto suggested in a session at the Thirty-sixth Medieval Congress), and he had access to the various Neoplatonic commentaries. Typically, though, those more directly Plotinian cosmogonies stress the role of three successively emanating hypostases (such as One, Intellect, and Soul) rather than the work of the angels, and thus the *Ainulindalë* by its nature resembles them less closely that it does *De Genesi*.

What is of interest, however, beyond the neat fit of this literary myth into the real history of Western thought, is the symmetry of opposed motives between Augustine's reading of Genesis and Tolkien's asterisked account of the Creation. Each man lives in a time that sees Genesis under attack from contemporary science: in Augustine's day, the story of Creation seemed to contradict the Stoic and Neoplatonist philosophers' picture of the world; in Tolkien's, as in our own, physical science and literary criticism seemed to converge in an attack on the myths of Western religion, in particular on the stories of Creation in Genesis. Tolkien, as we know from "On Fairy Stories," was concerned with establishing, or restoring, the power of myth (and, indeed, the power of language itself) by bringing us to look at words and concepts in a new light. Augustine, as we have seen, demonstrates that Genesis, when correctly read, agrees with such Neoplatonist and Stoic teachings as the doctrine of the seminal reasons. If myths convey powerful truths, then Augustine's analysis works to assert the truth, and Tolkien's mythopoesis, the power of the story of Creation.

These two activities represent two moments in the task of theology. On the one hand, as Augustine says, if Christians wish to have their neighbors believe the great miracles of the Gospel, it is necessary to avoid interpretations of Scripture that conflict with what the pagans know to be true from reason and experience (1.19.39). This is, to employ a term of art in a slightly uncommon way, the "demythologizing" aspect of theology. On the other hand, the theologian faces the task of recovery, of restoring the power of images and stories that have grown weak from cultural change or from mere familiarity. In this sense, the theologian's task is not demythologizing but mythopoesis as (in a word coined by theologian Sallie McFague) "re-mythologizing" (*Models of God*, 32), whether it takes the form of searching for a new language of theology (as, for example, in Paul Tillich's use of language of "depth" to replace images of "height" or in McFague's own work with the image of God as friend [*Metaphorical*, 174–92]) or the shape of telling new stories to express the old ideas (as most preachers do each Sunday).

The Christian theologian does not have a unique commitment to these two activities. Rather, every myth that retains its force, every myth that does not become a set of broken symbols, goes through a similar continuing process of interpretation and recovery. The fact that the underlying myths can and do live on through the ages, however, brings up a final point: interpretation and recovery are not replacement. Neither Augustine nor Tolkien would countenance for a moment the proposition that his work could supplant the foundational story of Genesis.[11] Ultimately, power lies not in translations but in the language of myth itself.

Notes

I gave an earlier version of this paper, as "Augustine and the *Ainulindalë*," at Mythcon 25 (6 August 1994), in Washington, D.C.; that version subsequently appeared in *Mythlore* 79 (1995): 4–8. For assistance with that version, I am indebted to Dr. Fabian Lochner, who invited me to speak on the subject to his freshman seminar at the University of Notre Dame in 1992, and to Dr. J. M. B. Porter, who read and commented on an earlier draft.

1 For a general overview of the Neoplatonist heritage, see Marenbon, *Early Medieval Philosophy*, 3–19. Flieger discusses the *Ainulindalë* in relation to Plotinus and Pseudo-Dionysius in "Naming," but on the meaning of the name "Eru", this 1986 essay is less accurate than the corresponding discussion in *Splintered Light* (49–50), from 1983.

2 Augustine's text of Genesis (1:2; the Vetus Latina, or Old Latin) has "terra invisibilis erat et incomposita, et tenebrae erant super abyssum. et spiritus dei superferebatur super aquas" [the earth was invisible and unordered, and darkness was over the abyss. And the Spirit of God was moving over the waters], representing the wording of the old Greek translation, the Septuagint. When Augustine's contemporary Saint Jerome made a new translation (the Vulgate) directly from the Hebrew, he wrote "terra autem erat inanis et vacua et tenebrae super faciem abyssi et spiritus Dei ferebatur super

aquas" [now the earth was void and empty and darkness {was} on the face of the abyss and the spirit of God was moving over the waters] (all translations are my own).

3 Whereas the initial reference to Creation of corporeal things as formless matter refers to the Second Person simply as "the Beginning," avoiding any reference to "the Word."

4 Thus "and so it was done" is omitted after "let light be made," since "let light be made" refers to the creation of spiritual creatures themselves, an event that the angels experience (rather than one that is revealed to them) (2.8.16–19).

5 For Augustine, as for the Neoplatonists generally, knowledge of the thing in itself is only a sort of dim echo of knowledge of the thing as an idea in God.

6 Flieger, considering this latter phrase in particular in light of the Neoplatonic tradition's concept of "emanations," says of the Ainur: "They are powers or principalities emanating directly from the godhead, and seem to be aspects of his nature" (*Splintered Light*, 50) and "As 'offspring' of Eru's thought, the Ainur are aspects of whole mind, differentiations of Eru's undifferentiated nature" ("Naming," 130). But Tolkien's use of "made" in the text parallels his reference to the Ainur as "created" and "angelical first-created," in letters from 1958 and 1964 (*Letters*, 284, 345), and Ilúvatar's declaration in *The Silmarillion* itself that Aulë has "being as a gift" (43). These instances would argue against an emanationist view of the Ainur or of their actually sharing the divine nature, though as creatures they may reflect parts of it.

7 Christopher Tolkien points out that the introduction of this separate moment of physical creation is one of few developments between the early and late versions of the *Ainulindalë* (J. R. R. Tolkien, *BLT*1, 62).

8 Tolkien himself calls it a hymn, and Elbereth, "'divine' or 'angelic,'" in J. R. R. Tolkien and Donald Swann, *The Road Goes Ever On* (63, 65).

9 See Augustine's *De Genesi ad litteram imperfectus liber* [An Unfinished Book on the Literal Sense of Genesis] (25), where he uses the image in discussing the division of light from darkness.

10 In presenting an earlier version of this paper at Mythcon 25, I was reminded by David Bratman and Anders Stenstrom that Arda, in that it reflects the disharmonies of the rebel Ainur, appears to be a flawed creation somewhat like those of subcreators in ancient religions. Stenstrom points out that, in a letter, Tolkien himself contrasts the "subcreatively introduced" evil of Eä with the place of evil in "Christian mythology," where Satan's rebellion does not change the nature of the world *per se* (*Letters*, 286). The world is, as one volume of the *History of Middle-earth* declares in its title, *Morgoth's Ring*. While the contrast is a legitimate one, it does not seem to me that Morgoth's pollution reaches to the level of a flaw in Creation. The evil in Eä, however primordial, still has a place in the pattern of Ilúvatar, while Augustine would say that God's assessment of the world as "very good" includes evil – it is a verdict on the whole of the universe as unfolded in time, not merely on the state of affairs at the moment of Creation (cf. *De Genesi* 3.24.37).

11 Indeed, in his oft-cited 1958 letter to Rhona Beare, Tolkien explicitly denies any primary-world religious status to his myths (*Letters*, 283).

12 The "music of the spheres"

Relationships between Tolkien's *The Silmarillion* and medieval cosmological and religious theory

Bradford Lee Eden

> [W]here there is no sorrow but only perpetual joy and what I might call a perennial mildness, we can guess that the most exquisite kind of singing is practiced by the holy Angels. Since joy almost never comes except from love, and since the highest love is the divine sort, there must also exist among the Angels that which serves to show the supreme love: which certainly cannot be better done than by heavenly music … . Since, therefore, the Angels perceive all his knowledge, love, and joy illuminated by divine radiance, they break out in untiring melody, singing to God.
>
> (Matthaeus Herbenus, *De natura cantus ac miraculis vocis*)

> There was Eru, the One, who in Arda is called Ilúvatar; and he made first the Ainur, the Holy Ones, that were the offspring of his thought, and they were with him before aught else was made. And he spoke to them, propounding to them themes of music; and they sang before him, and he was glad … . And it came to pass that Ilúvatar called together all the Ainur and declared to them a mighty theme … "Of the theme that I have declared to you, I will now that ye make in harmony together a Great Music." … Then the voices of the Ainur, like unto harps and lutes, and pipes and trumpets, and viols and organs, and like unto countless choirs singing with words, began to fashion the theme of Ilúvatar to a great music.
>
> (Tolkien, *Silmarillion*)

As a medievalist, Tolkien knew and recognized the importance of music as an anthropomorphic reality and creational material in many mythologies. The medieval concept of the "music of the spheres" was grounded in ancient and classical philosophy, discussed and theorized by Plato and Aristotle, through the early Christian writers and the third-century pagan philosopher Plotinus, up to its eventual standardization by Boethius in the early sixth century. A cursory examination of Tolkien's biography and letters indicates that Tolkien himself did not refer to his incorporation or philosophy regarding this theory in the construction of his mythology. Yet, as a classicist and medievalist, the "music of the spheres" concept would have been deeply ingrained in his educational training, and his Catholic background would also have influenced his thought and creative processes. Indeed, an examination of *The Silmarillion* illustrates that the creational power of music was a strong sub-thread throughout the stories, and whether it was inserted consciously or unconsciously has yet to be explored and discussed. Even further, the entire history of Middle-earth follows an interesting decay and descent in the uses and appearances of music that closely follow Boethius's model regarding the three types of music in medieval cosmological theory. By following Boethius's model of medieval cosmological theory, close parallels can be seen in the appearance of music throughout Tolkien's mythology. Finally, parallels between Jonathan Evans's writings on the development of dragon-lore in Middle-earth and the construction of Tolkien's musical cosmology throughout his writings are provided to support similar lines of evolution in Tolkien's mythology.

Music as mythological matter and content

In many mythologies, there is often one god or demigod whose main attribute is related to the power of music. In Greek mythology, for instance, the classic example is the demigod Orpheus, whose gift and power of music are able to affect the people and environment around him. So great is his musical ability that, when performing in front of Hades himself, Orpheus is able to obtain the soul/life of his wife, Euridice, from death (only to lose her again through his lack of faith). Other Greek mythological characters with musical powers include the Muses, the sirens, and Circe.

The power of music appears often in Celtic and Welsh mythology, and the playing or hearing of music is often a "bridge" between the worlds of man and faerie (Ralls-MacLeod, 2–4). Eastern mythological stories are similar in this respect, especially those of the Hindu and Japanese traditions. In the Judaic/Christian tradition, music is also featured in the cosmological drama, such as the poetic descriptions of music's power in the Psalms and Proverbs, the fall of the walls of Jericho at the hands of Joshua's trumpets, and the Final Judgment in the Book of Revelation.

The medieval concept of the "music of the spheres"

The most commonly quoted source concerning the medieval concept of the "music of the spheres" is Boethius (*c.* AD 480–524). Boethius was the first to state in his treatise *De institutione musica* that music was divided into three specific kinds, in order of priority and importance: the music of the universe, human music (vocal), and instrumental music. The first kind, the music of the universe, is embodied in the movement of celestial bodies, the harmony of the four elements, and the four seasons. About the movement of heavenly bodies Boethius argues:

> How indeed could the swift mechanism of the sky move silently in its course? And although this sound does not reach our ears (as must for many reasons be the case), the extremely rapid motion of such great bodies could

> not be altogether without sound, especially since the courses of the stars are joined together by such mutual adaptation that nothing more equally compacted or united could be imagined. For some are borne higher and others lower, and all are revolved with a just impulse, and from their different inequalities an established order of their courses may be deduced. For this reason an established order of modulation cannot be lacking in this celestial revolution.
>
> (Strunk, 84–85)

About the congruence of the four elements, earth, air, fire, and water, Boethius asks:

> Now unless a certain harmony united the differences and contrary powers of the four elements, how could they form a single body and mechanism? But all this diversity produces the variety of seasons and fruits, and thereby makes the year a unity. Wherefore if you could imagine any one of the factors which produce such a variety removed, all would perish, nor, so to speak, would they retain a vestige of consonance.
>
> (Strunk, 84–85)

For Boethius, the differences (or potential discord) among the four elements are harmonized by a chain of being that helps to balance and coordinate them in order to produce the plenitude of creation; this harmony is reflected in the music of the universe.

> And just as there is a measure of sound in low strings lest the lowness descend to inaudibility, and a measure of tenseness in high strings lest they be broken by the thinness of the sound, being too tense, and all is congruous and fitting, so we perceive that in the music of the universe nothing can be excessive and destroy some other part by its own excess, but each part brings its own contribution or aids others to bring theirs. For what winter binds, spring releases, summer heats, autumn ripens; and the seasons in turn bring forth their own fruits or help the others to bring forth theirs.
>
> (Strunk, 84–85)

The "music of the spheres" in Tolkien's *Ainulindalë*

In the *Ainulindalë*, or the creation story of Middle-earth in the *The Silmarillion*, the focus is on music as the creative and omnipotent force. The reader is an observer of the events that are transpiring at the beginning of time and space. The epigraph to this chapter is but a short summary of the "music of the spheres" that Eru encourages the Ainur to develop and compose upon. The medieval depiction of the various hierarchies of angels singing continuously around the throne of God is recalled in this creation story in *The Silmarillion*. Tolkien's creation of Arda through the melodies of Eru and the "variations" upon Eru's themes composed by the combined forces of the Ainur is a powerful exemplar of medieval cosmological theory in action. Indeed, when the Ainur/Valar first enter into Middle-earth, they greet a dark, unshaped world that has not yet begun:

> For the Great Music had been but the growth and flowering of thought in the Timeless Halls, and the Vision only a foreshadowing; but now they had entered in at the beginning of Time, and the Valar perceived that the World had been but foreshadowed and foresung, and they must achieve it.
>
> (*Silm*, 8)

That music is the creational and binding force that sets in motion the entire drama of Middle-earth as "Eä, the World that Is" (8), not only emphasizes the importance of the first type of music that Boethius describes, the music of the universe, but also binds Tolkien in the rest of his mythological work to construct and illustrate music's power through the other two types of music as well, that is, human/vocal music and instrumental music. For if Eru and the Ainur from the beginning are both bound and set free by the power of cosmological music, then even more so are the creations and creatures contained in Middle-earth.

The "music of the spheres" in Tolkien's *Quenta Silmarillion*

For those Ainur who choose to enter Middle-earth as Valar, the power of music comes to be the creational energy whereby they, in imitation of Eru, are able to bring to fruition the results of the Great Music, which they had only seen in vision but are now able to achieve. This creational energy is demonstrated by means of the Valar's respective powers in singing. In chapter 1 of the *Quenta Silmarillion*, "Of the Beginning of Days," Yavanna, who controls the production of fruits, sings on the green mound of Ezzellohar at the western gate: she

> sang a song of power, in which was set all her thought of things that grow in the earth … . And as they watched, upon the mound there came forth two slender shoots; and silence was over all the world in that hour, nor was there any other sound save the chanting of Yavanna. Under her song the saplings grew and became fair and tall, and thus there awoke in the world the Two Trees of Valinor.
>
> (*Silm*, 26)

In contrast to Yavanna is the Vala of water, Ulmo, whose solitary role (and power) gives rise to a different kind of music: "In the deep places he gives thought to music great and terrible; and the echo of that music runs through all the veins of the world in sorrow and in joy" (*Silm*, 28). Further, when the Valar depart forever to Eä, all music ends: "For it is said that after the departure of the Valar there was silence, and for an age Ilúvatar sat alone in thought" (30).

Indeed, Ilúvatar designs the fates of the Quendi (Elves) and the Atani (Men) during this silence after the departure of the Valar. Not only does music bring about great creational activity on a cosmological scale, but the silence or absence of music also appears to bring about cosmological implications as well.

Human/vocal music in Tolkien's *Quenta Silmarillion*

Moving to the second type of music, Boethius asserts that human music mirrors human nature, whose higher part is governed by reason and the soul.

> For what is that which unites the incorporeal activity of the reason with the body, unless it be a certain mutual adaptation and as it were a tempering of low and high sounds into a single consonance? What else joins together the parts of the soul itself, which in the opinion of Aristotle is a joining together of the rational and the irrational? What causes the blending of the body's elements or holds its parts together in established adaptation? … . He however is a musician who on reflection has taken to himself the science of singing, not by the servitude of work but by the rule of contemplation.
>
> (Strunk, 85–86)

In Tolkien, when the Valar discover the Firstborn, the importance of song to them is foreshadowed by the equivalence of their nature to features incarnated in external Nature.

> And the first sound that was heard by the Elves was the sound of water flowing, and the sound of water falling over stone … . Themselves they named the Quendi, signifying those that speak with voices; for as yet they had met no other living things that spoke or sang.
>
> (*Silm*, 39)

It is through the power of music and song, the "music of the spheres" philosophy of his educational and religious background, that Tolkien's concept of sub-creation comes to the fore in the drama that he creates through the lives and struggles of the peoples of Middle-earth. Many examples exist within *The Silmarillion* itself that music is the generational force out of which much of the drama of Middle-earth develops, both in its early history and in the future dramas of *The Hobbit* and *The Lord of the Rings*. For instance, not only is the entire unfolding of the Beren/Lúthien story framed by the power of song, but so also is the drama of Lúthien's parents, Thingol the Elf and Melian the Maia, falling in love: "Nightingales went always with her, and she taught them her song … and there suddenly he (Elwë) heard the song of nightingales. Then an enchantment fell on him" (*Silm*, 46–47). In another, analogous, passage, the Man Beren first discovers their daughter, Lúthien, dancing under the rise of the moon. Her singing reflects the song of the lark and of springtime regeneration as her mother's does that of the nightingale.

> In his heart he called her Tinúviel, that signifies Nightingale, daughter of twilight … . There came a time near dawn on the eve of spring, and Lúthien danced upon a green hill; and suddenly she began to sing. Keen, heart-piercing was her song as the song of the lark that rises from the gates of night and pours its voice among the dying stars, seeing the sun behind the walls of the world; and the song of Lúthien released the bonds of winter, and the frozen waters spoke, and flowers sprang from the cold earth where her feet had passed.
>
> (*Silm*, 161–62)

It is well known that the story of Beren and Lúthien emanates from Tolkien's own life and a specific incident with his wife, Edith. But there is a deeper and more significant meaning here.

Tolkien's scholarly and religious conviction regarding the power of music to affect and indeed engender drama in mythology and in real life comes to the fore in the Beren and Lúthien story, so much so that the three joinings of Elves/Men in *The Silmarillion* provide a significant portion of the history of Middle-earth and engender much of its conflicts and victories. And while the reader does not truly understand nor realize the intensity of the use of music throughout Tolkien's mythological drama, it becomes increasingly apparent as the reader is drawn into *The Silmarillion* that music is the ultimate power in the cosmological history of Middle-earth. The intensity with which Tolkien slowly yet intentionally weaves cosmological and human/vocal music throughout his mythology, in individual stories and dramas as well as through the ages of Middle-earth and the disparate timelines of his own output of the mythology, is a testimony to his understanding, knowledge, and indeed belief in music as a creational and cosmological power. His scholarly background as a medievalist, his strong religious belief and knowledge as a practicing Catholic, and his own life experiences come together to produce this powerful world whose sorrows and triumphs emanate from music.

The reader is drawn into this world by Tolkien's ability truly to draw parallels between his world and our world, for who has not been affected by the power of music in real life? This element of sub-creation in Tolkien's philosophy is an experience that all of us have had throughout our lives. A song that has become special between one and one's spouse or lover, music in a film that moves us to cry or draws us into the storyline, the tune that we hum throughout the day that we heard earlier from the radio – all of these experiences and more are a part of our daily lives. In fact, it is a sobering thought to think of what our world would be like without music. In the same way, Tolkien's mythology would be lifeless and uninteresting without music's presence as the generator and the thread that connects all dramas and histories and ages together.

Notice also the relationship between musical song and events in nature throughout the *The Silmarillion*. Lúthien's song above is but one example of her musical powers over nature; another example illustrates her musical prowess over even the emotions of the Valar themselves – and Melkor at that:

> She … offered her service to sing before him, after the manner of a minstrel … and out of the shadows began a song of such surpassing loveliness, and of such blinding power, that he listened perforce; and a blindness came upon him, as his eyes roamed to and fro, seeking her … . Then Lúthien catching up her winged robe sprang into the air, and her voice came dropping down like rain into pools, profound and dark.
>
> (*Silm*, 177)

And finally, like Orpheus before her (or after her, depending on which mythology you feel comes first!), Lúthien sorrowfully walks the Hall of Mandos to bring back Beren's spirit by means of her song to Mandos, which moves him to pity:

> The song of Lúthien before Mandos was the song most fair that ever in words was woven, and the song most sorrowful that ever the world shall hear. Unchanged, imperishable, it is sung still in Valinor beyond the hearing of the world, and listening the Valar are grieved. For Lúthien wove two themes of words, of the sorrow of the Eldar and the grief of Men, of the Two Kindreds that were made by Ilúvatar to dwell in Arda, the kingdom of Earth amid the innumerable stars.
>
> (*Silm*, 183)

Lúthien's two themes of grief reflect her two natures, Maia and Elf, and the love between Elf and Man that her relationship with Beren reflects – in effect, the power of her music even over death. Accordingly, she is given two choices: either to live in Valimar without Beren to forget her sorrows and griefs, for the gift of Ilúvatar could not be taken from him; or for both her and Beren to return to Middle-earth, where they would lead a second life, but she would become mortal and eventually die like him. Of course, Lúthien accepts the doom of the second choice, and as such she foreshadows the other two joinings of the Two Kindreds in *The Silmarillion*: that of Tuor and Idril Celebrindal, and that of Eärendil and Elwing, the half-Elf/half-human offspring of Beren/Lúthien and Tuor/Idril.

The adventures of these two other couples take up the majority of the rest of *The Silmarillion*, for they represent the best of both races, and as such their combined doings and their offspring are the stuff of legend. And as such, we find the link to the Third Age of Middle-earth, when we are introduced to the twin sons of Eärendil/Elwing, who are given the choice to be either Elven or human. Elrond, son of Eärendil and Elwing, chooses to become fully Elven and thus continues to fight Melkor's creations on Middle-earth into *The Hobbit* and *The Lord of the Rings*; while his brother Eros chooses to become fully human and the first king of Numenor in the Second Age. And it is Arwen who weds Aragorn in the final union of Elves and Men at the end of the Third Age of Middle-earth and thus brings the circle to full close.

Instrumental music in Tolkien's *Quenta Silmarillion*

Finally, Boethius's words on the third type of music describe music produced by instruments, which is for the most part missing in the *The Silmarillion*:

> This [music] is produced by tension, as in strings, or by blowing, as in the tibiae or in those instruments activated by water, or by some kind of percussion, as in instruments which are struck upon certain bronze concavities, by which means various sounds are produced.
>
> (Strunk, 85)

In contrast, in *The Silmarillion*, interestingly enough, there is no direct reference to the use of instruments. In the few references Tolkien emphasizes song as the primary musical power in the early history of Middle-earth, and he only indirectly refers to instrumental music. The few references Tolkien does make acknowledge two minstrels of renown among Elves: Maglor son of Fëanor, a Noldo Elf, and Daeron the minstrel of Thingol, a Teleri Elf. Although instruments are not mentioned when referring to these two minstrels, they would obviously have been used, especially by a court musician such as Daeron. With regard to the first, Maglor, of the Quendi, Tolkien indicates that he matches the Sindar in skill and voice:

> But the Sindar had the fairer voices and were more skilled in music, save only Maglor son of Fëanor, and they loved the woods and the riversides; and some of the Greyelves still wandered far and wide without settled abode, and they sang as they went.
>
> (*Silm*, 111)

With regard to the second, Daeron, Tolkien portrays this Teleri minstrel as wandering in despair and lamenting the departure of Lúthien, who has followed Beren on his quest of the Silmarils. Of interest in the second quotation is the vague indication of the art of courtly love among the Elves, given that there would have had to have been many minstrels for one to have been given the title of greatest, along with the idea of wandering from place to place:

> And it is told that in that time Daeron the minstrel of Thingol strayed from the land, and was seen no more. He it was that made music for the dance and song of Lúthien, before Beren came to Doriath; and he had loved her, and set all his thought of her in his music. He became the greatest of all the minstrels of the Elves east of the Sea, named even before Maglor son of Fëanor.
>
> (*Silm*, 180)

There may be an unconscious decay of cosmological theory written into *The Silmarillion* that can only be detected by one who is knowledgeable about the entire mythological reality that is Middle-earth. Each theoretical step taken away from the "Great Music," which set everything into motion, is a slow descent away from "the divine." This is a strong thread throughout the writings of Plato and Aristotle, that each gradation and division of music away from the "pure" or "universal" results in a type of gradual descent downward in spirit and soul. Looking at *The Silmarillion*, that time period in Middle-earth when the Valar actively walked and acted in the world and when Elves and Men, as races, were still young, the focus is on cosmological and human/Elven vocal music, with indirect reference to instrumental music. When reading the dramas contained in *The Hobbit* and *The Lord of the Rings*, the reader often finds reference to instrumental and human/Elven vocal music among Elves and Men, with little reference to cosmological music. There are stronger indications and examples of single songs and tales that have passed down to the Third Age, songs of power and light that in themselves are mere shadows of reality from a previous age. As such, Elves and Men are farther away in both time and space from the "music of the spheres" and closer to the third and lower type of music in the Third Age.

Of course, without an understanding of the entire content of Tolkien's oeuvre, it is difficult to see the line of thought through which he may consciously or unconsciously be leading the reader. However, I would argue that it is in this medieval cosmological "music of the spheres" philosophy that the life and drama of Middle-earth becomes believable – indeed, illustrates the sub-creation theory that Tolkien so greatly elucidated in his essay "On Fairy Stories."

Conclusion

The medieval philosophy of the "music of the spheres" makes its appearance throughout Tolkien's Middle-earth, similarly to his conception and construction of dragon lore, which Jonathan Evans so eloquently summarizes in his essay on "Medieval Dragon-lore" as a reflection as well of medieval legends about dragons, but "disassembled, taken down to its elementary components, rationalized and reconstituted, then reassembled to fit the larger thematic purposes of Tolkien's grand narrative design" (179). For Evans, Tolkien can do this because he adheres to a belief that the Middle Ages subscribed to a single unified worldview:

> Tolkien treated the disjointed inferences and disparate motifs found in medieval literature as if they were the *disjecta membra* of a once-unified whole, i.e., as if there really were a coherent underlying medieval conception of the dragon from which all scattered references drew information. This is in fact a fiction; but it is an example of what T. A. Shippey has described as the reconstruction of the hypothetical, original *Zusammenhang* (coherence) of "asterisk-reality" that characterizes Tolkien's vision and method. It is analogous to, and for Tolkien part and parcel of, comparative historical linguistic reconstruction of the lost words and the lost grammar of lost, or largely lost, languages and thus lost worlds (*Road,* 15–18, 48, 59). The dragon-lore embedded in the medieval literature of the external world (our

world) is *not* coherent; it springs from sources as diverse as medieval European geography, ancient Semitic and Hellenistic cosmology and cosmogony, Roman mythology and popular legend, Latin hagiography, and Germanic legend and folklore.

("Medieval Dragon-lore," 179, 181)

The only difference between the dragon-lore of Middle-earth and the "music of the spheres" philosophy that runs throughout Middle-earth is the fact that medieval cosmological and religious theory regarding music's place in the creation and structure of the external world (our world) was not a *disjecta membra* but a coherent and well-documented belief found throughout the sources that Evans so thoroughly lists at the end of the quotation. What Tolkien has done is merely to transfer the external world philosophy into his own world, so much so that it dramatically appears from the beginnings of his world into and through the Fourth Age. The "music of the spheres" philosophy itself is so thoroughly embedded in Tolkien's world that it is transparent not only to the reader but perhaps subconsciously to Tolkien himself. The gradations of music's power in Middle-earth from its appearance in the first page of *The Silmarillion* all the way down to the Fourth Age in *The Lord of the Rings* reflect a Neoplatonic hierarchy of being, from the highest form of music, universal or comic music, down to human/vocal music, and then down to instrumental music. This chain of musical being also embodies the diminution of cosmic love/harmony that ends with the most material and literal, in the instruments of Man.

Again, Evans elucidates for the history of dragons what can be described as a leitmotif or concept-development that appears throughout Tolkien's Middle-earth, an "asterisk-reality" of dragons beginning and near-waning in the First Age to their reappearance in the Third Age. About that fictionalized history Evans sees a parallel in our own medieval history:

> Tolkien's reconstructions thus set the stage for a Fourth Age – in Middle-earth the age in which the race of Men dominates – in which dragons survive only as a memory. To the extent that Middle-earth's Fourth Age is analogous to the ancient epoch of our own world – and Tolkien himself made this explicit – then his fictionalized history of dragons is meant to connect seamlessly with the actual status of dragons in medieval literature, where they appear as facts about an earlier time in a world accessible only through the imagination in epic, elegy, legend, and folklore.
>
> ("Medieval Dragon-lore," 189)

In this respect, Tolkien has imaginatively and selectively organized the medieval concept of the "music of the spheres" in his works. But where dragons were a fictionalized history in Middle-earth that he connected seamlessly with the actual status of dragons in medieval literature, as Evans states, what Tolkien actually does with the "music of the spheres" is to take a well-constructed historical and religious theory and belief from ancient and medieval literature and transplant it wholesale into his world. And he does this without so much as a conscious decision. The coherence between medieval concept and his fantasy mythology becomes so much a part of his belief, his education, his religion, his medieval background and research that the threads and strands throughout Middle-earth, once detected, make his genius transparent. The songs and ditties and musical recollections of past heroes and deeds that abound so frequently in *The Hobbit* and *The Lord of the Rings* and that capture the attention and emotions of the reader are the "memory" that have survived of music's creational and universal power from the First Age. The God and angels of our world and the Eru and Ainur of Tolkien's world create and organize their universes in similar and wonderful ways. Yet Tolkien's world is so much more alive and magical for its presence.

13 The anthropology of Arda

Creation, theology, and the race of Men

Jonathan Evans

One aspect of J. R. R. Tolkien's immense literary oeuvre that has often been commented upon as a key to its remarkable popular success – its textual, historical, and geographic complexity – has as a corresponding feature the sense of what we might call its cultural, racial, or *ethnic* depth. Although there are human beings among the sentient creatures in Arda, the imaginary world corresponding to our own – there are a number of other "races" portrayed there in addition to "Men."[1] These groups are in many ways similar to humans, but they also exhibit certain key differences; the complexities of their relationships in Tolkien's world mirror the anthropology of the real world and – as in our world – attest to deeper sources of meaning than the merely social, political, or cultural. Since most of the words for "people" in the Indo-European languages are informed by broadly human perspectives or by more narrow ethnic ones, the subject is difficult to discuss without the exercise of due care in our choice of terminology: terms such as "man" and "human" are not easily transferred to a discussion of non- or extrahuman races such as Elves, Dwarves, Orcs, Ents, Hobbits, and Wizards; on the other hand, in addition to the complexities of the linguistic evidence, we ourselves – Tolkien's readers – are human beings whose understanding of the human is necessarily limited: we tend naturally to take ourselves as our own reference point. But despite these difficulties, this essay attempts to explore Tolkien's conception of the race of Men in the development of his *legendarium* and in the narratives based upon it in terms of (1) the historical growth of the main concepts from the earliest stages of mythopoeic invention to the composition of *The Lord of the Rings* and *The Silmarillion* and (2) the fictive internal chronology of the world he invented. While in some ways Tolkien's works successfully overcome what is now referred to pejoratively as "anthropocentrism," and while the anthropology of his imaginary world is enriched by the coexistence of people of many races, nonetheless in the total framework of his literary invention, Tolkien's "Men" enjoy especially important status for one very good reason: Tolkien himself was a *man*.

Before going into detail concerning the anthropology of Arda and the theological principles underlying it, it will be instructive to consider some related concepts in the real-world relationship between human beings and the words they use to describe themselves and others. Tolkien would have been familiar with many of these ideas, and his imaginary universe must have been modeled deliberately upon certain aspects of them, particularly insofar as they involve linguistic nuances that for him were always central if not germinal. Special attention will be paid to nomenclature as a key to understanding inherent facts of what we must here call "anthropology," even though the application of this term to the diversity of races in Tolkien's imaginary world is in some ways inaccurate. The anthroponymy and the toponymy of both Arda and the real world provide powerful indications of underlying ethical and moral conceptions which, in turn, suggest principles with recognizable theological moorings in the doctrines of Christian orthodoxy. These, it will be seen, are deeply embedded in Tolkien's conception of artistic creation in the human world and the sometimes difficult relationship between creators – both human and divine – and their works.

It is a well-established fact of linguistic anthropology that the root meanings of words people use to describe their own tribe, clan, or ethnic groups often equate functionally, if not semantically, with something like "the people," or perhaps "the humans," default terms often implying unstated positive self-valorization. Concomitantly, terms applied to people outside a core *ethnos* are often pejorative in meaning. Emile Benveniste says this succinctly:

> All terms of an ethnic character were in ancient times differential and oppositive. The names which a people gives itself expresses, either clearly or otherwise, the intention of setting itself off from neighbouring peoples; it affirms that superiority inherent in the possession of a common, intelligible language.
>
> (Benveniste, *Indo-European Language and Society*, 299)

Etymologically, a powerful set of ethical distinctions is inscribed in such systems of terminology: according to this pattern, a given group says about itself, in effect, "We are *the people*, the only real humans; those over there are not people at all – they are not *us*."[2] Further, indigenous cultural groups may name their nearby competitors by using pejorative terms reflecting underlying patterns of self-aggrandizement and xenophobia. For example, several ethnic groups in the Indo-European community – ancestors of the modern Iranians and the *Alani* – described themselves by forms of the word *rya*, which means possibly "the hospitable ones" or "the venerable ones" and has been associated with the idea of "stranger" (Latin *alienus*), whether friend or enemy.[3] The Aryans, says Benveniste, are self-described as hospitable hosts of strangers, thus "contrasting their humanity with the barbarism of the people who surrounded them."[4] Further,

> When peoples give themselves names, these are divided, as far as we can understand them, into two categories; if we exclude names of a geographical character, they are either (1) an ethnic consisting of a complimentary epithet, e.g. "the valiant," "the strong," "the excellent," "the eminent" or (2) most often they simply call themselves "the men".
>
> (Benveniste, *Indo-European Language and Society*, 302)

The English word "barbarian," for example, derives from Latin *barbaria*, from earlier Greek βαρβαροι, βαρβαροσ, terms whose negative semantic developments are traced in the *OED*:

> The Gr. word had probably a primary reference to speech, and is compared with L. *balbus* "stammering." The sense-development in ancient times was (with the Greeks) "foreign, non-Hellenic," later "outlandish, rude, brutal"; (with the Romans) "not Latin nor Greek," then "pertaining to those outside the Roman empire"; hence "uncivilized, uncultured," and later "non-Christian," whence "Saracen, heathen"; and generally "savage, rude, savagely cruel, inhuman." The later uses occur first in Eng., the L. and Gr. senses appearing only in translators or historians.[5]

The Germanic-speaking "barbarians," then, were distinguished from the Roman *gens* initially in a gesture of linguistic xenophobia as a reflection of the perceived rudeness of their speech: the Proto-Indo-European root of both "barbarian" and "babble," likely, is **baba*, the reduplicative feature of this reconstructed form onomatopoeically imitating the supposed gibberish perceived in foreign speech.[6] From this pejorative characterization of the languages of non-Greeks or non-Romans, there arose later a broader cultural critique ascribing inferior anthropological status to nonmembership in those self-privileging cultures – whose languages to be sure must still have sounded like gibberish in the ears of Latin- and Greek-speaking Romans, and whose cultural deficiencies, while symbolized in terms of a difference in language, could not be overcome simply by linguistic adjustment. Thus, for example, the German-speaking Franks could adopt Latin as their spoken tongue, but they remained in all essential respects foreign to Roman culture.

Discernible through now fragmented evidence in mythic personal- and place-names including "Teuton" and "Aryan," these terms are meaningful not in isolation but as part of what Françoise Bader has described as a "complete system" of appellative principles related to Indo-European territorial expansion in prehistory. This system transcends the opposition of "other" and "self" or of "conquerors" and "conquered."[7] In the Germanic world, the early tribal name *Germani* (from prehistoric Germanic **gen-men-*, derived in turn from Proto-Indo-European **genə*, meaning "give birth," "beget") is related to a host of terms associated with the concepts implying close relations (compare, for example, "kin," "kind," "genus," "genre," "germane") and was first applied by non-Germans in Gaul to neighboring tribes, "men born nearby." The indigenous German term "Alemanni" translates literally to mean "all men," and the synonymous tribal name "Teuton" can be associated with underlying roots producing Latin *tōtus*, "complete," both terms suggesting the tribal unity of a group of people speaking a common tongue in contrast with foreign-sounding aliens.

Modern English words such as "man," "people," "folk," "human," "pagan," and "heathen" illustrate similar principles. "Human" derives from Proto-Indo-European **dhghem-*, "earth," and means "from the ground," "earthling" (compare Latin *hōmo, humus*); "folk," from **pelə*, may be related to variants producing Latin *plēnus* and Modern English "full" and seems to bespeak the same sense of racial unity or totality given in "Teuton" above. In "pagan" we can see the Latin word *pāgānus*, "rustic villager, country-dweller," whose reconstructed root **pag-* appears in *pāgus*, a "staked-out boundary" dividing a village or settlement-site from the unsettled area surrounding. The latter term was taken over in the ecclesiastical usage of Tertullian and Augustine in a pejorative sense for individuals – again, rural – who were *not* members of the *milites Christi*, the "soldiers of Christ." Pagans were pagans partly because they did not believe the doctrines of Christianity but also – speaking etymologically again – because they lived outside the places where Christians were more likely to live. It must be remembered that Christianity flourished early principally as an urban phenomenon, and so the social and cultural disapprobation of un*civil*ized people (i.e., people living outside *cities*) may be added in as part of this larger phenomenon. "Heathen," which appears in the *OED* note on "barbarian," derives from Old English *hǣð*, "heath"; thought by some to be a Germanic calque on *pāgānus* introduced (as *haiþnô*) in the fourth-century Gothic of Bishop Ulfilas, the word similarly describes people living in outlying, uncultivated lands and thus identifies them as culturally rustic and religiously heterodox.[8] "Man," finally, is a word associated with Latin *mens*, "mind." Owen Barfield says the etymology "hints at a dim consciousness among the Aryans that the essential function of the human being – at any rate of the Aryan human being – is to think" (*History in English Words*, 84).[9] We can scarcely surmise what the Aryans (that is, Indo-Europeans) must have thought the essential function of what they regarded as "non-human" beings – pagans, heathen, barbarians – was. Again and again in linguistic history in the real world we find patterns of identity, self-definition, inclusion, and exclusion inscribed in the lexical terms people employ in reference to themselves and the people around them, patterns aggrandizing as only truly human the local cultural perspective and ascribing special significance to *language* as an index of identification within or outside the ethnic group.

J. R. R. Tolkien's works of fiction, by contrast, display a great deal of sensitivity to these issues, revealing a remarkable capacity for decentering the anthropological perspective – the perspective of the race Tolkien describes as "Men" – in a culturally complex imagined world that, as said above, includes other kinds of people. Men are not the only race in Tolkien's imaginary world, and they are not the most important. Indeed, in terms of the internal chronology of the history of Middle-earth, the first sentient mortal beings in the created order were not Men but Elves (Eldar and Avari),[10] the Men appearing long afterwards. In a 1951 letter to Milton Waldman, long available in the Humphrey Carpenter edition of Tolkien's *Letters* but recently reprinted as the preface to the second edition of *The Silmarillion*, Tolkien said *The Silmarillion* "differs from all similar things that I know in not being anthropocentric." Further,

> Its centre of view and interest is not Men but "Elves." Men came in inevitably: after all the author is a man, and if he has an audience they will

> be Men and Men must come in to our tales, as such, and not merely transfigured or partially represented as Elves, Dwarves, Hobbits, etc. But they remain peripheral – late comers, and however growingly important, not principals.
>
> (*Letters*, 147)

We will return to the deeper implications of the casual concession "after all the author is a man" later in this chapter, but it is important to recognize throughout this discussion that, whether invented by him or adapted from other mythologies, each of Tolkien's races symbolizes a particular facet of the *human* beings in the real world, through which he provides insight into the problems faced by them.

The nomenclature of Arda and its people expresses a hierarchy of chronological succession and one of spiritual proximity to the Valar. While the Valar are immortal powers who share in making the world with the Creator (Eru Ilúvatar, "the One," the "Father of All"), the Elves – also immortal – are called Ilúvatar's "First Children." Men, however, a mortal race, are called both *Atani*, "the Second People," and *Hildor*, "the Followers," since they appear after the Elves. The Elves are also called *Eldar*, a name said to have been given to them by Oromë, one of the Valar, meaning "people of the stars"; *Quendi*, on the other hand, the name the Eldar give themselves in their own language, signifies "those that speak with voices." We may note here the inherent difference, and the apparent superiority – in terms laid out by Benveniste – of the Quendi as a race "in possession of a common, intelligible language" (*Indo-European Language and Society*, 299). The system of appellative terms used for Men in *The Silmarillion* also suggests something of the complex conception of this race in the mythology: the proper names *Apanónar*, *Engwar*, and *Fírimar* are translated as "After-born," "Sickly," and "Mortals," respectively; other epithets, given only in translation, include the "Usurpers," the "Inscrutable," the "Self-cursed," the "Heavy-handed," the "Night-fearers," the "Children of the Sun," and the "Strangers" – the latter being equivalent to at least one of the root meanings that has been suggested for the term "Aryan" in the real world. Some of these can be related to existing stories in *The Silmarillion*, but the others suggest otherwise undescribed narrative vistas whose unfolding of the meaning of these terms we can only imagine.

The fathers of Men, "who in the first years of the Sun and Moon wandered into the North of the world," are called the Atanatari (*Silm*, 103), and here is a point of connection between the languages of Middle-earth and human language in the real world that rewards some scrutiny. It is well known that amidst the complexity of invented languages and the narratives based upon them, Tolkien had to choose a real human language in which to communicate; English being his mother tongue, he naturally chose that for the composition of his stories. But he also chose to use the history of the Germanic languages as a model for the complex relationships between and among the languages of Arda: for the Elves, Quenya and Sindarin; for Men, the Adunaic speech of Númenór and Middle-earth.[11] In the Third Age of Middle-earth, Westron represents a late form of Númenórean degraded by time and influenced by various languages (both Eldarin and archaic forms of the language of the Edain) with which the eastward-migrating Númenoréans came into contact. Old English language is given as an approximation of the language of Rohan. As has been noted, to Gothic – the oldest attested Germanic language, a language and people that "haunted Tolkien all his life" (Shippey, *Road*, 14) – is assigned the language of the Woses of Druadan Forest and the Púkel-men of Dunharrow, last survivors and isolated cultural remnants of Men wandering Middle-earth before the arrival of Númenórean mariners from the west. Tolkien used Gothic as a linguistic resource for personal and tribal names. But Gothic *atta*, "father," coincidentally is almost identical with *atar*, a Quenya etymon also meaning "father" and appearing in such names as *Ilúvatar*, "Father of all," *Atanatari*, the "Fathers of Men," *Aratar*, "Exalted Ones" (the eight most powerful Valar; presumably, "royal fathers"), *Annatar*, "Father of Gifts" (a name Sauron gives himself), and others.[12] Tolkien seems to have been fascinated with this word in particular: in a letter concerning a paper his son Christopher had read, Tolkien commented on the light philology sheds on words and names. "[T]he thing that thrills my nerves," he said, "is the one you mentioned casually: *atta, attila*. Without those syllables the whole great drama both of history and legend loses savour for me" (*Letters*, 264). Thomas A. Shippey discusses Tolkien's fascination with Gothic and with this word especially, concluding, "*Atta, Attila*: what's in a name? One answer is, a total revaluation of history" (*Road*, 16). Another answer is a productive root linguistically connecting Arda, the imaginary world of Elves and Men, with our own world.[13]

The chronological status of Men as "aftercomers" is the source of much grief even before they appear: Melkor deceives some of the Noldor into believing Men are created by the Valar explicitly to displace the Eldar from their privileged position in Valinor.[14] There is enough truth in this to make the lie believable. Both the "Ainulindalë" and the "Valaquenta" describe a development that comes as a surprise to the Valar: the coming of the Elves and Men, children of Ilúvatar, the third theme in the cosmic music whose meaning and purpose the Ainur do not fully comprehend. Nor do the Elves, it seems. Though Ilúvatar blesses the Elves especially with the capacity to "conceive and bring forth more beauty than all my Children," Men are given "a new gift," the unquenchable desire to "seek beyond the world," finding rest only in death. Ilúvatar knows Men will "stray often" and "not use their gifts in harmony," and to the Elves "it seems … that Men resemble Melkor most of all the Ainur" (*Silm*, 41–42). But Ilúvatar does not tell the Elves where Men go when they die, nor does he reveal their ultimate role in the final stage in the history of Arda.

In the later history of Middle-earth, the linguistic dichotomy in the Third Age separating the Dunlendings from the Rohirrim (subcultures within the race of Men, though long estranged) reproduces these dynamics of inclusion, exclusion, and ethnic self-definition:

> Wholly alien was the speech of the Wild Men of Drúadan Forest. Alien, too, or only remotely akin, was the language of the Dunlendings … . Of their

> language nothing appears in this book, save the name *Forgoil* which they gave to the Rohirrim (meaning Strawheads, it is said).
>
> (*RK*, 407–8)

Like the appellative ethnic terminology in the primary world, the terms employed in Tolkien's secondary world indicate a specific moral weakness of human character; often, they are indicative of underlying antipathies between and within races; and they imply a spiritual definition that, while true of Men, is not exclusive to them: Tolkien's conception of all the races with which he populates the world of Arda stipulates one central unifying theological theme – all are *fallen*. More than an incidental affectation conducive to greater verisimilitude in relation to our world, however, the manner and the consequences of the fall of Men are connected deeply with Tolkien's anthropological conceptions, with his views concerning the powers and limits of human and divine creativity, and in particular with the nature of creative art exercised in the invention of myth and the making of literature.

Historically, the earliest reference to Men in the published writings of J. R. R. Tolkien is in the prose introduction to a poem entitled "Kortirion among the Trees," written in November 1915. There, in a prose introduction to what is probably the earliest expression of his conception of the earthly realm of Aman in the larger kingdom of Arda, reflecting something of the glory of the Blessed Realm of Valinor, Tolkien describes the city of Kortirion – "a fair city … girt with trees" in the center of the Lonely Isle (later to be called Tol Eressëa). The fairy inhabitants of that city, says the author, would have "rekindled once more the Magic Sun of Valinor *but for the treason and faint hearts of Men*" (*BLT*1, 25–emphasis mine). Here we see for the first time the description of human character as morally weak and prone to betrayal that would remain essentially unchanged through the great quantity of writing that would follow in the decades to come – in the myths and legends then developing into *The Book of Lost Tales* but which would later become *The Silmarillion* in its various prepublication and posthumous forms, and in the quest-romance *The Lord of the Rings*. In this first narrative venture, as a result of flawed human character, the Magic Sun is not revived; the Lonely Isle is "drawn back unto the confines of the Great Lands;" the fairies – prototypes of the race that would later emerge as the Eldar or "Elves" – are "scattered through all the wide unfriendly pathways of the world;" and the habitation of the Lonely Isle is given to Men, who "now … dwell even on this faded isle and care nought or know nought of its ancient days" (*BLT*1, 25).

It is to this island that Eriol, a "traveller from far countries, a man of great curiosity," comes in the opening scene of "The Cottage of Lost Play," written two years later in 1917. Eriol is described in the opening paragraph of that story as "a man of great curiosity" possessed of a "desire of strange lands and the ways and dwellings of unaccustomed folk" (*BLT*1, 13); the Lonely Island in which he has arrived, now named as Tol Eressëa, also bears the names "Dor Faidwen" and "the Land of Release," and – says the narrator – "a great tale hangs thereto." The "great tale" to which this sentence refers is nothing less than the whole of the history of Middle-earth, which would unfold over nine decades in the material published by Tolkien in *The Hobbit* and *The Lord of the Rings* and in the posthumous works edited by Christopher Tolkien as *The Silmarillion*, *Unfinished Tales*, and the twelve volumes of *The History of Middle-earth*. Eriol was later to disappear entirely from the actual text, and Tolkien explicitly describes the race of Men as marginal – "peripheral – late comers … not principals" – to the great narratives of Arda: "Of Men little is told in these tales, which concern the Eldest Days before the waxing of mortals and the waning of the Elves …" (*Silm*, 103). But in all these works Men play an important thematic role, the moral and theological characteristics of which are foreshadowed in the brief remarks of 1915–17. There we first meet Men as westward-travelers from an eastern home, curious and eager for adventure but at the same time by nature faint-hearted and treasonous. When they make their initial appearance much later in *The Silmarillion*, the chapter titled "Of Men" retains this essential definition: "Men feared the Valar rather than loved them, and have not understood the purposes of the Powers, being at variance with them and at strife with the world" (103).

Although to most readers Eriol is a shadowy figure at best, Thomas A. Shippey and Verlyn Flieger have written persuasively of his central importance as a touchstone to Tolkien's deepest themes.[15] The essential definition of the moral fallibility of the human race that Eriol represents would remain unchanged throughout all the writings, serving as the impetus and the driving force for the many complex narratives that would emerge. The frailty of the human spirit is one of the primary facts around which the vast narrative of all Tolkien's imaginative work – not only *The Silmarillion* but also *The Lord of the Rings* and many of the shorter stories and poems – is spun. In Tol Eressëa, Eriol encounters Lindo and Vairë – two Elves, storytellers – who propose to relate to their mortal visitor tales

> of the Great Lands, and of the dwellings of Men; of the Valar and Valinor; of the West and its mysteries, of the East and its glory, of the South and its untrodden wilds, of the North and its power and strength; or of this island and its folk, or of the old days of Kôr where our folk once dwelt.
>
> (*BLT*1, 18)

Valinor, Eriol learns, was "a place of fair gardens … beside a silver sea" to which a pathway, the "Olórë Mallë or Path of Dreams," "ran by devious routes" to the "homes of Men." In the middle of the garden there was a white cottage, thatched with gold, to which the "earliest children – the children of the fathers of the fathers of men" would come – guided by the Eldar – for joyful play, music, dancing, and mingling with the lush floral and animal life of the gardens. Those who strayed from the cottage into the city of Kôr "became enamoured of the glory of Valinor" and would stay there forever or "wander back and long for ever vainly, and become strange and wild among the children of Men" (18–19). Those who returned retained "misty aftermemories" of the things they saw and heard in Valinor, and "of their broken tales and snatches of song, came many strange legends that delighted Men for long, and still do, it may be; for of such were the poets of the Great Lands" (19). The path to Valinor has been "blocked forever with great impassable rocks," and the cottage stands empty "to this day," awaiting some future time when the path "shall be thronged with the sons and daughters of Men." In the meantime, Lindo and Vairë maintain their cottage, the Cottage of Lost Play, where "old tales, old songs, and elfin music are treasured and rehearsed" (20). Though they were to become marginal in the eventual form of the *legendarium*, clearly at the earliest stage of invention and development Men were already central to its imaginative vision. And in the internal chronological dimension of that vision, Men are described as gaining in importance progressively through the history of Middle-earth, becoming *narratively* prominent in the Third Age in *The Lord of the Rings*; the Fourth Age, of course, is specifically described as "the time … for the dominion of Men and the decline of all other 'speaking-peoples' in Middle-earth" (*RK*, 363).

As Christopher Tolkien writes, the "Eriol-story" is

> among the knottiest and most obscure matters in the whole history of Middle-earth … .My father abandoned the writing of the *Lost Tales* before he reached their end, and when he abandoned them he had also abandoned his original ideas for their conclusion.
>
> (*BLT* 1, 23)

In all the writing that later developed – *The Hobbit*, *The Lord of the Rings*, and so on – we do not get to see the great "Faring Forth," an expedition from Tol Eressëa to rescue Elves still wandering in the Great Lands (presumably, Europe); nor do we see the uprooting of the Isle and its relocation close to the western shores of the Great Lands to which the remaining Elves flee and fade after it is overtaken and populated by Men.[16] "The subsequent history of Tol Eressëa is the history of England," says Christopher.

> I shall not attempt any analysis or offer any elucidation of the ideas embodied in the "Cottages of the Children." The reader, however he interprets them, will in any case not need to be assisted in his perception of the personal and particular emotions in which all was still anchored.
>
> (*BLT* 1, 31)

But it seems clear that the original event giving rise to the story of Eriol is deeply connected to events during J. R. R. Tolkien's courtship of Edith Bratt, later his wife, who lived for a time in the city of Warwick, which is symbolized by the city of Kôr in *The Book of Lost Tales* and in separate poems composed at about the same time.

When we meet Men, then, they are already fallen, even in this earliest of narrative compositions from which Tolkien generated the rest of the mythology and history of Arda – of Aman and Middle-earth, the west and the east – and the stories that grew out of it. We can go even earlier than *The Book of Lost Tales*, though, to "what must be ... the very earliest" of the outlines from which Tolkien composed the *Lost Tales* – "a little pocket-book ... headed 'Story of Eriol's Life,'" – to learn more of who Eriol was supposed to be. "From these jottings we learn," Christopher tells us, that Eriol was originally named Ottor Wæfre, whose father Eoh was slain by his brother Beorn (23). The father of Eoh and Beorn was Heden, whose ancestry itself traced back to Woden or Oðinn of the Scandinavian pantheon. Ottor Wæfre settled on the North Sea island of Heligoland, married a woman called Cwén; their two sons Hengest and Horsa were born "to avenge Eoh." But Ottor was born under the beam of Eärendel and so was endowed with wanderlust; thus he sets out upon his expedition to find Tol Eressëa, "the unknown island." We might note in passing the echo here of the Cain/Abel feud; in the Christian tradition, significantly, the first sin after the Fall is a sin of violence – *murder* – the driving force in the heroic tradition for the human race in both the real world and the imaginary realm of Middle-earth.

Tolkien wrote a prose introduction to the 1915 "Kortirion among the Trees," sketching out the origins of Kortirion and its story, concluding with this:

> And it seems to the fairies and it seems to me who know that town and have often trodden its disfigured ways that autumn and the falling of the leaf is the season of the year when maybe here or there a heart among Men may be open, and an eye perceive how is the world's estate fallen from the laughter and the loveliness of old. Think on Kortirion and be sad – yet is there not hope?
>
> (*BLT*1, 26)

Tolkien's use of the word "fallen" is not accidental – we may be certain he means it in its fullest sense as a theological term describing the moral condition of human imperfection, which for Tolkien and many of his readers is central to the Christian myth. In the 1951 letter, Tolkien says of his work,

> Anyway all this stuff is mainly concerned with Fall, Mortality, and the Machine. With Fall inevitably, and that motive occurs in several modes. With Mortality, especially as it affects art and the creative (or as I should say, sub-creative) desire which seems to have no biological function, and to be apart from the satisfactions of plain ordinary biological life, with which, in our world, it is indeed usually at strife. This desire is at once wedded to a passionate love of the real primary world, and hence filled with the sense of mortality, and yet unsatisfied by it. It has various opportunities of "Fall." It may become possessive, clinging to the things made as "its own," the sub-creator wishes to be the Lord and God of his private creation. He will rebel against the laws of the Creator – especially against mortality. Both of these (alone or together) will lead to the desire for Power, for making the will more quickly effective, – and so the Machine (or Magic).
>
> (*Letters*, 145)

This paragraph provides a great deal of insight into the theological dimension of what Tolkien was trying to achieve. We may note at once the connection between creativity as a motif for, and mortality as a consequence of, the Fall. This motif works itself out in "several modes" in the actual narratives, where the Fall is connected both with love of the "primary world" and with artistic desire. Both of these involve a love of creation: that is, the world itself resulting from the creative acts of Ilúvatar – "Creation" with a capital *C* – and the artistic products resulting from the sub-creative acts of people *within* the created world. In both modes, illegitimate or inordinate love leads to dissatisfaction, possessiveness, rebellion, and death.

The Elves' love of artistic creation, the Dwarves' love of masonry and smithing, and Men's love for political domination and military conquest reflect one another as expressions of the same human sub-creative impulse. As David Llewellyn Dodds suggests, these are all expressions of the human drive toward technological manipulations of the primary world, exertions of the power of the will. In our world, what we might call the "technological imperative" is most often associated with the invention of mechanical devices to accomplish tasks of work; but in a more abstract sense it is also the essential motive behind artistic creativity and the design of the institutions of modern life: we must not think of "technology" simply in terms of "the making of tools and instruments – and not only hardware – or indeed software," but also in terms of "planning and organization … for production, communication, and so on" as well as for "the making of secondary worlds" (166). What Dodds calls "the technological representation of reality" is as much – perhaps more – a matter of how we think as it is a matter of the plans we make, the devices we invent, or the art we produce. Viewed in this way, the institutions of modern life together constitute an elaborate invented "mechanism" for the achievement of political, social, economic, and other goals, reflecting in an immense way the same fundamental impulse illustrated in more humble terms in the design of an automobile, the composition of a poem, the painting of a mural, or the preparation of a meal. More than simply an incidental feature of the modern cultural landscape, says Dodds, the free use of our reason and imagination "in analyzing and devising … to make what we have thought of, to put our designs into practice" has become "a basic feature of modern consciousness"; it is an impulse that can be employed by free agents toward ends that ultimately are either good or evil. Quoting Oliver O'Donovan, Dodds says our culture "is not 'technological' because its instruments of making are extraordinarily sophisticated," but because "it thinks of everything it does as a form of instrumental making," seeing everywhere it looks "nothing but the products of the human will" (168–69). The advanced technological societies of the modern world increasingly show signs of technological hubris, and one of the most important implications of Tolkien's imaginative work involves an essential critique of a modern culture that has forgotten that "our making activity … is 'sub-' to something else, depends on 'given' conditions":

> Whatever it may be, the world – including ourselves – is not the product of our instrumental making, no matter how dramatically we alter or manipulate it in fact, and no matter what we project upon it or how we represent it to ourselves.
>
> (Dodds, 171)

In Tolkien's secondary world, in Arda, this human impulse is represented in the *legendarium* in a number of ways through the diverse characteristics of the various races found within it – which, earlier, we said represent particular facets of fallen *human* character. The theological sources of this understanding of human nature are found in the Old Testament passages describing the Fall, expanded in the New Testament, and developed into Christian doctrine in patristic and medieval exegesis; *narratively* an important source for Tolkien, as for much of English-speaking Christendom, is probably not the Bible itself but John Milton's imaginative retelling in *Paradise Lost.* In many ways similar to Tolkien's *legendarium*, Milton's theological epic sought to render a literary vision of humanity at the level of all-encompassing cosmic scope that would explain the most difficult philosophical problem, perhaps the deepest source of human disquietude and "all our woe": the sin of Man.

For Tolkien, the artistic implications of the fallen definition of humanity were thematically central, both inside and outside his imaginary universe. Colin Duriez and Debbie Sly have written about the relationship between aesthetics and theology in Tolkien and in *Paradise Lost.* Duriez says "[each is] a study of evil" and "a defence of God's ways to mankind" ("Sub-creation and Tolkien's Theology of Story," 147). Sly suggests, "Both texts reflect what might be termed a creative struggle between religious orthodoxy and aesthetic imperatives, though these factors operate very differently in each case" ("Weaving Nets of Gloom," 109). Milton and Tolkien pursued similarly grand literary schemes, but they were different men with not always compatible views; though at bottom the theological principles are virtually identical, their aesthetic outworkings are rather different in the two writers. Shippey has written of Tolkien's probable dislike for Milton – "a Protestant, a divorcer, and a spokesman for regicides" – owing to his ignorance and even contempt for things Tolkien held most dear (*Road*, 200); but as Shippey also indicates, Tolkien solved part of the problem of how to write a story that could "reach out towards non-fictional truths about humanity – and perhaps about salvation" – without "forfeit[ing] its status as a story" or becoming either blasphemous or boring by taking cues from Milton (177). In *Paradise Lost*, Shippey says, "Milton … had managed to begin *his* epic very near the beginnings of time" (204). So does Tolkien; like Milton also, Tolkien portrays evil as originating not within the human world but in a time before time, in the fall of angelic beings (Tolkien's Valar). Shippey summarizes succinctly *The Silmarillion*'s relationship to the accounts of the Fall in *Genesis* and in Milton: "*The Silmarillion* … is a 'calque' … on the history of *Genesis*" and "an answer to *Paradise Lost* and *Paradise Regained*" (209). His exposition of the correspondence between it and key elements of Christian doctrine found in both is also broadly allusive. Not much more can be added to it, probably: in both works, God creates the world good, but perversion of the good through angelic pride produces rebellion and evil; fallen *daemones* corrupt an originally sinless race – in Tolkien, *races*, including Men. The motive force, the narrative engine energizing the plots of *The Lord of the Rings* and the heroic stories in *The Silmarillion* and others of Tolkien's fictional works merely present the ever more complicated ramifications – Milton's "all our woe" – flowing from the primordial cataclysm of Man's Fall.

In the middle of his development of these similarities, however, Shippey identifies a key difference that bears perhaps some expansion. Highlighting Tolkien's decision to avoid creating his *legendarium* as a "*rival* to the Christian story," Shippey says Tolkien deliberately kept the actual moment of the Fall out of the narrative:

> Significantly he left a gap in *The Silmarillion*, or designed a dovetail, for the Fall of Man as described in the Old Testament. In his work the human race does not originate "on stage" in Beleriand, but drifts into it, already sundered in speech, from the East. There something terrible has happened to them of which they will not speak: "A darkness lies behind us … and we have turned our backs on it."
>
> (Shippey, *Road*, 209)

Men, we learn, have been corrupted "off stage," so to speak, by Morgoth. "Clearly," says Shippey,

> one can … assume that the exploit of Morgoth of which the Eldar never learnt was the traditional seduction of Adam and Eve by the serpent, while the incoming Édain and Easterlings are all sons of Adam flying from Eden and subject to the curse of Babel.
>
> (Shippey, *Road*, 210)

Like Milton, Tolkien assumes the Fall of Man to be predicated on a prior fall – Satan's/Melkor's. But unlike Milton, Tolkien chooses *not* to make this event the central conflict of his story but only one of its many effects. In his 1951 letter, Tolkien said of his work, "Its centre of view and interest is not Men but 'Elves.' Men came in inevitably … . But they remain peripheral – late comers, and however growingly important, not principals" (*Letters*, 147).

This relegating of the Fall to an unnarrated scene – what I earlier described as an avoidance of overt anthropocentrism – no doubt has the effect Shippey ascribes to it: it allows an intentional "dovetail" connecting Tolkien's myth with Milton's to avert the danger of contradicting the biblical account of man's Fall and Redemption. "Tolkien … would not wish to go against what he accepted as doctrine universally true" (Shippey, *Road*, 210). But it is probably even more important than this, for it enables Tolkien, like Milton, in some respects to beg the complicated question of the role of human responsibility in the Fall by displacing the origins of it outside the human world into the prior world of angels and demons. In both *Paradise Lost* and *The Silmarillion*, the human Fall is secondary, growing out of the first Fall – the *really* "original" sin – of Satan and his followers. Although in Milton's work this secondary fall is narrated in great detail while in Tolkien's it is decidedly *not* told, both are the result of a seduction. Both writers choose deliberately ambiguous language when they give an account of the first Fall.

Just as in Milton's, in Tolkien's work there are two cataclysmic disruptions of the moral structure of the created order: the Fall of Men, and the earlier Fall of the archangelic powers from which the fallen state of humanity derives. In *The Silmarillion*, when the Noldor first encounter Men, they are already fallen into a state of spiritual darkness. The actual moment of the Fall – the central event in Milton's poem – is described only in a cryptic allusion, displaced to the periphery of Tolkien's narrative. In a different kind of literary displacement, but one equally pregnant with meaning, Milton puts the story of Satan's Fall in the mouth of Sin, figured allegorically as the female offspring and later the object of Satan's own incestuous lust. Leaving Pandemonium to depart hell for earth and the planned seduction of man, Satan encounters his daughter guarding the gates of hell. He does not recognize her, and she says:

> Hast thou forgot me then, and do I seem
> Now in thine eye, so foul, once deem'd so fair?
> In Heaven, when at th' Assembly, and in sight
> Of all the Seraphim with thee combin'd
> In bold conspiracy against Heav'n's King,
> All on a sudden miserable pain
> Surpris'd thee, dim thine eyes, and dizzy swum
> In darkness, while thy head flames thick and fast
> Threw Forth, till on thy left side op'ning wide,
> Likest to thee in shape and count'nance bright,
> Then shining heav'nly fair, a Goddess arm'd
> Out of thy head I sprung: amazement seiz'd
> All the Host of Heav'n; back they recoil'd afraid
> At first, and call'd me *Sin*.
>
> (Milton, *Paradise Lost*, 2.746–60)

Based on the account of Athena's birth from the head of Zeus in Hesiod's *Theogony*, the passage is visually arresting; like Tolkien's narrative, which leaves the reader only to guess at the deep psychological mechanism whereby Melkor came to prefer his own discordant music to the celestial harmony sanctioned by Eru, it doesn't give a satisfactory explanation for the most important philosophical or theological question addressed in the myth: *Why?* We might also observe that in giving us this account, Milton has *cheated*: Satan's offspring is represented as recalling the moment of her own birth – and the moments immediately beforehand – memories of which she could not possibly be in possession. Satan's Fall is stated simply as a *given*; it avoids the central issue concerning how a free creature created morally flawless can make a choice against the good, without responsibility for the evil inherent in that choice lying ultimately in the character of the deity who created him free in the first place. Similarly, in Tolkien's mythology the intrusion of evil into the world of Arda is not first or even foremost the fault of Men, nor is it that of their predecessors, the Eldar; it is the fault of one of the Valar, those who, as Eru's agents, assist in the creation of the universe. In the cosmogonic text entitled "Ainulindalë," just as in *Paradise Lost*, the account of the origins of evil begs the fundamental question *Why?* because, in our world as in Arda, both in terms of the general human condition and in individual psychological terms, the imperfection of the world and the fallen human condition are *givens* within which all our making must operate. It is one of the principal themes which mythopoeia – the creation of mythology and, within it, all literary invention – must struggle to express, even if its explanatory efforts finally fail.

After the initial act of creation whereby Eru creates the Ainur, "the Holy Ones" and "the first offspring of his thought," the process of sub-creation begins whereby the world of Arda is sung into existence through the themes of music that the Ainur compose at Eru's suggestion. All seems well at first – all is perfect – until the interruption of a discordant element. The passage in which the first hints of evil come into being at the instigation of a Vala called Melkor – equivalent to Satan in Tolkien's mythology – is subtle and complex, and it bears quoting at length:

> But now Ilúvatar sat and hearkened, and for a great while it seemed good to him, for in the music there were no flaws. But as the theme progressed, it came into the heart of Melkor to interweave matters of his own imagining that were not in accord with the theme of Ilúvatar; for he sought therein to increase the power and glory of the part assigned to himself. To Melkor among the Ainur had been given the greatest gifts of power and knowledge, and he had a share in all the gifts of his brethren. He had gone often alone into the void places seeking the Imperishable Flame; for desire grew hot within him to bring into Being things of his own, and it seemed to him that Ilúvatar took no thought for the Void, and he was impatient of its emptiness. Yet he found not the Fire, for it is with Ilúvatar. But being alone he had begun to conceive thoughts of his own unlike those of his brethren.
>
> (*Silm*, 16)

Melkor weaves these thoughts into his music, discord arises about him, and though their thoughts are "disturbed" and their music falters, "some began to attune their music to his rather than to the thought which they had at first" (*Silm*, 16). Melkor's theme gains strength, and two musics, "utterly at variance," compete before the throne of Ilúvatar (*Silm*, 16). As readers of *The Silmarillion* know well, the character of Melkor is thus launched on a downward moral trajectory, a "ruinous path" leading twice to his imprisonment and ultimately to his banishment from Arda itself into the void of everlasting night. But Melkor's first sin is presented so subtly as to obscure its nature and the precise moment of its occurrence. Here, it will be noted, all but one of the verbs connected with

Melkor are passive or past-perfect: the Fall "happens" to him. While in retrospect the attentive reader is able to reinterpret Melkor's actions as the self-alienating behavior of a being ultimately to be cut off from Eru, the ground of being itself, by being alone or thinking thoughts of his own, Melkor is behaving like Ilúvatar himself prior to the creation. Further, like Milton's Satan, Melkor's character traits are like those of his maker, Eru: the first fall of a created being is shown as concomitant with an act of *making*. Though presented as a distortion of Ilúvatar's intentions, Melkor's music-making is an act of creation, invalid not in and of itself but only insofar as its intentions and/or its effects prove to be at odds with the divine, creative will of Ilúvatar. Finally, Melkor himself might have objected (though he does not) that responsibility for the error that results from his exercise of the free will with which he was endowed must lie at least in part in his creation as a free being, and thus must have its ultimate source in the creator – Eru – himself. The very act of creation must contain within it at least the risk that something might go awry.

Tolkien was to return to this theme often. In *The Silmarillion*, we see the theme of the powers and limitations of sub-creation in the smithing of the three Silmarils – hallowed jewels described as "the most renowned of all the works of the Elves" – by Fëanor, one of the Noldorin Eldar. Fëanor's jealousy over these created works and Melkor's lust for them are the centerpiece in the history of what is called the First Age of Arda and the motive force driving the narrative through multiple tragedies. The inordinate love of an artisan for his art, one of the "modes" or motives for the moral fall to which Tolkien referred in his 1951 letter, appears elsewhere in the account of the creation of the race of Dwarves by Aulë, the smith. Because Aulë desires "learners to whom he could teach his lore and his crafts" and is "unwilling to await the fulfilment of the designs of Ilúvatar," he secretly creates the Seven Fathers of the Dwarves in a hall under the mountains in Middle-earth. Angered, Ilúvatar questions him concerning his motives, pointing out that the creatures Aulë has made are utterly dependent upon him, "moving [only] when thou thinkest to move them" but otherwise "standing idle." Aulë answers,

> I did not desire such lordship. I desired things other than I am, to love and to teach them, so that they too might perceive the beauty of Eä, which thou has caused to be. For it seemed to me that there is great room in Arda for many things that might rejoice in it, yet it is for the most part empty still, and dumb. And in my impatience I have fallen into folly.
>
> (*Silm*, 43)

Aulë objects that his desire to create is simply part of who he was created to be:

> Yet the making of things is in my heart from my own making by thee; and the child of little understanding that makes a play of the deeds of his father may do so without thought of mockery, but because he is the son of his father. But what shall I do now, so that thou be not angry with me for ever?

> As a child to his father, I offer to thee these things, the work of the hands which thou has made. Do with them what thou wilt. But should I not rather destroy the work of my presumption?
>
> (*Silm*, 43)

Aulë lifts his hammer to crush his unauthorized works of creativity, but because of Aulë's humility, Ilúvatar intervenes, granting the Dwarves independent being: "These things have now a life of their own and speak with their own voices" as "children of my adoption" alongside the Elves and Men, called here "children of my choice" (*Silm*, 43). An objection might be raised: there doesn't seem to be any real difference between Aulë's independent creation of the Dwarves and Melkor's solitary composition of musical themes at variance with Ilúvatar's propounded themes. Why is Melkor ultimately banished but Aulë not? The discrepancy is not resolved; the story of the creation of the Dwarves alludes effectively to the theme of the human tendency to idolize artistic creation; but it is also richly suggestive of the possibility for redemption of artistic creativity which (apart from in the "Ainulindalë") Tolkien seldom articulates. Dodds says,

> The story is not an explanation of the strange assumption in favour of making which is now so widespread, but it is an imaginative realization of the depth and power of the inclination toward making, even when it is recognized as a temptation.
>
> (Dodds, 183)

The Silmarillion, whose narrative fabric is overwhelmingly tragic, contains few hints of what we might call redemption or salvation.

Tolkien's poem "Mythopoeia" – first published in part in Humphrey Carpenter's *The Inklings*, but printed in full in the second edition of *Tree and Leaf* – summarizes these concerns. As a whole, the poem bears reading in the context of this discussion. The human heart is not "compound of lies," says Tolkien, and though now estranged from perfect intellectual communion with their creator, people are still capable of apprehending wisdom from its divine source ("the only Wise"). Of crucial importance is the prefatory statement that while it is permissible to worship neither the products of human artistic creativity nor the created world itself, "man, the sub-creator" preserves the remnants of his ruined lordship and expresses his divinely sanctioned dominion over the created order "by creative act." The roles of poet and mythmaker are thus granted extremely high status in Tolkien's world-view. The key lines, however, are as follows:

> Though all the crannies of the world we filled
> with Elves and goblins, though we dared to build
> gods and their houses out of dark and light,
> and sow the seed of dragons, 'twas our right
> (used or misused). The right has not decayed
> We make still by the law in which we're made.
>
> (*TL*, 98–99)

The "modes" of the Fall outlined in Tolkien's 1951 letter to Waldman are all operative here; the poem expresses some of the possibilities and dangers of human action expanded narratively in *The Silmarillion* and *The Lord of the Rings.* Though Man is described here as "changed," estranged from the Wise and disgraced, the rags of lost lordship are retained "by creative act." The word "dared" governs the lines describing the process of mythmaking, suggesting risks including the idolization of the created world itself ("not his to worship the great Artefact"), which is the particular temptation of the Elves. The temptations of political power to which Men are especially susceptible are hinted at in the references to "lordship" and "world-dominion," while the final line is a direct echo of the ideas expressed by Aulë to Ilúvatar after his creation of the Dwarves. All three modes of temptation include specific possibilities for Fall that are developed in various ways throughout Tolkien's literary corpus. The implications, though, for Tolkien's own art, are discussed in detail later.

The fact that Men emerge from the east of Middle-earth already fallen is central to the complex series of events tracing the implications of Melkor's cacophonous compositions in the "Ainulindalë": Melkor falls; he corrupts many of the Eldar, destroys the Two Trees, accelerates the moral corruption of Fëanor, and precipitates a series of cataclysms resulting in the Marring of Arda and the end of the First Age. Men are rewarded for their valor in the Elves' war against Morgoth: Ilúvatar gives them possession of Númenór, the westernmost island closest to Valinor. But during the Second Age, Sauron seduces these high, noble men to worship the darkness in temples of death. The flourishing of Númenórean culture culminates in the tyrannous reign of the proud king Tar-Celion – later renamed Ar-Pharazôn – who mounts a great armada, invading Tol Eressëa and landing by force on the shores of Valinor, breaking the Ban of the Valar whereby mortal Men are vouchsafed only glimpses of the Blessed Realm from afar but not permitted to set foot within it. His fleet is sunk and Númenór is engulfed by the sea; Aman is removed permanently from Arda, and the path to Valinor is forever hidden from Men.

This story, told in the "Akallabêth," the "Downfall of Númenor," is described by Tolkien in the 1951 letter as "the Second Fall of Man (or Man rehabilitated but still Mortal)," bringing the Second Age to a "catastrophic end." The Third Age of Middle-earth begins then as "a Twilight Age, a Medium Aevum," which, significantly, Tolkien describes as "the first of the broken and changed world; the last of the lingering dominion of visible, fully incarnate Elves, and the last also in which Evil assumes a single dominant incarnate shape" (*Letters*, 154). We should note here yet another connection between the world described in the fictional corpus and the real world: the implication of the statement that the Third Age is the *first* "Medium Aevum … of the broken and changed world" is that that world is our world, connected not only by isolated linguistic threads but as a matter of geographic fact. This may be set aside as merely another indication of Tolkien's genius in creating a sense of depth. But on a more profound level it is a *theological* fact, making a connection with both aesthetic and spiritual implications.

> The *Downfall* is partly the result of an inner weakness in Men – consequent, if you will, upon the first Fall (unrecorded in these tales), repented but not finally healed. Reward on earth is more dangerous for men than punishment! The Fall is achieved by the cunning of Sauron in exploiting this weakness. Its central theme is (inevitably, I think, in a story of Men) a Ban, or Prohibition.
>
> (*Letters*, 154)

But it also involves the simple desire for power, sway, dominion, and domination of others. The Second Age witnesses the rising of Sauron as a servant and vicarious manifestation of the spirit of Melkor himself; the forging of the One Ring – note, the work of a jewelsmith and, again, an act of artistic creation – occurs in this period, setting the stage for the history of the Third Age chronicled in *The Lord of the Rings*. In all epochs of the history of Middle-earth, Men are subject less to the allurements of artistry than they are to mere political power.

Fascinating though the details of Númenórean history may be as outworkings of original sin, they do not add materially to an understanding of the foundational components of the theology or anthropology of Arda already established here. What they do, though, is develop these essentially theological and anthropological concepts into a full narrative capable of expressing with great subtlety the nuances of what this might mean psychologically and emotionally in individual personal terms. As such, these narratives solicit and – if Tolkien's popularity is any measure – gain the deep sympathies of readers, real human beings in the real world whose personal moral crises can be projected onto the vivid tableaux presented in the fiction.

A particularly compelling instance of the outworking of this theme in the narrative *The Lord of the Rings* occurs about halfway through the journey of Frodo, Sam, and the others of their Company on their mission to destroy the One Ring in a crevice of Orodruin in Mordor. As a Man, Boromir is drawn with great subtlety as one of the truly three-dimensional characters in the book. Jane Chance has commented that, by contrast with the "acknowledgment of inner nobility gained by voluntary renunciation" on the part of the Dwarf Gimli,

> Such strength of character, such courtesy, is not witnessed in the man Boromir, who fails to control his own desire for the Precious – the Ring … . Boromir, the antitype of Gimli, deteriorates morally after the sojourn in Lórien. His mistake is to privilege his own need for the Ring, ostensibly to protect Minas Tirith from the Enemy but in reality to express his racial hostility toward Hobbits and his own sense of personal and national superiority.
>
> (Chance, *Mythology of Power*, 51–52)

As such, Boromir both represents himself as an individual Man enmeshed in the narrative fabric of the events surrounding him and epitomizes the particular temptations to which his race is subject. As Chance shows, Boromir is merely one in a long lineage of "capable but flawed ruler[s]" capitalized in his father Denethor – King of Minas Tirith – and evocative of a race of beings for which power, especially political power, provides overwhelmingly seductive temptation.

The event that precipitates Frodo and Sam's separation from the rest of the Company is Boromir's long conversation with Frodo concerning ownership of the One Ring and its potential power in the struggle of the Free Peoples of Middle-earth against the races under the sway of Sauron. As Frodo separates himself from the others to contemplate the next steps in his journey, he encounters Boromir, who has come quietly alongside him to help him reflect upon his dilemma. Boromir suggests Frodo should *not* go directly to Mordor but instead go with him to Minas Tirith; Frodo is reluctant. His heart warns him against delay, he says; further, it warns him, "well, if it must be said, against trust in the strength and truth of Men" (*FR*, 413). Boromir becomes angry and tries to snatch the Ring from Frodo, who then places it on his finger and by its power is rendered invisible. Boromir thrashes about recklessly looking for Frodo, then utters these words:

> "Curse you and all halflings to death and darkness." Then, catching his foot on a stone, he fell sprawling and lay upon his face. For a while he was as still as if his own curse had struck him down; then suddenly he wept.
>
> (*FR*, 414)

We may not be overreading this scene to lay rather heavy emphasis upon the symbolic significance of the choice of wording here: Boromir "fell," not only physically but also morally and spiritually in the quest for power and dominion – here, not only over Frodo himself, but also over many others through the Ring – the age-old temptation afflicting all of Boromir's race.

In the narrative continuation of these events at the beginning of *The Two Towers*, Boromir lies against a tree after defending the Hobbits from an Orc ambush. Speaking to Aragorn, who finds him dying, Boromir says: "Farewell, Aragorn! Go to Minas Tirith and save my people! I have failed." Aragorn's answer – "You have conquered. Few have gained such a victory. Be at peace" (16) – addresses the inner struggle in which, too late, Boromir overcomes his selfish desire for power justified by his political ambitions. Comforting though Aragorn's statement may be, it belies the gravity of the situation Boromir's treachery has created: many of the hazards faced subsequently by Merry and Pippin and by Frodo and Sam are the direct result of Boromir's fateful interview with Frodo at the top of Amon Hen. Treachery has bitter consequences for the traitor, but – sadly – often those around him suffer also in the wake of his treachery. Chance comments that Boromir's self-sacrifice is performed "to atone for his catastrophic moment of greed and desire," but in the end, "Boromir remains dead" (94–95).

In the example of Boromir, we see portrayed with psychological subtlety the moral temptations of a Man confronted with the desire to do good in the world but corrupted by the power he sees as necessary for doing it. It is only one of many such illustrations in *The Lord of the Rings*, and it reveals Tolkien as a writer skillfully able to evoke the psychological nuances of individuals playing their particular – often tragic – part in larger communal, social, cultural, and racial patterns in which they find themselves. In all Tolkien's works we see human beings and members of other races presented with opportunities for nobility, for heroic resistance against external forces of evil in which mustering the resolve to resist is as important as the success or failure of the outcome. And we see them presented with internal temptations to cowardice, pride, self-deception, and the tendency to regard others as somehow not quite human, not really men or women of infinite worth, but as objects – obstacles – or as tools for selfish personal achievement. The temptation is to regard ourselves, if not our culture or our race, as the only truly "human."

The focus of this essay is on Tolkien's Men, but by now the reader may be tempted to ask, What of the Hobbits? Are they fallen too? As suggested earlier, though the moral fallibility of Men is a touchstone for the deeper themes of the narratives set in Aman and Middle-earth, the peculiar susceptibilities of other races such as Elves and Dwarves contribute to a comprehension of Tolkien's anthropology in a wider sense. We have seen that Elves, Men, and Dwarves are fallen in particular ways; how are the Hobbits fallen? What are their special susceptibilities?

The first thing that must be said is that Hobbits may in fact be part of the race of Men. In his 1951 letter to Waldman, Tolkien said, "Their origin is unknown (even to themselves)," adding in a footnote "The Hobbits are … really meant to be a branch of the specifically *human* race." More ecologically minded, Hobbits live closer to nature and, "abnormally, for humans, [are] free from ambition or greed of wealth." They are small, says Tolkien, "partly to exhibit the pettiness of man, plain unimaginative parochial man" (*Letters*, 158). While Boromir's aspirations for political and military power are motivated in part by nationalism and, if not by outright xenophobia, at least by a settled conviction that Men are racially superior to Hobbits, Chance says, the Hobbits are shown to be limited in their anthropological perspective, too. Chance adds,

> The political problems in the Shire grow out of its deceptively "safe" isolation from the rest of Middle-earth. Its inhabitants distrust those who come from outside, who are different from them in ways they do not understand. A stranger … arouses mistrust, and the inhabitants band together.
>
> (Chance, *Mythology of Power*, 27–28)

Distinct from that of the Elves, Dwarves, and Men, the fallenness of the Hobbits is expressed in the bourgeois desire for comfort, safety, a preference for the familiar overriding even the necessity of sacrifice and hardship for the sake of noble achievement. In the Hobbits, Tolkien offers us an image of the domesticated side of the seemingly harmless devotion to self, clan, or race that is part of the universal human tendency toward the kind of ethnic self-aggrandizement with which this chapter begins.

So far, the focus of this chapter has been upon the anthropological dimension – enhanced by etymology – of Tolkien's invented world. The fall of Men in Tolkien's work is presented as a secondary fall, one event in a series of seductions, betrayals, and rebellions including not only Men but also Elves, Dwarves, and Valar, originating in the very creation of Arda. We said the fall of Melkor included an ambiguity: like Milton's Satan, Melkor is presented in some ways as already fallen – he is weak, certainly – before his fall. This artistic or narrative ambiguity reflects a problem that is a perennial intellectual puzzle at the heart of Christian doctrine. How can free but unfallen beings commit sin without the blame resting at least partly with the one who created them so? Artistically, as Christians, both Milton and Tolkien were in a difficult position: how can an author, an imperfect human being, explain the Fall of Man to readers – themselves also fallen – using a human language which is also imperfect due to the very Fall he is trying to explain?

In "The Marriage of Heaven and Hell," William Blake comments that Milton was "of the Devil's party without knowing it" (150), a view held generally by the Romantics including Shelley, Byron, and Hazlitt – all of whom in various ways regarded Satan as the real hero of *Paradise Lost.* Stanley Fish, however, in *Surprised by Sin: The Reader in Paradise Lost*, demonstrates convincingly that Milton was *not* unaware that he and his readers were implicated in the Fall his poem tries to explain: for Fish, "[T]he poem's center of reference is the reader who is also its subject." Milton's object is "to educate the reader to an awareness of his position and responsibilities as a fallen man," and his technique is "to re-create in the mind of the reader … the drama of the Fall, to make him fall again exactly as Adam did" (1). Fish suggests that the reader – and here, I would argue, Milton too – is "confronted with evidence of his corruption and becomes aware of his inability to respond adequately to spiritual conceptions, and … is asked to refine his perceptions so that his understanding will be once more proportionable to truth" (lxxi). Following this line of thinking, we can speculate further that Milton knew his attempt to "justify the ways of God to men" was doomed to fail because his perspective, like that of his readers, was already that of a fallen man. Over the course of twenty-six lines from the poem's beginning, Milton's choice of nouns moves from Man ("Of Man's First Disobedience") to men ("justify the ways of God to men"), suggesting that as a race "Man" is fallen, but the desire for redemption is a personal matter requiring instruction, acceptance, repentance, and devotion from individual people – "men." Milton intends his readers to be surprised to find their sympathies aligned with those of Adam and Eve in the psychological process of rational and rhetorical seduction, startled to find the figure of Satan so admirable. For Milton and his readers, these responses were calculable as effects of the Fall: we don't know ourselves as anything but already fallen.

As a matter of orthodox Catholic doctrine, Tolkien must have believed he, too, and all his readers were "of the Devil's party," and he illustrates this by casting his first Man, Eriol, into a mythic pattern as an already fallen human being and by bringing the Men of Hildorien into western Middle-earth already corrupted by Melkor's lies. What he suggests at the level of anthropological history operates also at the level of individual personality, and just as the fallenness of Men is offered as a "given" whose moment of origin is accessible to the memory of the race only through myth, so also is it unavailable for private inspection or rational explanation in the individual human person. In Milton's poem, Satan's attempts to shift the responsibility for his Fall onto his Maker are rebuked by Abdiel, who objects, "Shalt thou give law to God … who made / Thee what thou art?" (*Paradise Lost*, 5.822–24a). The problem for Satan, however, is that he cannot remember the moment of his own creation:

> Who saw
> When this creation was? remember'st thou
> Thy making, while the Maker gave thee being?
> We know no time when we were not as now;
> Know none before us, self-begot, self-rais'd.
> (*Paradise Lost*, 5.853, 855–60)

Satan's perspective is identical to that of Adam, says Fish:

> Recalling the moment not of his creation, but just after his creation, Adam reports "Myself I … perused … limb by limb" and found that I could speak and name, "But who I was, or where, or from what cause / Knew not."
> (Fish, *Surprised by Sin*, 8, 267, 270–71)
>
> Satan and Adam begin alike from a point of ignorance – they know nothing prior to (the precise word is "before") the perspective they currently occupy; and the direction each then takes from this acknowledged limitation follows with equal logic or illogic … . In neither case does the conclusion follow necessarily from the observed fact of imperfect knowledge. In both cases something is missing, a first premise, and in both cases reasoning can't get started until a first premise is put in place.
> (Fish, "Why We Can't All Just Get Along," 20)

Fish goes on to say, "The habit of identifying the limits of reality with the limits of his own horizons defines Satan" (22). In the Christian myth, it also defines Adam after the Fall and, as a result, all his race. It defines Tolkien and all his readers, and in order to be believable as myth, Tolkien's *legendarium* had to be true to this doctrine. Satan has a point: it also seems to be true *before* the Fall, and if Milton fails to provide a believable literary account of humankind's Fall, it is because his literary art is also tainted with its effects. For postlapsarian men, to *be* is to be *fallen*, to be conscious is to be conscious of ourselves as already corrupt, and to write – to compose poetry or mythology in which, as it must be, the Fall is a central theme – is to do so with tools of craftsmanship already tainted by it.

Thus, one of the foundational concepts in Tolkien's myth is the twofold implication of the fallenness of Men and the limitations upon artistic creation as a satisfactory fulfillment of deepest desire – in our world or in Arda. In Tolkien's view, the impulse toward artistic creativity and the motives for the Fall are inextricably wedded. Debbie Sly has said,

> When Tolkien declares that there "cannot be any 'story' without a fall" (*Letters,* 147), he means, of course, that all stories must reflect what for him is the essential truth about humanity: it is fallen. However … the statement has another, very simple meaning: without the Fall, there could be no stories, no art of any kind. Indeed, not only may evil be a prerequisite for aesthetic experience and its production through art, but the origins of evil … may be linked to the sub-creative impulse itself. Melkor's first sin is to insert his own discordant theme into the music of Ilúvatar. Tolkien, too, … introduces a "discordant" theme, but one … that adds considerably to the affective power of his work, just as the "discordant" attraction of Milton's Satan has, for so many readers, enriched *Paradise Lost.*
>
> (Sly, 118)

We return now to Eriol, the human character who played a key role in the early development of the anthropology of Tolkien's invented world. Eriol, we recall, appears as a mariner from England who hears the stories in Tol Eressëa first represented in *The Book of Lost Tales*. Verlyn Flieger has indicated Eriol's role is twofold: first, he serves as a crucial device linking the narrative with the reader:

> Why not just tell the story and allow it to stand on its own? First, because to Tolkien the value of a story is in its transmission as well as in its existence. Indeed, its transmission *is* its existence … . Tolkien was too knowledgeable a storyteller not to recognize and affirm the importance of the Teller to the Tale.
>
> (Flieger, "The Footsteps of Ælfwine," 185)

Additionally, though, while "by definition an editor or scholar can be in only one [world]," an outsider whose presentation of textual material results in "not stories but data," a linking character like Eriol "can participate in both worlds … neither wholly outside nor completely inside but in between." Eriol is a "true mediator," says Flieger, acting as "a semitransparent mask for the real Elf-friend, who is actually Tolkien himself" ("The Footsteps of Ælfwine," 185). This figure appears in a number of forms under different names throughout the texts of the developing *legendarium* of Arda and related stories in *The Notion Club Papers* and *The Lost Road.* Insightfully discussed by Flieger, these names include "Angol," "Wæfre," "Elendil," "Alboin Errol," "Alwin Lowdham," and "Ælfwine the Mariner." Though over time his role diminished, throughout the composition and revision of his work, Eriol remained for Tolkien "an essential part of the plan":

> In whatever tale he appeared … and whatever his particular character in the story, the Elf-friend figure provided a fictive persona through whose agency the author Tolkien could convey the stories to the reader and at the

> same time gratify some of his most deeply held desires – to participate in myth firsthand, to converse with other kinds of beings, to visit other dimensions of time and space, to experience, in human form and in human terms, something of the believer's sense of awe and wonder at the supernatural. Ælfwine provided Tolkien a way to participate in his own mythology.
>
> (Flieger, "The Footsteps of Ælfwine," 190)

Ultimately, the Eriol–Ælfwine character disappeared from the narrative texts, being reduced only to a faint echo in *The Lord of the Rings* when, on the outskirts of the Shire, the Elf Gildor addresses Frodo as "Elf-friend." Beyond his function as "witness" to the mythic events and as author of texts fictively "translated" by Tolkien, in terms of the anthropology and theology of Arda this figure contributes a meaning compounded of the themes expressed in the mythology and Tolkien's deeply held beliefs about human beings and their creative works.

How much good can creative works of fallen men hope to achieve in a fallen world? We have already noted the fact that themes of salvation or redemption – while present – are seldom expressed in Tolkien's work. For evidence of what Tolkien might have hoped to accomplish in his creative work, we may turn to his remarks about another writer whose creative efforts suggest similar preoccupations. In speaking about *Beowulf* in his 1936 lecture, "*Beowulf*: The Monsters and the Critics," Tolkien drew near to his conclusion by saying, "Beowulf is not … the hero of an heroic lay, precisely. He has no enmeshed loyalties, nor hapless love. *He is a man, and that for him and many is sufficient tragedy*" (18). He goes on to say concerning the *Beowulf* poet, "Its author is still concerned primarily with *man on earth*, rehandling in a new perspective an ancient theme: that man, each man and all men, and all their works shall die" (23). The emphatic italics in both statements are Tolkien's; they suggest something of the depth of Tolkien's convictions concerning fallen humanity and the sub-creative works of human authors.

> When new, *Beowulf* was already antiquarian, in a good sense, and it now produces a singular effect. For it is now to us itself ancient; and yet its maker was telling of things already old and weighted with regret, and he expended his art in making keen that touch upon the heart which sorrows have that are both poignant and remote. If the funeral of Beowulf moved once like the echo or an ancient dirge, far-off and hopeless, it is to us a memory brought over the hills, an echo of an echo … . It would still have power had it been written in some time or place unknown and without posterity, if it contained no name that could now be recognized or identified by research.
>
> ("*Beowulf*," 33)

Clearly Tolkien strove to create these same effects in his works and felt a kinship with the *Beowulf* poet; *mutatis mutandis*, in *The Lord of the Rings* and *The Silmarillion* as well may be heard the "echo of an echo" possessing the same "intense emotion of regret" he finds in *Beowulf*. If any single mood may be said to pervade all of Tolkien's fictions, it is, like *Beowulf*, that of the elegiac. In "Mythopoeia," which earlier we said expressed some of his key ideas on sub-creation, a similar attitude of regret dominates; yet the poem also raises a cautious note of hope. Humphrey Carpenter has established the context out of which the poem grew – a conversation on the subject of myth among Tolkien, Hugo Dyson, and an as yet unconverted C. S. Lewis in 1928 (*Inklings*, 43–45). Tolkien argued (against Lewis) that myths of human making could express eternal truths. "[P]agan myths were, in fact, God expressing himself through the minds of poets," says Carpenter, summarizing Tolkien's claim (*Inklings*, 43–45).

"Mythopoeia" betrays its origins in this conversation: it begins in the second-person voice addressing (presumably) Lewis himself and moves into a more distant, philosophical, third-person mode surveying, first, the creation of the world – "petreous rocks … arboreal trees, / tellurian earth … stellar stars" – including "homuncular men, who walk upon the ground." This rather base view of human beings is improved as the poem goes on to describe the ameliorating influence of speech, including simply the naming of things but also, more deeply, the composition of poetry and the creation of mythology, in "digging the fore-known from experience / and panning the vein of spirit out of sense" in order to "cheat / our timid hearts and ugly Fact defeat" (lines 19–21, 31, 39–40, 71–72). The artistic use of language is not vain nor idle, Tolkien says, and then he blesses "timid hearts" that quail in the shadow of evil "and yet shut the gate," implying that art can with some success hope to raise effective resistance. When he then blesses "men of Noah's race" in whose "little arks" they "steer through winds contrary towards a wraith, / a rumour of a harbour guessed by faith" (87–90), we may read not only an allusion to the medieval exegetical interpretation of the ark as a prefigurement of salvation but also a veiled reference to Eriol, a figure with whom Tolkien closely identified. The likelihood of this connection is further demonstrated in the next passage, where he blesses a third group, "legend-makers with their rhyme / of things not found within recorded time," which must include Tolkien himself. In lines 90–95 of the poem, Tolkien envisions poets and creators of myth "turn[ing] the lyre" and "kindl[ing] hearts" as bulwarks against retreat, despair, and ultimate defeat. At this point, the poem moves into the first-person singular mode of address, and while the persona of the poem steps forward to be revealed unmistakably as Tolkien himself, a line separating him from the figure of Eriol the mariner who arrived in Tol Eressëa in 1915 is impossible to draw:

> I would be with the mariners of the deep
> that cut their slender planks on mountains steep
> and voyage upon a vague and wandering quest,
> for some have passed beyond the fabled West.
>
> ("Mythopoeia," lines 98–101)

Admitting that such a choice entails the risk that the writer might be regarded as one of the "beleaguered fools," he nonetheless offers to take his place among those who, by virtue of their poetic art, weave the "fantastic banners" and emblems of a "distant king" and a "lord unseen."

We see Tolkien here, like his character Eriol – earlier the "wandering" Ottor Wæfre – whose journey by sea to the Lonely Isle and down "devious routes" from the homes of Men to the "Path of Dreams" acquaints him with tales now echoed only in "misty aftermemories" in poems such as *Beowulf*, the "Lay of Leithien," and the "Geste of Beren," and stories such as "Akallabêth" and *The Lord of the Rings*. Mythmaking of the kind represented in these works concerns treacherous and faint-hearted Men – Men of the fall whose external and internal struggles are not guaranteed victory – but it also concerns those who, in spite of all the woe that so easily besets them, refuse to surrender to despair and dare to assert creative power in the face of evil and death. In a final passage marked by an unmistakably bitter cynicism, Tolkien further refuses to walk "erect and sapient" with the "progressive apes" of the modern age, seeing only "the dark abyss to which their progress tends"; in an allusion to the satanic figure of Morgoth in the products of his own mythopoesis, he signals his final refusal thus: "I bow not yet before the Iron Crown / nor cast my own small golden sceptre down" (118–19). In these lines Tolkien fully casts himself as a character – another Eriol? – within his own mythology.

"*He is a man, and that for him and many is sufficient tragedy*," Tolkien said ("*Beowulf*," 18), speaking of the hero of a poem whose author struggles to present the highest achievement of the prehistoric heroic society in a reconstructed vision of the ancient Germanic world from the perspective of late Anglo-Saxon Catholic Christianity. A compendium of many of the dominant modes of Old English poetic tradition, *Beowulf* is often described in literary terms as something of a generic omnibus, a heroic-elegiac epic leavened with numerous expressions of gnomic or proverbial wisdom.

Tolkien's prose and poetic compositions may be regarded as a similar expression of the struggle to reconcile Christian hope with the fact that the highest achievements of human effort are often tragically undermined by the flaws of human character accounted for in Christian terms by the Fall. For some, *Beowulf* is about the hollow success of a hero committed to the defective heroic virtues of tribal Germanic society. Similarly, too, both the *Beowulf* poet and J. R. R. Tolkien – along with Milton – struggle to express the possibilities for art to overcome the flaws of human character and, in the transmission or the making of myths, to provide a salvific or at least salutary vision.

Though the 1915 poem "Kortirion among the Trees," in which the *legendarium* began to unfold, takes the fallen condition of Man as an essential given, with cautious optimism it expresses an idea that may be taken as an early programmatic formulation of the mythopoeic theory that seems to have guided Tolkien throughout his life.

> And it seems to the fairies and it seems to me who know that town and have often trodden its disfigured ways that autumn and the falling of the leaf is the season of the year when maybe here or there a heart among Men may be open, and an eye perceive how is the world's estate fallen from the

> laughter and the loveliness of old. Think on Kortirion and be sad – yet is there not hope?
>
> (*BLT* 1, 26)

The assertion is couched in the interrogative, and in the light of retrospection upon all his published work, we may still ask Tolkien's question along with him. What do *The Hobbit*, *The Lord of the Rings*, *The Silmarillion*, and the poems and stories published by the "Author of the Century" suggest concerning the capacity for literature – and, by extension, all artistic work and indeed all the works of effort – to circumvent tragedy? Put in another way, we may ask, *did Tolkien succeed?*

Shippey's recent interpretive discussion of "Leaf by Niggle" and "Smith of Wootton Major," two late stories, suggests that in his own terms Tolkien himself wasn't so sure. Shippey says that while "Leaf by Niggle" – something of an autobiographical allegory – "ends as a comedy," it nonetheless "springs from a sense of earthly tragedy: failure, anxiety, and frustration" (*Author of the Century*, 277). In "Smith of Wootton Major," which Shippey calls "another 'Valedictory Address,' or 'Farewell to Arms,'" Tolkien – like Smith – "lays aside his star," a symbol within the story acting as a "passport into Faery" and in the story of Tolkien's life his own "impulse towards fantasy," described elsewhere as his literary vision, his mythopoeic consciousness and aesthetic. In "Wootton Major," says Shippey, Tolkien

> defends the real-world utility of fantasy; insists that fantasy and faith are in harmony as visions of a higher world; hopes for a revival of both in a future in which the Nokeses of the world (the materialists and misologists) will have less power … .
>
> (Shippey, *Author of the Century*, 303)

Shippey says though Smith "lives a good life," it "ends in multiple disappointment – he can never return to Faery; the star is passed on; he cannot give it to Ned," and though the story concludes with a satisfying coda, "even then Nokes has the last word." The story represents a "mixture of success and failure, happiness and bereavement" (301). In "The Sea-Bell" or "Frodo's Dreme," the speaker follows a vision of immortality, but – "as a punishment for hubris," Shippey says – in an experience of disenchantment "the speaker realizes he is old."

> Not only is the speaker exiled; his vision has gone too. In "The Sea-Bell" one may see Tolkien turning his back on the very notion of the Great Escape, and on images which had been with him for close on fifty years.
>
> (Shippey, *Author of the Century*, 283)

In "Bilbo's Last Song," however, published posthumously, Bilbo says "'farewell' to his friends and to Middle-earth," says Shippey, "to take the Lost Road, to make the Great Escape," in the words of a man dying "contented with his life and what he had achieved, and confident of the existence of a world and a fate beyond Middle-earth" (304). Among all the races J. R. R. Tolkien created, the one that stands out as fundamental to his art was the one he was not free to invent, for Men already existed. Each one of his invented races – Hobbits, Wizards, Dwarves, Orcs, Elves, and Ents – illustrates in its own way the high stakes of *being* in a fallen world. But with fallible Men in particular lay Tolkien's deepest sympathies; as a writer among them, Tolkien gives his readers a glimpse of creative power transcending the narrow perspective of the merely human.

Notes

This essay is an expanded version of a lecture delivered in Middlebury, Vermont, on 24 April 1997. I extend grateful thanks to Professor Matthew Dickerson and to the Middlebury College Department of English, whose invitation and generous hospitality facilitated that event.

1 Tolkien always capitalizes the term when employing the word for "the human race," a usage well established in history and questioned only recently. It should not need to be said that from the earliest reconstructable period of Germanic usage, semantically, terms generated from underlying **man-* have been used both in the narrower sense to refer to human beings of male gender and, more broadly, collectively to human beings as a whole. An exception worth noting, however, is the Low German *minsk*, appearing in Modern English "minx," referring to a decidedly female "hussy" (Benveniste, *Indo-European*, 299).

2 This has penetrated popular consciousness. My colleague Carl Rapp reminded me that in the 1970 Twentieth-Century Fox movie *Little Big Man*, the Cheyenne Indians, whose language is a member of the Algonquian family, are shown describing themselves as "the human beings," as contrasted with surrounding Native American tribes and the whites. In the Thomas Berger novel upon which it is based, narrator Jack Crabbe says, "[I]n their spoken language Cheyenne don't ever call themselves 'Cheyenne' but rather, *Tsistsistas*, which means 'the People,' or 'the Human Beings.' What anybody else is doesn't concern them" (40). *Tsistsistas*, from *Tsétsêhestase*, the term by which the Cheyenne name themselves, means something approaching "those who are thusly from there," "those who are of that group," or more simply, "the people." *Cheyenne*, however, derives from a Dakota term through Canadian French, *sahíyena* (*sahíyela*), meaning "the little Cree," though folk etymologies suggest other meanings including "those who speak an alien tongue" and Fr. *chien*, "dog" (Riggs, *A Dakota–English Dictionary*; Glenmore and Leman, 201–2).

Similarly, in Comanche – an Uto-Aztecan language – the name by which the tribe is known to the whites means "those-who-are-always-against"; the word they apply to themselves is *Nmn*, a plural form of *nm*, "our," related to *nmi*, "us, people" (Robinson and Armagost, 29, 67–68).

3 In *Der Fremding im Rgveda*, Thieme translates *arí* as "stranger," suggesting it contains the dual meanings of "friend" and "enemy," much as the Proto-Indo-European root word **ghosti* contains the sense of both "guest" and "host." Benveniste summarizes,

> Based on *arí*, the derivative *arya* would signify "he who has a connexion with a stranger," hence "protector of the stranger," German *gastlich* "hospitable," and also "master of the household." Finally, from *arya-* the secondary derivative *rya* would literally mean "belonging to the guests"; hence hospitable.
>
> (Benveniste, *Indo-European Language and Society*, 301)

4 The etymology of this term has been hotly debated. Benveniste rejects Thieme's reconstruction of the associations of *arí* with "the stranger," preferring instead an association with Gk. άρι-, "excellent, supreme." See pp. 299–301 of *Indo-European Language and Society* for a summary of the controversy. Bader, whose 1994 essay on the subject is discussed below, accepts "stranger" for *arí*: "The name *rya-*, which, during the period of their community, designated the Indo-Iranians, is present in Sanskrit, on the one hand, in appellatives which are in the same formal relationship as, e.g., Latin *ali-* and *ali-o-*; on the other hand, *ari* was applied to all kinds of relations of alterity, good or bad: "friend" and "enemy," "host" and "rival" (73).

5 *Oxford English Dictionary*, 2nd edn., s.v. "barbarian."

6 The asterisk indicates a nonattested form reconstructed according to principles of comparative/historical linguistics. For an insightful discussion of the origins and development of these principles, see Shippey, *Road*.

7 Bader cites anthroponyms such as "Achilles," "Nestor," and "Herakles," and toponyms including "Delphos," "Pythia," "Pelasgus," "Veneti," "Teutones," "Alemanni," and "Arya" as evidence of the fact that

> [t]he Indo-European speakers gave themselves names which comprise a structural *ensemble* which has been fragmented by a process to which their naming system gives a great deal of other evidence … . The very existence of this structure poses an insoluble problem at the present time: in order for these people to have given themselves one of these names, they must necessarily have known of the existence of the others … . For none of these names receives its true semantic value except from the *ensemble* of which it forms a part. Indeed, it is this *ensemble*, as opposed to the appellative term that forms the basis of each of these names, which furnishes the semantic value to each one of them.
>
> (Bader, 65–66)

I thank Professor Jared Klein of the University of Georgia Classics Department for pointing me to this source.

8 The word may be a hybrid formed on Gothic *haiþi* with the Greek suffix -ινος; however, its origin may be older – Proto-Germanic **haiþanaz*, "living on the heath, wild," only later influenced by Latin *pāgānus*, a word which is not attested until the second half of the fourth century and thus could not be "the model on which the Gmc form was created" (Lehman, *Gothic Etymological Dictionary*, 172–73).

9 The Soviet linguist Nikolai Iakovlevich Marr, who is satirized in Aleksandr I. Solzhenitsyn's novel *The First Circle*, attempted to derive the *man* from the word for "hand" (Latin *mānus*) (Solzhenitsyn, 31). Tolkien himself commented on the etymology in a letter to Robert Murray, S.J., in May 1958, illustrating the problem of homologous roots with Proto-Indo-European **men* designating the concepts of both "stick out" and "think" (*Letters*, 269).

10 Properly speaking, the Eldar include the Vanyar, Noldor, and Teleri, who heard the summons of the Valar to the Blessed Realm of Aman. The Avari, or "Unwilling," are of the same created order but did not heed the call, remaining in the extreme eastern portion of Middle-earth. Among the three kindreds of the Elves, the Teleri – who delay the migration to Valinor – name themselves *Eglath*, "the Forsaken" (*Silm*, 58).

11 Shippey discusses Tolkien's drawing of secondary linguistic correspondences analogous to those of the primary world in *Road*, 105–6.

12 The appendix of "Elements in Quenya and Sindarin Names" in *The Silmarillion* provides several examples, and the index of names expands this. Also, Hyde's dissertation, "Linguistic Techniques", contains a useful list of morphemes in Quenya and Sindarin which was at the time of its publication complete for *Lord of the Rings* and *Silmarillion*. For *atar*, Hyde lists the following words, most of them onomastic: *alatar*,

alatariel, atar, atar aranya, atarinya, iluvatar, aratar, atanatar, atanatari, envinyatar, hini iluvataro, iluvataro, and *annatar* (2:577–78).

13 Shippey, *Road,* 16. Also, when they first encounter the Eldar in their westward wanderings, Bëor and his men call Finrod Felagund *Nóm* and the Elves as a whole *Nómin*, words evocative of both Greek γνόμέ, and NLat. *gnomus*, appearing as Mod. Eng. *gnome,* a word meaning both "wise saying," "proverb," and "a small dwarflike creature." In earlier versions of the stories in the *Book of Lost Tales*, the Elves were named "Gnomes"; the etymology of the name the Atani first give to the Elves thus provides another connection with the real world.

14 "[H]e [Fëanor] echoed the lies of Melkor, that the Valar had cozened them and would hold them captive so that Men might rule in Middle-earth. Many of the Eldar heard then for the first time of the Aftercomers" (*Silm*, 83).

15 Shippey, *Road*, 93, 268–69, 271, 286; Flieger, "Footsteps of Ælfwine," 183–98.

16 In the earliest versions, Tol Eressëa represents England – in the later history of what we could call the "real" world, a realm dominated by Men, from which Elves have departed *eastward* into what is now called Europe. As with many details, a version of this motif does survive into the later narratives, but in radically altered form. In *The Silmarillion*, Ulmo uproots the island of Tol Eressëa from the middle of the sea and moves it "as it were a mighty ship" east to Middle-earth, then west to Aman, transporting many of the Teleri to the shores of Valinor. Later he moves it east again, gathers the remnant Teleri, and transports them westward again, rooting the island permanently near the Blessed Realm (57–59). Ultimately, as narrated in "Akallabêth," it is removed forever from the confines of Arda.

14 "A land without stain"

Medieval images of Mary and their use in the characterization of Galadriel

Michael W. Maher, S.J.

In his introduction to *The Lord of the Rings*, J. R. R. Tolkien requests his readers not to consider his story analogous to events, past or present.[1] Therefore, to look at any character in the author's work as a representation of a real person is hazardous at best. Although Tolkien warns against the reading of his work as a direct analogy, he does not preclude the possibility that certain persons and stories from the great wealth of the medieval and classical literary tradition provided guides for the development of his characters and plot. In particular, the elements from the Christian tradition of salvation history frequently tempt readers into believing the work is a retelling of that history. When reading the trilogy, who could not think of Gandalf's descent into the pits of Moria and his return clothed in white as a death-resurrection motif? The Hobbits, particularly Sam and Frodo, representing the "little people," the smallest of all the sapient creatures of Middle-earth, are the instrumental cause of saving Middle-earth – recalling a central theme of the Christian Scriptures that the smallest and the least, the stone that was rejected, became the vehicle for salvation (Luke 20:17). Although Tolkien did not consider his story allegorical, he was not averse to using material from other sources to help the tales that earned him the title "the author of the century." In any discussion of analogy and the possible literary sources on which an analogy would be based, Tolkien's description of the character of Galadriel is worth repeating:

> I think it is true that I owe much of this character to Christian and Catholic teaching and imagination about Mary, but actually Galadriel was a penitent: in her youth a leader in the rebellion against the Valar (the angelic guardians). At the end of the first age she proudly refused forgiveness or permission to return. She was pardoned because of her resistance to the final and overwhelming temptation to take the Ring for herself.
>
> (Duriez, *The Tolkien and Middle Earth Handbook*, 100)[2]

Pride has never been a characteristic of the Virgin Mary. Commentators such as Bernard of Clairvaux and Thomas Aquinas have cited Mary's humility before the Divine Will as her paramount virtue. Artists who portrayed the Annunciation have employed a standard iconographic pose of a demure young woman with head bowed and hands folded.[3] In contrast to this passive attitude, Galadriel, this warrior-woman rebelling against the Valar, bears greater resemblance to Lucifer, the angel of light who chose to rule in hell rather than to serve in heaven. Also, Galadriel has borne children, Celebrían and Arwen Evenstar, without miraculous intervention; hence, there is no parallel with Mary's virginity. Considering these facts, a simple analogy between Galadriel and the Virgin Mary is impossible for two important reasons. First, Tolkien rejected any direct analogy; and second, the difference between Galadriel's story and Mary's renders such an analogy impossible.

What text or image was Tolkien possibly referring to when he identified "Catholic imagination" as crucial in the development of the character of Galadriel? Today the "Catholic imagination" of Tolkien's time is not very accessible to many, even to many Catholics. It is the purpose, therefore, of this chapter to examine a text that Tolkien may have had in mind when he stated that he owed "much of this character to Christian and Catholic imagination about Mary." In substantiating some relationship between a specific text used by Tolkien, we may come to a better understanding of Galadriel and her relation to the total narrative.

There is a vast body of medieval texts dealing with Mary, who, in many respects, is the central figure of the Middle Ages. Given the breadth of Tolkien's scholarship and his devout Catholic faith, one could suppose his familiarity with the major sources of medieval Marian piety, such as Bernard of Clairvaux's (d. 1153) great work *Homiliae in laudibus Virginis Matris*. For the purpose of this chapter I would like to examine the most common images of Mary and ones certainly known to Tolkien, the images of Mary found in the Loreto Litany.[4] A litany is a prayer in which a leader, not necessarily a priest, invokes a set of short petitions to which the congregation responds after each supplication with a specific response such as "Lord, have mercy" or "Ora /orate pro nobis." There is a long tradition in the church of the recitation of litanies, a practice that became codified during the pontificate of Gregory the Great (590–604) (Jungmann, 336–37). During the sixteenth century one litany in particular became very popular, the litany of Loreto. Loreto, Italy, holds the honor of having the original house of Mary first located in Nazareth, the very home where she received the Annunciation of the angel Gabriel. Not properly venerated at its original location, the house was allegedly moved by angels four times before arriving at its current location.[5] Although some modern Christians may question the veracity of the angelic transport, such doubts were not raised by thousands of faithful who flocked to the holy house. Prayers offered to the Virgin at the Holy House at Loreto took on many liturgical forms, one of which was a litany. The litany of Loreto originally included over forty titles given to Mary drawn from the Jewish and Christian scriptures as well as from popular devotions and medieval commentaries on her life.[6] This devotion to the Virgin gained further acclaim when it was set to print by the Jesuit Peter Canisius in 1558. The printed version of the litany was spread by pilgrims who carried the prayer back with them to their native towns all across Europe. Faithful Catholics have recited this litany ever since, and doubtless Tolkien himself would have been familiar with the litany since the usual rubric of saying the communal rosary included the Loreto Litany. In the pre-Vatican II church, the recitation of the litany was one of the most common devotions practiced by the laity. It presented the devout petitioner with many images of Mary and, as the following citations demonstrate, are similar to the images used by Tolkien in his description of Galadriel and the land she ruled, Lórien.

When the Fellowship of the Ring arrived at Lórien, their sadness at losing their comrade Gandalf was temporarily lifted by the murmuring waters and the "hint of fallow gold" which greeted them on their arrival (*FR*, 438). Lórien was the land of gold, the full brilliance of which was first described through the eyes of Frodo when he saw for the first time the splendid golden leaves of the mallorn trees. Even those who feared Galadriel referred to her as the "the Mistress of Magic, who dwells in the Golden Wood" (*TT*, 348), thus confirming the connection between gold and Lórien. This attribute of a golden home is found in the Loreto Litany, where Mary is spoken of as the *Domus Aurea*, the "House of Gold." The designation, however, is not directly given to Galadriel but to the land in which she dwells. Another attribute of the land of Lórien given to Mary is *Immaculata*, "without stain." Tolkien describes it as follows: "No blemish or sickness could be seen in anything that grew upon the earth. On the land of Lórien there was no stain" (*FR*, 455). This attribution of "without stain" comes from the Canticle of Canticles: "Tota pulchra es, Amica mea, et macula non est in te" (Song of Songs 4:7). Poetically translated it reads: "Thou art all fair, O my love, and there is not a stain on thee." Such an attribute could not be given to Galadriel, since her revolt, not mentioned in the text, renders her ineligible for this title. The land, however, received the title as unspotted, a designation given to Mary in the Loreto Litany as *Mater Inviolata*, "Mother undefiled."

Not all the designations given to Mary in the Loreto Litany are characteristic of the land of Lórien. Most attributes are bestowed only upon Galadriel herself rather than upon the land of Lórien. Although Galadriel may not be considered immaculate, Tolkien does identify her as not having any external *maculae*. Before any conversation between the travelers and Galadriel occurs, Tolkien provides a brief description of the Lady of Lórien as tall and clad in white (*FR*, 459). This echoes the attribution given to Mary in the Litany, *Turris Eburnea*, "Tower of Ivory." The name "Galadriel" itself comes from the combination of the two Hebrew words "gld" and "r'al," which when combined mean "smooth or polished skin."

One of the designations given to Mary in the Loreto Litany is *Stella Matutina*, "Morning Star." Mary is called "Morning Star" because of her arrival in the story of salvation history, like the morning star, the herald of the coming of the sun, which in Christian symbolism is the person of Jesus.[7] Linking Galadriel with the morning star raises some difficulties. Tolkien's geography has moral boundaries as well as natural ones. The "west" is designated as the land of goodness, while Mordor, with all its evil machinations, lies to the east. The morning star shines in the east and thus places itself geographically, according to Tolkien's world, in an evil place. If we disregard the adjective "morning" and remain only with the noun "star," then several texts point to a connection between Mary as "star" as found in the Loreto Litany and the association of a star with the character of Galadriel. In the litany Mary is the morning star, and in Tolkien's work Galadriel is the giver of a star – the star glass given to Frodo that shines with the bright light of Lórien in the darkest holds of Shelob's lair. The morning star and the star phial – both of them – give light at a time of darkness. The star phial serves as a guide for Sam just as another image of Mary does for seafarers, *Stella Maris*, "Star of the Sea." Although this image of *Stella Maris* is not in the Litany of Loreto, it was an important image of Mary, especially among sailors.

Even though the image *Stella Maris* is not in the litany, there is a reference to boats both in the Land of Lórien and the Loreto Litany. As the Fellowship are being brought to the Lord and Lady of Lórien, Tolkien describes their hall as similar to "the deck of a great ship." Ships are important for the Elves, for they are the means by which they will return to their home beyond the sea. This connection of a ship-like hall with the presence of Galadriel recalls one of the titles given to Mary in the Loreto Litany: *Foederis Arca*, "Ark of the Covenant." Among the ancient Hebrews and among modern Jews, the Ark of the Covenant was and is a chest holding the tablets of the Law, the presence of God among his chosen people. Mary, according to Christian symbolism, is the Ark because she held the presence of God in the person of Christ in her womb. In the Vulgate translation of the Bible, the word *arca* is used both for the Ark of the Covenant and for the Ark of Noah.[8] The association of Mary with the idea of "boat" would have been very obvious in the Middle Ages. The central part of the church is called a nave, from the Latin *navis*, or boat. The great "boats" of the high Middle Ages, the great cathedrals particularly in France but also England, were dedicated to Mary.

Some of the titles given to Mary in the Loreto Litany provided an eighteenth-century spiritual writer, Alphonsus Liguori (1696–1787), a framework for speaking about her qualities. Whereas the text of the litany provides only short phrases, Liguori's work, entitled *The Glories of Mary*, provides the reader with further elaboration of Mary's titles found in the Loreto Litany by using Scripture, patristic writings, and other devotions.[9] We may use Liguori's text as a commentary on the litany with confidence since it was a very popular devotional text, certainly known to Tolkien. In it Liguori provides the following gloss on the designation *Mater Inviolata*: "Hence she [Mary] was made the sinner's peace-maker, as she is called by St. Ephrem, 'Hail, peacemaker of the whole world'" (622). Galadriel, like Mary, became known as a peacemaker.

When Gimli and Legolas were about to enter Lórien, a torrent of accusations occurred between the two concerning the past. At their departure, they share a single boat since "they had now become fast friends" (*FR*, 481). The reconciliation and subsequent peace between Dwarf and Elf has occurred because they both love Galadriel. Galadriel is referred to as "Queen" (*TT*, 194) and Mary, in the litany, is called upon as *Regina Pacis*, "Queen of Peace." This designation of Galadriel as source or cause of peace is confirmed by her command to the travelers at the end of their first meeting with her: "Do not let your hearts be troubled … . Tonight you shall sleep in peace" (*FR*, 462).

Another important incident of peacemaking occurs when the conversation begins among the Company, Celeborn, and Galadriel. Celeborn berates Gimli – as the representative of the Dwarves – for stirring up the Balrog, Durin's Bane: "But had I known that the Dwarves had stirred up this evil in Moria again, I would have forbidden you to pass the northern borders, you and all that went with you" (*FR*, 461). Even Legolas, before their arrival at the fleet of Galadriel and Celeborn, recalls how the Dwarves "awakened the evil in the mountains" (442). Although the word "sin" is not used in the text, Celeborn blames Gimli for a deed done by his people that caused tremendous evil and hardship, an accusation Legolas likewise levels against the Dwarf. In response to the judgment of Celeborn, Galadriel recalls, in the Dwarf's native tongue, the beauties of the stony kingdom. Although the mention of these places stirs his heart, it is the glance of Galadriel that transforms the Dwarf:

> She looked at Gimli, who hearing the names given in his own ancient tongue, looked up and met her eyes; and it seemed to him that he looked suddenly into the heart of an enemy and saw there love and understanding.
>
> (*FR*, 461)

This was a transformative moment for Gimli. From this point onward any mention of the lady would be followed by rapture, and any discredit to her name was quickly followed by a glint of steel. Here Galadriel assumes not only the role of "Queen of Peace" but also another role attributed to Mary in the litany, *Refugium Peccatorum*, "Refuge of Sinners." In his commentary on this title from the Loreto Litany, Liguori cites Saint Bonaventure, the great medieval Marian theologian: "You embrace with maternal affection a sinner who is even despised by the whole world, nor do you cease your embrace until you have reconciled him with his judge" (622). At the end of Galadriel's discourse, Celeborn asks Gimli "to forget his harsh words" (*FR*, 462). Galadriel had been Gimli's refuge and the cause of his reconciliation before the judgment of the lord of Lórien.

Immediately following this reconciliation, Galadriel speaks to the Ring-bearer, stating that she and Celeborn know the purpose of the quest and that "not in vain will it prove, maybe, that you came to this Land seeking aid" (*FR*, 468). In the Loreto Litany, Mary is referred to as the *Auxilium Christianorum*, "Help of Christians." She is also called in the litany the *Mater Divinae Gratiae*, "Mother of Divine Grace." Liguori provides the following gloss for this title:

> Hence Saint Bernardine of Siena writes, that "all gifts and graces that we receive from God are dispensed by the hands of Mary, to whom, when, and as she pleases." This she herself says: "With me are riches … that I may enrich them that love me."
>
> (Liguori, 620)

Galadriel is the dispenser of graces to whom she chooses. By the end of the story, Legolas and Gimli have developed a deep friendship, and together they sail across the sea, a privilege normally not given to Dwarves. But, according to the appendix, "[Galadriel] being mighty among the Eldar obtained this grace for him" (FR, appendix, 451).

The role of Mary as powerful intercessor was a frequent theme in the Middle Ages, and it was for this reason that litanies were created in her honor. Another example of Galadriel as dispenser of graces occurs when the Fellowship prepares for their departure from Lórien. It is at this point that Gimli requests a strand of hair that he promises to set in imperishable crystal – a type of reliquary – a "pledge of good will between the mountain and the wood" (*FR*, 487). Another gift is a small box of dirt from Lórien given to Samwise, which he uses to heal the scourged shire. It is because of this gift, in part, that the shire returns to health. Mary, in the Loreto Litany, is known as the *Salus Infirmorum*, "Health of the Sick."

Following the recognition of the Ring and its mission, Galadriel makes a bold statement: "It was I who called the White Council" (*FR*, 462). The White Council may be considered the collective wisdom of Middle-earth, and by claiming the locus of the council, Galadriel claims for herself the seat or location of this collective wisdom. Medieval imagery, particularly Greek iconography, considers Mary the *Sedes Sapientiae*, "Seat of Wisdom," another appellation given to Mary in the Loreto Litany. Following Galadriel's recollection of calling the White Council, she dispenses counsel to the travelers:

> I will not give you counsel, saying do this, or do that. For not in doing or contriving, nor in choosing between this course and another, can I avail; but only knowing what was and is, and in part also what shall be. But this I will say to you: your Quest stands upon the edge of a knife. Stray but a little and it will fail, to the ruin of all. Yet hope remains while all the Company is true. (*FR*, 462)

Although her initial words seem to indicate that she will offer no advice, at the end of this brief discourse she does offer good counsel: do not stray or else ruin will prevail. Again Tolkien attributes to Galadriel a characteristic similar to one found in the Litany: *Mater Boni Consilii*, "Mother of Good Counsel."

After the meeting with the Lord and Lady of Lórien, the Fellowship gathers and discusses what occurred during the conversation. Boromir expresses his suspicions concerning Galadriel and is immediately reprimanded by Aragorn, who states that "there is in her and in her land no evil, unless a man bring it hither himself" (*FR*, 464). This identification of Galadriel as "without evil" is reminiscent of the title *Mater Intemerata*, "Mother Undefiled," as well as the titles *Virgo Veneranda*, "Virgin Most Venerable," and *Virgo Praedicanda*, "Virgin Most Renowned."

After a length of time in the Elven home, Frodo grows restless and realizes that it is time to continue with the quest entrusted to Elrond and the Council.

Samwise and Frodo wonder if they will see Galadriel before their departure. Thereupon, Galadriel arrives and invites them to follow her into an enclosed garden. This recalls a frequent image of Mary as the thornless rose in the enclosed garden. In the Loreto Litany Mary is invoked as the *Rosa Mystica*, "Mystical Rose." Liguori identifies her, as do other commentators on the Virgin Mary, as the inhabitant of the enclosed garden. This image is portrayed in many medieval Annunciation scenes in which Mary is seated in a small oratory surrounded by an enclosed garden. It is in an enclosed garden where Galadriel gathers Sam and Frodo toward a silver basin that she fills with water, Galadriel's Mirror. She invites both to gaze into the reflections that the Mirror provides. Samwise is the first to look, and in the reflections he sees various events, including the scourging of the Shire. Frodo follows, but to him the Mirror reveals the awful roving eye of the Dark Lord in search of the One Ring. This Mirror reveals, as Galadriel states, "things that were, and things that are, and things that yet may be" (*FR*, 468). It is a mirror of truth, although the truths of the Mirror, as she states, are hidden even to the wise. In the Loreto Litany, Mary is named *Speculum Justitiae*, "Mirror of Justice." This attribute is given to Mary because she conformed her will to God's at the Annunciation. In Thomistic philosophy, justice is understood as that which is due a person or due to God (Gilson, 379–81). Mary is a mirror because she renders or reflects back to God what is due to God. Here again, as in the case of the designation "without stain," the mirror image is not a direct attribute of the person of Galadriel; rather, it is something that is possessed in her land.

After viewing the scenes revealed in the Mirror, Galadriel informs Frodo what will occur if the Dark Lord takes the Ring or if it is destroyed. In either case, Lórien will be lost forever. Frodo becomes aware that Galadriel possesses one of the three remaining rings that are beyond the power of the Dark Lord as long as the One Ring remains unclaimed. Impressed with Galadriel, Frodo offers her the One Ring. What hitherto is only imagined or desired by Galadriel is now a reality: possible possession of the One Ring. Galadriel rises up tall and strong before Frodo, demonstrating the possibilities of her power (*FR*, 473). Here, too, is an echo of the Loreto Litany: *Virgo Potens*, "Virgin Most Powerful."

The attributes discussed above have been taken from chapters 6, 7, and 8 of the first volume of the trilogy. References to the Loreto Litany can be found elsewhere in Tolkien's work as well. When Gandalf returns as Gandalf the White and reveals himself to Aragorn, Legolas, and Gimli, he bears messages for each from the Lady of the Golden Wood (*TT*, 135). Although the Elf receives his solemn message with reserve, the message of greeting to Gimli sends the Dwarf capering with delight, overjoyed at the greeting. In the litany, Mary is referred to as *Causa Nostrae Laetitiae*, "Cause of Our Joy."

In the second book of the trilogy, the reader finds Frodo and Samwise struggling toward the cracks of doom. At one moment in their trek, Frodo falls over a cliff. Stunned, unable to see his surroundings, and unable to move, he calls out for Sam's help. When Sam sees Frodo below but out of his reach, he cries out, "What can I do, Mr. Frodo? What can I do?" (*TT*, 271). Frodo reminds Sam that he has a rope, by which he pulls Frodo up from the dark abyss. The rope serves the two well, enabling them to descend the cliff and continue on their appointed task. For Catholics, the rosary has played an analogous role as a spiritual "rope" as a means to enter heaven and as a means of fortification against adversaries, both spiritual and temporal.[10] The recently restored fresco of Michelangelo's Last Judgment in the Sistine chapel provides a striking illustration of this idea of the rosary as assisting in attaining salvation, an almost exact illustration of the episode in which Sam assists Frodo up from the cliff. Thanks to the recent cleaning of the Sistine Chapel we know that the rope extended and held by one person to assist souls toward salvation is actually a rosary. While the actual provenance of the rosary is a debated point, the pious faithful believe it was made by Mary and given to Saint Dominic for greater promotion as an efficacious means of moving souls toward heaven. Keeping this image painted by Michelangelo in mind along with the important role the rosary plays in Catholic devotion, let us return to the scene where Samwise lovingly holds his rope, the one that pulled Frodo from the cliff's edge, and notes that perhaps the rope may have been made by Galadriel herself (*TT*, 275). In the Loreto Litany Mary is known as *Regina Sacratissimi Rosarii*, "Queen of the Most Holy Rosary."

Tolkien himself has said that Catholic teaching and imagination influenced his shaping of the character of Galadriel. This brief chapter has identified images that are found in the Loreto Litany that were used by Tolkien to describe either Galadriel directly or the land in which she dwells. Although it is very possible that Tolkien could have used other sources – for example, the writings of well-known Marian commentators such as Saint Ambrose and Saint Bernard of Clairvaux – it is unlikely that such scholarly material would have been familiar to his readers. In any event, the images used by Saint Bernard and others in their texts are the same as those that found their way into the Loreto Litany. By using this litany as a source, Tolkien employed an important compilation of medieval imagery of Mary as well as a source familiar to devout Catholics.

As Tolkien himself admitted, he employed "Catholic teaching and imagination about Mary" in creating the character of Galadriel. Although he does not mention the Loreto Litany specifically, the presence of the images found in the litany, and their use in describing Galadriel and her land, point to the litany as a source used by Tolkien. The more important question remains in how this Marian imagery furthers our understanding of the character of Galadriel and the role she plays in the story. I would argue that, by evoking such Marian images as "Tower of Ivory" and "Refuge of Sinners," and by describing her land as "without stain" and her hall as a great boat, Tolkien associates Galadriel with Mary in order to move her toward the character of Mary. Galadriel, because of her rejection of goodness, is not an allegory of Mary, who was without sin. At this point in her life, however, she assumes some aspects of Mary's character: that is, she denies self and moves to accept the will of another in order to promote a greater good. At the Annunciation, Mary made herself completely open to the will of God. This was Mary's character. This denial of self-will is the opposite of the first great choice of Galadriel, who, before the story of the trilogy, was portrayed as disobedient to the forces of good. Even those unfamiliar with the history of Middle-earth, who have read only *The Hobbit* and the trilogy, are witnesses to the struggle she endures when Frodo offers her the One Ring, a possible reference to a past weakness. Galadriel is tempted to replace the Dark Lord with a dreadful queen but rejects this temptation and remains true to what she knows is best, even though this means destroying what is known for attaining that which is unknown. Galadriel's definite rejection of power takes place in a garden, just as Eve's act of disobedience took place in a garden. Medieval and Renaissance painters inspired by contemporary theology understood Mary's acceptance of God's will as the perfect reversal of Eve's denial of that same will. These two scenes, Eve's rejection of God's will in a garden and Mary's acceptance in a garden, were frequently painted in the same altar piece or single panel.[11] Galadriel's formal rejection of the Ring in the enclosed garden was anticipated when she offered the Company advice at their first meeting. At this meeting she did not recommend a particular choice of her own but advised them to be true to their own course. At this moment, and then again in the garden, Galadriel denies any inclinations towards her own self-will. This attribution of self-emptying, the single desire to do only the will of God, was given to Mary in the litany under the title of *Vas Insigne Devotionis*, "Singular Vessel of Devotion." Galadriel proves herself faithful to the call of a greater good when she denies the power of the Ring. By doing so she stands in contrast to those who seek to use its power to promote their own self-will. She is one of many characters who choose to deny what the Ring represents. For Gollum, this striving for the power brings only a prolonged and miserable existence that ends in a fiery death. But for Galadriel, there is to be a different ending. Because Galadriel denied her own self in order to promote a greater good, to her is given a beautiful place beyond the sea.

Table 14.1 Litany of the Blessed Virgin Mary, the Litany of Loreto

Antiphon: Sub tuum praesidium confugimus, sancta Dei Genitrix; nostras deprecationes ne despicias in necessitatibus nostris, sed a periculis cunctis libera nos, semper virgo glorisa et benedicta.	Antiphon: We fly to your patronage, O holy Mother of God; despise not our petitions in our need, but deliver us from all dangers, O ever glorious and blessed Virgin.
Kyrie eleison.	Lord have mercy.
R. Christe eleison.	R. Christ have mercy.
Kyrie eleison. Christe, audi nos.	Lord have mercy. Christ hear us.
R. Christe, exaudi nos.	Christ, graciously hear us.
Fili Redemptor mundi Deus:	God the Son, Redeemer of the world:
R. Miserere nobis.	R. Have mercy on us.
Spiritus Sancte Deus:	God the Holy Spirit:
R. Miserere nobis.	R. Have mercy on us.

Sancta Trinitas, unus Deus.	Holy Trinity, one God.
R. Miserere nobis.	R. Have mercy on us.
Sancta Maria, R. Ora pro nobis.	Holy Mary, R.
Sancta Dei Genitrix, R. (etc.).	Holy Mother of God, R. (etc.).
Sancta Virgo virginum,	Holy Virgin of Virgins,
Mater Christi,	Mother of Christ,
Mater divinae gratiae,	Mother of divine grace,
Mater purissima,	Mother most pure,
Mater castissima,	Mother most chaste,
Mater inviolata,	Mother inviolate,
Mater intemerata,	Mother undefiled,
Mater amabilis,	Mother most amiable,
Mater boni consilii,	Mother of good counsel,
Mater Creatoris,	Mother of the Creator,
Mater Salvatoris,	Mother of the Savior,
Virgo prudentissima,	Virgin most prudent,
Virgo veneranda,	Virgin most venerable,
Virgo praedicanda,	Virgin most renowned,
Virgo potens,	Virgin most powerful,
Virgin clemens,	Virgin most merciful,
Virgo fidelis,	Virgin most faithful,
Speculum justitiae,	Mirror of justice,
Sedes sapientiae,	Seat of wisdom,
Causa nostrae laetitiae,	Cause of our joy,
Vas spirituale,	Spiritual vessel,
Vas honorabile,	Vessel of honor,
Vas insigne devotionis,	Singular vessel of devotion,
Rosa mystica,	Mystical Rose,
Turris Davidica,	Tower of David,
Turris eburnea,	Tower of ivory,
Domus aurea,	House of gold,
Foederis arca,	Ark of the covenant,
Janua coeli,	Gate of Heaven,
Stella matutina,	Morning Star,
Salus infirmorum,	Health of the sick,
Refugium peccatorum,	Refuge of sinners,
Consolatrix afflictorum,	Comforter of the afflicted,
Auxilium Christianorum,	Help of Christians,
Regina angelorum,	Queen of the Angels,
Regina patriarcharum,	Queen of the Patriarchs,
Regina prophetarum,	Queen of the Prophets,

Regina apostolorum,	Queen of the Apostles,
Regina confessorum,	Queen of the Confessors,
Regina virginum	Queen of Virgins,
Regina sanctorum omnium	Queen of all the Saints,
Regina sine labe originali concepta,	Queen conceived without original sin,
Regina sacratissimi rosarii	Queen of the most holy rosary,
Regina pacis	Queen of peace,
Agnus Dei, qui tollis peccata mundi:	Lamb of God, Who takes away the sins of the world:
R. Parce nobis, Domine.	R. Spare us, O Lord.
Agnus Dei, qui tollis peccata mundi	Lamb of God, Who takes away the sins of the world:
R. Exaudi nos, Domine.	R. Graciously hear us, O Lord
Concede nos famulos tuos, quaesumus, Domine Deus, perpetua mentis et corporis sanitate gaudere: et gloriosa beatae Mariae semper Virginis intercessione, a praesenti liberari tristitia, et aeterna perfrui laetitia. Per Christum Dominum nostrum.	Grant, O Lord God, we beseech Thee, that we, your servants, may rejoice in continual health of mind and body; and through the intercession of the Blessed Mary ever Virgin, be freed from present sorrow and enjoy eternal happiness. Through Christ our Lord.
R. Amen.	R. Amen.

Notes

1 The text consulted for *The Lord of the Rings* is the Houghton Mifflin paperback edition (New York: Houghton Mifflin, 1973). Those wishing to avail themselves of a valuable concordance should consult Blackwelder's *A Tolkien Thesaurus.*

2 Concerning Mary and the character of Galadriel, see Kilby, "Tolkien as a Christian Writer," in *Tolkien and the Silmarillion*, 53–65. On p. 53 the author states, "Tolkien was a staunchly conservative Tridentine Roman Catholic." Kilby then continues to describe both J. R. R. Tolkien's and his wife's devotion to Mary. Other sources dealing with Roman Catholic features of Tolkien's writing include Miesel, 209–13; C. Madsen, 43–47; and Hostetter, 5–8.

3 The Annunciation was a favored subject for artists of the late Middle Ages and Renaissance. To demonstrate Mary's acceptance of God's will, depictions of the Annunciation portray her with her hands folded across her breast and head bowed. Portrayals of the Annunciation from the following artists typify this pose: Giovanni di Paolo (Washington, D.C., National Gallery of Art), Fra Filippo Lippi (Munich, Alte Pinakothek), and Titian (Venice, Scuolo San Rocco).

4 A note on the spelling of "Loreto." Some sources spell the name of this Italian city with one *t*, others with two. This work will standardize the spellings, using the word "Loreto" since this predominates, although this is by no means exclusive usage. Printed sources that use a variant spelling remain as published.

5 One may consult the following sources for further details concerning the House at Loreto: Kenrick, *Holy House of Loreto* and MacDonald, *Holy House of Loretto.* For more concise material on the House of Loreto, see entries in *New Catholic Encyclopedia*, "Litany of Loreto," and "Loreto."

6 There is one important exception to this general rule of considering Mary as the morning star. In the Holy Saturday liturgy, the ancient hymn that proclaims the coming of the Light of Christ, the "*Exsultet*," refers to Christ as the "morning star." In the "*Exsultet*," the darkness of sin is banished by the new light of the Resurrection.

The first light seen in the darkness is the morning star, an allegory for the risen Christ. For the text of the "*Exsultet*" see *The Roman Missal*, 182–86.

7 *Biblia Sacra iuxta Vulgatam Clementinam*, ed. Colunga and Turrado; and *The Holy Bible Translated from the Latin Vulgate* (Douay Rheims Version).

8 There are many editions of *The Glories of Mary*. See, for example, the one edited by Eugene Grimm. The material concerning the Loreto Litany is taken from part 5: "Meditations on the Litany of Loretto for the Nine Days Preceding Each of the Principal Festivals of the Divine Mother."

9 In the Encyclical *Ingravescentibus Malis* written by Pope Pius XI on 29 September 1937, the pontiff reminds the faithful of the important role the rosary plays in solving the "evergrowing evils of our day" as well as assisting souls towards their supernatural end. *The Papal Encyclicals*, ed. Carlen, 563–66.

10 An example of this juxtaposition of Eve and Mary's Annunciation can be seen in the work of Fra Angelico's Annunciation that hangs in the Prado, Madrid.

Part IV

J. R. R. Tolkien's *Silmarillion* mythology

Medievalized retextualization and theory

15 The great chain of reading

(Inter-)textual relations and the technique of mythopoesis in the Túrin story

Gergely Nagy

The term "mythopoeic," though now habitually attached to the works of J. R. R. Tolkien, seems still to be a problematic one, and this doubtless derives from difficulties in defining myth. Surely there is a "quality" that Tolkien's writings share with other literary works that we consider mythological (the *Iliad*, the *Metamorphoses*, the Eddas) that makes us apply the label – what exactly it is is hard to say. Myth has many aspects, facets, and consequently many definitions. We suppose that behind our mythological texts there are *mythologies*, religious-historical systems of belief, and the ability to *invoke* these background systems is one of the qualities of these texts: they can function as the remnant of these disappeared cultural phenomena, offering an insight into practices and beliefs that could hardly be gleaned in any other way. But the texts themselves are also *mythologies*: the "*telling* of myths." Individual myths seem to be the constituent parts of the background systems, which are consequently themselves called "mythologies" in the sense of "a collective body of myths." An ambiguity in the use of the term "mythology" is thus already apparent.

"Mythopoeic" means "productive of myth," and mythological texts have an effect of invoking their background mythological systems: to clarify the technique of mythopoesis in Tolkien's works (and consequently, what "mythopoeic" means), it may be worthwhile to examine parallels between the methods of *invocation* and *creation*. In what ways are Tolkien's texts like those antique and medieval corpora?[1] The meeting point is usually given as one of the effects produced. Tolkien's words that in *Beowulf* the poet uses reference and allusion to a body of "connected legends" "to give [a] sense of perspective, of antiquity with a greater and yet darker antiquity behind" ("*Beowulf*," 31, 27), to create an "impression of depth" (25) are customarily seen as central in the interpretation of his own mythopoeic art.[2] T. A. Shippey and Christopher Tolkien discuss the concept of depth in Tolkien's works extensively (Shippey, *Road*, 100–2, 107, 203–4, 272–81; Tolkien, *BLT* 1, vii–xvi), and Shippey summarizes it thus: "a sense that the author knew more than he was telling, that behind his immediate story there was a coherent, consistent, deeply fascinating world about which he had no time (then) to speak" (203). This is indeed an impression in *The Lord of the Rings* but becomes factual knowledge in the case of other Tolkien texts, for example, in the case of the Túrin Turambar story, where, unlike the case of

Beowulf but like that of Chaucer or Malory, the allusions can be traced, verified, and studied in other texts.

Beowulf and Malory may be taken as two paradigmatic models for the "techniques of depth" we see in Tolkien. In *Beowulf* we find digressions and episodes inserted into the main story, many of which (by recounting other stories) hardly advance the plot in any apparent way,[3] and there are also ongoing allusions to seemingly equally unrelated matters (for example, the Brosingamene, lines 1197–201). Adrien Bonjour's classic study (*The Digressions in "Beowulf"*) shows that these all have an artistic function: they "[render] the *background* of the poem extraordinarily alive" (71; italics mine) and, by links to the main theme, provide contrasts and parallels that continually comment on and clarify the main points. Bonjour differentiates between digressions and episodes, both of which may use allusions (xi–xii, xii n. 2),[4] in many of which we have to assume that the "story must have been very well known at the time when *Beowulf* was composed" (even if the main story line is told in the digression: 7; also 27, 31, 38, 41–42, 44, 61). But though contemporary audiences knew, we do not – the analogue is between us as an audience for *Beowulf* and as an audience for Tolkien's works. Tolkien "assumes" acquaintance with other stories in the same way as *Beowulf* does[5] and raises basically the same questions: the *Beowulf*-model is about other, perhaps thematically unrelated, *stories* which are connected to the one with which the reader is presented.

In cases like that of Chaucer or Malory, we frequently see reference to other texts as sources, implying that the connection is between texts that tell the same story. However, these references are often no more than a cover for the authors' own invention. The Malory-model is about *textual* history, where the source text has certain functions making it relevant to the interpretation of the adapted text.[6] The focus of interest is how exactly *Beowulf*'s invocation of stories and Malory's invocation of textual history are paralleled in Tolkien's *creation* of these.

In Tolkien's work both models are present, and it is their joined application that is largely responsible for our perception of an essentially "mythological" quality. Shippey's examination of the depth effect (*Road*, 274–78) results in the suggestion that, as with medieval textual corpora, versions of the story with their dissimilarities and inconsistencies form an "imaginative space" (277) where the story evolves through the contribution of several authors.[7] The imperfections of any version can generate another telling, while all versions stem ultimately from a "central event," the nontextual source of the story, which all authors attempt to communicate (280). While the centrality of *story* is apparent as a primary basis for comparison, the Túrin texts and Shippey's analogue show that it is not only stories but also texts that are to be treated in this way (where "story" means a narrative sequence in the teller's/reader's consciousness, abstracted from any textual manifestation). A related story necessarily implies a related text: the concern with story is only one aspect of depth.

In this chapter I will argue that the examination of Tolkien's several versions of the Túrin story brings out the other aspect where the concern with *texts* is dominant, and that the critical task is to clarify how implied texts and textual relations contribute to the perception of the whole interconnected system of texts as, in one sense, "mythology" and, in another, "mythopoeic literature." Closely analogous to the "imaginative space" of real corpora, a "philological space" is created (cf. Shippey, *Road*, 280) by the texts' claim to be either the context or the retextualization of other texts (comparable to the *Beowulf*- and the Malory-model, respectively). It will be necessary to examine how depth is created and maintained, and how it functions between the several versions: an analogy can be drawn between Tolkien's corpus, real-world corpora, and Tolkien's texts *as a corpus within the textual world*. The Túrin texts make it clear by the relations established between them that a multilayered understanding of depth (on the levels of primary world philology, readerly and critical inquiry, and parallel "secondary levels" inside the textual world) can explain the mythological quality and help considerably in the interpretation of particular texts. Further, we find implied texts in the provenance that are not extant and not even "lost" but that are *pseudo-texts*, invented by the author to serve as the basis of authentication (a device also found in medieval texts) and thematizing exactly the status and use of (background) traditions in which I am now interested. This status also turns out to be essentially similar to that of the primary world background systems. My concern is primarily critical in the way that it inquires about how we should interpret the effect of depth and the texts in its light: it should also illuminate the standards by which we should evaluate and appreciate Tolkien's works. It is not my aim now to engage in a critical analysis of any particular version of the story; I will also not provide a summary of it, for giving one in this critical context would problematize exactly the status of the different details from the different versions that I intend to deal with.

The two allusions to the Túrin story in *The Lord of the Rings* serve to connect the events into the legendary background and to enrich the possible interpretation of the scenes where they occur – however, these functions can only be realized by recourse to another text or other texts. In the first instance, Elrond comments at the Council that Frodo's place should be with the "mighty elf-friends of old, Hador, and Húrin, and Túrin, and Beren himself" (*LR*, 288). The second is when Sam attempts to stab Shelob: we are told that she had no soft spot like that of dragons and that "[her hide] could not be pierced by any strength of men, not though Elf or Dwarf should forge the steel or the hand of Beren or of Túrin wield it" (755–56). Not much about the actual *story* of Túrin can be gleaned from these, other than that he was a great hero: allusions by nature *compress* a story, and their proper functioning depends on the availability of their *content*. The reader will face a question of *comprehension*: one has to know the alluded story to understand the allusions and the text of which they are part. This content must be supplied in a text that explains the allusions, *expands* the story contained in their compressed form; that functions as a *context*. However, allusions could also serve to create depth by just this feeling of incomprehension, and this effect is the object of a *critical question* as opposed to the *readerly* one. We must inquire into the *status* of the context and the *relation* between these two texts.[8]

As for their status, allusions can be *contentless* or *genuine*. Contentless allusions might only be employed to create a sense of depth like that which is accessible for us in *Beowulf*; the context they imply is a *pseudo-context*, created by these very allusions. This might conceivably be their function in the text, and even if the reader does not understand them, the effect of a "yet darker antiquity" is achieved. But comprehension not being supplied anywhere, the readerly question is frustrated. Many of the *Beowulf* allusions (even the episodes sometimes) work similarly for us: the content of the allusions is sometimes inaccessible and not reconstructible (see Bonjour, 45, 54), and we need long explanations of the stories in the episodes (= their content).[9] *Genuine* allusions, on the other hand, would be expected to have content and point to an existing context. Depth is just as well created this way, but it is not confined to the readerly "sense of unknown story"; it is extended along a philological dimension to use text, context, and their relation in its functioning. So it grants comprehension and satisfies the critical question with an existing context and a real textual relation between the two. The foreword and the appendices of *The Lord of the Rings* suggest that the latter is the case, though they do not mention Túrin himself or his story (only the "three peoples of Men" [1071]). There are indications that the "mythology and legends of the Elder Days," where the story obviously belongs, had been "taking shape for some years" before the writing of the trilogy (9; see also 11); and the appendices say that the sources on the Elder Days are "very extensive" (1070; though "not recorded here" [1119]). However, we still get a pointer: "Of these things the full tale … is told in *The Silmarillion*" (1071).

In *The Silmarillion* – chapter 21, "Of Túrin Turambar" (henceforward *Túrin*) – the full story is given, which answers the immediate comprehension question and as a consequence makes possible a critical interpretation.[10] The story is a truly tragic one of a hero under the shadow of Morgoth: a great number of readers prove Gloriana St. Clair wrong in asserting that Túrin is not an "appealing character" and that "it is fairly difficult to care whether he triumphs or not" (St. Clair, *Volsunga Saga*, 69).[11] It gives the content (and thus the expansion) of the *Lord of the Rings* allusions, and the readerly question of comprehension is closed. At the same time it contextualizes those allusions (indeed, the whole *Lord of the Rings* story), apparently closing the critical question too: depth is in the relation of the two texts, the way they supplement each other in terms of comprehension (readerly) and interpretation (critical).

One readerly consequence is that, knowing the content, one sees how the context adds to the meaning of the allusions, or how the allusion, not wholly appropriate, produces further depth on another level by simulating the effects of the transmission of stories over great periods of time and many generations. Knowing Túrin's story one might wonder, for example, why Elrond named him among the "mighty elf-friends." Húrin's mention is more in place, though he is also much more culpable in the downfall of Doriath and Gondolin; but Túrin, after all, killed Saeros and Beleg, caused the fall of Nargothrond, and contributed liberally to other catastrophes. Inside the textual world, one can argue, the memory of his deeds was already faded when the story reached

Elrond, so that only Túrin's prowess in arms in the defense of Doriath and Nargothrond, along with his slaying of Glaurung, were remembered.[12] More interesting is the other example, since by the narrator's invoking the image of Túrin the dimension of the scene is greatly increased, and several other associations come into play as well. Sam, fighting with Shelob, becomes a reflection of Túrin slaying Glaurung:[13] the dragon's explicit allegiance to Morgoth strengthens the connection with evil that Shelob, as a descendant of Ungoliant, herself has in the *Silmarillion* context. Túrin's personal feud with the dragon also seems to be paralleled in Sam's case. By the invocation of Túrin, an embryonic *typological interpretation* is presented by the narrator, with Túrin as type and Sam as antitype, proving the affinity of these texts to each other.[14] This typological scheme is pertinent to both primary and textual worlds as far as we handle *The Lord of the Rings* as a "later account" of the happenings at the end of the Third Age[15] – the narrator/persona then presents events with an eye on their universal tradition. The persona in the textual world follows the same method of presentation that the *Beowulf*-poet uses, in giving us a contrast to Beowulf in Heremod (one of the stories that "must have been known" to audiences; see Bonjour, 6–7, also 25–27, 47, 48, 50–52, 53) or to Hygd in Modthrytho (53–55). An analogy is established not only between the effects of mythological texts (for example, those of *Beowulf*) and Tolkien's texts on us, but also between the personae narrating the stories: the effects and devices to achieve them are similar.

There are thus three textual levels on which conclusions can be formulated. First, from a philological point of view, the *Silmarillion* text is a precursor of and a context for *The Lord of the Rings*, which makes the allusions philologically genuine in an objective, primary world sense. Second, on a readerly/critical level, the relation between the texts is genuine and meaningful, since it both supplies comprehension (readerly) and facilitates interpretation (critical). Third, the relation is also functional *within the textual world*, as the lore of the Elder Days contextualizes the whole story and the allusions *for the characters themselves*, for whom the *Silmarillion* tradition is accessible, quite regardless of the reader in the primary world.[16]

But *Túrin* also has its own textual connections, of a different kind than those already seen, that give rise to further critical points. On the story level, the action of *The Lord of the Rings* spans a few years, but that of *The Silmarillion* several thousand, which means that in a sense it itself is a compression and becomes a primary text in its own right. This is the immediate context for the *Túrin*,[17] which, furthermore, claims to be an adaptation of an ancient lay, the *Narn i Hîn Húrin* (*The Lay of the Children of Húrin*), where the story "here told in brief" is "fulltold" (*Silm*, 243).[18] The implication is that *Túrin* is a compressed *retextualization* of another text.[19] This is where depth is again created by a claim of an unknown text and a corresponding textual relation. Along with *The Silmarillion*, *Túrin* itself also becomes a primary text with its own textual connections: in relation to *The Silmarillion as a whole*, the relation is that of text – context,[20] but in relation to *the claimed source*, the relation is that of (compressed) retext – (expanded) base-text. The numberless retext-claims in medieval literature may again serve as analogies. From a simple claim we often cannot tell whether the relation is genuine or unsubstantiated – but there is no comprehension problem, only the philological one of relatedness and the critical point of the evaluation of the relation.[21] Thus, a textual tradition is implied, in the same way as the legendary stories are implied in *Beowulf*: it is the text's *claim* again that produces depth. Critical effort must aim at discovering how this effect functions in *Túrin*; an important tool in that critical examination is to take the text's claims seriously, since the textual relation produced by these claims is the key to evaluation.

The three important considerations that emerge thus concern the existence of the relation; its nature as expansion – compression; and its cross-genre working – all important for a critical evaluation. The first of these is similar to the previous critical question: is the text's claim of being a retextualization a *genuine* or a *pseudo*-claim? If the latter, a *pseudo-text* is created and depth is used without its philological extension. It is appropriate at this point to differentiate between pseudo-text and lost source, since they are different and function in entirely different ways. A lost source is of course a text we know to have existed but that is not extant any more: the text–retext relationship is a philologically real one, though not verifiable in the absence of the base-text. A pseudo-text, on the other hand, is mainly a theoretical construct: it is a text we know never to have existed but to have been invented by the author. Needless to say, no real textual relation can exist between a text and a pseudo-text: its main function is to *create* one, to situate the author's text in a textual relation and thereby endow it with certain characteristics. In fact, the author's own text becomes a *transcript* of the pseudo-text. A lost source has a philological function, whereas a pseudo-text is really fictitious, and its main function is that of authentication and the *creation* of a (pseudo)philological textual relation. The phenomenon is observable in a number of medieval texts: Geoffrey of Monmouth's "liber vetustissimus" or Malory's "French book" can be considered examples of it. A lost source is in many cases more or less reconstructible (certainly much more so than the content of allusions); a pseudo-text is by nature not reconstructible since it is in fact *constructed* by the text that claims it as a source.

The second consideration relates to the claim of compression: is there an expanded text behind *Túrin*? Certainly the tale bears many traces of compression (see Shippey, *Road*, 232, cited in n. 19): a quick-paced narrative (Túrin's early years are told in two pages, his sojourn in Doriath in another two, and so on); few descriptive details; and little or summary dialogue and characterization (Túrin's description in a brief passage [*Silm*, 243] and some mere remarks [throughout]; some short dialogues [*Silm*, 245, 245–46, 246–47, 249, 257, 258–59, 276, 277). Indeed, overall, only the most effective situations are exploited dramatically (for example, the death of Beleg [*Silm*, 255]; Túrin's encounter with the dragon [*Silm*, 262–63]). This evidence suggests that an expansion text would not so much be expanded in *content* but rather in *form*, or the handling of that content. We expect a more leisurely narrative with more incidents (broken down to smaller narrative units), more descriptive detail, more vividly drawn characters, and more attention to their interactions, etc.[22]

The third problem, related to the supposition of an expanded form rather than content, is that of the generic claim. *Túrin* claims to be a *generic* retext: are we to expect a *poetic* text behind it? Certainly there are poetic elements in *Túrin* that might be remnants of its base-text: many phrases and sentences of alliterative pattern can be found (not only as far as alliteration itself but also as far as the rhythm is concerned),[23] and there are expressions that appear to be panels or formulae.[24] There is much poetically charged description and even some dialogue in central scenes[25] where one would expect poetic convention to be at its highest, even surviving after compression/adaptation (as in Malory's account of Arthur's Roman wars, which betrays its source, the alliterative *Morte Arthure*).

But the most intriguing detail is not that Tolkien, in texts that create their own textual world, alludes to and uses other texts of his about the same world; it is that these same texts, *just as they are*, are claimed to be not only representations of the textual world but also *texts inside it*, creating a "secondary philological level" of inquiry. The *Silmarillion* text is conceived as a "compilation, a compendious narrative, made long afterwards from sources of great diversity" (*Silm*, xii): our first question is a philological one, on both primary and secondary levels, dealing with texts. The other two considerations are genuinely *critical*, inquiring into issues of textual relations in the interpretation of depth. If an existing textual relation is found, we expect a philologically extended effect of depth, revealing and useful in the interpretation of both texts. Comparative analysis can then throw light on the compression, the differences in narrative technique, characterization, the handling of dramatic action or dialogue: features attributable to the author in the primary world and to the persona within the textual world, who are again placed in an analogical relation.

The *Narn i Hîn Húrin*, as it is entitled in *Unfinished Tales*, seems to match the claims. The story of Túrin told in it is, at any rate, essentially the same as that in *Túrin*.[26] It is certainly an expansion of *Túrin*: the narrative pace is slower, the summaries are expanded (the two-page story of Túrin's early years to eighteen pages; the sojourn in Doriath to ten; and so on), and many minor details are introduced (Sador, the old servant, with his affinity to proverbial language; the relationships of Túrin to his parents and of his parents to each other; etc.). Much dialogue and description are added or are more detailed (Túrin's description expanded to a longer passage [*UT*, 81–82, also 63]; longer and more dramatic dialogues [63–64, 64–66, 67–68, 70–72, 75–77, 78, 83, 85, 86–87, 88–89, 90–91, 93, 93–94, etc.]); and situations more appropriately exploited. Verbal parallels, often verbatim correspondences, are also found.[27] From a philological point of view, *Túrin*'s claim is justified: the two texts are in the relation of (compressed) retext to (expanded) base-text. Within the textual world, *Túrin* is a redaction made from the *Narn* by a "later redactor" (= persona); in the primary world, it is the editor Christopher Tolkien's production of a continuous, "coherent and internally self-consistent narrative" (*Silm*, xii) from the discontinuous and sometimes fragmentary *Narn* (cf. *UT*, 7). Both processes are authorial/editorial reworking, demonstrable by way of collation, so the claim of retextualization proves to be genuine on the whole, though the fact that the *Narn* is unfinished shows that other texts must also be present in the history of *Túrin*. The effect of depth is here functional in the sense of a real tradition of story and text standing behind, a primarily philological fact with results mainly on the *textual* level (and interpretive conclusions through that).

But in spite of the demonstrable connectedness of the texts, the claim of generic retextualization is not wholly satisfied, and consequently the equation of the *Narn* with the ancient lay that *Túrin* claims to retextualize remains problematic. By its title the *Narn* claims to be that lay, but it is actually written *in prose*. Christopher Tolkien reports that the lay was supposed to be written by one Dírhavel in a specific Elvish verse-form (*UT*, 153),[28] suggesting that this "prose *Narn*" might not have been conceived as that. It does not in fact fulfill all the criteria established for the base-text of *Túrin*. It is expanded; there are many more poetic elements in it than in *Túrin*; but it is not in verse (where "poetic" refers to linguistic and stylistic features and "in verse" to metrical form). It might be argued that the Elvish verse-form was not thought to be reproducible in translation (= in English) and that the *Narn* can be accepted as its *representation* in the primary world[29] – but then again, the text as we have it is one remove from the original lay, as its prose translation. Both if it is a redaction of the lay in the textual world and if it is a prose translation meant to represent it in the primary world, the discrepancy is a new claim of a textual relation. The critical question is thus concerned with the existence of a poetic *and metrical* base-text that would function as the Dírhavel *Narn* in both worlds, still a question of existent base-text versus pseudo-text.[30] Depth is again produced and maintained by claims of texts to stand in a certain relation to other texts, with the implication that others underlie the currently read one. A critical examination of the concept of depth must always be interested in the elusive base-texts, since it is in these that, seeking for the *origin* of stories and their effect on us, we see how this origin is always relegated into other texts, in some cases exactly by the *creation* of one (a pseudo-text).

To summarize how depth has up to now been treated, it will be useful to differentiate clearly between the levels in the discussion: the (primary) philological, the readerly/critical, and the secondary philological levels were distinguished. On the *philological* level we inquire whether the textual relations claimed by the texts exist *in the primary world*. On the *readerly/critical* level we are concerned with the way these relations function in our perception, understanding, and evaluation of the text(s). The reader's attention is focused on stories strictly on the comprehension level, and the critic's on texts and their working: how they and their relations participate in meaning production. Depth for the reader suggests that there are other stories than the one currently read, that this one is in fact at a junction of other stories, in a vast system of "connected legends."[31] This body of stories is closely paralleled in the mythological systems of the primary world, which also tend to be organized into comprehensive linear narrative (from creation to Apocalypse, Ragnarök, or some unspecified future), with the individual stories (its constituents, individual myths) connecting at various points: at the junction of shared characters, thematic similarity, chronological succession, etc.[32] For the critic, on the other hand, depth means that a set of other texts is in fact or in fiction connected to the presently examined one, which together form not only a corpus but in a way a cohesive *unity*, where the connections, real or illusory, are a functional part of the effect the whole is supposed to convey.

There is a clear analogy between Tolkien's texts and real-world mythological corpora, and that means that the same levels of examination apply in the textual world too. Tolkien's texts, inside the textual world, have exactly the same effect of invoking the background mythological system that we find in the primary world; as texts *in the primary world*, they in fact serve to *create* that mythological system. Our present problem arises mainly on the *secondary philological level*: seemingly we cannot find a place for the prose *Narn* in the provenance of texts in the textual world. We are never told of a redactor who reworked Dírhavel's *Narn* into prose, and even though in the primary world it may "represent" Dírhavel's lay, it will not completely suffice as the base-text of *Túrin*, and its status is problematic also in the primary world. In a complete enumeration of levels, furthermore, a *secondary readerly level* is also to be supposed, where story relations *within the textual world* are situated (Elrond's mention of Túrin and the narrator's typological interpretation, already discussed, constitute proof of its existence and working).

However, in the textual world the situation is more complex: there these are not simply *stories* but *history*, with the result that depth acts there as a constitutive factor. Supposed readers in the textual world do not only contextualize the Túrin story in the larger framework or see it as a context of allusions in texts they are presented with; *they themselves* are also contextualized in that framework.[33] In this they are like the original audience of *Beowulf* who "must have known" the stories in the episodes and the allusions as their own historical/legendary context – that made the poem relevant to them. At this point the effect of depth, introduced into the textual world, *explodes* the textual reading of the context and broadens it into a cultural/historical/social horizon. The textual world, so to say, substantiates itself. Stories and texts interact and evolve in it, determined by those other aspects of the context. It is precisely because of the prose *Narn*'s claim that we can see the same story having been retextualized in the textual world – what is more, retextualized sometimes in terms of content, sometimes in terms of form: a history for the story, with its own stations and rules of transmission.

The secondary levels of textual relations supply some preliminary conclusions about historicity and broadened effect of depth as a constitutive force. First, it is obvious that philological examination in both worlds cannot be anything but historical, the very idea of retextualization presupposing temporal sequence. Second, cross-genre retextualization, again in both worlds, implies a tradition of story that can be given a different form in different genres without essentially being changed in content. The effect of depth, in the sense of both unknown/connected stories and preceding/connected texts, does not only exist in the textual world as well; it is also essential in *creating* that world when it ceases to be purely story-oriented or textual and expands into historical and cultural depth. *Creating* a mythological system is done essentially in the same way as *invoking* one.

The only extant treatment of the Túrin story in metrical form is an unfinished alliterative poem in *The Lays of Beleriand*,[34] which could possibly be the Dírhavel *Narn*; but it fails to make claims that would identify it as that. The prose *Narn* certainly draws heavily on it,[35] as the general story line (as far as the poem goes) is mostly the same and characterization is very similar.[36] Textual similarities can also be found.[37] But although the title of its second version is "The Children of Húrin" (= Hîn Húrin, changed from *Túrin* [*Lays of Beleriand*, 5]), the poem never claims to be the Dírhavel lay. The fact that it is not an expansion of the prose *Narn* does not mean much in itself (Dírhavel's work need not be an expansion of the prose *Narn* but only of *Túrin*), but it is clear that no redactor could have worked from this poem alone, unless he added much of his own. The poem cannot be the Dírhavel *Narn*: a primary philological suggestion is that when it was written (in 1920–25[38] [*Lays of Beleriand*, 2]) the idea of Dírhavel had not yet emerged. On the secondary philological level we might suppose that the poem either represents (1) a precedent to Dírhavel's work; (2) a later tradition of verse redactions from it; or (3) a completely different verse tradition stemming (ultimately) from the same source.[39]

Dírhavel's *Narn* thus seems to be a pseudo-text, and depth in the prose *Narn* and *Túrin* seems to be illusory; but a glance at the secondary levels will cast light on how the pseudo-text is covered by depth in the textual world. In neither world can we produce a text that would fit in the philological place of the Dírhavel *Narn*, although a basic narrative structure and some passages might be reconstructed. But the poem can nevertheless be seen as a *functional* base-text in primary world terms;[40] in the textual world we can suppose the prose *Narn* to be an "anonymous redaction" (a plausible supposition: we are crowded with such redactions in primary-world philological work, and there is no reason to suppose that it is impossible in the textual world). In the light of the fact that Tolkien preserved "a very high proportion of all that he ever wrote" (*Shaping*, 47), I think it unlikely that an unknown poem could exist – the Dírhavel *Narn* is certainly a pseudo-text in primary philology, but there is no evidence against its being a lost source in secondary philology. What we could reconstruct on the basis of narrative lines, characters, and common textual items is Dírhavel's poem *in the textual world*: we could never reconstruct a "lost Tolkien text" that probably never existed. Primary and secondary philology separate: there is a pseudo-text in the primary philological provenance, but this is transmuted into a lost source through the philologically extended effect of depth in the textual world. The pseudo-text serves to authenticate the *Narn* and *Túrin* by situating them in a net of textual relations: in the secondary provenance created by this net of textual relations, it is transformed into a lost source, which lends further authentication to the relations.

But the poem itself has depth too, which means that it itself claims to have its own textual relations, in ways we have already seen at work. By its unexplained allusions to stories, concepts, and characters,[41] it produces just the same effect of depth that we saw in the *Lord of the Rings*'s allusions, implying a context to enable comprehension. A philological (and thus historical) concept of depth is also present. In primary-world terms, the poem represents a stage in the development of Middle-earth and the Túrin story preceding the prose *Narn* and *Túrin*, which are both retexts of the poem's story and text. In the textual world the poem occupies a philological position in the secondary provenance (see n. 39), and itself must go back to sources, not only because of its implication of a context, but also because some structural and authorial devices (such as the use of unlinked dialogue, stock elements both in narration and as epithets applied to heroes; digressions and episodic matter used in a *Beowulf*-like way, etc.)[42] strongly suggest sources and a developed poetic convention. The poem must exist in a context, at a stage of the development of texts (evolving in the textual world, reported not by the author but by the persona) earlier than that which we have up to now seen, and it clearly has an audience for which the context would be in other texts. This context is not only a *textual* one, but, as we have already seen, it is also one that broadens into a cultural/historical horizon. In primary-world terms, the textual context of the poem (Tolkien's other writings on the Túrin story) is in this way seen as invoking the broadened context inside the textual world – for us, in fact, *creating* it through this invocation. There is again a strong resemblance in this to real-world mythological texts invoking their background mythological systems. The existence of depth *within the textual world* can be seen as the effect of depth in the primary world. The critical question is supplemented by a historical aspect in both worlds: within the textual world this is indeed *history*, and what we are after is not only a textual but also a *historical* tradition. In the primary world it is for the same historical reasons that we cannot accept *The Silmarillion* as a context: it represents a later stage in the textual and conceptual development of Tolkien's text where the poem would not fit in.

Many of the poem's textual connections may be recovered by primary philology, and the relevant texts can also serve as the textual history of the prose *Narn* and *Túrin*. On the one hand, we can accept the *Lost Tales* as a context for the poem and "Turambar and the Foalókë" in them (*BLT* 2, 70–145) as the ultimate base-text for it (there are many similarities in narrative as well as in wording that suggest derivation).[43] But on the other hand, there are other base-texts for *The Silmarillion*, which themselves ultimately go back to the *Lost Tales*: the "Sketch of the Mythology" (written in 1926), the "Quenta Noldorinwa" (c. 1930), the "Earliest Annals of Beleriand" (1930s),[44] the "Later Annals of Beleriand" (1930s), and the "Quenta Silmarillion" (1937).[45] In these we find a prose tradition of the Túrin story, and taken together with the poem, the evidence suggests that a verse tradition detached from this at some point around 1920. Later it turned into a *fictional verse tradition* (the pseudo-tradition of the Dírhavel pseudo-text in the primary world and the "lost tradition" containing the lost source of the poem in the textual world), integrated again into the extant prose tradition in the prose *Narn* and finally editorially in the *Silmarillion* synthesis.[46] In these several cross-genre retexts of the story of Túrin, a historical narrative is told in texts of various genres (legend, chronicle, annalistic historiography and its translation, heroic lay, prose redaction of that lay, etc.), all connected by their retext – base-text relations. Similarly, mythological systems in the primary world usually manifested in texts of various genres are often then retextualized into other texts: Greek mythology, for example, came to be recorded in texts generically varying from epic (Homer) and tragedy (Aeschylus, Sophocles, and Euripides) to choral song (Pindar) and comprehensive synopsis (the late Greek *Bibliotheke* formerly attributed to the Athenian Apollodorus).

The Túrin story evolved through its retexts, in both primary and textual worlds (see *BLT* 2, xvii, xviii); what remained central in the inter-textual tangle is the story used in the (re)texts. Of course, it took a great number of smaller or greater changes to reach *Túrin* from "Turambar and the Foalókë" (though the general story lines are the same, quite a few details are not shared by these two accounts).[47] On the other hand, as can be seen from a collation of the Túrin texts, a significant number of *textual* details (phrases, epithets, especially speeches and central scenes) can be traced at least as far back as the poem, so the textual affinity (even derivation) between the versions is unquestionable. By parallel, real mythological texts also show a great variation of detail but still remain the "same story": contrast Aeschylus's and Euripides' versions of the Electra story. There is, however, no ultimate "Electra text": all versions are legitimate and authentic retextualizations of the Greek myth.

By combining the two main factors that keep the system together, that of *texts/versions* and the textual relations between them, and the centrality of *story* as a basis for comparison, we arrive at a multilayer definition of depth, which is a key to the technique of mythopoesis. The effect of depth is generated by the texts' claims to be in certain textual relations with other texts (on both primary- and textual-world levels) and is founded on the concept of story as a linking factor and on common textual features – the philological and the readerly concepts of depth are clearly differentiated. The result is not only a corpus of texts representing the stages of composition but also an interconnected system that has its counterpart in the textual world as well: both the *Beowulf*- and the Malory-models are at work. We may add that there are also differences in the *handling* of the story, which is not only a philological but also a critical concern. The technique of mythopoesis, I would suggest, is for a large measure dependent on this textual tangle, responsible for the creation of the textual world in the same way as mythological texts in the primary world are responsible for the invocation of their background mythological systems.

All historical recession must arrive finally at a starting point, an "Ur-Text," the earliest form and base to all retexts, where retextualization ends and the *textualization of event* is supposed to have taken place. In the textual world where all the Túrin texts are used as history, it is not difficult to see the *Lost Tales* as the earliest *textualized* form of those historical events. In the primary world, the *Lost Tales* are the philological Ur-Text anyway, being Tolkien's "first substantial work of imaginative fiction" (*BLT* 2, vii), within sight of literary creation, the *textualization* of ideas by the author. Thus, through the analogy of author and persona and the duplication of texts into the textual world, the corpus not only simulates the evolution of stories and texts within the textual world (presenting what is treated as history *within that world* as the history *of that world*) but does it in just the same terms that we can use to describe the actual evolution in real-world text corpora.

The further claims of the texts show the establishment of a story tradition reaching into another definition of textuality, again in ways very similar to real-world techniques. Not only do the "Earliest" and "Later Annals of Beleriand" claim to be founded on the work of "Pengolod the Wise" (*Shaping*, 311; *Lost Road*, 201–4); the "Quenta Noldorinwa" on Eriol's "Book of Lost Tales" (itself drawing on the "Golden Book" of Kortirion; *Shaping*, 94); and the "Quenta Silmarillion" variously on the work of Pengolod (*Lost Road*, 201), Rúmil (*Lost Road*, 223), and the "Golden Book" (*Lost Road*, 203–4; differing in the versions of the title page),[48] but the *Lost Tales* themselves, though apparently contained in the "Golden Book" in some form, are orally *told* to Eriol at first. Before all textualized versions we discover a preceding oral tradition, which also explains many of the formal features of the texts (alliterative fixed phrases, narrative devices, epithets, meter in the poem and some subtly rhythmical parts in the *Lost Tales*, etc.) and adds further depth. This claim means a proliferation of pseudo-texts, as far as primary philology is concerned, and a number of lost sources for secondary philology. A pseudo-text in the provenance of real-world texts can in fact account for an understanding of invention and the (fictitious) status of tradition: tradition is always what the author chooses it to be, since writing it into the pseudo-text (and transcribing it into his own text) authenticates invention and incorporates it into the undifferentiated concept of "tradition."[49] Tolkien *creates* a tradition in an exactly similar way for the works of Eriol, relegating it into pseudo-texts and making them (lost) sources in the textual world.

Having seen how the concept of depth can be differentiated and extended into the textual world where it broadens into a cultural and historical concept from a purely textual one, the conclusions concerning the technique of mythopoesis may now be formulated, starting with the relation of all texts to their ultimate base. Primary mythological texts (either from Greek, Roman, or Germanic mythology) usually show the same effect of depth in the sense of interconnected texts and endlessly retextualized stories (also apparent in medieval corpora like the texts of the Arthurian legend), at the end receding into oral tradition. In the treatment of mythology as history, textualization is also a necessary starting point of tradition, since the first instance of the manifestation of the story (either in oral or, later, in written form) cannot be put back in time indefinitely. An Ur-Text, or rather, "Ur-Version," is a theoretical starting point of the linguistic articulation of events, which is, then, endlessly recycled into other (oral or textual) *versions*. Ultimately, the nonconstraining nature of the Ur-Version provides Shippey's "imaginative space" to authors of the different versions, but this nature is the result of the social context, the *uses* to which the story/text is put: their cultural role and the many aspects of that role. Mythology, the "telling of myths" is in this sense the continual retextualization, in different genres and different forms (depending on the cultural role assigned to the particular versions), of culturally important stories, of hypothetically historical, textualized events (cf. Shippey, *Road*, 279, 280), referring to events in an intermediary way: what we get is always a version but never a *one-to-one transcript* of the Ur-Version.

Tolkien's texts and the background mythological system they succeed in creating are essentially similar to real-world mythological corpora and the way they invoke their mythological system because of the basically similar relation of text to myth. Mythology traverses the definitions of textuality in the overlay of textual on oral and makes it clear that *no text is myth by genre.* The texts are *mythological*, and together they form a *mythology*, the "*telling* of myths" contained in the background mythological system. They are assigned this status by the user community's relation to them, their cultural (/religious/political) use as such, and the relation they are supposed to have to their base-text: myth is always in the base-text, but however deep we delve into the philological descent of mythological texts, there will always be a base, a source. The texts are just the *telling* of the myth – they are not the *myth itself.* We do not seem to be able to grasp *myth as text.* All its retextualizations are made on the content/form axes, with not much restriction on either: competing versions of the same story can stand alongside each other without being "inauthentic," "uncanonical," or "false," demonstrating the nonconstraining nature that enables this variety. Apart from very general narrative lines and characterizations, we cannot reconstruct the implied version of which all mythological stories claim to be retexts. What I propose is the handling of *myth as a pseudo-text,* with an indefinite number of retexts, which is a way to account for both the differing story versions and the complex textual tangle. As mythology is the articulation of (in that form doubtless fictitious) events in linguistic form, oral or textual, which is then used for various cultural aims and is retextualized in various forms and genres, it is not in any way different from the retextualizations of an ultimate "pseudo-event" that we see in Tolkien's texts, where even the cultural, historical, and political context of the texts is supplied and simulated.[50]

The effect of depth that I have examined in Tolkien's works proves to be analogous to the effect found in primary-world textual corpora in the connectedness of stories (readerly) and texts (philological) that together form a *critical* definition. Interpreting the corpus as a system of interconnected texts with specific textual relations that are relevant to the interpretation of the particular texts and the evaluation and appreciation of the whole, we can say that Tolkien's works are essentially similar to primary-world mythological corpora. The methods he uses have been noted by historians and literary historians alike in texts and corpora such as *Beowulf* and the Arthurian legend, and the application of two models, here called after *Beowulf* and Malory, to Tolkien's texts have proved usable and efficient in clarifying both the concept of depth and the techniques of mythopoesis. The fact that illusory depth also appears should not detract from the feeling of completeness: the ultimate base-text, as we have seen, is *always* a pseudo-text. This understanding of mythology as continual retextualization on the content/form axes means that depth is always where textual relations are produced, to be exploited in various ways. The duplication of texts in(to) the textual world means that it can also be exploited there to indicate (in fact, to *create*) not only a textual but also a broader historical-cultural context, purely by the philological-historical implications of the effect of depth as applying in the textual world. To say that this gives Tolkien's texts their "mythological quality" is to realize that mythopoesis happens in the process and is for a large part in the system; to call Tolkien's texts "mythopoeic" is to assign equal importance to *all texts* in the corpus and their interrelations – because it is precisely their interrelatedness and their claims to textual relations that make them mythological. Our recognition of this is the way to appreciate both his understanding of mythology, and his artistic method and technique used to create this extraordinarily complex effect: to construct, in the process to uncover, and in that process to *use* the Great Chain of Reading.

Notes

All the *Mythlore* and *Mallorn* articles, as well as those from the volume *Proceedings of the J. R. R. Tolkien Centenary Conference, Oxford, 1992* (ed. Patricia Reynolds and Glen GoodKnight), that I use in this essay became available to me through the kind and generous help of Prof. Theodore J. Sherman, current editor of *Mythlore*, for which I would here like to express my gratitude.

1 Some studies dealing with the question of mythology/mythological quality in Tolkien are Hyde, "Mythos" (especially interesting is the section "Mythology and Myth: Coming to Terms with a Definition," 27–28); Betteridge, "Tolkien's New Mythology"; Chris Seeman, "Tolkien and Campbell Compared" (focusing specifically on the comparison of the views of Tolkien and Joseph Campbell): these work with a mainly literary or general culture-historical definition of myth. Hostetter and Smith, in "A Mythology for England?" use a definition which is rather drawn from the history of religion and supplemented by a philological method (closer to my view, as will be seen).

2 The effect was observed by some early reviews of *The Lord of the Rings*: see Donald Barr, "Shadowy World of Men and Hobbits" (*New York Times Book Review*, 1 May 1955), 4 (quoted in Hammond, "Critical Response," 228).

3 For example, Beowulf's swimming contest with Breca (lines 499–603) and the references to Hygelac's fall (lines 1202–14, 2354–59) and to the tragical end of Heremod (lines 1709–22), and so forth.

4 From the "historical standpoint," these digressions, as "documents of Germanic history and legend" (Bonjour, xiv; see also 12–13, 65–66), are extremely important: we see in them the function of mythological texts as the remnant of a lost or unattested mythological system. That history and legendary matter is conflated in this respect points out the use of mythology as history in the society for which *Beowulf* was composed; this use will also appear in Tolkien's textual world.

5 See Shippey's examination of the verbal techniques of how this is done in *The Hobbit* (*Road*, 51–86).

6 These connections in many cases have been studied extensively. Chaucer's use of Lollius as a cover in *Troilus and Criseyde* has been discussed almost exhaustively (see Benson *et al.*, *Riverside Chaucer*, 1022, for references); so has Malory's use of his sources, though not in an overall fashion explaining the explicit references to the "French book" exactly at points where Malory inserts his own invention. In a paper read at the Fifth Conference of the Hungarian Association for the Study of English, "The Fictitious Text: Malory's Construction of the Source through References," I attempt to outline an explanation of the fictitious source as an implied "pseudo-text," used mainly as an authentication device but also throwing light on the nature of invention and the (ultimately fictitious) status of tradition.

7 For Tolkien's conception of the author of each of the versions as centrally important in this process, see Morus, "'Uprooting the Golden Bough,'" 8: "Tolkien took it for granted that any specific item of mythology would have an individual author."

8 We have to note, though, that the order in which the discussion proceeds on the texts is in some measure arbitrary. Publication chronology is in Tolkien's case entirely different from writing chronology; the order in which the texts are treated here could be said to represent the succession in which most readers will probably encounter them. But this does not have much critical significance; the relations established will be the same (for they are ultimately founded on writing chronology), whatever order the texts are read in.

9 *Beowulf* might not be the best instance to cite for this phenomenon, but I use it since Tolkien seems to have been fond of the example. The allusions in *Beowulf* must have had content for audiences (readers) when the poem was written (see above, on p. 240, also n. 4); it is just us for whom this content is not accessible, but as we will see, even this gap between reader and text is used by Tolkien.

10 Critical studies of the Túrin story have uncovered many primary-world texts and stories that affected Tolkien: Gloriana St. Clair, in "*Volsunga Saga*," examines the influence that versions of the Sigurd story had on *Túrin* (though her conclusions and parallels are sometimes very far from convincing); Barnfield's "Túrin Turambar and the Tale of the Fosterling" lists numerous parallels from various medieval texts (some of which are perhaps pushed too far or are far-fetched from the beginning). Shippey, in his discussion of the story (*Road*, 231–38), cites the *Kalevala* and *Egil's Saga* as ultimate sources (232, 235–36). The role of the *Kalevala* is supported by Tolkien's own letters, cited in West's essay "Túrin's *Ofermod*," 236–38. (I have been able to use this essay through the kind help of Prof. West, who sent me a copy of it, for which my thanks are due.) Broadwell, in "Esse and Narn," gives a very thorough and illuminating analysis of the connection of names and stories, producing an excellent critical reading of the Túrin story. These studies usually use more than one version of the story, looking for sources (St. Clair, Barfield) and/or working out an interpretation (Shippey, West, Broadwell).

11 Wicher, in " Artificial Mythology," 405, suggests that *The Silmarillion* has a "prevailing tragic mood," and that "[t]he story of Túrin presents the narrative scheme of the book in a condensed form." (This little-known article is, by the way, a very interesting inquiry into the "mythological status" of *The Silmarillion*.)

12 This gives the story a history *within* the textual world, implying a transmission where the unfavorable details were dropped and Túrin became assimilated to the stereotype of the "great hero" and the "elf-friend" – something that also happens in preliterate cultures when historical(/legendary) material, orally transmitted, is exploited in a variety of ways. In oral composition/transmission, the fixity of a text does not put restrictions on the fixity of story, and the author is free to shape performance according to the standards and aspects that seem to be relevant at any given moment (see Clanchy, "Remembering the Past," 165–66, 170). In some measure, the argument can be countered from within, by raising the objection that Elrond was in a position to know: he could easily talk to witnesses himself! The very nature of Elves modifies what we take to be the processes of oral transmission: since they do not die, Elves are a kind of "incarnate tradition" and for some measure a warrant against distortions. However, the mere mention of Túrin in such a context shows that it was thought of as possible to interpret him so. Elrond may know the story well enough, but the situation is such that it seems to him to be applicable, even if suppressing some details.

13 Bard's killing of Smaug in *The Hobbit* may also be recalled.

14 It also justifies the reader who, in the foreword to the *Book of Lost Tales*, part 1, is reported by Christopher Tolkien to have said that *The Silmarillion* was "like the Old Testament!" (ix). Wicher also remarks that biblical analogies are appropriately applied to *The Silmarillion*: it resembles "a holy writ rather than a novel" (399). In this scheme, Sam's action receives dimension from that of Túrin, who acts in defense of his small, immediate environment and from personal pride; Túrin's deed gains significance

from the parallel with the solemn aim of Sam's action (to save Frodo, to be able to continue the mission that would liberate Middle-earth), whose motivation is not purely personal but also grounded in his mission. The contrast is in a way treated in Evans, "Tolkien's World-Creation," 8 (the article has otherwise very dubious conclusions, with a number of factual errors and some suppressed counterevidence).

15 The runic script on the title page indeed reads, "The Lord of the Rings, Translated from the Red Book" (see also *LR*, appendix, 1167; prologue, 13, 26–28; and 1064–65).

16 See Zgorzelski, "A Fairy Tale Modified,"128–35, especially 132.

17 *The Lord of the Rings* itself is essentially an extended version of *The Silmarillion* section "Of the Rings of Power and the Third Age."

18 The phrasing of the *Lord of the Rings* appendix (that "of these things the *full tale* … is *told* in *The Silmarillion*" (*LR*,1071; italics mine) will be recalled.

19 Cf. Shippey: "'Of Túrin' has been selectively compressed with regard to its major features" (*Road*, 232).

20 Analogous to the *Lord of the Rings–Silmarillion* relation, which is also that of text and context.

21 Wace's and Layamon's *Brut* may supply an example of genuine relatedness, demonstrable by collation; the case of Chaucer's *Troilus* is more complicated, since after all there is no Lollius, but there definitely *is* a Boccaccio! Malory's claims, if checked against the extant French sources, often produce a critically highly significant discrepancy between claim and reality. Retext-claims, much more than context-claims, are a matter of critical consideration.

22 Cf. West's remark about the "remarkable consistency" of the versions of the story: "Apparently the basic narrative was set very early on … and thereafter grew largely by extension, not only with some additional material but with fuller description of incidents and motives, polishing of style, and changes in the nomenclature and geography" ("Túrin's *Ofermod*," 240).

23 "[H]e listened to his lore and the tale of his life" (*Silm*, 249); "in the dim dusk of a winter's day" (250); "Then Túrin stood stone-still and silent" (255); "[H]e walked as one without wish or purpose, while the year waned and winter drew on," and "[O]n Ivrin's lake is endless laughter … fed from crystal fountains unfailing" (256); "yearned for brave strokes and battle in the open" (259); "Tall and terrible on that day looked Túrin, and the heart of the host was upheld, as he rode on the right of king Orodreth" (261); "treacherous to foes, faithless to friends, and a curse unto his kin" (275); "Wilt thou slay me swiftly?" (278), etc.

24 "[G]uard him and guide him" (*Silm*, 246, 256; "[F]ind her and guard her" (267); "under wood and over stream" (252, one of Tolkien's favorites); "So he ended, of the house of Haleth not the least valiant" (273), etc.

25 Saeros's taunting (*Silm*, 244); Beleg's death and aftermath (255–56); Ulmo's message (260); Gwindor's death (261); Túrin's encounter with Glaurung (262–63); Brodda's killing (265); Nienor's last encounter with Glaurung (275), etc.

26 Apart from the place(s) where the *Narn* is fragmentary – Christopher Tolkien in the notes explains that at those places where the *Narn* lacks parts of the story, the extant texts are much the same as that given in *The Silmarillion*. Cf. West, "Túrin*'s Ofermod*," 240–41; Broadwell in her interpretation handles the versions of the story as supplementing each other and hardly differentiates them at all.

27 "[D]uring that time his grief grew less" (*Silm*, 243; cf. *UT*, 82); Saeros's taunting (*Silm*, 244; *UT*, 85); "Túrin son of Húrin loves me not; nor will" (*Silm*, 259; cf. *UT*, 165); Ulmo's message (*Silm*, 260; *UT*, 168); the description of Hithlum ("Bare and bleak it was," etc.; *Silm*, 264; *UT*, 110); "[A] shadow I cast wheresoever I come … Let Melian keep them! And I will leave them in peace unshadowed for a while" and "roaming the woods, … wild and wary as a beast" (*Silm*, 265; *UT*, 115); "put his shadow behind him" (*Silm*, 266; *UT*, 118); "Tell the Mormegil that Finduilas is here" (*Silm*, 266; *UT*, 117); the adjective "fey" applied to Morwen in Doriath (*Silm*, 267; *UT*, 122) and to

Túrin (*Silm*, 277; *UT*, 152); "ordered things as he would" (*Silm*, 271; *UT*, 133); "So he ended, of the house of Haleth not the least valiant" (*Silm*, 273; *UT*, 141); Glaurung's dying speech (*Silm*, 275; *UT*, 145); Túrin's death (*Silm*, 278; *UT*, 152). These parallels and correspondences cluster around the centrally important and most clearly fixed parts of the story.

28 Dírhavel is not mentioned in *Túrin*, but his authorship is asserted in the index of names, under *Narn i Hîn Húrin* (*Silm*, 427). The brief biography and the generic traits of a *Narn* given there correspond with what we find in *Unfinished Tales*.

29 Cf. Tolkien's remark in one of his letters that he would have "preferred writing in Elvish" (*Letters*, 219), quoted in Greenman, "*Silmarillion*," 21.

30 Christopher Tolkien's inserting the note at the end of the *Narn* might conceivably mean that the case was perhaps neither, and that Tolkien himself considered the *Narn* in *Unfinished Tales* as Dírhavel's work. Even if he thought so, on philological grounds that view must be disregarded, in keeping with our principle to take the texts' claims seriously. Tolkien might have thought of the *Narn* as Dírhavel's lay, so to speak, "provisionally," in the absence of anything else on which to put that label. It is easy to see that even that thought, if indeed it ever occurred to him, held in itself the implication of a "real," "*not* provisional" Dírhavel text, which would surely be in some kind of textual relation with the prose *Narn*.

31 This is basically what Tolkien speaks about in "*Beowulf*: The Monsters and the Critics" and what Shippey formulates as quoted above on p. 239.

32 Wicher treats the resemblance of *The Silmarillion* to "genuine mythologies" on the basis of Eliade's formal criteria of myths (399) and argues that Tolkien tries "to revive the mood of ancient legendary tradition without any effort to modernize it" (400).

33 See Zgorzelski, 134 (the discussion contains a summary of the view of the Polish critic P. Kuncewicz).

34 The poem's text will be cited by the line numbers of the first version (*Lays of Beleriand*, 6–94). Though it is unfinished, a fragment from the beginning of a revised version is also given; initially this is only in minor variance with the first version, but as it progresses it becomes substantially different.

35 The poem is commented on by Christopher Tolkien in J. R. R. Tolkien, *Lays of Beleriand*, 21–9, 48–56, 79–94 (see also the preface, 1–2), where he also highlights differences and correspondences to *Túrin*. Commentary on the second version can be found in *Lays of Beleriand*, 102–4, 118–27 (introduction at 94–95). See also West, "Túrin*'s Ofermod*," 241; it should be remembered, as West warns, that "some of Tolkien's finest poetry" is in this lay.

36 Some minor differences from the later works: Húrin's knowledge of Gondolin is not present (lines 18–21; cf. *Lays of Beleriand*, 6); Nienor is born while young Túrin is still in Dor-Lómin (lines 116–18; cf. *Lays of Beleriand*, 9); Beleg is less of a high-ranking warrior of Thingol than a hunter, a "son of the wilderness who wist no sire" (lines 192–200, 222, 398–99, 416; cf. *Lays of Beleriand*, 10); Túrin in Doriath learns not only the use of weapons but also minstrelsy (lines 353–55; cf. *Lays of Beleriand*, 14); Orgof (= Saeros) is killed right at the feast and not the day after (lines 502–7), etc. Túrin's grief over the slaying of Beleg is brought out most poignantly and expressively in this version (lines 1248–338 and further in part 3, lines 1339–698; cf. *Lays of Beleriand*, 46–8, 56–65). Túrin, Húrin, Morwen, and other major characters are essentially drawn along the same lines (see, for example, the description of Túrin, lines 341–51).

37 Thingol's welcome to young Túrin (lines 252–59; *UT*, 79); the "alms-guest" motif (lines 282–89; *UT*, 75, 79); Morwen's listening to the hoped-for footfall of Húrin (lines 286–90; *UT*, 74–75); Thingol's reception of the Dragonhelm as if "his hoard were scant" (lines 310–14; *UT*, 80) and Túrin's inability to lift the helm (lines 325–26; *UT*, 81); "[H[is mood was lightened" ("lot" in line 334; *UT*, 81); the description of young Túrin (lines 341–51, also 1979–83, 2141–43; cf. *UT*, 81–82); Orgof's taunting (lines 489–90; Saeros in *UT*, 85), etc.

38 Not in 1918 as St. Clair asserts ("*Volsunga Saga*," 68).

39

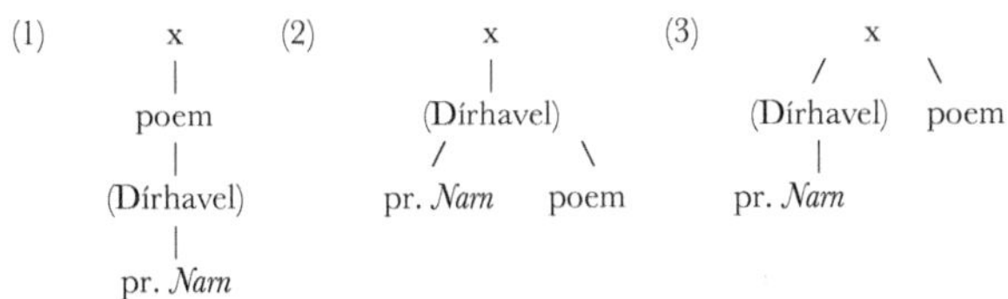

40 There are clear traces of its use in the other texts apart from the narrative and characterizational correspondences: "Gumlin his guardian, who guided him hither" (line 331) and "he guarded and guided his grim comrade" (line 1427; cf. "guard him and guide him" [*Silm*, 246, 256, 267; *UT*, 79]); "as tall as are the Men from the misty hills of Hithlum" (*Silm*, 254; cf. "in stature tall / as are Hithlum's men of the misty hills" [lines 853–54]); "and that grief was graven on the face of Túrin and never faded" (*Silm*, 256; cf. "[t]hat grief was graven with grim token / on his face and form, nor faded ever" [lines 1419–20]); "On Ivrin's lake is endless laughter. / Lo! cool and clear by crystal fountains / she is fed unfailing" (lines 1524–665; cf. *Silm*, 256, cited above in n. 23); even Túrin's walking "without wish or purpose," cited as a poetic instance in *Túrin*, has its origin in the poem, where he "wandered witless without wish or purpose" (line 1422).

41 Such allusions are to the gods (lines 215, 244, 432, 629, 883, 1130, 1410, 1479–80); to the famous Dorwinion wine (lines 224–27, 425–26); and to the "secret songs of the sons of Ing" (line 421). There are unexplained references in the minstrel's songs (lines 430–35) and in Beleg's song in the outlaw camp (lines 627–32). There are also references to Cuiviénen (line 450); to the fate of Orgof after death (lines 545–49), to Tain-Gwethil (lines 431, 636, 1409); to the Dwarves and Belegost (lines 1147–49); to the ten races of Hithlum (lines 1164–65); and to Beleg's fate after death (lines 1283–84 [repeated verbatim, lines 1696–97], 1408–11); and so forth.

42 The use of direct speech and unlinked dialogue (lines 56–57, 74–75, 77–78, 82–83, 604–5, 609–10, 872–73, 884, 888, 899, 919, 1357–58, 1363–64) is something that could easily mark a poetic convention. Stock/formulaic phrases both in narration ("Now tales have told" [line 666]; "The tale tells not of their travel weary" [line 1431]) and as epithets customarily attached to heroes (Húrin: [Thalion] Erithámrod [lines 313, 963] "and his thanes like gods" [lines 17, 208]; Húrin Thalion [lines 863, 1956, 1976]; Húrin the steadfast [line 248]; Túrin: Túrin Thalion [lines 653, 720, 1324, 1335, 1773, 2009, 2045, 2055]; Túrin the tall [lines 1015, 1103, 2072, 2214]; Beleg: "son of the wilderness who wist no sire" [lines 200, 399]), along with the occasional appearance of the historic present (for example, lines 162–64) and the "Lo!" exclamation at the start of structurally/thematically important parts (lines 1, 8, 105, 137, 323, 595, 1064, 1224, 1248, 1260, 1504, 1527, 1987, 2088; cf. *Beowulf*'s "Eala!" and "Hwaet!") strengthen the case. There are also allusions to unknown concepts (for example, the recurring and unexplained role of the number 3, apparently a ritual or sacral number [lines 243, 313, 547, 1220]; "three times three" [lines 1370, 1455]); and elements (see previous note), as well as digressions and stories, both historical and mythological (Beren's story [lines 1545–46]; the "doom of the Gnomes" [lines 359–61]; the Gnomes' skills in crafts and their history [lines 781–83]; the history of Nargothrond [lines 1540–44, 1708–22]; the scenes from Elvish history depicted on the Nargothrond cup [lines 2016–40]). Further, some of these are set in songs, recanted by minstrels (lines 429–35) or in camp by Beleg (lines 627–32). Túrin himself makes a "historical lay" in memory of Beleg (lines 1652–65; "wondrous wove he

words enchanted" [line 1659]; cf. the scop's procedure in *Beowulf* [lines 867–74]). These not only suggest a poetic convention: they go further and put the poem in a sort of analogy with *Beowulf*.

43 See Christopher Tolkien's introduction to and commentary on "Turambar and the Foalókë" (J. R. R. Tolkien, *BLT*2, 70–71, 119–45; especially 119–37, on the "primary narrative," where both *Túrin* and the prose *Narn* are used for the aims of comparison). Similarities include Túrin's description (*BLT*2, 75); "he stood as one stricken to stone" (*BLT*2, 81; cf. "Túrin stood stone-still" [*Silm*, 255]); the final encounter of Glómund and Nienor (*BLT*2, 109; Glaurung in *Silm*, 275); Nienor's question to the waters of Teiglin (*BLT*2, 109; cf. *UT*, 145); Túrin's speech to his sword (*BLT*2, 111–12; *UT*, 152; *Silm*, 278), etc. The most important difference is probably the assertion that "Turambar indeed shall stand beside Fionwë in the Great Wrack [at the end of the First Age], and Melko [= Morgoth] and his drakes shall curse the sword of Mormakil" (*BLT*2, 115), attributing to Túrin a central role in the great eschatological myth.

44 *Shaping*, 11–91 ("Sketch"), 92–268 ("Quenta Noldorinwa"), 351–411 ("Earliest Annals").

45 *The Lost Road*, 124–54 ("Later Annals"), 199–338 ("Quenta Silmarillion").

46 The "Quenta Silmarillion" version of the story is in fact derived from the poem (*Lost Road*, 316, 322) and even refers to it (*Lost Road*, 317; see 322).

47 See the commentaries to the "Turambar and the Foalókë," in *BLT*2, 119–45; to the poem in *Lays of Beleriand*, 25–34, 57–65, 96–113; to the relevant parts of the "Sketch" in *Shaping*, 69–73, 88–90; to the relevant part of the "Quenta Noldorinwa" in *Shaping*, 220–27, 251; to the relevant part of the "Earlier Annals" in *Shaping*, 386–90; to the relevant sections of the "Later Annals" in *Lost Road*, 151–52; and to the relevant section of the "Quenta Silmarillion" in *Lost Road*, 322–23.

48 Though in the Túrin part it also claims to be based on an ancient lay, given here as *iChúrinien* ("The Children of Húrin"; *Lost Road*, 349; cf. 355 on the history of the title), which is exactly the title given to the poem (see *Lays of Beleriand*, 4). As the "Quenta Silmarillion" does not claim a Dírhavel lay as source, this is another point where the poetic tradition was integrated into the prose one.

49 In the paper referred to in n. 6 ("Fictitious Text," 8), I argue that this is why Malory cannot be said to "rewrite" his source; rather, he "overwrites" it. In a way, the same thing happens in *Beowulf* (lines 867–915), when in the lay praising the hero's deeds, Hrothgar's scop sings at length about Sigemund and Heremod (see Moisl, 69–71; also Bonjour, 46–47). Moisl calls attention to the fact that this song is at the same time a "medium for the *propagation* and *generation* of historical tradition" (71; italics mine); Beowulf's praise is sung with historical parallels, and the whole new lay is passed off as "tradition" then. The status of the end product is exactly the same as that of the material from which it is built: tradition.

50 See Zgorzelski, 130, about the way the "non-existent *events* of non-existent history" are turned into an essential aspect of the creation of history by the "construction of chronicle time" in *The Lord of the Rings*. Wicher also notes that *The Silmarillion* attains a "pseudohistorical authenticity" by Tolkien's "artistic approach," which is the same as that of "the ancient mythographers" (400).

16 Real-world myth in a secondary world

Mythological aspects in the story of Beren and Lúthien

Richard C. West

Late in 1917, Edith Bratt Tolkien moved into furnished rooms in the village of Roos, north of the Humber estuary in Yorkshire and close to the army camp where her husband Ronald was stationed. Both were to some extent convalescent. Early that year Ronald had gone on sick leave from the trenches of the Great War and had been in and out of hospitals for months with chronic illness; but he had also recently been promoted to full lieutenant and had duties in the camp. Edith had given birth to their first child a couple of weeks before, on 16 November in Cheltenham, a boy they named John Francis Reuel; and it had been a difficult birth. Nonetheless, when Lieutenant Tolkien could get leave, and his wife a babysitter, the couple loved to take long walks in the woods, a favorite spot being a glade with an undergrowth of hemlock. Here Edith danced and sang for her husband, and this lived in their memories as a golden time.[1]

Almost fifty-five years later, on 11 July 1972, John Ronald Reuel Tolkien wrote to his third son, Christopher, about his late wife in that period: "In those days her hair was raven, her skin clear, her eyes brighter than you have seen them, and she could sing – and *dance*" (*Letters*, 420). He stresses the last word: Edith must have been a wonderful dancer. In the same letter he says, very revealingly, that it is his nature to express itself "about things deepest felt in tales and myths" rather than in other forms of discourse. He did not write a biography of Edith, but she was the inspiration for what was probably the favorite of his stories of Middle-earth. He maintained that "the kernel of [his] mythology, the matter of *Lúthien Tinúviel* and *Beren*, arose from a small woodland glade filled with 'hemlocks' (or other white umbellifers) near Roos on the Holderness peninsula" (221). No doubt it was a favorite in large part because on some level he identified (or at least very closely associated) the character of Lúthien Tinúviel with his wife.[2] As he wrote to his son in the letter from which I have been quoting, "she was (and knew she was) my Lúthien."

It is not the first of his tales: it is preceded by his saga of Túrin and a recounting of some sort of the fall of the Elvish kingdom of Gondolin. But it occupies a central place in his legendarium: the greatest victory of the Elves in their long struggle against the satanic Morgoth, when they penetrate to the deepest recesses of his stronghold and recover one of the three Silmarils, or Jewels of Power that contain divine light, which he has set in his iron crown.

With irony typical of Tolkien, this victory leads not only to the death of King Thingol and the destruction of his kingdom of Doriath but also, later, to the successful voyage of Eärendil the Mariner to plead with the Valar (godlike or angelic beings) for the aid that ultimately overthrows Morgoth. And the repercussions continue throughout the history of Middle-earth. Tolkien observed in 1954 that in a sense even *The Lord of the Rings* is a sequel to the story of Beren and Lúthien (*Letters*, 180).

Where, now, can we find the "tale or myth" that grew out of Edith Tolkien's dance in the woodland glade? Tolkien wrote it over and over again, and he revised it over and over again, but unfortunately, as is true for so many of his voluminous writings, he never really finished it. The earliest version we have is the "Tale of Tinúviel" in *The Book of Lost Tales*, part 2. It is not the first, which Tolkien said he began in 1917, but a rewriting from no earlier than 1918.[3] It is, however, a complete story, but one that was subsequently to be added to and changed. Tolkien told the story in verse form in rhyming couplets as what he called "The Lay of Leithian" (meaning "Release from Bondage"), written mostly between 1925 and 1931 but with later revisions amounting to a fresh start after he had completed *The Lord of the Rings*. These verses are in *The Lays of Beleriand*. There are bits of the story in chapter 10 of "The Earliest Silmarillion" (*Shaping*, 24–25; to use the editorial title assigned by Christopher Tolkien), in chapter 10 of the "Quenta Silmarillion" (109–15), and in "The Earliest Annals of Beleriand" (300–1, 307), all published in *The Shaping of Middle-earth* and in "The Later Annals of Beleriand," which appears in *The Lost Road* (134–35). Indeed, every one of the twelve volumes of Christopher Tolkien's magisterial edition of *The History of Middle-earth* has something about the development of the story. The fullest version, but a highly compressed one, is "Of Beren and Lúthien," chapter 19 in *The Silmarillion*.[4]

And, of course, Strider recounts the tale to the four Hobbits as they camp on Weathertop while en route to Rivendell in the first volume of *The Lord of the Rings*.

> The leaves were long, the grass was green,
> The hemlock-umbels tall and fair,
> And in the glade a light was seen
> Of stars in shadow shimmering.
> Tinúviel was dancing there
> To music of a pipe unseen,
> And light of stars was in her hair,
> And in her raiment glimmering.
>
> (*FR*, 204–6)

That is the first of nine stanzas we are given, and the second begins "There Beren came from mountains cold." But there is an evolution of some thirty years behind these verses, which go back at least to Tolkien's poem "Light as Leaf on Lindentree," published in *The Gryphon* in 1925. Compare the opening stanza as it was in an earlier draft of this chapter written perhaps during the early 1940s:

The leaves were long, the grass was thin,
The fall of many years lay thick,
The tree-roots twisted out and in,
The rising moon was glimmering.
Her feet went lilting light and quick
To the silver flute of Ilverin:
Beneath the hemlock-umbels thick
Tinúviel was shimmering.

(*Shadow*, 180)

Where the final version as published has grown out of the woodland glade near Roos, it is fully a picture of the dancing Elf-princess. The medial version, while just as romantic, could be a description of Edith dancing for her husband, if we could substitute her name and take out the silver flute of Ilverin. But this unseen piper is part of the story, though it will not surprise anyone who knows Tolkien's habits of composition that his name went through many changes. "Ilverin" is one of the variant names of Daeron, one of the finest minstrels of the Elves, who in the earliest "Tale of Tinúviel" is her brother who is happy to play music with and for her. But apparently Tolkien decided that it made a better story if Daeron was a rival suitor for her hand, and such he becomes in the "Lay of Leithian" and thereafter. His fate was never to return from searching the wilderness for Lúthien after she eloped, and he is said never to have been seen again, but only sometimes detected by travelers who hear the strains of his music in the distance.

This encounter in the woods is a constant feature in all versions, and that fact alone shows its importance to the author in encapsulating his idyllic memory of Edith. But also Tolkien, who liked repeated patterns, also gives similar scenes to a number of his other characters who are lovers. It is significant that Lúthien's parents also meet in this way, and that Thingol, though one of the greatest lords among the Eldar (Tolkien's version of Elves), is yet a lesser being than Melian the Maia (a quasi-angelic being in Tolkien's mythology, of the same kind as Gandalf in *The Lord of the Rings*). To some extent, then, Lúthien's union with Beren recapitulates that of her parents. The first meeting of Aragorn and Arwen repeats the pattern. They are *both* descendants of Beren and Lúthien,[5] and Tolkien draws deliberate parallels between these two marriages of Elf and Human. The careful reader should remember this when Strider tells their story on Weathertop, for his pensive mood on that occasion is due in part to his recognition that his case has similarities to that of his ancestors, and to his hope (only partially borne out) that it may have as relatively happy an issue among all the sad tales of Middle-earth. In the history of the composition of *The Lord of the Rings*, Arwen was a very late addition to the cast of characters, and all references to her are examples of what Tolkien called "constant re-writing backwards" (*Letters*, 258). We may not always recognize that Arwen, even though she is not mentioned, is very much present in the subtext of this scene on any reading after the first one, so long as one has paid attention at least to the appendices, and the more so the more familiar one is with the *Silmarillion* material.

Strider, once he has chanted part of the song of Beren and Lúthien, goes on to give a précis of the story. He says,

> Beren was a mortal man, but Lúthien was the daughter of Thingol, a King of Elves upon Middle-earth when the world was young; and she was the fairest maiden that has ever been among all the children of this world. As the stars above the mists of the Northern lands was her loveliness, and in her face was a shining light.
>
> (*FR*, 206)

There are several points to make about this passage.

"Beren was a mortal man": the evidence indicates that he was in the lost original version, but in the "Tale of Tinúviel" of about 1918, which is the earliest extant version, he is an Elf, albeit of a lesser house than the royal one into which he wishes to marry. By the mid-1920s, when we have the next recension in the "Lay of Leithian," Beren had become a mortal man again, though this went back and forth for quite a while before the matter was settled. But ultimately Tolkien decided, apparently, that the greater disparity between mortal and immortal beings made for a better story than one involving merely differing rank among beings of much the same kind. Also, he wanted his myth of a marriage between Elf and Human, of which Beren and Lúthien are the first of a very small number of examples in his own legendarium. As he explained to Milton Waldman,

> [A] recurrent theme is the idea that in Men (as they now are) there is a strand of "blood" and inheritance, derived from the Elves, and that the art and poetry of Men is largely dependent on it, or modified by it. Of course in reality this only means that my "elves" are only a representation or an apprehension of a part of human nature, but that is not the legendary mode of talking.
>
> (*Letters*, 149)

Lúthien "was the fairest maiden that has ever been." Aragorn's own beloved Arwen is said to resemble Lúthien (*RK*, 338), so he has a personal stake in this. A man falling in love with a supernally beautiful woman is a well-nigh universal theme in literature (at least, that written by men), and boy-meets-girl is our most common plot (by either male or female authors). But the "shining light" in her face is something more than a metaphor to Tolkien, when engaged in "the legendary mode of talking." See Verlyn Flieger's book *Splintered Light* for an extended discussion of the theme of light and darkness as very sensitively treated throughout Tolkien's work. Flieger observes that "Lúthien is the last glimmer of the true light, in human form what the Silmarils are as jewels – embodiment of all the remaining light" (119). I think this may be why Lúthien has a brief stint as a blonde at one stage in the composition, because of the association of golden hair with light. But Edith was Tolkien's Lúthien, so the raven tresses soon came back to stay.

Now, Lúthien's other name, Tinúviel, means "daughter of twilight" in one possible translation of Elvish (Sindarin),[6] associating her, as Flieger points out, with the time of diminished light. It is also a poetic term for the nightingale, which all readers of Hans Christian Andersen know is an exceptional songbird, even if they have never heard one. In the earliest "Tale of Tinúviel" this is actually her name, but in all later versions it is a cognomen given to her by Beren, apt because she is singing as well as dancing when he comes upon her. Thus on one level it functions as a term of endearment between lovers. But also it is when Beren gives her this name that she stops flitting away and allows him to approach her. On one level this is because he has thereby both praised her and piqued her curiosity, but on another because he has *named her* – and no one knew better than Tolkien the power of names or the significance of being able to assign names. But it is misleading to suggest that Beren has "power over" Lúthien other than their reciprocal love (each puts the other before all else, even life): rather what he has done is recognize her mythic "true name" and shown it to her. For in mythic terms song is powerful: think of the singing contests in *The Kalevala*, for example, where magicians may sing people into an enchanted sleep, and so forth. And Lúthien the Nightingale, daughter of an Elf-king and an angel, is one of the most powerful singers of any age in Tolkien's world.

After the quest of the Silmaril begins, Beren soon finds himself imprisoned – in the earliest version by Tevildo, Prince of Cats (who has perhaps a hint of the monstrous, giant cat whom King Arthur overcomes in one of the legends), but later by Sauron, the chief servant of Morgoth. When Lúthien seeks for a way to rescue him, her worried father asks her to promise to stop thinking of Beren and not to go after him alone nor tempt anyone else to go with her. She promises only not to tempt anyone else to go with her (*BLT*2, 16). This is the resolute answer of a hero, but it is not what Daddy wants to hear. He has a comfortable prison built for her in the great beech Hirilorn (this feature is constant in all versions), a tree house that can only be reached by long ladders that are taken away when not in use to bring her her daily needs. She contrives to include magical ingredients among her daily needs. She sings a spell to lengthen her dark hair so that it reaches to the ground, and then she cuts it off and weaves from it a cloak and a cord. She uses the cloak to shroud herself in darkness – and so go about invisible – and the long cord, which she drops, to put a sleeping spell on the guards below. Then she climbs down the cord and dances away into the hinterlands.

Is there anyone who isn't reminded of Rapunzel? Everybody mentions this fairy-tale resonance from what was probably the first published essay on this story on (Kocher, *Reader's Guide*, 132). And I think rightly: certainly Tolkien was familiar with the *Märchen* of the Brothers Grimm. Nevertheless, the differences are far more marked than the similarities. Nowadays we are quite accustomed to what Jay Williams called "the practical princess" who does not sit around waiting to be rescued, but this must have been unusual in 1918. Lúthien lets her hair down not just to allow her lover to reach her but to enable *her* to reach *him*. The situation is full of resonances from other traditional tales: the enchanted sleep in such stories as *Sleeping Beauty*; the cloak of invisibility in *The Twelve Dancing Princesses*, also suggestive of such magical devices as the Tarnhelm in *The Nibelungenlied*, or the Ring of Gyges in Plato's *Republic*, or the ring of invisibility in Chrétien's *Yvain*, or its analogue in *The Mabinogion* – even looking forward to the magic ring in *The Hobbit*, where its use is so much more benign than the One Ring later became.

Tolkien is always teasing us with this sort of skein of almost-correspondences. Many articles and books have been written by authors who have become aware of yet another possible source for something in Tolkien's fiction, most of these sources being more or less plausible because Tolkien was so well and widely read. For many modern fantasy authors it is indeed valuable to study their direct sources to see how they have handled them, but with Tolkien what I think we get is more of a sense of an addition to the corpus in the same vein.

Source studies are a chancy business, but especially so with Tolkien. Randel Helms suggests a source for the story of Beren and Lúthien in the Welsh tale of *Culhwch and Olwen*, in which Chief Giant Ysbaddaden demands that the hero Culhwch perform numerous seemingly impossible tasks before gaining the hand of his daughter Olwen (Helms, *Tolkien and the Silmarils*, 15). Brian Dunsire, dubious about this, observes:

> Both episodes also involve the aid of a King [Arthur], a dog [Cavall], a ring and a magic blade, but in my view such comparison is specious. A sufficient level of abstraction will reveal "parallels" anywhere. The motif of the impossible task set by the king as the price of his daughter is surely common enough elsewhere.
>
> (Dunsire, 9)

Indeed, with Tolkien we can only be confident of a direct source when he has borrowed a feature that is unique to some particular story or he has told us what was in his mind, and both of those circumstances are rare. What I think we do get over and over are echoes, even when we cannot pinpoint an exact source. Tolkien studied and taught myths and legends and fairy tales all his life, and they were an integral part of his mental furniture and imaginative make-up.

The earliest "Tale of Tinúviel" has no back story for Beren, and Tolkien added one making him a noted hero in the struggle against Morgoth, the last survivor of a band of guerrillas resisting the invader. There seems to me to be an underlying taste of Robin Hood and his outlaw band driven by oppressors into the forest, and also a whiff of James Fenimore Cooper's Hawkeye tracking down marauders in the wilderness. There is also something of those other devoted lovers, Tristan and Iseut, in Tolkien's pair (Lúthien is willing simply to go on living with Beren in the woods, should he abandon the quest). And we may remember that Tristan was a great hunter, said to have invented much of the terminology of the hunt, much as Beren early on is a skillful hunter and trapper (although he later develops rather into a friend of beasts and birds). When Beren and his Elf companions are in Sauron's dungeon where a wolf comes each night to devour them one by one until only Beren and Finrod are left, it is strongly reminiscent of the sons of King Völsung being killed one each night until only Sigmund survives. *Völsunga saga*, from which this scene comes, also features a lot of shape-shifting, but Tolkien could have found that in many other sources. When Sauron shifts shape repeatedly in an effort to escape from the jaws of Huan, it suggests the Norse god Loki's shape-shifting when trying to elude Heimdall and also the Greek Nereus, the Old Man of the Sea, who has to be held onto through various transformations before he will reveal hidden wisdom (as Sauron yields the spell that binds his castle together so that Lúthien is able to cast it down). When Carcharoth bites off the hand of Beren that holds a Silmaril, there is an echo of Tyr losing a hand to Fenris Wolf. But in all such matters our focus on the event is strongly on its place in Tolkien's mythology of the Silmarils: these tastes and whiffs and echoes resonating from other mythologies only add to the appropriateness of their setting in Tolkien's own mosaic. His myth seems like the real thing.

To return to Lúthien's position in the story, which is something far more than to be a damsel in distress or a prize to be won by the hero, I might remind you of the advice given by Jack Zipes: don't bet on the prince. Zipes means this for modern fantasies, but, while Tolkien is far from being a feminist author, his women characters are stronger than they are often made out to be. And Lúthien is, I think, his strongest. She does far more to achieve the quest of the Silmaril than does Beren, even urging him on when he is ready to abandon it rather than put her at risk. It is true that she has the help of Huan, the Hound of Valinor, to escape from Curufin and Celegorm and to overcome Sauron, but all this means is that she enjoys the aid of a magical animal helper much as the hero of many another tale, from the crafty Puss-in-Boots to the wise Firebird. It is Lúthien who gets them past the wolf guardian of Morgoth's stronghold by putting Carcharoth into an enchanted sleep, and it is Lúthien's dancing that enspells the Dark Lord's retainers and Morgoth himself, while Beren is hiding beneath the throne in perfectly understandable terror. When they have made their way back to her father's court and Thingol learns all that has happened, it is no wonder that "he marvelled at the love that had awakened in the heart of Tinúviel so that she had done greater deeds and more daring than any of the warriors of his folk" (*BLT* 2, 37).

But she has to achieve yet a greater deed. When the wolf Carcharoth, maddened by the Silmaril burning in his belly, ravages Thingol's kingdom of Doriath, a picked band of heroes mounts a hunt. Think of the Calydonian boar hunt in Greek mythology or the hunt for the great boar Twrch Trwyth in the Welsh *Culhwch and Olwen*. The Silmaril is recovered, but Beren is mortally wounded. Lúthien casts a mighty spell so that Beren's spirit will remain in the halls of Mandos, the Vala who oversees the dead, until she comes. She then pleads so eloquently with inexorable Mandos that the couple is allowed to return to the world of the living, though this time both as mortals. Thus Lúthien reenacts the descent into the underworld of Orpheus in Greek mythology or of Ishtar in Babylonian to recover a loved one, but with a happier result: much as in the Middle English *Sir Orfeo*, itself derived from the myth of Orpheus and a favorite romance of Tolkien's, the hero is successful in retrieving his wife. Tolkien himself drew a parallel between this episode and the Greek myth of Alcestis, who bravely and nobly volunteered to die in place of her husband but was saved when Heracles wrestled with Death to prevent her being taken.

To get Lúthien to the halls of Mandos, Tolkien ultimately decided on the easiest method: that she die of grief, like the Irish Deirdre of the Sorrows after the slaying of her heroic husband. But he had considered having her carried there by the great eagle Thorondor. This would have been one more example of a variation of the "helpful magical animal" motif, where one or more eagles swoop down to rescue a desperate situation. (I think of it as Tolkien's "eagle ex machina.") He deliberately made this a repeated pattern to symbolize a kind of divine grace; I suspect the germ of the idea is in the biblical words, "I carried you on eagle's wings" (Exodus 19:4). But Tolkien did prefer to employ the device sparingly, and he had already used the eagles once in this story to airlift the maimed Beren and exhausted Lúthien away from Morgoth's fortress. Also, by deciding against this motif, he thus preserved the uniqueness of Eärendil the Mariner[7] as the only messenger from Middle-earth to reach the Valar.

It is said in *The Silmarillion* that

> Among the tales of sorrow and of ruin that have come down to us from those days there are yet some in which amid weeping there is joy and under the shadow of death light that endures. And of these histories most fair still in the ears of the Elves is the tale of Beren and Lúthien.
>
> (*Silm*, 195)

Now Aragorn says, "So it is that Lúthien Tinúviel alone of the Elf-kindred has died indeed and left the world, and they have lost her whom they most loved" (*FR*, 206). But that tragic observation is the only knowledge possible from the perspective of a pre-Christian world such as Middle-earth. From Tolkien's Christian viewpoint, Beren and Lúthien, who died once but were restored by the Valar, to live again for a time but receive death a final time as the Gift of the One to Men, would have gone on to a true immortality with God.

To return again to J. R. R. Tolkien's letter in 1972 with which we began this chapter, he wrote to his son Christopher that he had decided to have the name "Lúthien" inscribed below Edith's on her tombstone, "which says for me more than a multitude of words: for she was, and knew she was, my Lúthien … . I hope none of my children will feel that the use of this name is a sentimental fancy" (*Letters*, 420). Evidently they all understood the significance. When, a year after this, Tolkien's body was buried with that of his wife and his own name added to the grave marker, they had the name "Beren" added to the inscription as a suitably succinct mythic correlative of a love that lasted a lifetime and would endure beyond the grave.

Notes

This chapter was originally presented as a paper at the Nineteenth International Conference on the Fantastic in the Arts, Ft. Lauderdale, FL, March 1998.

1 Carpenter, *Biography*, 97. Or so the Tolkiens remembered it, but this seems to have taken on a mythological status of its own. I am indebted to Christina Scull for pointing out to me that these flowers would not have been in bloom in November, and that the weather in Yorkshire at that season would have been too cold to be conducive to dancing outdoors. It seems likely that the Tolkien family memory was conflating events from different times.

2 As Carpenter avers (*Biography*, 97), and as many others have noticed.

3 See Christopher Tolkien's discussion of the date of composition in his "Note on the Order of the Tales," in Tolkien, *BLT* 1, 202–4.

4 Shippey has an excellent discussion of the textual versions in the second edition of *The Road to Middle-earth*, 277–80.

5 Arwen is the daughter of Elrond, son of Eärendil and of Elwing, daughter of Dior, son of Lúthien and Beren. Aragorn is many more generations removed, being descended from Elrond's brother Elros, founder of the line of the kings of Númenor.

6 "Star-mantled" is another translation that Tolkien considered.

7 Husband of Lúthien's granddaughter Elwing and inheritor of the Silmaril recovered by Beren and Lúthien.

References

Abbott, Joe. "Tolkien's Monsters: Concept and Function in *The Lord of the Rings*, Part II: Shelob the Great." *Mythlore* 16, no. 2 (winter 1989): 40–47.

Aciman, André, ed. *Letters of Transit: Reflections on Exile, Identity, Language, and Loss*. New York: New York Press, 1999.

Ælfric, Abbot of Eynsham. *Exameron Anglice; or, The Old English Hexameron*. Ed. with an introduction, a collation of all the manuscripts, a modern English translation, parallel passages from the other works of Ælfric, and notes on the sources by S. J. Crawford. 1921; rpt., Darmstadt: Wissenschaftliche Buchgesellschaft, 1968.

Alcuin of York. *Interrogationes Sigeuulfi in Genesin. Patrologia Latina* 100: 515–66.

Ambrose. *Hexameron, Paradise and Cain and Abel*. Trans. John J. Savage. Fathers of the Church, 42. New York: Fathers of the Church, 1961.

Anderson, O. S. "*The Seafarer*: An Interpretation." *Humanistiska Vetenskapssarmfundets I Lund Ärsberättelse* 1 (1937–38): 1–49.

Armstrong, Helen. "Good Guys, Bad Guys, Fantasy and Reality." In Reynolds and Good-Knight. 247–52.

Augustine. *Confessiones*. Ed. Pius Knöll. Bibliotheca Scriptorum Graecorum et Romanorum. Leipzig: B. G. Teubner, 1915.

——. *Confessions*. Trans. with an introduction R. S. Pine-Coffin. Baltimore, MD: Penguin, 1961.

——. *De Civitate Dei, Libri I–XXII. Aurelii Augustini opera*, pars 14, 1,2. Ed. Corpus Christianorum, Series Latina 47. Turnhout: Brepols, 1955.

——. *De Genesi ad litteram imperfectus liber* and *De Genesi ad litteram libri duodecim*. Ed. Josephus Zycha. Corpus Scriptorum Ecclesiasticorum Latinorum 28,1. Vienna and Prague: F. Tempsky: C. Freytag, 1894.

——. *The Literal Meaning of Genesis*. Trans. and annot. John Hammond Taylor. 2 vols. Ancient Christian Writers, 41 and 42. New York: Newman Press, 1982.

——. *De Genesi contra Manicheos. Patrologia Latina* 34: 173–220.

——. *Enarratio in Psalmum CXXV. Aurelii Augustini opera,* pars 10. Ed. Corpus Christianorum, Series Latina 40. Turnhout: Brepols, 1956.

——. *Epistulae*. Ed. Al. Golbacher. Corpus Scriptorum Ecclesiasticorum Latinorum 44. Vienna and Prague: F. Tempsky; Leipzig: C Freytag, 1904.

——. Vol. 4 of *Letters*. Trans. Wilfrid Parsons. Fathers of the Church, Writings of Saint Augustine, 12. New York: Fathers of the Church, 1955.

Austin, J. L. *How to Do Things with Words*. Cambridge, MA: Harvard University Press, 1975.

——. *Philosophical Papers*. 2nd ed. London: Oxford University Press, 1970.

Ayçoberry, Pierre. *The Social History of the Third Reich, 19331945* . Trans. Janet Lloyd. New York: New Press, 1999.

Bader, Françoise. "Les noms des Aryens: Ethniques et expansion." In *Langues indo-européenes* . Paris: CNRS Editions, 1994. 65–83

Barber, Charles C. *An Old High German Reader.* Oxford: Basil Blackwell, 1964.

Barfield, Owen. *History in English Words.* New York: Doran, 1926.

——. *Owen Barfield on C. S. Lewis.* Middletown, CT: Wesleyan University Press, 1989.

——. *Poetic Diction.* London: Faber & Gwyer, 1928.

Barman, Jean. *Sojourning Sisters: The Lives and Letters of Jessie and Annie McQueen* (Toronto: University of Toronto Press, 2002).

Barnfield, Marie. "Celtic Influences on the History of the First Age." *Mallorn* 28 (September 1991): 2–6

——. "Túrin Turambar and the Tale of the Fosterling." *Mallorn* 31 (1994): 29–36.

Barthes, Roland. "*To Write*: An Intransitive Verb?" In *Structuralist Controversy*, ed. Richard Macksey and Eugenio Donato. Baltimore, MD: Johns Hopkins University Press, 1972, 134–45.

Basadonna, Giorgio. *Litanie Lauretane.* Città del Vaticano: Libreria Editrice Vaticana, 1997.

Basil. *Homilien zum Hexaemeron.* Ed. Emmanuel Amand de Mendieta and Stig Y. Rudberg. Die griechischen christlichen Schriftsteller der ersten Jahrhunderte, n.s., 2. Berlin: Akademie Verlag, 1997.

——. *Homilies on the Hexameron* from *Exegetic Homilies.* Trans. Agnes Clare Way. Fathers of the Church, 46. Washington, D.C.: Catholic University of America Press, 1963.

Battarbee, K. J., ed. *Scholarship and Fantasy: Proceedings of the Tolkien Phenomenon, May 1992, Turku, Finland.* Anglicana Turkuensia, 12. Turku: University of Turku, 1993.

Bede, the Venerable. *In Genesim. (Libri quatuor in principium genesis usque ad nativitatem Isaac et electionem Ismahelis adnotationum).* Ed. Ch. W. Jones. *Bedae Opera*, pars II, *Opera Exegetica*, 1. Corpus Christianorum, Series Latina 118a. Turnhout: Brepols Press, 1967.

Benjamin, Walter. *The Origins of German Tragic Drama.* Trans. John Osborne. London, New York: Verso, 1977.

Benson, Larry D. *et al.*, eds. *The Riverside Chaucer.* 3rd ed. Boston: Houghton Mifflin, 1987.

Benveniste, Emile. "Active and Middle Voice in the Verb." In *Problems in General Linguistics*, trans. Mary Elizabeth Meek. Miami, FA: University of Miami Press, 1971.

——. *Indo-European Language and Society.* Trans. Elizabeth Palmer. Coral Gables, FA: University of Miami Press, 1973.

Beowulf. See Donaldson; Klaeber.

Berger, Thomas. *Little Big Man.* New York: Dial, 1964.

Berlin, Isaiah. *Essays on J. L. Austin.* London: Oxford University Press, 1973.

Bernheimer, Richard. *Wild Men in the Middle Ages.* Cambridge, MA: Harvard University Press, 1952.

Betteridge, William Edwin. "Tolkien's New Mythology." *Mythlore* 16, no. 4 (1990): 27–31.

Biblia Sacra iuxta Vulgatam Versionem. Ed. Robert Weber with B. Fischer, J. Gribomont, H. F. D. Sparks, and W. Thiele. 2 vols. Stuttgart, 1969; 4th ed., rev. R. Gryson, 1994.

Biblia Sacra iuxta Vulgatam Clementinam. Ed. Alberto Colunga and Laurentio Turrado. 4th ed. Madrid: Biblioteca de Autores Cristianos, 1965.

The Holy Bible Translated from the Latin Vulgate (Douay Rheims Version). 1899. Rpt. Rockford, IL: Tan Books, 1971.

Blackwelder, Richard. *A Tolkien Thesaurus.* New York: Garland Publishing, 1990.

Blake, William. *Blake's Complete Writings* . Ed. Geoffrey Keynes. London: Oxford University Press, 1972.

Blisset, William. "Despots of the Rings." *South Atlantic Quarterly* 58 (1959): 448–56.

Bloom, Harold, ed. *Modern Critical Interpretations: J. R. R. Tolkien's "Lord of the Rings*." Philadelphia, PA: Chelsea House, 2000.

Boenig, Robert. "Tolkien and Old Germanic Ethics." *Mythlore* 13, no. 2 (winter 1986): 9–12.

Boethius. *De institutione musica*. Excerpted in Strunk.

Bonjour, Adrien. *The Digressions in "Beowulf."* Medium Aevum Monographs, 5. Oxford: Basil Blackwell, 1950.

Boyle, Andrew, ed. *Everyman Encyclopedia*. London: J. M. Dent & Sons, 1913.

Branch, M. A. Introduction to *Kalevala*, comp. Elias Lönnrot and trans. W. F. Kirby. London: Athlone Press, 1985.

Brewer, Derek. E-mail to Andrew Lazo. 16 April 2000.

Broadwell, Elizabeth. "Esse and Narn: Name, Identity and Narrative in the 'Tale of Túrin Turambar.' " *Mythlore* 17, no. 2 (1990): 34–44.

Brooke-Rose, Christine. *A Rhetoric of the Unreal: Studies in Narrative and Structure Especially of the Fantastic*. Cambridge: Cambridge University Press, 1981.

Bryce, Lynn. "The Influence of Scandinavian Mythology on the Works of J. R. R. Tolkien." *Edda: Nordisk Tidsskrift for Literaturforskning* 2 (1983): 113–19.

Buck-Morss, Susan. *The Dialectics of Seeing*. Cambridge, MA; London: MIT Press, 1991.

Burns, Marjorie. "Gandalf and Odin." In Flieger and Hostetter. 219–32.

Byock, Jesse L. trans. *The Saga of the Volsungs*. Harmondsworth: Penguin, 1990.

Campbell, A. *Old English Grammar*. Oxford: Clarendon Press, 1959.

Campbell, John Francis. *Popular Tales of the West Highlands*. 4 vols. Edinburgh, 1860–2. Reissued London, 1889.

Carlen, Claudia, ed. *The Papal Encyclicals*. Wilmington, NC: McGrath Publishing Co., 1981.

Carnell, Corbin Scott. *Bright Shadow of Reality: C. S. Lewis and the Feeling Intellect*. Grand Rapids, MI: William B. Eerdmans, 1974.

Carpenter, H. *The Inklings: C. S. Lewis, J. R. R. Tolkien, Charles Williams and Their Friends*. Boston: Houghton Mifflin, 1978.

——. *Tolkien: A Biography*. London: George Allen & Unwin; Boston: Houghton Mifflin, 1977.

Carter, Angela. "The Better to Eat You With." In *Shaking a Leg: Collected Writings*. New York, London: Penguin Books, 1998. 451–54.

Catholic University of America. *New Catholic Encyclopedia*. Detroit, MI: Gale Group, 2001.

Chambers, R. W., M. Förster, and R. Flower, eds. *The Exeter Book of Old English Poetry*. London: Percy Lund, Humphries, 1933.

Chance, Jane. "Grendel's Mother as Epic Anti-type of the Virgin and the Queen." In *Interpretations of Beowulf: A Critical Anthology*, ed. R. D. Fulk. Bloomington: Indiana University Press, 1991. 251–63.

——. "*The Lord of the Rings*": *The Mythology of Power*. New York: Twayne/Maxwell Macmillan, 1992. Rev. ed., Lexington: University Press of Kentucky, 2001.

Chance (Nitzsche), Jane. *Tolkien's Art: A Mythology for England*. London: Macmillan, 1979; New York: St. Martin's, 1980. Rev. ed., Lexington: University Press of Kentucky, 2001.

Chance, Jane and David Day. "Medievalism in Tolkien: Two Decades of Criticism in Review." In *Medievalism: Inklings and Others* (special issue). *Studies in Medievalism* 3, no. 3 (1991): 375–88.

Cheah, Pheng. "Mattering." *Diacritics* 26, no. 1 (1996): 108–39.

Child, Francis James. *The English and Scottish Popular Ballads.* 5 vols. New York: Cooper Square Publishers, Inc., 1962.

Chrétien de Troyes. *Le Chevalier au Lion (Yvain).* In *Les Romans de Chrétien de Troyes*, Édités d'Après la Copie De Guiot. Paris: Librairie Honoré Champion, 1968.

——. *Yvain, or The Knight with the Lion.* Trans. Ruth Harwood Cline. Athens: University of Georgia Press, 1984.

Christensen, Bonniejean. "Gollum's Character Transformation in *The Hobbit.*" In *A Tolkien Compass*, ed. Jared Lobdell. La Salle, IL: Open Court, 1975. 9–28.

Clanchy, M. T. "Remembering the Past and the Good Old Law." *History* 55 (1970): 165–76.

Clark, George. "J. R. R. Tolkien and the True Hero." In Clark and Timmons. 39–52.

Clark, George and Daniel Timmons, eds. *J. R. R. Tolkien and his Literary Resonances: Views of Middle-earth.* Contributions to the Study of Science Fiction and Fantasy, vol. 89. Westport, CT and London: Greenwood Press, 2000.

Cockayne, Thomas Oswald. *The Shrine.* London: Williams & Norgate, 1864–70. Microfilm.

Crabbe, Katharyn W. *J. R. R. Tolkien.* Rev. and exp. ed., New York: Frederick Ungar, 1988.

Cross, J. "On the Allegory in *The Seafarer.*" *Medium Ævum* 28 (1959): 104–6.

Crowe, Edith L. "Power in Arda: Sources, Uses, and Misuses." In Reynolds and GoodKnight. 272–77.

Curry, Patrick. " 'Less Noise and More Green': Tolkien's Ideology for England." In Reynolds and GoodKnight. 126–38.

Curtin, Jeremiah. *Myths and Folklore of Ireland.* Boston, 1899; rpt. New York: Weathervane Books, 1975.

Damico, Helen. *"Beowulf"'s Wealhtheow and the Valkyrie Tradition.* Madison: University of Wisconsin Press, 1984.

——. "The Valkyrie Reflex in Old English Literature." In *New Readings on Women in Old English Literature*, ed. Helen Damico and Alexandra Hennessey Olsen. Bloomington: Indiana University Press, 1990, 176–90.

d'Ardenne, S. R. T. O. [S. T .R. O.] "An Edition of Þe Liflade ant te Passiun of Seinte Iuliene (MS Bodley 34)." B.Litt. diss. University of Oxford, 1933. Dir. J. R. R. Tolkien.

——. ed. *An Edition of Þe Liflade ant te Passiun of Seinte Iuliene.* Liège and Paris: Facultéde philosophie et letters; E. Droz, 1936. Rpt, as by S. R. T. O. d'Ardenne, as: *Þe Liflade ant te Passiun of Seinte Iuliene.* Early English Text Society, 248. London: Early English Text Society and Oxford University Press, 1961.

d'Ardenne, S. R. T. O. and E. J. Dobson, eds. *Seinte Katerine. Re-edited from MS Bodley 34 and the Other Manuscripts.* Early English Text Society, SS 7. London: Early English Text Society and Oxford University Press, 1981.

Dasent, George. *Popular Tales from the Norse.* With an introductory essay on the origin and diffusion of popular tales. 2nd ed., enlarged. Edinburgh: Edmonton and Douglas, 1859.

Davidson, Hilda Ellis. *Roles of the Northern Goddess.* London: Routledge, 1998.

Davis, Norman and C. L. Wrenn. *English and Medieval Studies Presented to J. R. R. Tolkien on the Occasion of his Seventieth Birthday.* London: George Allen & Unwin, 1962.

de Koster, Katie, ed. *Readings on J. R. R. Tolkien.* Greenhaven Press Literary Companion to British Authors. San Diego, CA: Greenhaven Press, 2000.

Dobbie, Elliott Van Kirk, ed. *The Anglo-Saxon Minor Poems.* New York: Columbia University Press; London: Routledge and Kegan Paul, 1942.

Dockray-Miller, Mary. "The Masculine Queen of *Beowulf.*" *Women and Language* 21, no. 2 (fall 1998): 31–38.

——. *Motherhood and Mothering in Anglo-Saxon England.* New York: St. Martin's, 2000.

Dodds, David Llewellyn. "Technology and Sub-creation: Tolkien's Alternative to the Dominant Worldview." In Battarbee. 165–86.

Donaldson, E. T., trans. *Beowulf*, ed. Joseph Tuso. New York: Norton, 1975.

Dorson, Richard M. *The British Folklorists: A History*. 2 vols. Chicago, IL: University of Chicago Press, 1968.

——, ed. *Peasant Customs and Savage Myths: Selections from the British Folklorists*. 2 vols. Chicago, IL: University of Chicago Press, 1968.

Dunning, T. P. and A. J. Bliss. *The Wanderer*. London: Methuen, 1969.

Dunsire, Brian. "… And *The Mabinogion*… ." *Amon Hen* 54 (February 1982): 7–10.

Duriez, Colin. *The C. S. Lewis Encyclopedia*. Wheaton, IL: Crossway Books, 2000.

——. "Sub-creation and Tolkien's Theology of Story." In Battarbee. 133–50.

——. *The Tolkien and Middle Earth Handbook*. Tunbridge Wells: Baker Book House, 1992.

——. "Tolkien and the Other Inklings." In Reynolds and GoodKnight. 360–63.

Eagleton, Terry. *The Ideology of Aesthetic*. Oxford: Basil Blackwell, 1990.

Ehrismann, G. "Religionsgeschichtliche Beiträge zum germanischen Frühchristentum." *Beiträge zur Geschichte der Deutschen Sprache und Literatur* 35 (1909): 209–39.

Evans, Jonathan. "The Dragon-lore of Middle-earth: Tolkien and Old English and Old Norse Traditions." In Clark and Timmons. 21–38.

——. "Medieval Dragon-lore in Middle-earth." *Journal of the Fantastic in the Arts* 9 (1998): 175–91.

Evans, Robley. "Tolkien's World-creation: Degenerative Recurrence." *Mythlore* 14, no. 1 (1987): 4–8, 47.

Felton, D. *Haunted Greece and Rome: Ghost Stories from Classical Antiquity*. Austin: University of Texas Press, 1999.

Fenwick, Mac. "Breastplates of Silk: Homeric Women in *The Lord of the Rings*." *Mythlore* 21, no. 3 (summer 1996): 17–23.

Fifield, Merle. "Fantasy in and for the Sixties." *English Journal* 55, October (1966): 841–44.

Fish, Stanley. *Surprised by Sin: The Reader in Paradise Lost*. 2nd ed. Cambridge, MA: Harvard University Press, 1997.

——. "Why We Can't All Just Get Along." *First Things* 60 (February 1996): 18–26.

Flieger, Verlyn. "The Footsteps of Ælfwine." In Flieger and Hostetter. 183–98

——. "Naming the Unnameable: The Neoplatonic 'One' in Tolkien's *Silmarillion*." In *Diakonia: Studies in Honor of Robert T. Meyer*, ed. Thomas Halton and Joseph P. Williman. Washington, DC: Catholic University of America Press, 1986. 127–32.

——. *A Question of Time: J. R. R. Tolkien's Road to Faërie*. Kent, OH: Kent State University Press, 1997.

——. *Splintered Light: Logos and Language in Tolkien's World*. Grand Rapids, MI: Eerdmans, 1983.

Flieger, Verlyn and Carl F. Hostetter. *Tolkien's Legendarium: Essays on "The History of Middle-earth."* Contributions to the Study of Science Fiction and Fantasy, 86. Westport, CT and London: Greenwood Press, 2000.

Ford, Paul F. *Companion to Narnia*. New York: HarperCollins, 1994.

Frederick, Candace and Sam McBride. *Women among the Inklings: Gender in C. S. Lewis, J. R. R. Tolkien, and Charles Williams*. Contributions in Women's Studies, vol. 191. Westport, CT: Greenwood Press, 2001.

Fuller, Edmund. "The Lord of the Hobbits: J. R. R. Tolkien." In *Books with Men behind Them*. New York: Random House, 1962. 159–96.

Furberg, Mats. *Saying and Meaning*. Totowa, NJ: Rowman and Littlefield, 1971.

Gallin, Alice. *Midwives to Nazism: University Professors in Weimar Germany, 1925–1933.* Macon, GA: Mercer University Press, 1986.

Geoffrey of Monmouth. *Life of Merlin.* Cardiff: University of Wales Press, 1973.

Gerald of Wales. [Giraldus Cambrensis.] *Expugnatio Hibernica.* Ed. and trans. A. B. Scott and F. X. Martin. Dublin: Royal Irish Academy, 1978.

Giddings, Robert, ed. *J. R. R. Tolkien: This Far Land.* London: Vision; Totowa, NJ: Barnes and Noble, 1983.

Gilson, Etienne. *History of Christian Philosophy in the Middle Ages.* New York: Random House, 1955.

Glenmore, Josephine Stands In Timber, and Wayne Leman. *Cheyenne Topical Dictionary.* Busby, MT: Cheyenne Translation Project, 1984.

Godwin, Joscelyn. *Harmonies of Heaven and Earth: The Spiritual Dimension of Music from Antiquity to the Avant-Garde.* London: Thames and Hudson, 1987.

Goffar, Janine. *The C. S. Lewis Index.* Wheaton, IL: Crossway Books, 1995.

Gordon, E. V. "A Ballad of Tristram." *Gryphon* 4, no. 3 (December 1922): 94. Rpt. in *Leeds University Verse, 1914–1924*, comp. by the English School Association. Leeds: Swan Press, 1924. 23–26.

——. "The Date of Æthelred's Treaty with the Vikings: Olaf Trygvasson and the Battle of Maldon." *Modern Language Review* 32, no. 1 (January 1937): 24–32.

——. "The Date of Hofuðlausn." *Proceedings of the Leeds Philosophical and Literary Society* 1 (1925): 12–14.

——. *An Introduction to Old Norse.* Oxford: Clarendon Press, 1927. 2nd ed., rev. by A. R. Taylor. Oxford: Clarendon Press, 1957.

——. Introduction to *The Saga of Hrolf Kraki.* Trans. Stella M. Mills. Oxford: Basil Blackwell, 1933. vii–xii.

——. "The Lay of Attila." [Translation from the Elder Edda of *Atlakviđa.*] *Microcosm* 7, no. 4 (winter 1922): 22–25.

——. "The Lay of Thrym." [Translation from the Elder Edda of *Thrymskviđa.*] *Microcosm* 7, no. 3 (autumn 1922): 3–5.

——. "The Lay of Wayland." [Translation from the Elder Edda of *Volundarkviđa.*] *Microcosm* 8, no. 3 (autumn 1923): 20–23.

——. "Old English Studies" and "Middle English." In *The Year's Work in English Studies, 1924*, ed. F. S. Boas and C. H. Herford. London: Oxford University Press, 1926. 66–77, 78–98.

——. "Old English Studies." In *The Year's Work in English Studies, 1925*, ed. F. S. Boas and C. H. Herford. London: Oxford University Press, 1927. 67–82.

——. "On *Hrafnkels Saga Freysgoða.*" *Medium Ævum* 8, no. 1 (February 1939): 1–32.

——. "Philology: General Works." In *The Year's Work in English Studies, 1922*, ed. Sir Sidney Lee and F. S. Boas. London: Oxford University Press, 1923. 18–24.

——. Review of *Doctrinal Terms in Ælfric's Homilies*, by Nelius O. Halvorson. *Review of English Studies* 9, no. 33 (January 1933): 87–89.

——. Review of *Egils saga Skalla-Grímssonar*, ed. Sigurður Nordal; *Laxdœla saga, Halldórs Þættir Snorrasonar, Stúfs Þáttr*, ed. by Einar and lafur Sveinsson; and *Eyrbyggja saga, Brands Þáttr Orva; Eiríks saga Rauða, Grœnlendinga saga, Grœnlendinga Þáttr*, ed. Einar Ólafur Sveinsson and Matthías Þorðarson. *Medium Ævum* 4, no. 3 (September 1935): 209–18.

——. Review of *English Place-names in –ing of Scandinavian Origin, Some English Place-name Etymologies*, and *Some English Place-names in a French Garb* by R. E. Zachrisson. *Modern Language Review* 21, no. 1 (January 1926): 76–77.

——. Review of *Nordiska Ortnamn i språklig och saklig Belysning* by Jöran Sahlgren. *Modern Language Review* 20, no. 4 (October 1925): 500.

——. Review of *An Old Icelandic Medical Miscellany*, ed. Henning Larsen. *Medium Ævum* 2, no. 1 (February 1933): 74–81.

——. Review of *Om Anglo-Frisiske, Heruliske og Burgundiske Indskrifter med de Ældre Runer fra Nordens tre Riger* by Th. Jørgensen. *Review of English Studies* 3, no. 11 (July 1927): 352–55.

——. Reviews of *Geoffrey Chaucer* by John Livingston Lowes; of *Seinte Marherete, Þe Meiden ant Martyr*, ed. Francis M. Mack; and *An Edition of Þe Liflade ant te Passiun of Seinte Iuliene*, by S. T. R. O. d'Ardenne. *Medium Ævum* 6, no. 2 (June 1937): 125–30, 131–43.

——. Reviews of *The Prose Edda*, trans. A. C. Brodeur; *The Arnamagnean Manuscript*, ed. G. T. Flom; *The Language of the Konungs Skuggsja* by G. T. Flom; *The King's Mirror*, trans. L. M. Larson; *The Place Names of Lancashire* by Eilert Ekwall; *The Poetic Edda*, trans. Henry Adams Bellows; *English Place-names in –ing* by Eilert Ekwall; and *Introduction to the Survey of English Place-names*, ed. A. Mawer and F. M. Stenton. *Year-Book of the Viking Club* 6 (1924): 55–58, 91–95, 97–101, 104–7, 107–9, 115–19.

——. "Scandinavian Influence in Yorkshire Dialects." *Transactions of the Yorkshire Dialect Society* 4, no. 24 (1923): 5–22.

——. "Scarborough and Flamborough." *Acta Philologica Scandinavica* 1 (1926–27): 320–23.

——. "A Skald's Impromptu" and "They Sat There." In *A Northern Venture: Verses by Members of the Leeds University English School Association*. Leeds: Swan Press, 1923. 6–7.

——. "Su Klukka Heljar" and "When I'm Dead." In *Songs for the Philologists*, by J. R. R. Tolkien, E. V. Gordon and others. London: Department of English at University College, 1936. 16, 26.

——. "The Traditions of *Kormáks Saga*." In *Transactions of the Philological Society, 1931–32* London: David Nutt, 1933. 39–67.

——. "The University of Iceland." *Universities Review* 5 (1932): 26–30.

——. "*Wealhþeow* and Related Names." *Medium Ævum* 4, no. 3 (September 1935): 169–75.

——., ed. *The Battle of Maldon*. London: Methuen, 1937. Rev. ed., with a supplement by D. G. Scragg. Manchester: Manchester University Press, 1976.

——, ed. *Pearl*. Oxford: Clarendon Press, 1953.

——, trans. *Scandinavian Archaeology* by Haakon Shetelig and Hjalmar Falk. Oxford: Clarendon Press, 1937.

Gordon, E. V. and C. T. Onions. "Notes on the Text and Interpretation of *Pearl*." *Medium Ævum* 1, no. 2 (September 1932): 126–36; 2, no. 3 (October 1933): 165–88.

Gordon, E. V. and A. H. Smith. "The River Names of Yorkshire." *Transactions of the Yorkshire Dialect Society* 4, no. 26 (1925): 5–30.

Gordon, E. V. and J. R. R. Tolkien, eds. *Sir Gawain and the Green Knight*. See Tolkien, J. R. R.

Gordon, E. V. and Eugène Vinaver. "New Light on the Text of the Alliterative *Morte Arthure*." *Medium Ævum* 6, no. 2 (June 1937): 81–98.

Gordon, Ida L. *The Double Sorrow of Troilus: A Study of Ambiguities in "Troilus and Criseyde."* Oxford: Clarendon Press, 1970.

——. Letter [Unpublished] to John D. Rateliff, April 20, 1982.

——. "The Murder of Thorgrímr in *Gíslasaga Súrssonar*." *Medium Ævum* 3, no. 2 (June 1934): 79–94.

——. "The Narrative Function of Irony in Chaucer's *Troilus and Criseyde*." In *Medieval Miscellany Presented to Eugène Vinaver*, ed. F. Whitehead, A. H. Diverres, and F. E. Sutcliffe. Manchester: Manchester University Press, 1965. 146–56.

——. "Oral Tradition and the Sagas of Poets." In *Studia centenalia in honorem memoriae Benedikt S. Thorarinson*, ed. B. S. Benedikz. Reykjavik: Typis Isafoldianis, 1961. 69–76.

——. "The Origins of *Gíslasaga*." *Saga-Book* 13, pt. 3 (1949–50): 183–205.

——. "Traditional Themes in *The Wanderer* and *The Seafarer*." *Review of English Studies*, n.s., 5 (1954): 225–35.

——, ed. *The Seafarer*. London: Methuen, 1960. New ed., with bibliography by Mary Clayton. Exeter: University of Exeter Press, 1996.

——, trans. *The Dream of the Rood*. Rosemarkie: Groam House Museum, 1993.

Goselin, Peter Damien. "Two Faces of Eve: Galadriel and Shelob as Anima Figures." *Mythlore* 6, no. 3 (summer 1979): 3–4.

Greenfield, Stanley. *Hero and Exile*. London: Hambledon Press, 1989.

Greenman, David. "*The Silmarillion* as Aristotelian Epic-Tragedy." *Mythlore* 14, no. 3 (1988): 20–25.

Grimm, Jacob and Wilhelm. *Kinder- und Hausmärchen*. 3 vols. Berlin: 1812–22.

Gross, John. *The Oxford Book of Aphorisms*. New York: Oxford University Press, 1983.

Grotta-Kurska, Daniel. *J. R. R. Tolkien: Architect of Middle Earth, A Biography*. Ed. Frank Wilson. Philadelphia, PA: Running Press, 1976.

Grunberger, Richard. *The Twelve-year Reich: A Social History of Nazi Germany, 1933–1945*. New York: Da Capo Press, 1971, 1995.

Gutman, Robert. *Richard Wagner: The Man, his Mind, and his Music*. San Diego, CA, New York, and London: Harcourt Brace Jovanovich, 1968, 1990.

Hall, Robert A., Jr. "Tolkien's Hobbit Tetralogy as 'Anti-Nibelungen.'" *Western Humanities Review* 32 (1978): 351–59.

Hammond, Wayne G. "A Critical Response to Tolkien's Fiction." In Reynolds and GoodKnight. 226–32.

Hammond, Wayne G., with Douglas A. Anderson. *J. R. R. Tolkien: A Descriptive Bibliography*. Winchester, U.K. St. Paul's Bibliographies; New Castle, DE: Oak Knoll Books, 1993.

Hammond, Wayne G. and Christina Scull. *J. R. R. Tolkien: Artist and Illustrator*. London: HarperCollins, 1995.

Harvey, David. *The Song of Middle-earth*. London: George Allen & Unwin, 1985.

Heaney, Seamus, trans. *Beowulf*. London: Faber and Faber, 1999.

Helms, Randel. *Tolkien and the Silmarils*. Boston: Houghton Mifflin, 1981.

——. *Tolkien's World*. Boston: Houghton Mifflin, 1974.

Herbenus, Matthaeus. *Herbeni Traiectensis De natura cantus ac miraculis vocis*, ed. Joseph Smits van Waesberghe. Cologne: Arno, 1957. Quoted in Joscelyn Godwin, ed., *Music, Mysticism and Magic: A Sourcebook*. London: Routledge & Kegan Paul, 1986. 123–26.

Herrnstein-Smith, Barbara. *Contingencies of Value: Alternative Perspectives for Critical Theory*. Cambridge, MA: Harvard University Press, 1988.

Hillegas, Mark R., ed. *Shadows of Imagination: The Fantasies of C. S. Lewis, J. R. R. Tolkien, and Charles Williams*. Carbondale: Southern Illinois University Press; London and Amsterdam: Feffer and Simons, 1969.

Hitler, Adolf, *Mein Kampf*. London: Hutchinson, 1985.

Holder-Egger, O., ed. *De fundatione monasterii S. Fidis Sletstatenis*. XV-s S. S. Hanover: M. G. H., 1888.

Hood, Gwyneth E. "Sauron as Gorgon and Basilisk." *Seven* 8 (1987): 59–71.

Hooper, Walter. *C. S. Lewis: Companion and Guide*. San Francisco, CA: HarperSanFrancisco, 1996.

Hope, Michael, comp. *Index to the Proceedings of the British Academy: Vols. 1–63*. London: Oxford University Press, 1980.

Hopkins, Lisa. "Female Authority Figures in the Works of Tolkien, C. S. Lewis and Charles Williams." In Reynolds and GoodKnight. 364–66.

Hostetter, Carl F. "Over Middle-earth Sent unto Men," *Mythlore* 65 (spring): 5–8.

Hostetter, Carl F. and Arden Smith. "A Mythology for England?" In Reynolds and Good-Knight. 281–90.

Housden, Martyn. *Hitler, Study of a Revolutionary*. London and New York: Routledge, 2000.

Hughes, Daniel, "Pieties and Giant Forms in *The Lord of the Rings*." In Hillegas. 81–96.

Hyde, Paul Nolan. "Linguistic Techniques Used in Character Development in the Works of J. R. R. Tolkien." Ph.D. diss., Purdue University, 1982.

——. "Mythos: The Daughter of Mountains, the Mother of Pearls." *Mythlore* 16, no. 1 (1989): 27–33.

Isaacs, Neil D. and Rose A. Zimbardo, eds. *Tolkien and the Critics: Essays on J. R. R. Tolkien's "The Lord of the Rings."* Notre Dame, IN: University of Notre Dame Press, 1968.

Jay, Martin. *The Dialectical Imagination: A History of the Frankfurt School and the Institute of Social Research, 1923–1950.* Weimar and Now, 10. 1973; rpt. Berkeley, Los Angeles, and London: University of California Press, 1996.

Jochens, Jenny. *Old Norse Images of Women.* Philadelphia: University of Pennsylvania Press, 1996.

Joly, M. A. *De la condition des vilains au Moyen Age d'après les fabliaux en Mémoires de l'Académie nationale des sciences, arts, et belles-lettres de Caen, 1882.* Caen: Académie nationale des sciences, arts et belles-lettres de Caen, 1882.

Jónsson, Guðni, ed. *Hrólfs saga Gautrekssonar.* In *Fornaldar sögur Norðurlanda.* Vol. 4. 1954. Rpt., Reykjavik: Íslendinga-sagnaútgáfan, 1981.

——. *Völsunga saga.* In *Fornaldar sögur Norðurlanda.* Vol. 1. 1954. Rpt., Reykjavik: Íslendinga-sagnaútgáfan, 1981.

Jungman, Josef, A. *The Mass of the Roman Rite.* Trans. Francis Brunner. New York: Benzinger, 1951–55.

Keightley, Thomas. *The Fairy Mythology*, new ed. revised and enlarged. London: George Bell & Sons, 1882.

Kennedy, Charles W. *The Earliest English Poetry.* London: Oxford University Press, 1943.

——. *The Old English Elegies.* Princeton, NJ: Princeton University Press, 1936.

Kenrick, Peter. *The Holy House of Loretto; or, An Examination of the Historical Evidence of its Miraculous Translation.* Philadelphia, PA: E. Cummiskey, 1841.

Ker, Neil R. *Catalogue of Manuscripts Containing Anglo-Saxon.* Oxford: Clarendon Press, 1957.

Kershaw, Nora, ed. *Anglo-Saxon and Norse Poems.* Cambridge: Cambridge University Press, 1922.

Kilby, Clyde S. *Tolkien and the Silmarillion.* Wheaton, IL: Harold Shaw, 1976.

——. "Traditional Themes in *The Wanderer* and *The Seafarer.*" *Review of English Studies*, n.s., 5 (1954): 225–35.

Klaeber, Fr., ed. *"Beowulf" and "The Fight at Finnsburg."* 3rd ed., with 1st and 2nd supplements. Lexington, MA: D. C. Heath, 1950.

Knowles, Sebastian D. G. *A Purgatorial Flame: Seven British Writers in the Second World War.* Philadelphia: University of Pennsylvania Press, 1990.

Kocher, Paul H. *Master of Middle-earth: The Fiction of J. R. R. Tolkien.* New York: Ballantine, 1972.

——. *A Reader's Guide to "The Silmarillion."* Boston: Houghton Mifflin, 1980.

Köhler, Joachim. *Wagner as Hitler: The Prophet and his Disciple*, trans. Ronald Taylor. Malden, MA; Cambridge, U.K.: Polity Press, 2000.

Krapp, G. P. and E. V. K. Dobbie, eds. *The Exeter Book.* Anglo-Saxon Poetic Records 3. New York: Columbia University Press, 1936.

Kvingedal, Helge. "Utviklingen av historien om Lúthien og Beren." *Angerthas* 39 (October 1995): 16–18.

Lang, Andrew. *Custom and Myth*. London: Longmans, Green & Co., 1893.

——. "Mythology and Fairy Tales." *Fortnightly Review* 19 (May 1873): 618–31.

Lawlor, John. *C. S. Lewis: Memories and Reflections*. Dallas, TX: Spence, 1998; Westport, CT and London: Greenwood Press, 2000.

Lawrence, W. W. "*The Wanderer* and *The Seafarer*." *Journal of English and Germanic Philology* 4 (1902): 460–80.

Lehman, Winfred P. *A Gothic Etymological Dictionary*. Leiden: Brill, 1986.

Lentricchia, Frank, Jr. "Some Coordinates of Modern Literature." *Poetry* 108 (1966): 65–67.

Levine, George. *Aesthetics and Ideology*. New Brunswick, NJ: Rutgers University Press, 1994.

Lewis, C. S. *All my Road before Me: The Diary of C. S. Lewis, 1922–1927*. Ed. Walter Hooper. London: HarperCollins, 1991.

——. *The Allegory of Love: A Study in Medieval Tradition*. Oxford: Oxford University Press, 1936 (revised 1938).

——. *C. S. Lewis: Collected Letters*. Ed. Walter Hooper. Vol. 1, *Family Letters, 1905–1931*. London: HarperCollins, 2000.

——. *The Discarded Image*. Cambridge: Cambridge University Press, 1964.

——. *English Literature in the Sixteenth Century*. Oxford: Oxford University Press, 1954.

——. *An Experiment in Criticism*. Cambridge: Cambridge University Press, 1961.

——. *The Four Loves*. London: Geoffrey Bles, 1960.

——. *George MacDonald: An Anthology*. London: Bles, 1946.

——. *The Great Divorce*. London: Bles, 1946.

——. *The Last Battle*. New York: HarperCollins, 1994.

——. *Letters of C. S. Lewis*. Ed. Walter Hooper. San Diego: Harcourt Brace, 1993.

——. *Letters of C. S. Lewis*. Edited, with a memoir by W. H. Lewis. New York: Harcourt, Brace & World, 1966.

——. *Mere Christianity*. New York: Macmillan, 1952.

——. *Narrative Poems*. Ed. Walter Hooper. London: Bles, 1969.

——. *On Stories*. Ed. Walter Hooper. New York: Harcourt Brace Jovanovich, 1982

——. *Out of the Silent Planet*. New York: Macmillan, 1967.

——. *Perelandra*. New York: MacMillan, 1958.

——. *Poems*. Ed. Walter Hooper. London: Bles, 1964.

——. *A Preface to "Paradise Lost."* Oxford: Oxford University Press, 1942.

——. *The Silver Chair*. New York: HarperCollins, 1994.

——. *Studies in Medieval and Renaissance Literature*. Ed. Walter Hooper. Cambridge: Cambridge University Press, 1966.

——. *Surprised by Joy: The Shape of My Early Life*. London: Bles, 1955.

——. *That Hideous Strength*. New York: Macmillan, 1946.

——. *They Asked for a Paper: Papers and Addresses*. London: Bles, 1962.

——. *They Stand Together: The Letters of C. S. Lewis to Arthur Greeves (1914–1963)*. Ed. Walter Hooper. New York: Macmillan, 1979.

——. *Undeceptions*. London: Bles, 1971.

——. *The Voyage of the "Dawn Treader."* New York: HarperCollins, 1994.

——. *Prince Caspian, The Return to Narnia*. London: Geoffrey Bles, 1951.

Lewis, W. H. *Brothers and Friends: The Diaries of Major Warren Hamilton Lewis*. Ed. Clyde S. Kilby and Marjorie Lamp Mead. San Francisco, CA: Harper and Row, 1982.

Liguori, Alphonsus de. *The Glories of Mary*. Trans and ed. Eugene Grimm. New York: Benzinger, 1887.

Liu, Alan. *Wordsworth: The Sense of History*. Stanford, CA: Stanford University Press, 1989.

Lobdell, Jared. *England and Always: Tolkien's World of the Rings*. Grand Rapids, MI: William B. Eerdman's, 1981.

——. *A Tolkien Compass*. La Salle: Open Court, 1975.

Lönnrot, Elias. *Kalevala*. Helsinki, 1849. English trans. Francis Peabody Magoun. Cambridge, MA: Harvard University Press, 1963.

Loyn, H. R. *The Making of the English Nation*. London: Thames and Hudson, 1991.

Lukacs, John, *The Hitler of History*. New York: Vintage, 1997.

MacDonald, Alexander. *The Holy House of Loretto: A Study of Documents and Traditions*. New York: Christian Press Association, 1913.

Madsen, Catherine. "Light from an Invisible Lamp: Natural Religion in *The Lord of the Rings*." *Mythlore* 53 (spring): 43–47.

Madsen, D. L. *Rereading Allegory: A Narrative Approach to Genre*. New York: St. Martin's Press, 1994.

Malory, Sir Thomas. *Works*. Ed. Eugène Vinaver. 2nd ed. London: Oxford University Press, 1971.

Map, Walter. *De nugis curialium*. Ed. C. N. L. Brooke and R. A. B. Mynors and trans. M. R. James. Oxford: Oxford University Press, 1983.

Marenbon, John. *Early Medieval Philosophy, 480-1150: An Introduction*. Rev. ed. New York: Routledge, 1988.

McFague, Sallie. *Metaphorical Theology: Models of God in Religious Language*. Philadelphia: Fortress, 1982.

——. *Models of God: Theology for an Ecological Nuclear Age*. Philadelphia: Fortress, 1987.

McKinnon, James. *Music in Early Christian Literature*. Cambridge: Cambridge University Press, 1987.

Miesel, Sandra. "Some Religious Aspects of *Lord of the Rings*. *Mythlore* 53 (spring): 209–13.

Miller, Miriam Youngerman, and Jane Chance, eds. *Approaches to Teaching "Sir Gawain and the Green Knight."* New York: MLA, 1986.

Milton, John. *Paradise Lost, a Poem in Twelve Books*. Ed. Merritt Y. Hughes. New ed. New York: Odyssey Press, 1962.

Mitchell, Bruce. "J. R. R. Tolkien and Old English Studies: An Appreciation." In Reynolds and GoodKnight, 206–12.

Mitchell, Bruce and Fred Robinson, eds. *Beowulf: An Edition*. Oxford: Blackwell, 1998.

Moisl, Hermann. *Lordship and Tradition in Barbarian Europe*. Lewiston, Queenston, and Lampeter, U.S.A.: Edwin Mellen Press, 1999.

Moorman, Charles. "The Shire, Mordor, and Minas Tirith." In Isaacs and Zimbardo. 201–17.

Morris, R., ed. *Blickling Homilies*. 3 vols. Early English Text Society, 58, 63, 73. London: Early English Text Society, 1874–80.

Morus, Iwan Rhys. "The Tale of Beren and Lúthien." *Mallorn* 20 (September 1983): 19–22.

——. "'Uprooting the Golden Bough': J. R. R. Tolkien's Response to Nineteenth-century Folklore and Comparative Mythology." *Mallorn* 27 (1990): 5–9.

Muir, B. J., ed. *The Exeter Anthology of Old English Poetry: An Edition of Exeter Dean and Chapter MS 3501*. Exeter: University of Exeter Press, 1994.

Müller, (Friederich) Max. *Chips from a German Workshop*. 4 vols. New York: Scribner, Armstrong, 1871–76; Oxford and London; 1867–1875.

——. *Comparative Mythology, An Essay*. Ed. Abram Smythe Palmer. London and New York: 1909.

Nagy, Gergely. "The Fictitious Text: Malory's Construction of the Source through References." Paper delivered at the Fifth Conference of the Hungarian Association for the Study of English. January 2001, Eger, Hungary.

Neckel, Gustav, ed. *Edda: Die Lieder des Codex Regius nebst verwandten Denkmälern*. 4th ed., rev. Hans Kuhn. Heidelberg: Carl Winter, 1962.

Nitzsche, Jane Chance. See Chance, Jane.

Noel, Ruth S. *The Mythology of Middle-earth*. Boston: Houghton Mifflin, 1977.

O'Brien, Donald. "*The Mabinogion* and Middle-earth," parts 1–3. *Beyond Bree* (October 1991): 5–7; (November 1991): 1–3; (December 1991): 2–5.

Orchard, Andy. *Pride and Prodigies: Studies in the Monsters of the "Beowulf"-Manuscript*. Cambridge: D. S. Brewer, 1995.

Orderic Vitalis. *The Ecclesiastical History of Orderic Vitalis*. Vol. 2, bks. 7 and 8. Ed. and trans. Marjorie Chibnall. Oxford: Clarendon Press, 1973.

Overing, Gillian. "The Women of *Beowulf*: A Context for Interpretation." In *Beowulf: Basic Readings*, ed. Peter S. Baker. New York: Garland, 1995. 219–60.

Pearce, Joseph. *Tolkien: Man and Myth*. London: HarperCollins, 1998.

Percy, Thomas. *Reliques of Ancient English Poetry*. 3 vols. London, 1765.

Petty, Anne C. *One Ring to Bind Them All: Tolkien's Mythology*. University: The University of Alabama Press, 1979.

Pope, John C. "Dramatic Voices in *The Wanderer* and *The Seafarer*." In *Franciplegius: Medieval and Linguistic Studies in Honor of Francis Peabody Morgoun, Jr.*, ed. J. B. Bessinger, Jr., and R. P. Creed. New York: New York University Press, 1965. 164–93.

——, ed. *Seven Old English Poems*. New York: W. W. Norton, 1981.

Ralls-MacLeod, Karen. *Music and the Celtic Otherworld: From Ireland to Iona*. New York: St. Martin's Press, 2000.

Rawls, Melanie. "Arwen, Shadow Bride." *Mythlore* 43 (autumn 1985): 24–25, 37.

——. "The Feminine Principle in Tolkien." *Mythlore* 10, no. 4 (spring 1984): 5–13.

Reynolds, Patricia and Glen H. GoodKnight, eds. *Proceedings of the J. R. R. Tolkien Centenary Conference, Keble College, Oxford, 1992*. Combined issue of *Mythlore* 80; *Mallorn* 30. Milton Keynes, U.K.: Tolkien Society; Altadena, CA: Mythopoeic Press, 1995.

Ricks, Christopher. "Austin's Swink." *University of Toronto Quarterly* 61 (1992): 297–315.

Ricoeur, Paul. *Time and Narrative*. Trans. Kathleen Blamey and David Pellauer. Vol. 3. Chicago, IL: University of Chicago Press, 1988.

Riggs, Stephen Return. *A Dakota–English Dictionary*. Ed. James Owen Dorsey. Minneapolis, MN: Ross & Haines, 1968.

Robinson, Lila Wistrand and James Armagost. *Comanche Dictionary and Grammar*. Arlington, TX: Summer Institute in Linguistics, 1990.

Roman Missal, The. New York: Catholic Book Publishing Co., 1974.

Rosebury, Brian. *Tolkien: A Critical Assessment*. Basingstoke: Macmillan; New York: St. Martin's Press, 1992.

Rosenberg, Alfred. *Race and Race History and Other Essays*. Ed. Robert Pois. New York: Harper and Row, 1970.

——. *Der Mythus des 20. Jahrhunderts: Eine Wertung der seelischgeistigen Gestaltkämpfe unserer Zeit*. Munich: Hoheneichen Verlag, 1930.

Rossi, Lee D. *The Politics of Fantasy: C. S.Lewis and J. R. R. Tolkien.* Studies in Speculative Fiction, 10. Ann Arbor, MI: UMI Research Press, 1984.

Rowse. A. L. *Oxford in the History of England.* New York: Putnam's Sons, 1975.

Saga of Hrolf Kraki, The. Trans. Stella M. Mills. Oxford: Basil Blackwell, 1933.

Salu, Mary and Robert T. Farrell, eds. *J. R. R. Tolkien, Scholar and Story-teller: Essays in Memoriam.* Ithaca and London: Cornell University Press, 1979.

Sandner, David. "'Joy beyond the Walls of the World': The Secondary World-making of J. R. R. Tolkien and C. S. Lewis." In Clark and Timmons. 133–46.

Sanford, Len. "The Fall from Grace – Decline and Fall in Middle-Earth: Metaphors for Nordic and Christian Theology in *The Lord of the Rings* and *The Silmarillion.*" *Mallorn* 32 (September 1995): 15–20.

Saunders, Corinne J. *The Forest of Medieval Romance.* Suffolk: Boydell & Brewer, 1993.

Scarry, Elaine. *Dreaming by the Book.* New York: Farrar, Straus, Giroux, 1999.

——. *On Beauty and Being Just.* Princeton, NJ: Princeton University Press, 1999.

Schakel, Peter J., ed. *The Longing for a Form: Essays on the Fiction of C. S. Lewis.* Kent: Kent State University Press, 1977.

Schlobin, Roger C. "The Monsters Are Talismans and Transgressions: Tolkien and *Sir Gawain and the Green Knight.*" In Clark and Timmons. 71–82.

Schmitt, Jean-Claude. *Ghosts in the Middle Ages.* Trans. Teresa Lavender Fagan. Chicago: Chicago University Press, 1998.

Schoenbaum, David. *Hitler's Social Revolution: Class and Status in Nazi Germany, 1933–1939.* New York, London: W. W. Norton and Co., 1966, 1980.

Schücking, L. L. "Die altenglische Elegie." *Englische Studien* 51 (1917): 97–115.

Schueller, Herbert M. *The Idea of Music: An Introduction to Musical Aesthetics in Antiquity and the Middle Ages.* Kalamazoo, MI: Medieval Institute Publications, 1988.

Seeman, Chris. "Tolkien and Campbell Compared." *Mythlore* 18, no. 1 (1991): 43–48.

Seidel, Michael. *Exile and the Narrative Imagination.* New Haven, CT: Yale University Press, 1986.

Senior, W. A. "Loss Eternal in J. R. R. Tolkien's Middle-Earth." In Clark and Timmons. 173–82.

Shippey, T[homas] A. *J. R. R. Tolkien: Author of the Century.* London: HarperCollins, 2000.

——. "Long Evolution: The History of Middle-earth and its Merits." In *Arda*, ed. Anders Stenström. Stockholm: Forodrim, 1987.

——. "Noblesse Oblige: Images of Class in Tolkien." *Lembas Extra* 93/94 (1995): 27–43.

——. *The Road to Middle-earth.* London: Allen and Unwin; Boston: Houghton Mifflin, 1982. Rev. ed., Hammersmith: Grafton, 1992.

——. "Tolkien and the *Gawain*-Poet." In Reynolds and GoodKnight. 213–20.

——. "Tolkien and 'The Homecoming of Beorhtnoth.'" In *Leaves from the Tree: J. R. R. Tolkien's Shorter Fiction.* London: Tolkien Society, 1991.

——. "Tolkien's Academic Reputation Now." *Amon Hen*, no. 100 (November 1989): 18–22.

——. "Tolkien's Sources: The True Tradition." In de Koster. 153–61.

Sillars, Stuart. *British Romantic Art and the Second World War.* New York: St. Martin's Press, 1991.

Sisam, Kenneth. "The Structure of *Beowulf.*" In *Beowulf*, ed. Joseph Tuso. New York: Norton, 1975. 113–17.

Sly, Debbie. "Weaving Nets of Gloom: 'Darkness Profound' in Tolkien and Milton." In Clark and Timmons. 109–19.

Smithers, G. V. "The Meaning of *The Seafarer* and *The Wanderer.*" *Medium Ævum* 26 (1957): 137–53.

Smyth, Herbert Weir. *Greek Grammar.* 1920; rpt. Cambridge, MA: Harvard University Press, 1984.

——. "J. R. R. Tolkien: The 'Monstrous' in the Mirror." *Journal of the Fantastic in the Arts* 9 (1998): 229–46.

Solzhenitsyn, Aleksandr I. *The First Circle.* New York: Harper & Row, 1968.

Spitzer, Leo. *Classical and Christian Ideas of World Harmony.* Baltimore, MD: Johns Hopkins University Press, 1963.

Stanley, E. G. "Old English Poetic Diction and the Interpretation of *The Wanderer, The Seafarer*, and *The Penitent's Prayer.*" *Anglia* 73 (1955): 413–66.

St. Clair, Gloriana. "An Overview of the Northern Influence on Tolkien's Works." In Reynolds and GoodKnight. 63–67.

——. "Tolkien as Reviser: A Case Study." In Reynolds and GoodKnight. 145–50.

——. "*Volsunga Saga* and Narn: Some Analogies." In Reynolds and GoodKnight. 68–72.

Stenström, Anders. "A Mythology? For England?" In Reynolds and GoodKnight. 310–14.

Stevens, David and Carol D. *J. R. R. Tolkien.* Mercer Island, WA: Starmont House, 1992.

Stimpson, Catherine R. *J. R. R. Tolkien.* Columbia Essays on Modern Writers, vol. 41. New York: Columbia University Press, 1969.

——. "The Meaning of *The Seafarer* and *The Wanderer.*" *Medium Ævum* 28 (1959): 1–22, 99–104.

Strunk, Oliver, ed. *Antiquity and the Middle Ages.* Source Readings in Music History, vol. 1. New York: W. W. Norton, 1965.

Sturluson, Snorri. *Edda: Prologue and Gylfaginning.* Ed. Anthony Faulkes. Oxford: Clarendon Press, 1982.

Sullivan, C. W., III. "Tolkien the Bard: His Tale Grew in the Telling." In Clark and Timmons. 11–20.

Sutcliffe, Peter. *The Oxford University Press: An Informal History.* Oxford: Oxford University Press, 1978.

Sveinsson, Einar Ól., ed. *Brennu-Njáls saga.* Íslenzk Fornrit. Vol. 12. 1954. Rpt., Reykjavík: Hið Íslenzka Fornritafélag, 1971.

Theweleit, Klaus. *Male Fantasies.* Volume 2: *Psychoanalyzing the White Terror.* Trans. Erica Carter and Chris Turner. Minneapolis: University of Minnesota Press, 1989.

Thieme, Paul. *Der Fremding im Rgveda: Eine Studie über die Bedeutung der Worte ari, arya, aryaman und arya.* Leipzig: Deutsche Morgenländische Gesellschaft, 1938.

Thorpe, Benjamin, ed. *Codex Exoniensis.* London: W. Pickering (Society of Antiquaries of London), 1842.

Tillich, Paul. "The Depth of Existence." In *The Shaking of the Foundations.* New York: Scribners, 1948. 52–63.

Timmer, B. J. "The Elegiac Mood in Old English Poetry." *English Studies* 24 (1942): 33–44.

——, ed. *Judith.* Exeter: University of Exeter Press, 1966.

Timmons, Daniel. "J. R. R. Tolkien: The 'Monstrous' in the Mirror." *Journal of the Fantastic in the Arts* 9, no. 3 (1998): 229–46.

Tolkien, Christopher, ed. and trans. *The Saga of King Heidrek the Wise.* London: Thomas Nelson and Sons, 1960.

Tolkien, J. R. R. *The Adventures of Tom Bombadil.* London: Allen & Unwin, 1961; Boston: Houghton Mifflin, 1962. Rpt. in *The Tolkien Reader.*

——. "*Beowulf*: The Monsters and the Critics." *Proceedings of the British Academy* 22 (1937): 245–95. Rpt. in *An Anthology of Beowulf Criticism*, ed. Lewis E. Nicholson. Notre Dame, IN: University of Notre Dame Press, 1963; rpt. in *The Beowulf Poet*, ed. Donald K. Fry. Englewood Cliffs, NJ: Prentice Hall, 1968; rpt. in R. Fulk, ed. *Interpretations of*

Beowulf: A Critical Anthology. Bloomington and Indianapolis: Indiana University Press, 1991. 14–44; and rpt. in abbreviated form, in *Readings on "Beowulf"*. Greenhaven Press Literary Companion to British Literature. San Diego, CA: Greenhaven Press, 1998. 24–30.

——. *The Book of Lost Tales, Part 1*. Ed. Christopher Tolkien. *The History of Middle-earth*, vol. 1. London: George Allen & Unwin, 1983; Boston: Houghton Mifflin, 1984.

——. *The Book of Lost Tales, Part 2*. Ed. Christopher Tolkien. *The History of Middle-earth*, vol. 2. London: George Allen & Unwin, 1984; Boston: Houghton Mifflin, 1984.

——. *Farmer Giles of Ham*. London: Allen & Unwin, 1949; Boston: Houghton Mifflin, 1950. Rpt. in *The Tolkien Reader* and in *Smith of Wootton Major and Farmer Giles of Ham*. New York: Ballantine, 1969.

——. *The Fellowship of the Ring, Being the first part of The Lord of the Rings*. 2nd ed. London: Allen & Unwin, 1966; Boston: Houghton Mifflin, 1967.

——. *Finn and Hengest: The Fragment and the Episode*. Ed. Alan Bliss. London: Allen & Unwin, 1982; Boston: Houghton Mifflin, 1983.

——. *The History of Middle-earth*. Ed. Christopher Tolkien. 12 vols. London: Allen & Unwin, 1983–95; Boston: Houghton Mifflin, 1984–96.

——. *The Hobbit; or There and Back Again*. 2nd ed. London: Allen & Unwin, 1937, 1951; Boston: Houghton Mifflin, 1938, 1958; 1965. Rpt., New York: Ballantine, 1974.

——. "The Homecoming of Beorhtnoth Beorhthelm's Son." *Essays and Studies by Members of the English Association*, n.s., 6 (1953): 1–18. Rpt. in *The Tolkien Reader*.

——. *The Lays of Beleriand*. Ed. Christopher Tolkien. *The History of Middle-earth*, vol. 3. London: George Allen & Unwin, 1985; Boston: Houghton Mifflin, 1985.

——. "Leaf by Niggle." *Dublin Review* 216 (1945): 46–61. Rpt. in *Tree and Leaf*. London: Allen & Unwin, 1964; Boston: Houghton Mifflin, 1965; and in *The Tolkien Reader*.

——. *The Letters of J. R. R. Tolkien*. Selected and ed. by Humphrey Carpenter with the assistance of Christopher Tolkien. London: George Allen & Unwin, 1980; Boston: Houghton Mifflin, 1981.

——. *The Lord of the Rings*. 3 vols. London: George Allen & Unwin, 1954–55; Boston: Houghton Mifflin, 1954–56. 2nd ed. London: Allen & Unwin, 1966; Boston: Houghton Mifflin, 1967. One-volume ed. London: HarperCollins, 1993. Reset ed., HarperCollins, 1994. Seven-volume HarperCollins ed., 1999.

——. *The Lost Road and Other Writings*. Ed. Christopher Tolkien, *The History of Middle-earth*, vol. 5. London: George Allen & Unwin, 1987; Boston: Houghton Mifflin, 1987.

——. *"The Monsters and the Critics" and Other Essays*. Ed. Christopher Tolkien. London: Allen & Unwin, 1983; Boston: Houghton Mifflin, 1984.

——. *Mr. Bliss*. London: Allen & Unwin, 1982; Boston: Houghton Mifflin, 1983.

——. *Morgoth's Ring: The Later Silmarillion, Part 1*. Ed. Christopher Tolkien. *The History of Middle-earth*, vol. 10. London: HarperCollins; Boston: Houghton Mifflin, 1993.

——. "Mythopoeia." In *Tree and Leaf, Including the Poem "Mythopoeia."* Introduction by Christopher Tolkien. Rev. ed. London: Allen & Unwin, 1988; Boston: Houghton Mifflin, 1989. 97–101.

——. *The Old English Exodus: Text, Translation, and Commentary by J. R. R. Tolkien*. Ed. Joan Turville-Petre. Oxford: Oxford University Press, 1981.

——. "On Fairy-Stories." In *Essays Presented to Charles Williams*, ed. C. S. Lewis. 38–89. London: Oxford University Press, 1947. Rpt., Grand Rapids, MI: William B. Eerdmans, 1966. Rev. and rpt. in *Tree and Leaf* and in *The Tolkien Reader*.

——. *The Peoples of Middle-earth*. Ed. Christopher Tolkien. *The History of Middle-earth*, vol. 12. London: HarperCollins, 1996; Boston: Houghton Mifflin, 1996.

——. *The Return of the King, Being the third part of The Lord of the Rings.* 2nd ed. Boston: Houghton Mifflin, 1965.

——. *The Return of the Shadow: The History of The Lord of the Rings, Part One.* Ed. Christopher Tolkien. *The History of Middle-earth,* vol. 6. London: Unwin Hyman; Boston: Houghton Mifflin, 1988.

——. *Roverandom.* London: Allen & Unwin, 1992; Boston: Houghton Mifflin, 1998.

——. *Sauron Defeated: The End of the Third Age (The History of the "Lord of the Rings," Part Four).* Ed. Christopher Tolkien. *The History of Middle-earth,* vol. 9. London: HarperCollins, 1992; Boston: Houghton Mifflin, 1992.

——. *The Shaping of Middle-earth: The Quenta, The Ambarkanta, and the Annals.* Ed. Christopher Tolkien. *The History of Middle-earth,* vol. 4. London: Unwin Hyman, 1986; Boston: Houghton Mifflin, 1986.

——. *The Silmarillion.* Ed. Christopher Tolkien. London: Allen & Unwin, 1976; Boston: Houghton Mifflin, 1977.

——. *Smith of Wootton Major.* London: Allen & Unwin; Boston: Houghton Mifflin, 1967; *Redbook* 130 (1967): 58–61, 101, 103–7. Rpt. in *The Tolkien Reader*; rpt. in *Smith of Wootton Major and Farmer Giles of Ham.*

——. *Smith of Wootton Major and Farmer Giles of Ham.* New York: Ballantine, 1969.

——. *The Tolkien Reader.* New York: Ballantine, 1966.

——. *The Treason of Isengard: The History of "The Lord of the Rings," Part Two.* Ed. Christopher Tolkien. *The History of Middle-earth,* vol. 7. London: Unwin Hyman, 1989; Boston: Houghton Mifflin, 1989.

——. *Tree and Leaf.* 2nd ed. London: HarperCollins, 1988.

——. "Tree and Leaf: On Fairy Stories." In *The Tolkien Reader.* 33–99.

——. *The Two Towers, Being the second part of The Lord of the Rings.* 2nd ed. Boston: Houghton Mifflin, 1965.

——. *Unfinished Tales of Númenor and Middle-earth.* Ed. Christopher Tolkien. London: Allen & Unwin, 1979; Boston: Houghton Mifflin, 1980.

——. *The War of the Jewels: The Later Silmarillion, Part Two.* Ed. Christopher Tolkien. *The History of Middle-earth,* vol. 11. London: HarperCollins, 1994; Boston: Houghton Mifflin, 1994.

——. *The War of the Ring: The History of "The Lord of the Rings," Part Three.* Ed. Christopher Tolkien. *The History of Middle-earth,* vol. 8. London: Unwin Hyman, 1990; Boston: Houghton Mifflin, 1990.

——, trans. *"Sir Gawain and the Green Knight," "Pearl," and "Sir Orfeo."* Ed. Christopher Tolkien. London: Allen & Unwin, 1974; Boston: Houghton Mifflin, 1975.

Tolkien, J. R. R. and E. V. Gordon, eds. *Sir Gawain and the Green Knight.* Oxford: Clarendon Press, 1925. 2nd ed. Rev. Norman Davis. Oxford: Clarendon Press, 1967.

Tolkien, J. R. R. and Donald Swann. *The Road Goes Ever On.* New York: Ballantine, 1967.

Toller, T. Northcote, ed. *An Anglo-Saxon Dictionary: Based on the Manuscript Collections of the Late Joseph Bosworth.* Oxford: Oxford University Press, 1898.

——. "The Meaning of *The Seafarer* and *The Wanderer.*" *Medium Ævum* 28 (1959): 1–22, 99–104.

Tuchman, Barbara. *A Distant Mirror.* New York: Alfred A. Knopf, 1978.

Ugolnik, Anthony J. "*Wordhord Onleac:* The Medieval Sources of J. R. R. Tolkien's Linguistic Aesthetic." *Mosaic* 10 (winter 1977): 15–31.

Van Horn Melton, James. "From Folk History to Structural History: Otto Brunner (1898–1982) and the Radical-Conservative Roots of German Social History." In *Paths of Continuity: Central European Historiography from the 1930s to the 1950s,* eds. Hartmut

Lehmann and James Van Horn Melton. Cambridge, New York, Melbourne: Cambridge University Press, 1994. 263–92.

Wagner, Richard. *Wagner's Ring of the Nibelung, A Companion*. Eds. Stewart Spencer and Barry Millington. Trans. Steward Spencer. New York: Thames and Hudson, 1993.

Walsh, Chad. *The Literary Legacy of C. S. Lewis.* New York: Harcourt Brace Jovanich, 1979.

West, Richard C. "Túrin's *Ofermod.*" In Flieger and Hostetter. 233–46.

Wheeler, Mortimer. *The British Academy, 1949-1968*. London: Oxford University Press, 1970.

Whitelock, Dorothy. "The Interpretation of *The Seafarer.*" In *Early Cultures of North-West Europe (H. M. Chadwick Memorial Studies).* Cambridge: Cambridge University Press, 1950. 261–72.

Whitman, Jon, ed. *Interpretation and Allegory: Antiquity to the Modern Period.* Leiden: Brill, 2000.

Whittier, P. G. "Spring in *The Seafarer* 48–50." *Notes and Queries* 15 (1968): 407–9.

Wicher, Andrzej. "The Artificial Mythology of *The Silmarillion* by J. R. R. Tolkien." *Kwartalnik Neofilologiczny* 28 (1981): 399–405.

Williams, Charles and C. S. Lewis. *Arthurian Torso: Containing the Posthumous Fragment of the "Figure of Arthur" by Charles Williams and a Commentary on the Arthurian Poems of Charles Williams by C. S. Lewis.* Oxford: Oxford University Press, 1948.

Williams, Jay. *The Practical Princess.* New York: Parents' Magazine Press, 1969.

Woolf, Rosemary, ed. *Cynewulf's Juliana*. Exeter: University of Exeter Press, 1966.

Wynne, Patrick and Carl F. Hostetter. "And Still at Large There Were Giants," pts. 1–2. *Vinyar Tengwar* 21 (January 1992): 14–20; 22 (March 1992): 12–18.

Zgorzelski, Andrej. "A Fairy Tale Modified: Time and Space as Syncretic Factors in J. R. R. Tolkien's Trilogy." *Zeitschrift fü Literaturwissenschaft und Linguistik* 92 (1993): 126–40.

Zipes, Jack, ed. *Don't Bet on the Prince: Contemporary Feminist Fairy Tales in North America and England.* New York: Methuen, 1986.

Zogby, Edward G. "Triadic Patterns in Lewis's Life and Thought." In Schakel.

Index

For Product Safety Concerns and Information please contact our EU representative GPSR@taylorandfrancis.com
Taylor & Francis Verlag GmbH, Kaufingerstraße 24, 80331 München, Germany

www.ingramcontent.com/pod-product-compliance
Lightning Source LLC
Chambersburg PA
CBHW071447110726
47908CB00003B/543

* 9 7 8 0 4 1 5 4 7 3 4 8 4 *